The fiery brilliance of the Zebra Hologram Heart you see on the cover is created by revolutionary process in which a powerful laser beam records light waves in diamond-like facets so tiny that 9,000,000 fit in a square inch. No print or photograph can match the vibrant colors and radiant glow of a hologram.

So look for the Zebra Hologram Heart whenever you buy a historical romance. It is a shimmering reflection of our guarantee that you'll find consistent quality between the covers!

PRIMITIVE PASSIONS

"Mr. Cutter, if we have to, my father and I will go alone to find the Pawnee. I'm sorry I provoked your anger, and if you do accompany us, I'll try not to do so in the future."

"I'm afraid that would be impossible, Miss Magruder. You provoke me just by being here, wearing those enormous, poufed sleeves and that tightly laced corset. You just don't belong here."

His assumption that she wore a corset when she did not infuriated her. "I fail to see why my undergarments should so fascinate you, Mr. Cutter, and can only conclude it's because you are low-minded!"

"That's what I've been trying to tell you, Miss Magruder. And to prove it, I *will* steal that kiss from you."

"Mr. Cut—!" she shrieked, but her cry of outrage was muffled as his mouth came down hard upon hers.

A perilous weakness invaded her limbs. Though she had never fainted before in her life, she feared she might do so now. Beneath her splayed hands—she had dropped her bonnet but managed to wedge her hands between their bodies—Luke Cutter's chest was brick-hard and unyielding.

When the kiss ended, she stared at him, and he stared back. Something primitive and violent vibrated in the air between them, and it came to her in a flash that this was what young women were so often warned about: This was why a woman should never allow herself to be alone with a man.

NEBRASKA EMBRACE

KATHARINE KINCAID

ZEBRA BOOKS
KENSINGTON PUBLISHING CORP.

previous works by Pamela Daoust include:

Violet Smoke
Ruby Orchid
Defiant Vixen
Sea Flame

ZEBRA BOOKS

are published by

Kensington Publishing Corp.
475 Park Avenue South
New York, NY 10016

First printing: October 1989

Printed in the United States of America

For my dear daughter, Maria
Wishing you joy and happiness.
Thank you for the beautiful grandchild.

Prologue

It was the hour before dawn, and Morning Star winked with a cold cruel beauty above the rim of the eastern horizon. The plains lay dark and silent, stretching away from a high rocky bluff, the only natural protuberance on the otherwise endlessly-flat terrain. Atop the bluff, Pitale-sharo, Knife Chief, gazed down at the silver glint of a river snaking across the prairie.

A deep sigh escaped him. The day he had been dreading had finally come. Before first light, he must leave the peaceful village nestled beside the river and embark on a long journey whose purpose was dark and evil. He did not want to go, but refusal was unthinkable. If he remained — or if he failed to achieve his goal — the wrath of Tirawa, fierce god of the Morning Star, would fall upon the Wolf River band of the Skidi Pawnee, and none would survive the god's terrible vengeance.

A voice behind him intruded upon Pitale-sharo's grim thoughts. "She is out there, my son, she whom Tirawa desires."

Turning, Pitale-sharo saw his grandfather, so bent and wrinkled with age that he resembled a withered old walking stalk. Wetara-sharo, Old Man Chief, came closer. In the dim starlight, his eyes shone like polished black stones, and his teeth glinted like a wolf's. Starlight also silvered his scalp lock, pulled back and made to stand erect in the distinctive Skidi manner, but it did nothing to enhance his sagging skin, which hung in folds around brittle bones and slack, aging muscles.

"I wish I did not have to go," Pitale-sharo said.

The old man nodded and touched his shoulder in sympathy. "Neither did I rejoice in going. Neither did your father. If he still lived, he would tell you how he, too, hated it. It is our burden, my son—our hidden sorrow, the penalty for being chief. My heart weeps for your distress, but you dare not defy the gods. . . . Look out there. What do you see?"

Wetara-sharo pointed to the vast panorama of the plains, spread like a blanket at their feet. Pitale-sharo examined it closely, searching for whatever it was his grandfather saw that he himself did not see.

Beside the silver-glinting river stood the circular, dome-shaped lodges of his people, the Skidi Pawnee, and scattered around the lodges were the moving, shifting shapes of ponies, the buffalo-runners. Past them, the sea of waving grass rolled away to the distant horizon. At this season, the plains were still lush and green, spangled with wildflowers. The new shoots of corn growing along the riverbank were strong and sturdy. Yet Pitale-sharo knew that the appearance of abundance and fertility was deceiving. The dry season was just beginning, following a spring which had not yielded as much rain as everyone had hoped.

The Nebraska Territory, or Land of Shallow Rivers, was teetering on the brink of a massive drought that could shrivel the corn shoots, suck dry the rivers, and drive the buffalo far to the west. The Plains had entered an arid cycle, in which famine, plague, and hordes of destructive grasshoppers threatened. By the next planting season, four summers would have passed since the last sacrifice to Tirawa. Each passing day offered increasing evidence that the god of Morning Star was growing restless, eager for his sacrifice of human blood.

8

His grandfather's thoughts precisely echoed his own. "The land is dry, my son, thirsting for blood. The blood of a virgin. Make certain she is also beautiful."

"Beautiful," Pitale-sharo repeated, remembering the last Morning Star maiden, the first he himself had captured. She had had long black hair and soft brown eyes that followed him wherever he went. He had stolen her from the Sioux, their enemies, but she had come to relish life among the Pawnee. Rather, she had relished the idea of becoming the wife of a Pawnee chieftain, an idea he had nurtured in her until the very last moment.

Feeling sick, Pitale-sharo turned his back on the scene below. "The Black Robes say that Tirawa does not exist. They say there is another god, more powerful than any of ours, who teaches kindness and forgiveness of one's enemies."

"Can you forgive the Sioux warrior from whose lodge pole hangs the scalp lock of your own father? Can you forgive the White-Eyes who sell us firewater that poisons our bodies and enflames our minds?"

"You know I cannot."

"Then you have no choice. The ways of our ancestors are all we have. If we abandon them, what shall become of us?"

"I do not know, Grandfather. But life is no longer simple and easy, as it was when you were a young man."

"It was never simple and easy, Pitale-sharo. Though my memory holds a time when there were no Black Robes, no White-Eyes, and no doubts to cloud the mind, there have always been droughts, prairie fires, storms, and raids by our enemies to test our strength and courage. And through it all, the Skidi Pawnee have remained strong and powerful because we have clung tightly to the ancient ways. The stars have guided us, and Tirawa has watched over us—making the corn grow and the buffalo multiply and the rivers flow freely with life-giving water. Is the life of a worthless maiden, demanded only once every four years, too much to pay for the bounty we have always enjoyed?"

Pitale-sharo studied the rock-strewn ground, as stark and barren as the hidden reaches of his own soul. "It is a thing that shames me, Grandfather, the taking of an innocent life."

"Pah! You have spent too much time with Great Heart. You have begun to think like a White-Eyes."

"Great Heart does not try to change my thinking. He knows nothing of sacrificing maidens to Tirawa, though if he did, no doubt he would call us animals and savages, as do the rest of his people."

"It is not good to make a friend of a possible enemy," Wetara-sharo snorted.

"It is worse yet to make an enemy of a possible friend. . . . I will not do it, not even to please you, Grandfather."

His grandfather heaved a sigh that sounded like dry leaves whispering in the wind. "I do not ask you to give up your friendship with Great Heart, my son. I ask only that you fulfill your responsibility to your people. Go and capture a maiden. Bring her home and let her live among us and learn to think kindly of the Skidi Pawnee, so that she will plead our cause when she stands before Tirawa."

"I have never understood why she should do so when her last memory of us will be one of treachery, her last breath one of agony."

The deep lines in Wetara-sharo's forehead conveyed sharp disapproval of Pitale-sharo's obstinate attitude. "Once Tirawa takes her to himself, all her tears will turn to joy, all her pain to pleasure. She will *thank* the Skidi Pawnee for the honor of being Morning Star maiden."

"Do you know that for a fact, Grandfather? Have any of the maidens ever returned from death to tell you so?"

Wetara-sharo made a cutting motion with his hand. "Enough! You show no respect for your elders. Perhaps it would be better if some other man went in your place."

"Who, Grandfather? Bon-son-gee? Would you send that

sly, whining dog who never fails to remind you that his name means The New Fire? He desires to replace me, have no doubt. No matter where I go or what I do, I have only to glance over my shoulder, and he is there, waiting for the slightest mistake, the smallest error. When he can, he runs ahead of me to count coup on an enemy I myself have brought down."

Swept with bitterness, Pitale-sharo fell silent. It was unfair of his grandfather to suggest sending someone else. He knew his duty, and he would go, but that did not mean he had to like it.

For several moments, neither man spoke. Then, Wetaro-sharo coughed and cleared his throat. "Forgive me, my son. . . . I understand your reluctance. But you must realize how important it is that you show our people strength, not weakness. From every side, we are beset with new ideas, new ways of thinking. In the old days, we needed no one. We lived complete unto ourselves. And we were strong, invincible before our enemies. Now, we desire things belonging to the White-Eyes — their iron tools and weapons, their beads, cloth, blankets, and firewater. Our women want iron pots to cook in, our braves want guns instead of bows and arrows. . . . Our whole way of life is threatened. Once we forget how to live without these things, we will become as slaves to the White-Eyes, doing whatever they demand in order to obtain them."

"So you think that if we continue to sacrifice maidens to Tirawa, this will not happen."

"I think if we continue to practice the old ways, in time we will remember who we are, and when the day comes when we must choose between old and new, we will choose the old and survive, instead of choosing the new and destroying ourselves."

"Is there no other choice, Grandfather?"

"No, my son. There isn't. All of the White-Eyes are not like your friend, Great Heart, who respects our people and wishes only to learn more about us. Nor are they like Major Dougherty in the village the whites call Belle-vue. They are the only two White-Eyes I trust. The rest smile at us and bring us gifts, but all the while their eyes roam over our land, coveting our furs, our horses, our women, and yes, even the land itself. If you would know the character of the White-Eyes, watch how they shoot the buffalo. They kill for the sport of it, not out of necessity, and leave the carcasses to rot in the sun. . . . Ah, my son, the day is fast approaching when no longer can we call the White-Eyes friends and welcome them among us. We shall be at war with one another, forced to defend all we hold dear against them."

"I hope it does not happen in my lifetime, Grandfather. I would be a man of peace, not war."

"So would we all, Pitale-sharo. But our destiny is written in the stars. We cannot change what fate has decreed for us. So it is with the Morning Star maiden. From the hour she first drew breath, she was marked to belong to Tirawa. . . . Go now, and find her. The dawn is coming. Let it not discover you still doubting and hesitant. Go forth with purpose."

"Give me your blessing, Grandfather!" Pitale-sharo cried. A sense of cold foreboding and impending disaster consumed him.

Wetara-sharo laid his gnarled, bony hands on Pitale-sharo's shoulders, then raised his voice in a singsong chant. In it, he called upon Tirawa to guide his grandson's footsteps, to help him find a suitable, pleasing maiden for the secret ceremony, to be held on the eve of the summer solstice one year hence. He implored Tirawa to give Pitale-sharo courage and clearness of thinking, so that he would never waver from the path of his ancestors or disgrace his proud name and heritage.

By the time Wetaro-sharo had finished, Pitale-sharo's resolve had baked and hardened in the fire of his grandfather's faith in him. Wetaro-sharo touched his dry, withered cheek to Pitale-sharo's and whispered huskily. "Good hunting, my son."

Pitale-sharo only nodded; there was nothing left to say. Borrowing a gesture he had learned from the White-Eyes, he stepped back and saluted his grandfather. Then he strode past him to his patiently waiting buffalo-runner, the piebald pony who carried him on all his most important missions and journeys. Effortlessly, he swung up on the pony's bare back and touched his heels to its shaggy sides.

The animal snorted, half-reared on its hind legs, wheeled in place, and then shot forward at a gallop toward the narrow, twisting, rocky path leading down to the plain below. Pitale-sharo never once looked back, not even when he reached the flat grasslands and allowed his eager mount to stretch and run. He did not have to; he could *feel* his grandfather's eyes upon him, following his progress and urging him onward.

When the sun split the eastern horizon with a dazzling gold bar of light, Pitale-sharo was seized with a wild, inexplicable elation. He threw back his head and shouted a war cry—the cry of his forebears. It was a sound akin to the howl of a wolf, the totem of his tribe. From far off in the distance came an answering cry, echoing and re-echoing across the misty plains. In the sky above the rising sun, Morning Star glowed its brightest, a shimmering jewel suspended between heaven and earth.

For the space of several thundering heartbeats, Tirawa held sway over everything, more brilliant than sun or moon. Then the god's radiance began to fade, and so also did Pitale-sharo's elation. Gloom once more descended, and he rode into the freshening morning with a sad and heavy heart.

Chapter One

Missouri River, 1832

"My dear Miss Magruder, are you looking forward to beginning your sojourn among the savages?"

Whirling from the railing of the steamship, the *Yellowstone,* Maura Elizabeth Magruder saw a dapper man dressed in a shooting costume — a knee-length, embroidered frock coat, gaiters, and an odd little cap with a long pointed brim and turned-up earflaps. He was George Catlin, a fellow explorer who would be traveling two thousand miles up the Missouri to the Yellowstone River, while she and her father, Eben Magruder, were disembarking that very afternoon at Bellevue, a tiny settlement and military outpost some two hundred miles from St. Louis.

"Mr. Catlin, you startled me. I was just watching the passing scenery — and yes, thinking about my future. Ever since I was a little girl, I've wanted to accompany my father on one of his expeditions to study the aborigines. Now that I'm finally here, I'm *most* eager to begin."

George Catlin grinned. He had bright blue eyes, a prominent nose, and from what Maura had seen of him so far, an insatiable curiosity. "The scenery has been spectacular, hasn't it? Have you been capturing the bluffs and prairies in your sketchbook? I haven't seen a single one of your drawings, yet you and your father have already seen a dozen or more of my paintings."

Maura smiled back, but clutched her sketchbook a bit tighter to her bosom. With her free hand, she maintained her hold on the rough, yellow pine railing. The vibrations of the engine made the entire boat shake, and twin smokestacks near the bow belched huge puffs of noxious, black smoke that soiled everything, including her sketches. No, she did not want to show her smudged, amateurish efforts to George Catlin, a professional painter whose vivid oils far surpassed her humble charcoal and pen and ink renderings.

"I find it difficult to draw a straight line when the engine is running, Mr. Catlin. I haven't your control, I'm sorry to say."

The sudden loud clacking of the paddle wheel made it necessary for her to shout. A moment later, the frantic clang of the ship's bell rendered all conversation impossible. Maura braced herself for the inevitable jolt. The ship lurched and shuddered. Her timbers creaked protestingly. Maura heard a loud thud and felt a bump. It was not as bad as some that had occurred during the journey, but annoying and frightening just the same.

Clinging to the rail beside her, George Catlin leaned far out and looked toward the bow. "Another snag, I fear, or a shoal. Though it's impossible to see anything in these churning, muddy waters, one would think we could avoid at least a few of these mishaps." He withdrew and sighed. "I don't blame you for not working when we're underway, Miss Magruder. However, one could paint an entire portfolio during one of these interminable delays while the ship is being freed."

Underscoring his complaint, the paddle wheel clacked slowly and aimlessly, and Maura had to press herself into the rail as several roustabouts raced past them. From the wheelhouse forty feet above the water, the pilot roared commands to his rapidly assembling crew.

"Ah, well. . . ." George Catlin good-naturedly clucked his tongue and shook his head. "Would you care to accompany me to the stern, Miss Magruder? While our doughty captain conquers this latest challenge, we may as well sit down and be comfortable. T'will give us a chance to become better acquainted."

Without waiting for an answer, he took Maura's arm and led her through a narrow companionway. She had to turn sideways to allow for her stylish, leg-o'-mutton sleeves that otherwise would have filled the entire doorway. In anticipation of their arrival in Bellevue, Maura had worn her second-best gown of bright blue taffeta, but now had reason to regret her choice. Eager to see what new danger threatened the steamboat, men jostled and shoved past them in the opposite direction.

"Mind the lady! Mind the lady!" George called out admonishingly.

He pressed steadily forward, and finally, they came to an empty, dimly lit salon lined with pine benches and several tables. Wondering where her father was, Maura glanced uneasily at the half-empty whiskey mugs and abandoned playing cards lying face down on the littered tables. Usually she spent her time on deck or in their cabin, leaving Eben on his own to enjoy the rowdy comradery of the other passengers. She was all too uncomfortably aware of being the only woman aboard and possibly the only white woman ever to have journeyed this far west of the Mississippi, let alone the Missouri.

Smiling encouragingly, George Catlin led her to the cleanest table in the place and then indicated a chair placed a discreet distance away from the one he obviously intended to sit upon. "Don't worry, Miss Magruder. In your father's absence, I shall look after you. He's probably on deck with everyone else, watching the show. I do hope we don't have to leave the boat again while they lighten her and float her over whatever obstacle we've encountered this time. Somehow, I

17

never imagined steamboat travel to be this fraught with inconvenience, did you, my dear?"

Maura sat down gingerly and placed her precious sketchbook on the floor beside her chair. "It *was* so much easier on the Ohio," she agreed. "We hardly had to stop for anything."

Like most travelers journeying west from Philadelphia, Maura and her father had used water routes where steamboat travel was relatively common and tranquil. Nothing had prepared them for the tumultuous Missouri, a shallow, shifting, tree-clogged river that steamboats were only just beginning to navigate.

George Catlin leaned back in his chair and regarded her jovially, seeming most interested to have her all to himself, without her father to monopolize the conversation. Maura recalled that Mr. Catlin was thirty-three years old—practically *ancient*—and married, though his wife had remained in the east. He reminded her of a kindly uncle on her mother's side, and she relaxed a little and began to enjoy herself.

"Many still believe that only flat-bottomed mackinaws, keelboats, dugout canoes, or bullboats are suitable methods of transportation on this wild, unsettled waterway," he began. "And at times like these, I'm inclined to agree. Why, we left St. Louis over a month ago—March 26, wasn't it?—just after the breakup of the river ice. At the ship's present rate of speed, it won't reach its final destination on the Yellowstone River until the end of June."

"The unexpected snags, shoals, and rapids don't bother me so much," Maura confided. "But I do mind the possibility of being steamed like a lobster or blown to bits if something should go wrong with the ship's boiler. Sometimes, I worry about it."

"You do?" George Catlin waggled his eyebrows in amazement. "Why, I thought you were imperturbable, Miss Magruder. Indeed, I had been hoping to have this opportunity of speaking privately with you. Aren't you just a wee bit afraid of all the dangers and hardships you will face living alone among the Pawnee for a year or more? Burying oneself in the wilderness and relying solely upon one's own resources is a daunting prospect that would scare off most men. I find it incredible that a lovely young woman such as yourself should wish to do so."

Maura self-consciously sat up straighter. She knew that when people looked at her they saw a slim, blond, fragile young woman with blue-gray eyes, even features, and a carefully arranged coronet of braids. She was the image of her deceased mother, except for one substantial difference only her closest friends ever noticed; she had her father's spirit of adventure and tenacious determination shining in her eyes.

By the time she was twelve years old, she had already made up her mind to follow in her father's footsteps and become a renowned anthropologist and historian like Eben Matthew Magruder. Just as he had made the study of the North American aborigines his life's work, so would she, beginning by illustrating his treatises with precise, if not exactly artistic, drawings.

Unbeknownst to anyone, even her father, she also intended to record her observations of aboriginal women, about whom almost nothing had ever been written—and someday, hopefully in her own lifetime, the jottings in the brown leather journal in her baggage would find an eager audience and establish her as a gifted scholar in her own right.

Blushing beneath George Catlin's blatantly curious gaze, Maura cast about for the right words to explain her unusual ambitions to her fellow traveler. "No, I'm not afraid, Mr. Catlin. If anything, I'm most excited. I relish the idea of seeing places and people few whites have ever encountered. The Pawnee are especially fascinating because we know so little about them. They are more secretive than the rest of the Plains tribes—or so I gather from what the trappers and missionaries have to say about them."

George Catlin's blue eyes twinkled. "And just what do the trappers and missionaries say?"

Having grown accustomed to people not taking her seriously, Maura overlooked his faintly teasing tone. One day, they would. One day, the whole world would listen to her; her name would be as famous as her father's.

"The missionaries and trappers say that the Pawnee have many mysterious religious rituals related to the growing of crops and the hunting of buffalo. White men are never permitted to attend these rituals, so we know little about them. Other tribes are sometimes reticent about their ceremonies, too, but none so much as the Pawnee."

"And you think they will make an exception for you and your father?"

"Perhaps . . . with a more gentle persuasion than has been employed by arrogant missionaries who regard them as heathen devils."

George Catlin laughed and smacked his knee. "Miss Magruder, I do wish you and your father would change your plans and join forces with me! I would so love to see you exercising your considerable charm upon the unsuspecting savages. General William Clark himself has recommended the two guides who are awaiting me at Fort Union. Think of what a jolly company we should make! Going our separate ways in this dangerous land makes no sense."

"I believe you have discussed this already with my father, Mr. Catlin, and he refused. You wish to paint the Mandan and the Sioux, while we wish to concentrate primarily on the Pawnee. It isn't just their religious ceremonies that intrigue us; as you know, the Pawnee are the only Plains Indians who combine agrarian interests with the nomadic pursuits of the buffalo hunters. In a sense, they are already half-converted to the ways of the white man. By expanding on their ability to farm the land as we do, they would stand an excellent chance of surviving the westward flow of migration that we all know is coming. And perhaps they could survive it better than did their eastern counterparts."

"Ah, now I see the significant difference between us, Miss Magruder. I only want to paint the Indians, to record the way they now are. You obviously desire to improve them. Why, you almost sound like one of those arrogant missionaries to whom you just referred."

"On the contrary, Mr. Catlin. What I want is to *understand* them, and for them to understand us. Their only hope for survival lies in adaptation, *not* subjugation."

As she warmed to her subject, Maura's voice rose. For nearly all of her twenty years, she had been frustrated by people's ignorant, uncaring attitude toward the Indians and what was happening to them. Leaning across the table, she earnestly expounded the theories that so rarely found an interested, let alone sympathetic ear.

"The American Fur Company has already stripped the land of beaver in every territory east of the Mississippi. How long before they do it here? And *then* what will the Indians do to obtain whiskey, tools, and guns? Having forgotten how to live without such things, they will soon resort to stealing. Then we shall be forced to destroy or remove them—tribe by tribe—as we've had to do back home, God forgive us!"

George Catlin stared at her, open-mouthed. "Miss Magruder, you are even more radical than your father—or myself! Every post between St. Louis, Missouri and Fort Union on the Yellowstone River was built by the American Fur Company. So was this boat. Every man aboard, excepting me and your father, is in some way connected to the fur trade. Are you accusing John Jacob Astor or Manuel Lisa of being responsible for the ultimate annihilation of the red man?"

Maura hesitated. The two men George Catlin had mentioned were giants of the fur industry. Privately, she did hold them to blame for the debauchery of the eastern tribes of Indians and now, of the western. However, even her father did not go so far as she did in her opinions. In any case, she hoped to air her views in a more scholarly fashion, with tact and discretion, and not get carried away arguing them to a near stranger over spilled whiskey and playing cards.

"Mr. Catlin, I had rather accuse all those foolish men in Europe and America who are only too willing to pay outrageous sums of up to fifty dollars for a beaver hat. In their eagerness to be fashionable, they do not always count the cost to primitive peoples—or to poor dumb animals. I'm sorry if I've offended you. I should take better care to guard my tongue."

"You have not offended me, Miss Magruder. In truth, you have astounded and delighted me. One rarely finds a beautiful woman capable of discussing such a complex, difficult subject. You and your father are the first persons I've met who share my respect and concern for the noble savage. I do not delude myself into thinking I can stay the march of progress; I will be content if I can merely capture the dignity of the Plains Indians on canvas. But *you*, Miss Magruder. . . . Something tells me you will leave your mark here in this untamed land. Whether it will be for good or ill I cannot say. I only hope you have an able and understanding guide to lead you among the Pawnee. If you come to harm, it will be a tragic waste."

Maura smiled widely. Her dimples never failed to distract a man from her admittedly unorthodox ideas—or her brashness in stating them. Men were such dunces to think a woman incapable of having her own thoughts! Still, she must be more careful. Intelligence and outspokenness in a woman were not usually admired. For that very reason, she had considered publishing her findings under a male pseudonym—at least, at first.

"Luke Cutter is supposed to be the best guide in the Nebraska Territory, Mr. Catlin. Major Dougherty at Bellevue made the necessary arrangements. My father wrote to the major and offered a princely sum—but only for someone who has the confidence of the Pawnee. Mr. Cutter has lived

22

among them."

"So your father told me, my dear. But I would feel much better if your fiancé had accompanied you as planned. What is his name—Nathaniel something or other?"

"Nathaniel Hibbert," Maura said quietly, twisting the ring on the third finger of her left hand.

Disappointment flooded her in a hot, familiar wave. At the last moment, Nate had decided not to join their expedition because he did not want to leave his work. He had studied botany under John Bartram at the College of Philadelphia and was engaged in botanical experimentation, the nature of which could establish him as an authority in his field. In pursuing her dream, Maura could hardly begrudge the man she loved the fulfillment of his own dreams, yet she missed Nate terribly and worried about the effects of their prolonged absence from each other; more precisely, she worried that Nate might fall in love with someone else while she was gone.

Studying her intently, George Catlin pursed his lips and frowned. "Yes, I wish Mr. Hibbert had come west with you, Miss Magruder. Happily, your father is in excellent health, but I would still feel better knowing you had more protection. Didn't your mother voice some complaint about your traveling to so wild a place?"

"My mother died of smallpox when I was four years old," Maura bluntly informed him. Idly, she left off twisting her ring and began to stroke a small, white, sickle-shaped scar on her wrist. Similar scars marred the smoothness of skin on both her forearms, necessitating the wearing of long sleeves or concealing, fingerless mits, even in warm weather.

Abruptly realizing what she was doing, Maura stopped and carefully rearranged her skirt. "I, too, contracted the pox, and so did my father. We escaped with only minimal scars, thank heaven, and I expect to emerge from this adventure in quite the same fashion. You see, Mr. Catlin," she flashed her dimples once more, "we Magruders are survivors as well as explorers and scholars. . . . Now, hadn't we better go and find my father? These delays make him even more impatient than they do me. If we don't make Bellevue by this evening, he'll be most upset."

Due to the necessity of having to "grasshopper" or pole the steamship past the obstruction in the river, it was noon of the following day before the *Yellowstone* came within sight of Bellevue, a compound of storehouses and traders' cabins nine miles above the juncture of the two mighty rivers, the Missouri and the Platte.

On deck, Eben Magruder stood listening to the animated conversation between his daughter, Maura, and the painter, George Catlin. The two were speculating on the tribal identities of the Indians lining the bank to watch their approach. Clearly in awe of the vessel, furred and feathered figures were racing up and down the gentle bluffs, each man, woman, and child trying to find the optimum viewing position.

Scanning the rustic little settlement for some sign of Major Dougherty, Eben saw a number of white men dressed in the inevitable homespun trousers, shirts, waistcoats, and wide-brimmed floppy hats. A few sported fringed leather hunting jackets and coonskin caps. Eben identified two or three Frenchmen by their distinctive woolen stocking caps and brightly colored, full-sleeved shirts, and noted with surprise the several women in plain poke bonnets, capes, and long white aprons. At this distance, it was hard to tell if the women were white or Indian, but as the vessel drew closer, the women's dark skins and heavy black braids indicated that they were squaws dressed in clothing probably obtained from lonely white men.

Nowhere did Eben see anyone dressed in a military uniform or the alternate costume of authority—frock coat, high, stiff collar, cravat, and beaver or silk hat—signifying a

24

gentleman in appropriate daywear.

Worriedly, he glanced at his daughter; had he been a fool to bring her along? He had sojourned among the Sacs and Foxes in Illinois, the Seminoles in Florida, and the Cherokee in Tennessee. He had often been far from any outpost of civilization, yet never quite this far. Between the riverfront posts, with their modest cornfields and orchards, he had witnessed nothing but mile upon mile of wilderness — towering bluffs and canyons, immense stretches of straight, flat plains, and undulating prairies extending as far as the eye could see.

He had hoped Bellevue would be bigger and more developed. At the same time, he had known that if it was, he would have to go even farther into the interior to find the untouched primitives he hoped to study.

Today's attack of anxiousness was entirely due to Maura's presence, and Eben covertly watched her from the corner of his eye. On this warm sunny day, his daughter wore a charming bonnet of Tuscan straw, faced with blue taffeta and trimmed with ribbons and silk flowers in the same shade of blue as her gown and her eyes. The gown was the same she had worn yesterday — the one she believed would create a good impression on Major Dougherty and their guide, Luke Cutter, who were to meet them in Bellevue.

A printed, white muslin fichu discreetly skimmed her neck and bosom. She had discarded her long wool cloak and hood in favor of a stylish short cape called a pelerine, and Eben saw that it, too, brought out the blue of her eyes. Silver-gold curls escaping her coronet of braids framed both sides of her perfectly oval face set off by the coy bonnet. Her blondness came from him, and like his, her hair would probably turn completely silver when she reached the wrong side of forty, but on her, the effect would doubtless be stunning, as it had been on his own mother.

Eben's chest constricted at the mere sight of his lovely, well-turned-out daughter. The blue of her sparkling eyes was made even bluer with excitement, and her cheeks had a rosy tinge, most becoming to her exquisite, white complexion. She was beautiful and delicate, like a rare woodland flower, and he wondered for the thousandth time why he had permitted her to talk him into this.

Probably his age had something to do with it. At fifty-two, he could not help but realize that his daughter would soon leave his protection. Every moment in her charming company was therefore fleeting and precious. Had Maura remained in Philadelphia, she most certainly would have married Nate Hibbert, and Eben did not think Nate was a strong enough man for his high-spirited, strong-willed daughter. Nate had only one passion—his work, and by the time Maura discovered this, it might be too late.

Eben counted it a blessing that Nate had backed out of the expedition at the last minute. As soon as time and distance had dulled Maura's infatuation, she, too, would see it as a blessing and return his betrothal ring posthaste. At least, Eben hoped she would.

"Father, do you think they are Pawnee?" Maura waved a lacy handkerchief in the direction of the Indians craning their necks on the riverbank.

"It's possible, Maura. This is Pawnee territory."

George Catlin could not take his eyes from the savages. "These tribesmen are taller than I expected. I can't wait to paint them. . . . Look at that fellow over there. He has the bearing of a king."

Just then, the steamboat belched an unusually large cloud of steam and smoke. The regal Indian leaped a foot into the air, then clawed and scrambled his way up the steep bank as if pursued by devils. The onlookers laughed and jeered. The ship's bell clanged. Dogs barked. Cats yowled. The dogs were romping on the bank, and the cats were confined to a wooden crate on deck. Eben recalled hearing that the inhabitants of a fort upriver had ordered the felines in hopes of preserving their flour supply from rats.

"Oh, Father, this is so exciting!" Maura plucked at Eben's sleeve. "It's almost like a homecoming—just the way I imagined it would be!"

Her bright-eyed attention flew back to shore. The roustabouts were tossing lines to people on the riverbank, but only white men leaped to grab them. The Indians flinched away, their bronze faces reflecting a fear and awe that further undermined Eben's confidence in his latest undertaking. Always before, his arrival among the subjects of his newest study had occasioned a feeling of exhilaration akin to his daughter's, but this time, he felt close to panic.

Maura was so young, precious, and untried. If anything should happen to her, he would never forgive himself. He slid his hand in his vest pocket and rubbed his thumb along the rim of his round gold watch fob. Maura's mother, Lucille, had given it to him on their wedding day. Lucille, too, had been young, precious, and untried, no older than Maura when they married, while he had been in his thirties.

Despite his love for his young wife, he had been unable to keep her safe. The disease that had killed Lucille and scarred both him and Maura had come like a thief in the night to steal his most precious possession. Ever since, he had been holding his breath, praying that a similar tragedy would not befall his darling daughter.

Quickly, he withdrew a silk handkerchief, blew his nose, and wiped his eyes.

"Father, are you all right?" Maura's face clouded with sudden concern.

"Don't mind me, dear. The combination of noonday sun and smoke is making my eyes water. I must be getting old, to be so sensitive."

"Oh, pooh! You'll never be old. That's one of the things I love most about you." Maura gave him a quick hug. "The other is that you grant my dearest wishes. Oh, thank you, Father, for letting me come!"

On shore, Luke Cutter watched the arrival of the *Yellowstone* and wished he knew more about the famous E.M. Magruder than what Major Dougherty had been able to tell him. Magruder's experiences among the eastern tribes of Indians would probably have the same relevance to living among the Plains Indians as traveling on a steamboat down the placid Ohio had to traveling on the cranky Missouri. New arrivals always complained about the unexpected rigors of the journey.

Were he not so in need of money, Luke would have refused to lead Magruder's expedition. Now was not a good time to be venturing across the unmarked plains in search of scholarship. Hostility against whites had been running high ever since the previous autumn, when a barrel of tainted whiskey had caused the deaths of two Osages and blindness in three other Indians.

Dismally, Luke wondered how he himself had ever been so naive as to think he could make an honest living in the fur trade. It was a more violent, cut-throat business than the one he had fled in Boston — the manufacture and sale of weapons, gun powder, and dangerous, unproven explosives. His stepfather would slap his knee and burst a blood vessel laughing if he ever learned that his idealistic stepson had found far greater greed and corruption out west than he had ever found back home.

Fortunately, Major Dougherty was a decent man who dealt fairly with Indians and white men alike. Luke knew he and the major made a good team. For the most part, despite the fact that competition between rivals in the fur trade had led to theft and unauthorized trading away from the post, they managed to keep the Indians from being cheated.

*Un*fortunately, every keelboat — and now, the new steamship — laboring upriver, disgorged more scoundrels and fortune-seekers, swelling the volume of potential troublemakers to unmanageable proportions. In moments of grim prescience, Luke wondered where it would all end. He was ashamed of being a part of the fur trade, but even more ashamed to think of leaving Major Dougherty to cope with the problem alone. And so he stayed on, taking advantage of the few opportunities for earning an honest dollar that also gave him a temporary respite from settling trade disputes with diplomacy when possible, and with fists or rifle when not.

"You see anybody who looks like an important eastern gentleman?" Major Dougherty asked beside him.

The benevolent-looking, round-faced major squinted against the bright April sunlight and wiped his brow with his homespun shirt sleeve. Dougherty never put on airs; it was one of the secrets of his success. People instinctively felt he could be trusted. The major dressed and acted no differently from the rough frontier types who frequented his post. What set him apart was the sharp intelligence sparkling in his calm hazel eyes.

"Not yet," Luke answered.

He narrowed his own eyes and scanned the steamboat, finally spotting a short gentleman in a distinctive brimmed cap with turned-up earflaps. The man was dressed as if for a day of grouse shooting in the east, and to his right, stood a taller, more distinguished-looking fellow with a thatch of silver hair. Luke's gaze roamed further and stopped in shock when it came to a flower-trimmed bonnet.

"There's a young woman aboard," he muttered.

"A young woman? Where? Ah, now I see her. A little bit of a thing, ain't she? Wonder what she's doin' here." The major frowned. "I hope she's not with the Magruder party. Maybe she's just makin' the river journey to see the sights and won't even be coming ashore."

"Crazy damn tourists," Luke growled. "People think the wilderness is some kind of circus where they can pay to see all the dangerous critters, but don't have to worry about getting clawed or bitten."

He resumed his search of the crowded decks for Eben Magruder. There were supposed to be three in the Magruder party: Magruder himself, his assistant, and a botanist named Nathaniel Hibbert.

"She's already drawin' quite a bit of attention," Major Dougherty said, nodding toward the bobbing bonnet of the young woman on the *Yellowstone*. "Can't make out whether those curls peekin' from inside her hat are gold or silver. Sure hope she stays on the boat. I don't want to be responsible for lookin' after her."

Luke's gaze returned to the young woman, who was as pretty and delicate as a prairie wildflower, and as out of place in this rough setting as a china teacup. She was dressed, he saw, like the greenest easterner in a gown with huge, impractical sleeves. Lace foamed at her throat and wrists, and her waist was so tiny it was a wonder she could even breathe with a such a tightly cinched corset. Already the Indians were gawking at her.

Exasperation clenched Luke's jaw; whoever had brought the girl this far ought to be staked out on an ant hill in consequence, and very likely would be if he stayed here. More than one of the young bucks admiring her was probably busy tallying how many furs he would need in order to buy the girl—or else he was planning how to steal her.

"A tart like that should be kept under lock and key," Luke snarled half under his breath. "Or maybe it would just be better to drown her in the river and be done with it. Save a lot of trouble all around."

"My, my. . . ." Major Dougherty slanted Luke an inquiring glance. "Do I detect a touch of bitterness? You sound as if you don't much appreciate the gentler sex."

"I don't," Luke responded curtly.

The major's eyes held questions, but Luke was not giving any answers. No one but himself need know all the reasons why he had fled the comforts of Boston to seek his fortune in the west. The slender blond beauty on the *Yellowstone* stirred memories he would rather forget, and he was suddenly impatient to gather the damn anthropologist, his assistant, and the botanist, and set forth across the plains. The only place he managed to find any peace was beneath the endless, burning blue sky. Alone on the grasslands, he could erase the memory of another beautiful female who had soured him on nearly all women, except for his mother and his younger sister, Celina.

"Come on," he snapped. "Let's find Magruder and get the hell out of here."

Without even waiting to see if Major Dougherty was following, Luke began to shoulder his way through the throng.

Chapter Two

Trembling with excitement, Maura could scarcely believe they had finally arrived at Bellevue, the jumping-off place for their journey across the plains in search of knowledge, adventure, and academic recognition. When she and her father left this little outpost, they would be entering a world unknown to most whites, and the near achievement of this long-held dream made Maura feel as if she had downed three successive glasses of her father's precious, secret store of French brandy.

"Father, these Indians *must* be Pawnee, don't you think? They're so strong and healthy-looking—nothing like our poor tribesmen back home. Instead of slinking about like whipped dogs, they stand tall and proud, staring us straight in the eye. Oh, I hope they are Pawnee; imagine living among such noble creatures."

On the other side of her strangely silent father, George Catlin grinned, his eyes shining with shared enthusiasm. "T'will be a magnificent adventure, I warrant, Miss Magruder. After I explore the upper river, I may return here to paint these fellows. Look at that man's hair. I've never in my life seen hair as long as that."

George pointed to a brave on horseback. The Indian's long black hair trailed behind him, mingling with his horse's white tail and sweeping the ground at his horse's feet. Other braves sported hair equally as long, but most wore their impressive tresses rolled up into more manageable lengths and decorated with feathers, quills, and other ornaments.

The steamship was firmly secured to shore now, and a gangplank was being maneuvered into place. Near it, Maura noticed a tall, lean, broad-shouldered, white man standing on the bank, impatiently awaiting the completion of the final docking procedures. Something about him compelled her attention. In his own way, he was as striking as any of the Indians, but unlike most of the onlookers, he was not smiling or admiring the steamboat. Rather, he was scowling, and as she watched, wondering at the hostility emanating from him, he caught her eye, and she shivered involuntarily.

His eyes were a clear, cold gray, the color of river ice in late winter. Boldly, he perused her, his scowl deepening, and her cheeks grew hot beneath the intensity of his gaze. He had a lean, brown, hawkish face, too harsh and predatory to be counted handsome, and his dark hair, gleaming with chestnut highlights, was too windblown and unruly to belong to a gentleman. He wore a fringed leather hunting jacket of a warm brown color, open halfway to his waist, and stretched taut over rippling chest muscles. The jacket tapered in at his mid-section and fit snugly over a flat belly.

Her eyes stopped at his hips, and quickly, she returned her gaze to his face. No real lady would wantonly assess a man's hips and thighs—or anything else in that region, yet she had to concede that he was blatantly and attractively male. Guiltily, Maura tried to conjure a less disturbing image: that of her fiancé, Nate, whose pale cheeks, straw-colored hair and slender, impeccably clothed figure were the very antithesis of this bold stranger.

Despite her fascination with Indians, Maura had never enjoyed the company of challenging, rustic men; they always made her feel distinctly uncomfortable, and she longed to see them taken down a peg or two. They were usually unbearably arrogant, not given to polite discourse, nor even capable of intelligent conversation. Experience had taught her that they usually wanted only one thing, and she had long ago learned to avoid them.

Again, her glance collided with the bold stranger's, and slowly, mockingly, he grinned, as if he knew exactly what effect he was having upon her self-possession. She glared back at him, drawing her lips into a prim, thin line, but he only grinned more broadly, revealing perfect white teeth that unfavorably recalled Nate's slightly crooked, yellowish ones, her fiancé's single imperfection. Bristling inside, Maura realized she ought never to have begun this silent war between herself and this beastly fellow. She hated to lose at anything, and the infuriating brute seemed to know it.

Instinctively, she knew that *he* would *never* be first to look away, and if *she* did, he would think he had won something. Mustering all her dignity, she forced herself to smile at him and flash her dimples. Amazingly, it worked. His insolent smirk vanished in an instant. His lips thinned, and his dark brows plunged downward over his penetrating, icy gray eyes.

Preening over the victory, she turned to her father. "The gangplank is in place now, Father. Shall I see to our things in the cabin?"

"The captain will send someone to get them, Maura. There's no cause for worry. Nothing will be lost or forgotten."

Maura stole another glance at the stranger, but to her surprise, he had disappeared. She was vaguely disappointed and decided to go to the cabin, anyhow. Of the pitifully few belongings she had so carefully and sparingly packed, she did not want to lose her sketch book, her journal, or her father's journal. These were irreplaceable.

"I'll return in a few moments, Father. I just want to make certain we leave nothing behind."

"If you must, then go ahead, my dear. Meanwhile, Mr.

34

Catlin and I will try to find Major Dougherty. I had expected him to meet the ship, but I suppose the precise time of our arrival was impossible to predict."

Picking up her skirts, Maura hurried away to their cabin, and by the time she returned, valuables in arms, Mr. Catlin and her father were engaged in animated conversation with two men. The first was an amiable, balding, round-faced gentleman wearing a plain homespun shirt, a wrinkled waistcoat, and trousers that had not seen a crease in months. The second had his back to her — a very broad back clad in soft leather of a faintly familiar, buttery nut-brown color, quite distinct from the stiff, waterproof, malodorous buckskins worn by most of the traders and trappers.

"Here is my daughter, now," Eben said, catching sight of her. "Maura, this is Major Dougherty." He nodded toward the shorter, balding man, then inclined his head toward the taller figure. "And this other gentleman is our guide, Mr. Cutter. Gentlemen, may I present my daughter, Maura Magruder."

The tall, buckskinned man turned, and Maura found herself looking up into the icy gray eyes of the stranger who had been watching her from shore. His eyes swept her face and figure like a scythe mowing down tender blades of grass, and he gave her only the barest of nods before turning back to her father.

"As I was saying, Magruder, no way in hell am I going to lead you and your daughter into Pawnee territory. In your letter to the major, you said nothing about bringing along a female, and if you had, I would have refused to be your guide right then and there."

Maura saw her father stiffen. The faint pox scars on his cheeks turned white — a sure sign of his anger — but gentleman that he was, he did not raise his voice as Luke Cutter had done.

"Mr. Cutter, I most certainly did inform Major Dougherty about Maura. She is the assistant to whom I

35

referred, a position she has admirably held since she was old enough to take pen in hand and neatly copy all my notes."

"You mean she's accompanied you on previous expeditions?" Luke Cutter shot Maura a scornful glance that condemned her puffed sleeves and bonnet as completely frivolous, if not downright ridiculous.

"No, she has not. This is the first time. But nonetheless she is adequately prepared. Do not let her appearance of fragility deceive you. She has spent many long hours on horseback in order to toughen herself for the coming ordeal. And she has also read and studied extensively about the Plains Indian culture. As much as anyone can know about it beforehand, she knows. She anticipates a certain amount of hardship and inconvenience, don't you, Maura?"

Before Maura could answer, Luke Cutter's eyes again swept her disdainfully; he did not believe a word of her father's praise, or else he had decided she could not measure up no matter what anyone said.

"Do you anticipate abduction, enslavement, rape, torture, and a slow, agonizing death, Miss Magruder? Those are very real possibilities. Even the squaws here at the post rarely venture far from Bellevue without an army of friends or relatives to protect them. And they are much tougher than you appear to be."

"Really, Mr. Cutter," Maura responded as coolly as she could manage. "Don't you think you are exaggerating the potential for danger and tragedy? A woman accompanied Meriwether Lewis and William Clark all the way to the Pacific Ocean, and no harm came to her."

"You are referring, of course, to Sacajawea, an *Indian,* and that journey took place nearly thirty years ago. Today, the rare female of any race in these parts not only has to worry about the red-skinned savages, but also the white-skinned. Tell me, do you know how to shoot?"

Maura flushed beneath Luke Cutter's hawk-eyed scrutiny and was glad she could answer affirmatively. "I can handle a small pistol better than most women, Indian *or* white. I have one packed in my luggage."

"I don't mean one of those pepperbox toys ladies use to fend off ungallant admirers, Miss Magruder. I mean, can you shoot a rifle? Can you load one, and if so, are you capable of hitting anything?"

Unable to answer yes, Maura momentarily dropped her gaze to the quilled embroidery decorating the yoke of Luke Cutter's hunting jacket. Red, blue, and white symbols had been worked into the soft-looking, supple leather, and it struck her that Mr. Cutter must have a wife — an *Indian* wife; who else would have performed such a difficult, painstaking task?

Lifting her chin, she fixed the boorish guide with a withering stare. "I was not aware I was supposed to defend us on this expedition, Mr. Cutter. I thought that was *your* job. Since you seem to be unwilling or incapable of performing your duties, we'll have to find someone else."

"Maura . . . ," her father said warningly, his frown deepening as he listened to their exchange.

From the corner of her eye, Maura saw George Catlin's grin. Major Dougherty was biting down hard on his lower lip. Despite or perhaps because of Luke Cutter's ferocious glare, Maura felt a spurt of perverse satisfaction. "Is there anyone you would recommend to take your place, Mr. Cutter? We shall, of course, demand a demonstration of his ability to shoot accurately."

"You can demand any damn thing you please, Miss Magruder. You can also find your own guide. I've no desire to risk my neck playing nursemaid to a spoiled brat, and if I don't want to do it, I certainly won't ask a friend to go in my place. In all likelihood, anyone attempting to look after *you* will just get himself killed. Good day, gentlemen. Major, if you need me, you know where to find me." With a curt nod, Luke Cutter spun on his heel and stalked away.

His rapid departure was followed by a moment of stunned

37

silence, during which the sun's rays suddenly felt as if they were blistering Maura's face and body, penetrating even her clothes.

"Good heavens, Maura, what have you done?" Eben exploded.

Amazed and chagrined, Maura simply gaped at her father. It had all happened so fast. What, in the space of only a minute or two, *had* she done? Destroyed the entire expedition?

Wending his way through the crowd, Luke bypassed the official log and sod buildings and headed for the tall tepees fringing the settlement. Several Indian children scampered at his heels, grinning and calling his name, but as he did not stop to josh with them as he usually did, they soon backed off and resumed watching the exciting scene on shore.

Luke kept walking until he reached a richly decorated tepee set a short distance apart from the others. Without preamble, he ducked through the east-facing entrance, then stood still a moment, allowing his eyes to adjust to the cool, shadowed interior.

Not in the least surprised that he should come barging into her quarters, the person he had come to see rose to greet him. Across a stone-ringed cooking pit where no fire burned at this hour, the tall woman silently regarded him, her dark eyes registering only the faintest polite inquiry.

Luke returned her gaze without speaking. Elk-Runner was a handsome, lithe, muscular woman whose name derived from her ability to track game as well as any man of her tribe. Because of this special skill, she had not been required to marry again after her second husband followed her first to the Happy Hunting Grounds.

Now, she slept with whom she chose, hunted when she wanted, and was regarded as something of a seeress. Whenever the Blackfeet came to trade or discuss problems with

Major Dougherty, Elk-Runner welcomed Luke into her lodge, and the two shared meals and a fur-lined bed, then parted without any recriminations. Luke enjoyed the tall woman's company and respected her — all the more so because she never made demands upon him; demands would only have spoiled a pleasant relationship that allowed each to stave off loneliness and satisfy their physical needs before returning to their solitary lives.

Holding something out to him, Elk-Runner said in the Blackfoot tongue: "This came for you a moment ago. A boy brought it from the Canoe-That-Walks-On-Water."

Only marginally surprised that the mail had been distributed so rapidly, Luke took the letter. Whenever a mackinaw or keelboat arrived from St. Louis, its first order of business was the distribution of news from home. Everyone in Bellevue, including Luke, had family, friends, and loved ones worrying if they were still alive. Nonetheless, his hand trembled slightly as he held the letter and studied the writing on it.

He knew it was useless; it had been four years, but he never could break of himself of the hope that one day the writing on his mail would be Margaret's. She would be writing to say she was sorry, and it was all a mistake. She still loved him and wanted him to come back east and take her away with him, freeing her forever from her brutish lout of a husband, whom she had married in a childish fit of anger and disappointment, because Luke had not inherited his father's business.

Elk-Runner touched his hand, her black eyes warm with sympathy. "Do not read it if it will only bring you pain, Great Heart."

Luke flinched at her use of his Indian name, bestowed in recognition of his having endured several tribal manhood rites and supposedly proven his bravery many times over. The name embarrassed him, for he felt he did not truly deserve it. The Indians thought he was courageous, but he knew he was merely reckless, relishing danger and finding a morbid fascination in seeing how close he could come to being killed without actually dying.

Then, noticing Elk-Runner's characteristically timid disdain for the written word, he smiled reassuringly. Like most Indians, she was highly suspicious of the white man's way of communicating, believing that the alphabet held great power for evil and abuse. Too many treaties had been written on paper, signed by whites and Indians alike, and then broken or deliberately misquoted. Since none among the Indians could read, they feared this strange magic that so often put them at great disadvantage.

"Relax, Elk-Runner. This letter is from my sister. I have nothing to fear from her."

"Then I shall leave you in peace to read it. I have no wish to know the meaning of those strange markings that resemble hen tracks, even if they are from your sister."

Elk-Runner gave a slight bow and departed the lodge as quietly as a mountain cat padding on cushioned claws. She pulled the flap closed behind her, and as soon as he was alone, Luke tore open the stained and travel-worn missive.

"My dear stubborn, pig-headed brother . . ." the letter began, and despite the long years and great distances separating them, Luke could almost hear Celina's gay, teasing voice. They had been very close, though Celina was eight years younger and as different from him as day from night.

She was sunlight, laughter, and sparkling good fun, while he had always been an introspective, brooding personality sadly lacking in a sense of humor, as Celina was always quick to point out. Yet she had been able to make him laugh and be lighthearted when no one else could. No matter how terrible things seemed, Celina had made life bearable—a joy, actually, and Luke hoped her new husband would love and cherish her as she deserved.

The first half of Celina's letter dealt with her recent marriage to a man Luke had never met. Happiness bubbled

40

from every line, and Luke could not keep from smiling, even when his sister scolded him for failing to come home for her wedding. *"Mama longs to see you again, Luke. You don't write to her nearly as often as you should, and all she does is talk about you and wonder if you are all right. Isn't it about time you forgave her for marrying Walter? She can't help being a silly, gullible woman who fell in love with the wrong man after Papa died. In her grief, I don't think she knew what she was doing—and it certainly wasn't her fault that Walter turned out to be everything you accused him of being: a money-grubbing charlatan."*

The mention of his mother's folly and his stepfather's greedy nature made Luke narrow his eyes in disgust. Walter Cardoway had taken over the family munitions business and almost overnight had destroyed its reputation as a small, respected, gunpowder and firearms manufacturing firm. Now, it was a huge, unwieldy, unsavory operation which specialized in selling oft-times faulty, untested merchandise to unsuspecting buyers headed west, where complaints of rifles misfiring or powder that would not ignite could not possibly reach the ears of anyone back east.

"Business is business," Walter had told Luke when he first discovered what was happening. "But don't worry. Close to home, I sell only first-rate stuff. Only to fools do I pass on the cheap goods. Most men headed west can't afford better anyway, so I'm doing them a favor in a manner of speaking. At least they're not traveling empty-handed."

Remembering that conversation, Luke's stomach knotted with helpless frustration; his own father had been killed while testing the safety of the new percussion cap pistols. Four months later, his mother had married Walter, and after Margaret's disaffection, Luke himself had headed west—and never looked back, except occasionally when he heard from Celina.

After describing her wedding, her new home and husband, and the state of their mother's health, Celina tackled a new subject, and as he read onward, Luke's breathing accelerated, and his palms became sweaty.

"Margaret came to the wedding, Luke, and she has grown quite plump and matronly after the birth of their first child. She has a son now, and her husband is ecstatic about his heir. They bored everyone to tears talking about how rich their little Reginald will one day be, and all I could think of was thank God you didn't marry her. No matter how much it hurt at the time, when she jilted you and eloped with a corset manufacturer of all things, it was for the best. She is a vain, silly, shallow woman, Luke, unworthy of your affection. I pray you have forgotten her.

Enough about Margaret. The family business is doing marvelously well, and Walter is making money hand over fist. I don't know why someone hasn't come gunning for him yet, but I suppose he has been careful not to sell shoddy merchandise close to home. He is now manufacturing the very same percussion cap pistols that blew up on Papa. Says he can't afford not to because there's such a demand for them. I wonder how many people will have to be maimed or killed before the dangerous things are banned. As usual, Mama defends Walter whenever I question his business practices. You know how ignorant she is of weapons, and sometimes I think she is still quite muddled in her thinking . . . I don't think she'll ever completely recover from Papa's death. Nor will I. He was always so vital, alive, and healthy. Probably that's why he never got around to amending the will he made when he and Mama were first married. I'm sure he never intended to overlook his own children; he just assumed he would live to be a hundred!"

Celina continued for another two pages, but Luke only skimmed it. The news about Margaret greatly upset him. He had not known she was pregnant, much less already delivered of a son and heir. Somehow, it was the final blow. Until now, he could still fantasize that she would grow weary of the crude, pompous dandy she had married and remember how deeply in love they had been that summer before his father's death.

How could she forget the long rides in his new cabriolet, that wonderfully springy, two-wheeled carriage that had borne them to so many picnics in the country . . . the promises and plans they had made . . . and the heady, sun-drenched kisses in the pear orchard, with the bees droning all about them?

Those memories would forever haunt him, but less than six months later, when Margaret learned that he had *not* inherited his father's business, she had tearfully broken off their engagement and begun seeing other men. Wealthy men. Men of property and promise. He had begged her not to give up on him; he would find another way to make his fortune. But goaded by her parents, she had soon stopped seeing him altogether and would not even respond to his desperate letters.

He had been twenty-four years old then, still naive and idealistic. When he heard of Margaret's elopement, he had stubbornly refused to accept that it was truly over between them. He would go west, make his fortune in the lucrative fur trade, and one day return to Boston and reclaim Margaret, married or not.

Now, he knew he never would. Nor would he ever be as rich as the man she had married. Money made by cheating Indians or gullible white men sickened and revolted him. His first year on the plains had monumentally changed him; he had gone to the mountains, been snowed in, chased by wolves, and nearly starved to death. It had been the longest, loneliest winter of his life—and the most meaningful. In the spring, he had thought to return to civilization, but a chance encounter with a grizzly bear had left him half-dead in the bottom of a ravine. Had he not been discovered and taken home by a young Pawnee brave named Pitale-sharo, his bones would be lying there still. His stay among the Indians had changed him further in ways he was still trying to understand.

More than ever, he wanted fame and wealth, but he wanted it honestly and honorably. And until today, he had harbored a secret vision of himself one day sweeping beautiful, vivacious Margaret into his arms and making her his own. Today, when he read that she now had a son—someone else's son—he knew with stone-cold certainty that it was over, and that he'd been a fool. He had lived twenty-eight years, the last four of them clinging to a stupid dream, and he had nothing to show for his life—not home, wife, family, children, wealth, success, or anything else by which a man measured himself.

"Damn fool!" he muttered under his breath.

Crumpling Celina's letter in his clenched fist, he hurled it across the tepee. A moment later, a soft voice outside the dwelling called his name: "Mr. Cutter? Are you in there, Mr. Cutter? It's Maura Magruder. Please, may I speak with you? It's very important."

Too upset to immediately answer, Luke ran his hands through his hair in an effort to regain his composure and focus on this rude interruption. The voice came again, soft and pleading: "Please, Mr. Cutter. My father didn't want me to come, and Major Dougherty said it was useless to try and change your mind, but I had to try. You've made a terrible mistake, Mr. Cutter, and if I could just speak with you a moment. . . ."

Luke crossed the tepee in two strides and jerked open the flap. Maura Magruder stood uncertainly before him. She had taken off her straw bonnet and was holding it in one hand while, with the other, she nervously plucked at its blue silk ribbons. The sun shone full upon her golden head, and her eyes were the bluest blue he had ever seen.

"Mr. Cutter . . . ," she sighed, endowing his name with a breathy, sensual quality. "I'm so glad I picked the right tepee and found you here. Please, may I come in?"

Chapter Three

At first, Maura thought Luke Cutter was going to refuse outright. The planes of his face seemed chiseled from stone, his eyes hewn from flint. Half afraid of him, she retreated a step and then chided herself for lacking in courage. If she allowed him to scare her away, she might as well start planning the journey back home. Major Dougherty had already told her that Luke Cutter was the only man in the entire area capable of safely leading them to the Pawnee. Not only was he the only one who knew the whereabouts of the tribe at any given season during the year, but he was also the only man the major would trust to see that they came to no harm.

Maura *had* to convince Luke Cutter to change his mind. "I came to apologize, Mr. Cutter. I'd like to do so privately, but if you feel that's impossible, I suppose we can hold this discussion right out here in front of everyone."

She nodded in the direction of a score or more of curious Indians who had been trailing her since her breathless arrival in the midst of their tepees. Following her glance, Luke Cutter acknowledged the onlookers with a negligent shrug. His unyielding gray eyes again pierced her to the core.

"I can think of a dozen reasons why you shouldn't set foot inside this lodge alone with me, Miss Magruder. However, I can also think of one compelling reason why I *should* allow it."

He stepped back and held open the flap, and Maura was suddenly hesitant to enter. She had not thought he would be alone, nor that his manner would be so suggestive of possible improprieties. Doubtless, he was using every tactic available to discourage her from pleading her case. Briskly stepping inside the tepee, she immediately turned and faced him. "What reason is that, Mr. Cutter?"

Too late she realized that she had not left much space for him to stand between her and the doorway; he was mere inches away, and as he allowed the flap to fall shut again, cool, dim shadows encased them, and every nerve ending she possessed thrummed in awareness of his tall, perfectly proportioned body standing so near her. Trying desperately to remain calm, she inhaled deeply of the scent of leather and horse, excitingly intermingled with *male* — and underlaced with tangy, conflicting odors from the bunches of dried herbs hanging from the side poles of the lodge.

His eyes bored into hers, then with slow, insolent calculation roamed each feature of her face, starting with her cheek bones, then her nose, then her forehead. Everywhere he looked, she felt his glance like a burning, intimate touch.

"You're a stunning manifestation of eastern womanhood, Miss Magruder," he drawled provocatively. "A man would have to be standing waist-deep in a half-frozen stream in mid-January not to want to be alone with you in a teepee — where *anything* can happen."

He had incredibly long lashes, Maura noticed, and as his glance fastened on her mouth she felt an odd tightening sensation in her lower abdomen. It was difficult to focus on what he was saying, but gathering her wits about her, she endured his appraisal with an outwardly icy calm.

"Nothing is going to happen, Mr. Cutter. Major Dougherty assured me that you were completely trustworthy, which is why I felt I had to come here and try and change your mind."

His eyes came back to her eyes. "No man is completely trustworthy where a beautiful young woman such as yourself is concerned, Miss Magruder. Beautiful young women have a way of making men think and behave like utter jackasses. I myself for example have a sudden powerful urge to steal a kiss from your tempting pink lips, while at the same time, I would actually like to boot your fanny out of here and send you back east where you belong."

His crude language shocked her, but Maura was determined not to let him know it. She had expected as much from him. What she had *not* expected was to feel the way she did — all fluttery and melting inside, as if she were a lump of butter left atop a hot stove.

"Mr. Cutter, if we have to, my father and I will go alone to find the Pawnee. However, we would prefer that you accompany us. I am sorry that I . . . I provoked your anger, and if you do accompany us, I will try very hard not to do so in the future."

"I'm afraid that would be impossible, Miss Magruder. You provoke me just by being here, wearing those enormous, poufed sleeves and that tightly laced corset. You don't *belong* here . . . and nothing you say can make me think otherwise."

Maura knew he had not approved of her clothing; earlier, she had read his scorn on his face. But his assumption that she wore a corset when she did not infuriated her into making another rash retort. "I fail to see why my undergarments should so fascinate you, Mr. Cutter, and can only conclude it's because you *are* a low-minded fellow, not at all of the high, moral character Major Dougherty claims."

"That's what I've been trying to tell you, Miss Magruder. I *am* a low-minded fellow, and to prove it, I *will* steal a kiss from you."

Before she could protest or even blink, Luke Cutter's large hands spanned her waist, seized it, and dragged her closer, so that her breasts were crushed against his wide chest. "Mr. Cut—!" she shrieked, but her cry of outrage was muffled as his mouth came down hard upon hers.

He kissed her with a savage urgency never before encountered in her limited experience of kissing. Nate had always kissed her closed-mouth, with dry, respectful lips. Luke Cutter's mouth was hot, damp, and open. While her head swam with these realizations, his tongue somehow forced itself between her lips and thoroughly ravaged the inside of her mouth, exploring first her tongue, then her teeth, then plunging into her throat. Gasping, she tried to push away, but he held her so tightly she could scarcely breathe, much less escape.

The buzzing of a thousand bees began in her ears, and a perilous weakness invaded her limbs. Though she had never fainted in her life, she feared she might do so now. Beneath her splayed hands—she had dropped her bonnet but managed to wedge her hands between their bodies—Luke Cutter's chest was brick-hard and unyielding. Pushing against it was like shoving at a wall, only this wall was warm and alive, rigid with muscle, and thumping like a drum. His buckskin jacket was softer than it looked, and she clutched at it to keep her balance and maintain a secure, upright position.

The kiss ended almost as suddenly as it had begun.

With an animalistic growl, Luke Cutter severed the intimate contact and drew back, glaring down at her. She stumbled forward and would have fallen were it not for his hands moving quickly to grip her wrists. She stared at him, and he stared back. Something primitive and violent vibrated in the air between them, and it came to her in a flash that this was what young women were so often warned about: this was why a woman should never allow herself to be alone with a man, not even when they were betrothed.

In the pit of her stomach, she felt a coiling, slithering heat, an insidious throbbing and wanting. . . . His dark, seductive power held her in thrall, even as she fought to be escape it. For the first time in her life, she knew what it was to be *tempted*. Her lips felt afire where he had kissed them, and her breasts tingled from being crushed against his chest. His virile odor enveloped her, so that she had the unnerving sensation of inhaling him each time she breathed. This was danger such as she had never imagined, and to make matters worse, she could no longer even think of the name of her fiancé, nor could she remember his chaste, gentlemanly kisses. They had been wiped from her memory by Luke Cutter's savage branding of her lips and body.

Wrenching free of him, she searched frantically about the tepee for some means to defend herself should he decide to kiss her again. Near her feet stood a beautifully woven basket filled with gourds in all sizes and shapes. Sparing no time to think, she bent and grasped the sides of the basket in both hands, swung it aloft, and flung it at him. The gourds flew in all directions, harmlessly glancing off him and rolling across the matted floor.

Flicking a piece of gourd shell off his shoulder, Luke Cutter grinned the slow, mocking grin that was fast becoming his most noticeable attribute. "I suppose I deserved that ineffectual but nonetheless unladylike attack, Miss Magruder. But a kiss is no more than *you* deserve for barging in here, uninvited."

"You . . . you held open the flap!" she reminded him incredulously.

"Did I? Yes, I guess I did. But no woman concerned for her virtue and reputation would have stepped inside — unless she was extremely gullible. Which proves my point. I repeat, Miss Magruder, you don't belong here. What you got from me was only the mildest of the tragedies sure to befall you if you stubbornly insist on remaining in the Land of Shallow Rivers."

"Well, we *are* remaining here, Mr. Cutter, so you had better get used to it! As to your serving as our guide, you can forget we ever asked. We wouldn't have you now if you *begged* us to take you!"

"You wouldn't?" He had the audacity to touch his finger to the corner of her mouth. She slapped his hand away as hard as she could, but his grin only widened. "Your response to my kiss tells me you wouldn't mind at all if I accompanied you as planned. Indeed, it tells me you wouldn't mind if I stole into your blankets one fine night. Tell me, does your father sleep soundly?"

"Why, you . . . you unprincipled rake! You will never know my father's sleeping habits — or mine, either, for that matter!" Backing away, Maura inhaled deeply and almost choked on her suppressed ire. Since losing control only made him laugh at her, she was determined to regain her lost dignity. "I'm sorry I disturbed you, sir. Please give my regards — rather, my *sympathy* — to your poor, unfortunate wife."

"My *wife?*"

Intensely gratified to see him recoil in shock, Maura bestowed a chilly smile. Obviously, he had intended for her to think him unmarried, despite the perfectly plain evidence. He was living in an Indian tepee, and wore Indian clothing. The tepee itself bore the unmistakable imprint of a woman's occupancy. When she had bent to pick up the basket of gourds, she had spotted a pair of beaded, fringed moccasins — too small to be his — peeping out from beneath the nearest fur-heaped platform.

Brushing past him, Maura crossed to the doorway. "Good day, Mr. Cutter. I hope this is the last I ever see of you, because meeting you has been anything but pleasant."

"Likewise, Miss Magruder."

Brushing by her, almost knocking her down as he did so, Luke Cutter grabbed the tent flap and with mock politeness, held it open. Maura longed to break a chair over his head, but no chairs were in sight. Furthermore, her desire to escape his odious presence was suddenly stronger than the need for retaliation. Head held high, she exited the tepee and stalked away without once looking back.

"So you're actually going to let them go off by themselves to find the Pawnee." Major Dougherty leaned back in the chair, lifted his booted feet, and placed them on the cluttered desk in front of him, using them like a pair of paperweights to hold down a pile of papers.

"*Their* decision, not mine," Luke growled. "I told them both what *I* thought."

"Hmmm. . . ." The major clasped his hands behind his head and benevolently gazed out the open window of his cramped, untidy office. The shutters had been flung wide to admit the fresh spring breezes and the golden light of early evening. The ever-present sounds of horses whinnying and people going to and fro were also clearly audible.

"They're leavin' first thing in the mornin', as soon as they finish gettin' supplies together," Dougherty informed Luke. "I already had horses lined up and the basics assembled, but they insisted upon addin' a few things besides."

"Figures," Luke snorted. "If I were you, I would have hidden the lot of it, and let them discover for themselves how difficult it is to choose items that might make the difference between life and death. Also give them a few days to think about the folly of what they're doing."

"Hmmm. . . ."

The major's noncommittal responses infuriated Luke. "You aren't siding with them, surely!" he exploded. "What you ought to do is *insist* they get right back on the steamship and keep going upriver. Isn't that what the painter wants them to do anyway? Catlin has guides waiting for him on the other end, he says, and the three of them together plus the guides would be a hell of a lot safer than the Magruders here by themselves."

"Mr. Catlin does want the Magruders to accompany him," Dougherty acknowledged. "But they're bent on studyin' the

Pawnee along the Loup River. I tried talkin' old man Magruder out of it, but his daughter simply wouldn't listen. Whatever occurred between the two of you in Elk-Runner's lodge set her mind so firm upon goin' that nothin' I say can change it." The major's hazel eyes scrutinized Luke. "What *did* happen in that tepee, Luke?"

"Nothing," Luke coldly denied. "Except that I gave her a mild demonstration of the sort of behavior she can expect on the trail from any strangers she might encounter."

Sighing, the major shook his head and ran the fingers of one hand over his bald spot. "Was that really necessary, Luke?"

"I thought so at the time," Luke ground out, remembering the incredible softness and sweetness of Maura Magruder's lips and body. To his surprise, she had *not* been wearing a corset, and the very embrace by which he had intended to teach her a lesson had taught *him* a lesson, too. The girl was definitely capable of rattling his self-control; he had nearly lost his head while kissing her, a reaction he had *never* expected, and even now, the recollection of that kiss was enough to make his blood thunder through his veins.

"I kissed her — that's *all*. But you know what any other red-blooded man in these parts would have done to her. She's a fetching piece of skirt, *too* fetching to be left alone for long. I give her a week, maybe less, before she gets raped. I just hope her father has quick reflexes and a damn good aim with a pistol or rifle."

"I hear Shon-ka, The Dog, has offered himself as a guide." Major Dougherty laced his fingers together and stared down at them as if they interested him immensely.

"Shon-ka! When did he arrive in Bellevue?"

"This afternoon, about the same time as the *Yellowstone*. He and three other braves brought in a fine passle of furs. The first thing he did was trade for 'em, and the second was to find out what the White-Eyes woman was doin' here. After he found out, he hied himself right over to the

Magruders and offered his services as a guide. Must say his English is gettin' quite good."

"Of course you advised them of the danger of hiring a Sioux when they're riding out to find the Pawnee." Luke leaned over the desk, supporting his weight on both hands.

The major shot him a nonchalant look. "Of course. However, to their credit, the Magruders already knew of the enmity between the two tribes. They politely refused. But you know Shon-ka . . . I doubt he will take no for an answer."

"Yes, I know Shon-ka."

While considering this latest development, Luke straightened and gazed out the window. Shon-ka was trouble with a capital T and always had been. The Sioux and the Pawnee honored the most recent truce only within the neutral area around Bellevue. For the sake of the fur trade, all of the different tribes honored the settlement's neutrality, but away from Bellevue, one pack of Indians was just as likely to swoop down upon another as the sun was likely to rise each morning.

Raiding for furs, women, and horses was a way of life for the Plains Indians, the only avenue for achieving wealth, status, and whatever necessities they could not gain in trade. Few braves were as good at it as Shon-ka, The Dog. As a tribe, the Sioux were fierce and warlike, often taking scalps as part of their booty, and among the various Sioux factions, Shon-ka's name was legendary. Shon-ka and Pitale-sharo, Luke's friend, were sworn enemies; it was from Shon-ka's lodge pole that the scalp of Pitale-sharo's father hung.

"So he's taken a fancy to Maura Magruder, has he?" Luke mused aloud.

Major Dougherty did not have to ask who he meant. "It would seem so. Out on the plains, she could simply disappear, and no one could prove a thing against him. In all likelihood, we'd never even find Eben Magruder's bones."

"Hell and damnation!" Luke swore.

"Does that mean what I think it means?" Dougherty took his feet off the desk, his glance quizzical.

"If you mean that I've reconsidered and intend to go hat in hand and *beg* the Magruders to let me accompany them after all, no, it doesn't. What it *does* mean is that I *will* tail them some distance from the post and make sure Shon-ka isn't tailing them when they leave tomorrow morning."

"That's certainly better than nothin', though I had hoped for more."

"Sorry, but that's all you or the Magruders are going to get. I'll see them safely partway, but after that, they're on their own. Once I know no one from the post is following, I'm coming back here and, not sparing a second thought for people too stupid and stubborn to take my advice in the first place."

"All right, Luke. If that's the way you want it, so be it. I'm havin' dinner with the Magruders this evening, and I'll continue to try and talk 'em out of it. Mr. Catlin will doubtless help. Maybe, between the two of us, we can still convince them to board the *Yellowstone* in the morning instead of riding out on a mission that can only end in tragedy."

"I hope you succeed, Major, because tragedy *is* the only end their mission can have."

"Good night, Maura, my dear." Eben paused before the closed wooden door and lifted his daughter's hand to his lips. Gently, he pressed a kiss upon her open palm. "I hope you can sleep tonight."

"Oh, Father, please stop worrying!" Maura's blue eyes flashed in the light of the tallow candle she held to illuminate the narrow dark passageways of Major Dougherty's cramped, sparsely furnished, log and sod house. "Don't tell me you *aren't* worrying, because I know better. You frowned through dinner. I had to advance all the arguments for why

54

we should continue on our way tomorrow as if nothing had happened to change our plans."

"Well, we can't just ignore what has happened, Maura. We've lost our guide *and* a protector we very well might need."

"We *don't* need Mr. Cutter, Father. I've already told you he isn't the sort of man upon whom we can or should rely."

Maura's glance dropped to the flickering flame of her candle, and Eben wondered what she was trying so hard to hide. She had not accused Luke Cutter of doing anything rude or scandalous, but she *had* implied that his speech and conduct left much to be desired. He ought to have accompanied his daughter to the surly guide's lodgings, but Maura had impulsively hurried off to confront Mr. Cutter by herself. Whatever had occurred between them this afternoon now caused a rosy stain to darken Maura's fair cheeks whenever the man's name was mentioned.

"Maura, while it's true we have a compass to chart our way and keep us from getting lost on the plains—as you so charmingly pointed out to Major Dougherty and Mr. Catlin—it is *not* true that a compass can find the Pawnee if they've gone off to hunt or visit friends and relatives in some other tribe. Only Mr. Cutter can do that. I didn't want to contradict or embarrass you in front of the major, but I am seriously considering whether we ought to abandon this whole venture."

"Father, no!" Maura grasped his arm with her free hand, her face expressing a horror and disappointment that cut Eben to the quick. Unwittingly, he remembered all the promises he had made to her as she was growing up—that one day she would accompany him, and they would do important, scholarly work together. This trip was the culmination of her girlhood dreams.

"We *could* do as Mr. Catlin suggests, and journey along with him, at least for the time being—"

"But what about the Pawnee, Father? We didn't come here

just to *sightsee* and paint scenery. You're only suggesting we quit because of *me*, aren't you? If you were by yourself, nothing on earth would stop you."

"Now, Maura," Eben demurred, but he could not look his all-knowing daughter in the eye. She was right, of course; were he by himself, the loss of Luke Cutter as guide would never give him pause. Nor would Cutter have had reason to walk out on him. "You can't blame me for worrying about you, Maura. Major Dougherty, Mr. Cutter, and Mr. Catlin are merely saying what I've secretly feared ever since we embarked on the *Yellowstone*. This country is so big . . . so wild. I can't imagine what I was thinking of to bring you this far. It's simply too dangerous for us to proceed; *anything* might happen."

"If you won't go with me, then I'll go by myself!"

Maura's voice cracked and ended in a sob. Disbelieving she had actually said such a thing but terribly afraid he had heard aright, Eben studied her face. Her enormous blue eyes were brimming with tears and a stubborn will he recognized all too readily. In the past, whenever he had denied her something she desperately wanted—learning to ride astride, to swim in the creek behind the house, to climb the tall willow in the backyard—her responses had been similar. If he refused permission, she did it anyway, when he was not there to stop her.

Finally, he had learned *not* to refuse permission in the autocratic way fathers of the time usually did. Maura was far more likely to allow herself to be reasoned out of things than to be *ordered* not to do them—except that she was also devilishly good at applying her own brand of logic to persuade him to accept her point of view over his own. Eben often wondered if Maura would succeed so well in getting her own way if her mother were still alive to discipline and influence her.

"You can't mean that, Maura," he began cajolingly, but Maura only held her candleholder more tightly and shook

56

her blond head.

"Yes, I do, Father. I'll find another guide, if I have to, but I *will* locate the Pawnee, live among them, and study their customs. After all these years, this is finally my chance, and I won't let it slip through my fingers without a fight. I'm going at least as far as their main village on the Loup River, and I don't even need a compass to do that. All I have to do is follow the Platte."

"You would do it, wouldn't you?" Eben could hardly keep the hurt out of his voice. He had thought her eagerness for this journey was due entirely to the fact that she would be with him, not left home alone and missing him. Her ambition came as a shock, though he had suspected it for some time. He just had not realized how great it was—or that it would cause her to challenge and defy him.

"Only if I have to, Father." Maura bit her trembling lower lip. Tears glistened in her eyes. "But you know that is not what I want. I want *both* of us to go. I want it to be the way I always dreamed it would be—the two of us working side by side, sharing everything, discovering it all together. . . . I've waited a lifetime for this to happen. Please don't disappoint me when we're finally so close to our goal. Please, Papa, don't spoil it."

It was the Papa that did it. Maura had not called him Papa since she was a little girl. When she reached her thirteenth birthday, she had informed him that from then on, she would only call him Father. Father was so much more dignified and grown up. And she had ceased following him around and hanging on his every word. He had sorely missed that wide-eyed adoration, and even longed to hear her call him in the dead of night, as she had done when she was small, scared, and lonely: "Papa? Papa, can I come sit on your bed for a little while? Just until I feel sleepy?"

After she had fallen asleep, he had always gathered her into his arms and carried her back to her own bed and tucked her under the quilts. When she no longer needed

57

that from him anymore, he had felt bereft, old, and useless. Now, he knew how much she still needed him. *Papa.* For the sake of the little girl he had loved and lost, for the sake of the beautiful albeit stubborn young woman she had become, in order to make her smile and be happy, he would do anything, even if it went against his better judgement.

"All right, Maura. We'll go tomorrow, just as I promised." He leaned forward and kissed her brow, where the golden wisps of hair curled so charmingly.

"Oh, thank you, Father! Thank you!" She hugged and kissed him, then leaned back, smiling radiantly. "Nothing will happen to us. You'll see. Major Dougherty is just a pessimist. And that awful Luke Cutter probably *invites* trouble. We're lucky to be rid of him. Good night, Father. I'll be up early. Shall I knock on your door to wake you?"

"No," Eben said. "That won't be necessary."

He did not say it, but he had the uncomfortable feeling he would be wide awake all night. Worrying was not conducive to a good night's sleep, and he *was* worried. But about what and whom? He did not really believe they would come to harm — did he? Maura may be green as grass but he was not. He could handle weapons better than most men. More importantly, he knew how to avoid having to use them. He treated Indians with respect, and in return, received respect. Why should this venture be any different from a hundred others from which he had emerged unscathed?

But he knew as he proceeded down the dark corridor to his own room that it *was* different; Maura made it different. Maura made it doubly dangerous. And he tossed and turned sleeplessly the entire night.

Chapter Four

No sooner had Maura and her father ridden out of Bellevue, when they came perilously close to another argument. Bellevue lay nine miles north of the juncture of the Missouri River with the Platte, so Maura favored retracing the nine miles on horseback and then following the course of the Platte to the juncture of the Loup or Wolf River. From there, she reasoned, it would be an easy matter to follow the Loup until they stumbled upon the Skidi Pawnee, the particular branch of the Pawnee tribe they had selected to study.

"I think we should head straight west, Maura. Look here," Eben tapped one of Major Dougherty's rudimentary maps. "The Platte may join the Missouri south of Bellevue, but the juncture of the Platte with the Loup lies further north. If we cut west, we should be able to intersect it without riding so far out of our way."

"But, Father, if we ride west, we can't really be certain *where* we'll find the Platte. The river's known for being wide, shallow, and constantly splitting itself into smaller streams. From year to year, it shifts its location."

"Trust me, Maura. I think I can find a river as big as the Platte."

Eben's tone had a biting edge that persuaded Maura to quietly acquiesce. Her father was, after all, embarking on the journey with a noticeable lack of enthusiasm, its having been doused by Major Dougherty's dire warnings and George Catlin's last minute pleadings. Mr. Catlin had bade them good-bye and good luck, but Major Dougherty had not appeared for coffee and cold biscuits at the long wooden table in the main room of his house. Nor had Luke Cutter sought them out. They had quickly saddled the two riding horses, loaded the pack horses, mounted, and within a short time, reached the rolling grasslands.

Fearing her father might still change his mind about going, Maura was much relieved when the last signs of civilization—orchards, cornfields, squawking chickens, and rooting pigs—began to fade from view. It was a beautiful morning, with the sun shining warmly and the sky a pristine blue. Maura soon discarded her short woolen cape and rode only in her traveling costume—a brown, broadcloth dress with a specially designed skirt that permitted her to ride astride, and sensibly non-padded sleeves of which even Luke Cutter would have approved. Sturdy, brown boots, patterned after a man's riding boots, completed the practical ensemble.

Her horse was a small, quiet mare, surefooted and plain in appearance. She was brown, like Maura's riding costume, and had a single white stocking on her left foreleg and a thin white stripe running down her nose. Major Dougherty had not known the mare's name, so Maura had decided to call her Cinnamon, and she had dubbed their two pack horses Zeke and Jack. They were also plain, no-nonsense horses, one a dun and the other a darker brown than Cinnamon. Her father rode a leggy, good-looking bay that kept trying to snatch mouthfuls of the long green grass, so they settled on Greedy for him.

Once out on the plains, Maura marveled at the waving sea of grass. Away from Bellevue, not a single tree pierced the blue sky. On close inspection of the grass, however, she could identify multi-colored phloxes and spiderworts, intermixed with shooting stars and violets. Wildlife abounded.

They flushed prairie dogs, coyotes, ferrets, badgers, raccoons, jack rabbits, ground squirrels, and voles, stocky cousins to the rat. Once, Maura thought she saw pronghorn antelope springing away into the far distance, and the dark, blotchy shapes skirting the horizon might have been buffalo.

Speaking little, they rode until noon. By the time Eben called a halt, the sun was beating down mercilessly, and Maura's stomach was growling with hunger. As she dismounted, she felt stiff and sore, but, swallowing any complaints, only smiled when her father held out a leather-jacketed canteen of water. She drank sparingly from it, aware that if it took them longer than two days to reach the Platte, they would be running short. Expecting to be near rivers for most of the journey, they had not burdened themselves with any more water than was absolutely necessary.

"It's grown warm, hasn't it?" her father commented, wiping his perspiring brow with the back of his sleeve.

He was wearing a plain, fringeless, hunting jacket of finely tanned leather over sturdy, dark gray pantaloons tucked into black Wellington boots. The jacket was a souvenir of his stay among the Indians of Illinois, and he had always claimed it was the most comfortable and practical way to dress in the wilderness. Maura felt it changed his looks completely. She was so accustomed to seeing him in meticulously stylish frock coats that she could scarcely believe that this tall man with the windblown, silver hair and sky-blue eyes was actually her academically renowned father. Without a stiff collar and beaver top hat, he seemed too casual — half-undressed.

Beneath the jacket, he was still wearing a carefully tied cravat, she noticed, and her smile grew wider. That single gentlemanly detail set him apart from all the other men dressed in buckskins that she had seen in Bellevue or on the *Yellowstone* — that and the fact that his jacket was supple and clean, though not nearly as velvet-soft as Luke Cutter's had

61

been.

Tearing her thoughts away from the disturbing Mr. Cutter, Maura agreed with her father that yes, the day was indeed growing warm. Then she helped him hobble the horses so the animals could graze for the short time it would take to eat a light lunch. The meal consisted of more dry biscuits and Maura's first taste of pemmican, which reminded her of boot leather in consistency, though the flavor was slightly better. Again, she did not complain. Dried buffalo or deer meat seasoned with fat and berries was probably all she was going to get until they reached the Pawnee, unless her father stopped to hunt, which she doubted he would do.

"This afternoon we'll keep our eyes open for a rabbit or something else we might cook for dinner," Eben said. Maura sighed with unspoken relief. One morning on the trail, and already she was starved for fresh meat.

After a brief rest, they remounted and rode onward. Maura amused herself by studying the shifting shapes of clouds gathering in the sky. The sky itself was an inverted blue bowl, inside which great puffs of fluffy white clouds slowly drifted, assuming fantastic sizes and shapes. To her right, the clouds resembled the profile of a stern, frowning giant. To her left, they formed a buffalo with not one but two humps. An hour or more slid by as she lazily contemplated the clouds. Looking back over her shoulder, she saw four Indians on horseback silhouetted against the sky.

"Father? Look behind us. . . . We're being followed by some Indians."

Her father stopped his horse, half-turned in the saddle, and peered at the horizon. "You're right, but they're too far away yet to guess at their tribal identities — or their intentions. Perhaps they aren't following us at all. They may just be out hunting."

He spoke in a reassuring tone of voice, but at the same time kneed the leggy bay horse into a fast trot. Maura did the same to Cinnamon, and the pack horses clumsily followed. They trotted some distance, but when they turned to look again, the Indians were closer than before.

"What do you think they want?" Despite her efforts to sound calm and unafraid, Maura's voice trembled.

Eben was already reaching for his gun and checking to make certain it was ready to fire in case he needed it. He then slid it back into its leather scabbard alongside his saddle. "If they're friendly, we'll only anger them by making it difficult for them to catch up. If they're unfriendly, we might as well defend ourselves here and now, while we can see clearly, rather than later tonight after we make camp."

Maura's heart pounded in her throat. Only a half day's ride from Bellevue and already they were facing potential trouble! She squinted her eyes and studied their pursuers. At home, she had read that the Plains Indians often painted themselves before raiding or riding into battle. As the four drew closer, she could see they were not painted, and one of the Indians looked familiar.

"Father, isn't that the Sioux brave who volunteered himself to be our guide?"

"I believe you're right. He said his name meant The Dog, or something like that. Let's wait and see what he wants—though I hope he doesn't intend to talk us into hiring him as our guide. I thought I had already made myself clear on that point."

Keeping a snug rein on their horses, they sat in their saddles and watched the four braves approach. There could be no doubt who the leader was; the man they had first met in Bellevue was taller, more impressive, and better dressed than the other three. A profusion of porcupine quills and scalp locks decorated his fine, elk-skin shirt and breeches. A large shell necklace hung around his neck, and his hair, very long and thick, had been divided into two parts, lifted up and crossed over the top of his head, and then tied in place, like a Turkish turban.

His nose was large, his lips full, and his expression self-confident. Maura thought he had a proud aspect; certainly, his imposing, muscular figure gave him the look of a chieftain. She had been sorry he could *not* be their guide as he would have made an interesting travel companion. Quelling her anxiety, she smiled at him as he lifted one hand in greeting.

"Silver-Hair!" he called to her father. "I'm glad you wait. Shon-ka afraid he not find you."

The big brave rode his black and white spotted pony past Maura and the two pack horses, leaned over, and clasped Eben's hand at the wrist, as if intending to shake hands white-man's style. "*How-ke-che-wa?* How goes it, Silver-Hair? I come fast behind you make trade."

"Trade?" Eben kept one hand on his reins and dropped the other to the scabbard containing his rifle. "I have nothing I wish to trade, Shon-ka. We carry a few presents for the Pawnee, but nothing *you* would like."

He made it sound as if presents intended for the Pawnee would not be good enough to interest the Sioux. Shon-ka grinned, displaying a row of teeth as white as his shell necklace. "We ride with you 'til sunset. Tonight make talk-talk around fire. Silver-Hair have something Shon-ka want plenty much."

"I can't imagine what that might be, Shon-ka." Eben shot Maura a worried glance.

While Eben and Shon-ka had been talking, Shon-ka's three half-naked companions had totally surrounded Maura. One now rode on each side, and the third brought up the rear, trailing the two pack horses. The braves' faces were impassive, and they looked neither at Maura nor her father, but Maura had the uncomfortable feeling they were making certain she did not run away.

"We smoke peace pipe like brothers. Eat from same pot. Silver-Hair and Shon-ka good friends. Tomorrow we part, go separate ways." Shon-ka entwined his fingers to show unity and then parted them, indicating that he would go north and Eben west.

Unable to refuse without offending Shon-ka, Maura's father politely agreed. But Maura could read his suspicion and reluctance in the downward slant of his mouth. "Your company is welcome then, my friend," he lied smoothly. "We would be honored to have you and your companions ride part way with us."

The afternoon proved long and wearisome. Surrounded by the fierce-looking braves, Maura was no longer able to enjoy the scenery or cloud shapes. The Indians did not talk among themselves or pay any attention to Maura, except that occasionally, one or the other would ride too close and brush a muscled leg encased in buckskin against her knee.

Startled, Maura would dart a glance at whoever had done it, but the brave never acknowledged or excused his clumsiness. Furtively, Maura studied her four silent escorts. Shon-ka might be the leader, but the other braves could hardly be dismissed. Beneath their necklaces of animal teeth, feathers, and amulets, their bare, bronzed chests rippled with muscles. Any one of them could probably best her father; she herself must seem weak as a child to them.

Late in the afternoon, one of the braves removed an old musket from its leather scabbard and calmly shot a small antelope hiding in a clump of buffalo grass. The noise of the gun going off startled other animals, who recklessly bounded away. Maura felt like joining them in their headlong flight to safety, but she knew she could not outrun the Indians' guns or their sturdy, tireless ponies. Whatever was going to happen tonight was going to happen; she could think of no way to stop it.

They dismounted and set up camp before dark. Maura had intended to impress her father with her willingness to shoulder an equal share of the work. But Shon-ka and his companions did everything so quickly and efficiently that she had no time to think, much less help. Within minutes, one brave had gathered enough buffalo chips to start a fire, another was cleaning and gutting the antelope, and the third was fashioning a spit on which to roast the meat.

The Indians acted as if Maura and her father were not even present. Maura fetched blankets and two large squares of oilskin from the pack horses, and set up sleeping pallets for herself and Eben. She also unsaddled Cinnamon and Greedy, rubbed them down with handfuls of grass, and gave them water, while her father looked after Zeke and Jack. By the time she had finished slipping leather hobbles on the front and rear legs of the horses, the Indians already had a haunch of meat roasting. Maura found the coffee pot, filled it with water and ground coffee beans, and then hung the pot to boil on one end of the spit.

She turned suddenly to find Shon-ka watching her every move. Hairs prickled on the back of her neck. As the Indian stared at her unblinkingly, admiration lit his black eyes, and his full lips curved into a sly half-smile. Maura quickly looked away.

The roasted meat filled the night air with tempting odors, but Maura had lost her appetite. Shon-ka offered the first piece of the burnt-on-the-outside, raw-on-the-inside meat to her father, and the second piece to her. This occasioned a scowl from the Indian who had shot the antelope, and Maura wondered if Indian women customarily ate *after* Indian men. She pretended to nibble at the meat, and was glad when the coffee was done and she could busy herself pouring, sugaring, and passing it around. Having only two tin mugs, she gave one to Eben and Shon-ka to share, and the other to the remaining three Indians.

Her father insisted she drink some, too, and she gulped a mouthful of the boiling-hot liquid and burned her mouth and throat. The strong brew did fortify her flagging courage, however, and while the men drank coffee and ate, Maura furtively dug her pistol out of her pack, loaded it, and hid it in the pocket of her skirt. Then she resumed her place beside her father, and with pounding heart, waited to see what would happen next.

After he had finished his meal, Shon-ka grinned and moved closer to her father. "Look you at these," he said, fingering the long tufts of human hair sprouting from his fringed shirt. "Shon-ka great warrior . . . kill many enemies, count many coups. In the land of the Sioux, Shon-ka is chief. Great hunter. No one kill more buffalo than Shon-ka. Lodge always filled with meat and skins. If you do not believe, ask Walking Bear."

Shon-ka pointed to the man who had killed the antelope, and the brave grunted in response, then continued picking at his teeth with a splinter of bone he had taken from a leather pouch hanging at his side.

"I believe all you say, Shon-ka," Eben responded. "But what has that to do with us? We are en route to the village of the Skidi Pawnee. Though we would enjoy visiting *your* tribe, we cannot do so at this time. I'm very sorry, but we have other commitments."

"What is 'commit-ments'?" Shon-ka asked. "Does this mean Silver-Hair's daughter already promised to other man?"

In the firelight, Eben's face blanched. The lines at his mouth and eyes tightened. "My daughter, Maura, is, as you say, promised to another. A White-Eyes man who lives where we come from, a large city in the east. But that is not what I mean by commitments. We came here to study the ways of the Pawnee, not the Sioux. I intend to write down everything I learn about them, so that all the White-Eyes who have never seen an Indian can learn about them, too."

"Why Sioux not good enough for study?" Shon-ka demanded belligerently. "Sioux much better tribe, much stronger, than old-women-Pawnee."

"Perhaps we will one day study the Sioux. I'm sure they are a better tribe. But we could only choose one tribe for this first study, and we decided on the Pawnee because there is even less known about them than there is about your people. *Everyone* has heard of the mighty Sioux, but almost *no* one has heard of the Pawnee." Eben's tone dripped diplomacy.

"Hmph!" Shon-ka snorted. "No one hear of Pawnee because they cowards and old women. Stay home and dig in earth instead of following buffalo. Live in lodges made of dirt instead of fine skins. They afraid of own shadows. The Sioux fear nothing; we ride, hunt, and take wives when and where we choose."

When he said "wives," Shon-ka looked at Maura. He lifted his hand and pointed at her. "This woman called Moe-ra, this White-Eyes woman with hair like moonbeams. Shon-ka want for wife. Give Silver-Hair five horses for her, and best bow to shoot buffalo. Also, ten arrows."

"That . . . is a very generous offer," Eben said carefully. "But as I just said, she is already promised to another. It would be dishonorable to give her to you when she belongs to someone else."

"Who she belong to? Where I find him?" Shon-ka leaned forward, his face ferocious in the flickering firelight.

"His name is Nathaniel Hibbert, and he lives in Philadelphia, a long, long way from here."

"He bring gifts? He give you plenty horses?"

Maura's father looked nonplussed, but he quickly recovered and nodded. "Of course. It has all been arranged between our two families. When we go back east, Maura will marry Mr. Hibbert."

"How many horses? Whatever he offer you, I offer double. You send presents back to him. Tell him Moe-ra no want to be his wife."

"But that's not true. Maura *does* want to marry Mr. Hibbert. Don't you, Maura?"

Maura vigorously nodded. "Yes . . . yes, I do. I am honored by your offer, Shon-ka. Any woman would be. But I have pledged myself to Mr. Hibbert. See here . . . I wear his ring."

She held out her left hand. On her ring finger gleamed the tiny, perfect pearl that had belonged to Nate's grandmother. The gem had been set into a thin band of gold; her wedding ring would bear a second pearl surrounded by diamonds. She had tried it on before they left Philadelphia, and Nate had then kissed her hand. Maura remembered wishing he had kissed her lips. But Nate was *always* careful of her virtue; it was one of the things she loved about him. Unlike Luke Cutter, Nate treated her like a lady.

Shon-ka peered at the ring in the semi-darkness. He seized her hand and turned it this way and that, then flung it back at her, grunting contemptuously. "What good is tiny, round shell? I give you bigger shell, much better."

He removed his shell necklace and tossed it at Maura. "Here. Put on. Then you belong Shon-ka, and everyone who see you, know it. Shell is powerful medicine. Protect you from evil spirits."

Maura stared at the necklace. A large, round, white sea shell with a pearly pink interior hung suspended from a leather thong. No doubt among the Indians the shell was considered quite valuable; where on the dry plains had it come from?

Eben reached down, picked up the necklace, and gravely handed it back to Shon-ka. "I am sorry, Shon-ka, but it would make no difference how many shell necklaces or how many horses you brought. I am a man of honor and must keep my word. Maura will wed no one but Mr. Hibbert."

In a flash, Shon-ka leaped to his feet. Towering over them, he looked twice as tall, twice as fierce in the firelight as he had in daylight. "Then I take her from you. We are four and you are only two. You cannot stop me."

Maura plunged her hand into her pocket and wrapped her fingers around the pistol. Her father reached for his rifle, but before he could grab it, Shon-ka kicked his arm. While two of the Indians attacked her father, the third flung himself at Maura, knocking her backwards and pinning her to the ground.

Maura struggled to get her hand out of her pocket. Even when she succeeded, she could not see where to aim the pistol. Walking Bear's face loomed in front of her, his breath smelling of antelope meat. She flailed at him with the gun. It went off, followed almost immediately by a second retort, much louder and more powerful than the small pistol's. Walking Bear screamed and rolled away from her.

For a moment. Maura could not move. She took several deep, gasping breaths. Her ribs hurt from being crushed beneath the Indian, and her head was spinning. With great effort, she scrambled to her feet. Across the fire from her stood a tall figure half-concealed in darkness and shadow. She recognized Luke Cutter. He held a still-smoking rifle.

"Get up, Shon-ka, or my next target will be your backside. Maura, get away from that wounded Indian."

At Maura's feet, Walking Bear lay writhing on the ground and holding his bloody shoulder. She stepped back. Then she saw her father still struggling beneath the three Indians. "Papa!" she screamed.

"Stay back!" Luke shouted. He fired into the air over the heads of the men on the ground. "Damn you, Shon-ka! I said, get up!"

The struggling stopped. Sullenly, their faces masks of fury, the three Indians got to their feet. Panting, Maura's father lay still. Luke motioned with his rifle, and as the Indians moved away from Eben, Maura ran to him. "Father . . . Father, are you all right?"

Dropping to her knees beside her father, Maura heard Luke ordering Shon-ka to pick up his wounded comrade and "clear the hell out of here."

"Maura . . . Maura." With Maura's help, Eben managed to sit up.

Frantically searching for injuries, Maura touched his shoulders, his head, his hands. Her father's silver hair was mussed, and his upper lip bleeding, but she could discover no evidence of serious injury. Overwhelmed with relief, realizing for the first time how close to dying Eben had come, Maura began to sob. Eben put his arms around her and held her close. "There, there, my dear . . . I am really quite all right. I just got the wind knocked out of me."

"But they meant to kill you! Maybe even scalp you!"

"Hush, now. I am unharmed. Let us see what we can do to help Mr. Cutter."

Maura assisted her father in rising to his feet, only then glancing over her shoulder to see what was happening behind her. The tall, surly guide did not seem to need their help. As he waited for the Indians to catch and mount their horses, he stood with his back to Maura and her father, his broad shoulders a wall shielding them from danger.

"If you come back tonight, I'll be waiting for you, Shon-ka. And next time, I'll shoot to kill. If I so much as see a shadow on the horizon, I'll fire. I suggest you ride north. Go home to your people. And don't think to come back later and raid the Pawnee. I'll warn them to watch out for you. Besides, the Magruders won't be there. They're going back to Bellevue, and from there, to Philadelphia. You'll never see this particular White-Eyes woman again."

Shon-ka's voice, grating and vengeful, came to them out of the darkness. "I go, Great Heart. This time, you win. But Shon-ka not forget tonight. Now you are enemy of all Sioux. I tell my people, and never again will you be safe on plains. . . . I am Shon-ka, and I have spoken."

The Indians rode away, their hoofbeats echoing in the still night air. Then all was silent, save the crackling of the fire and the distant howl of a wolf hunting beneath the rising full moon.

Chapter Five

Maura did not say one word to Luke Cutter as he unsaddled and hobbled his horse for the night, then sat down by the dying fire and helped himself to some leftover antelope meat. She did not know what to say; the man had saved her father's life and rescued her from a horrible fate. She was grateful, but she still did not like or trust him. Nor did she want to hear him say, "I told you so."

While she retrieved her pistol and pocketed it, her father did the talking for both of them. "We are beholden to you, Mr. Cutter. Had you not come along when you did, I would be dead, and Maura would be in the hands of that heathen scoundrel. I don't know how to thank you."

Luke Cutter chewed and swallowed. "Don't try, Magruder. I don't want or need your thanks. All I do want is your solemn promise to return to Bellevue in the morning while I ride on to warn the Pawnee to expect a raid from Shon-ka."

"Do you really think he'll raid the Pawnee when he knows we won't be there?"

"Of course. His pride is stung, and the only way he can redeem it is to attack an enemy."

"What do you mean, Father—we won't be there?" Kneeling down beside her father, Maura touched Eben's arm. "Surely, you don't intend to *quit*. Granted, now we must constantly be on guard, but I see no reason to return to

Bellevue. If anything, we should leave at once and press onward. With a full moon, we can find our way."

"Maura, we *can't* continue. Have you learned nothing from what happened tonight? I am only one man; I don't stand a chance of defending us against so many."

"We can do it!" Maura disputed. "Our mistake was in being friendly and allowing them to catch up to us. What we should have done was hold them off with our guns. We behaved foolishly, but next time—"

"Next time *what*, Miss Magruder?" Luke Cutter rudely interrupted. "If you hadn't invited them to join you, sooner or later they would have crept up on you and attacked."

"Perhaps so, but they would not have won. We saw them coming from a long way off. We could have prepared ourselves for an attack. Next time, we will be prepared."

"Did you see me? Did you know *I* was trailing you?" Luke speared a second piece of meat with the tip of his hunting knife, but paused before popping it into his mouth. His gray eyes skewered her as neatly as he had just skewered the strip of meat. Maura dropped her glance. Across Luke's knees, ready when and if it was needed, lay his rifle, a handsome weapon, gleaming with brass. Instead of staring at him, she stared at it, despising the blush that reddened her cheeks whenever he looked at her.

"No, Mr. Cutter," she conceded. "I never thought to check if anyone else was following us. Now, I will. After today, no one will sneak up on us undetected—not even you. Especially not you."

"Hah!" Luke snorted. "If I don't want you to hear or see me, you won't. The same is true of Shon-ka. Give it up, Miss Magruder. Be sensible for once, and listen to your father."

Biting her lip to keep from screaming invective at the arrogant scout, Maura again turned to her father. "I won't go back to Bellevue, Father. You know I won't."

Eben shook his head. "You *must,* Maura. Just this once,

for your own good, I must insist that you obey me."

"I won't go back," Maura repeated stubbornly.

"Doesn't mind too well, does she?" Luke Cutter drawled infuriatingly. "I'd say she needs a bit of persuading right on her backside."

"Please keep out of this, Mr. Cutter," Eben said calmly. "This is between my daughter and me. We are perfectly capable of handling this matter in our own way."

Ignoring Luke Cutter, Maura once more lay her hand on her father's arm. "Father, I am not a child, who can be told what to do or *spanked* if she doesn't do it. I am a grown woman, and I *demand* to be treated as such. Since Mr. Cutter is going to find the Pawnee anyway, we can simply ride along with him — or follow him if he refuses to wait for us. That's the safest thing to do. After all, what is to prevent Shon-ka from doubling back and intercepting us before we arrive in Bellevue? Mr. Cutter *did* tell him we would be returning there — a rather stupid error in judgment, if you ask me."

"Who the hell *asked* you?" Jamming his knife into the scabbard at his waist, Luke rose to his feet, his face dark as a thundercloud. "I only told him that so he wouldn't be so quick to gather his whole tribe together and descend on the Pawnee en masse, which I suspect he'll do anyway."

Sensing the argument was swinging her way, Maura also stood, hands on hips, glaring at him. "What difference does it make *why* you told him? The truth is, we would be in less danger if we stayed with you and kept going than if we returned to Bellevue by ourselves, as Shon-ka now anticipates."

"She does have a point there, Mr. Cutter," Eben said. "At least, if we keep going, we could help the Pawnee fight off the Sioux. The harm of our coming here in the first place has already been done. Since we can't undo it, we might as well stay and make the best of things."

"My opinion exactly, Father!" Maura's jubilant smile soon

faded when she caught sight of Luke Cutter's face. He looked mad enough to spit nails.

"How can you allow this spoiled little bitch to manipulate you so shamelessly?" he roared.

Still seated before the fire, Maura's father sedately looked up at the furious guide. "My daughter may be spoiled, Mr. Cutter, and I may in fact be to blame. But she most certainly is not a bitch. If you do not apologize to both of us, I shall have to call you out, sir, though it would grieve me sorely to have to shoot a man who just saved my life."

"Are you actually proposing a *duel*, Magruder? I can't believe it. Shon-ka should have stayed around to watch. I'm sure it would fulfill his fondest dream to witness the two of us killing each other. Then he could have Maura without lifting a finger. And on cold winter nights, he could also entertain his people with tales of the idiocy of white men."

"Will you apologize or not, Mr. Cutter?"

Eben's voice never wavered, and Maura did not doubt that her father *would* shoot Luke Cutter if no apology were forthcoming. Steel-gray eyes probed icy blue ones, the tension between the two men as palpable as a living presence. Maura was proud of her father for standing up to Luke Cutter.

After a long moment, Luke Cutter finally said: "All right, Magruder. I apologize for calling your daughter a bitch. But I hope you know I'm doing it only to avert needless bloodshed — *yours,* not mine. I don't think I would lose the duel."

"Apology accepted, Mr. Cutter. And if indeed you *are* the better marksman, I am doubly in your debt. But you should also know that I count my life as worthless when it comes to defending my daughter's honor. I would gladly die for her sake."

"If you stay here, Magruder, you may get that chance."

"Whatever happens, we will not blame you, sir. This decision is *ours,* not yours. . . . Well, Maura? You have seen the danger, and you have heard Mr. Cutter's opinion. You also know mine. I would be far happier to return to Belle-vue. Taking all that into account, do you still wish to proceed?"

Maura hesitated only a moment, and then only because Luke Cutter's eyes held an unspoken but very clear and piercing accusation: *If your father dies out here defending you, his death will be* your *fault, no one else's.*

"Yes," she said. "Yes, I do. I'm not afraid of taking risks, Father. The risks are worth it; I *believe* in what we're doing. For years, you yourself took risks—and you took them alone, with no one to share them or help you. Now, I am here. We'll face the risks together. Please, let's not talk of quitting anymore."

Eben sighed. "Spoken like a true Magruder. I don't know how I can be angry when I know very well where you get your stubbornness and determination."

He held out his arms to her, and she went to him. They hugged and kissed, renewing their will to succeed in a loving embrace that made further discussion superfluous.

Behind her, Maura heard Luke Cutter's low, angry mutter. "A pretty speech, Miss Magruder. I'll grant you that. I just hope you never have cause to regret it."

The following morning, Maura awoke to find Luke Cutter in almost the same position she had left him the previous night. With his back straight and his legs folded beneath him, he sat still and watchful before the fading embers of the tiny, banked fire, his eyes constantly scanning the horizon.

Feeling guilty, she quickly sat up. "Have you been awake all night?" She bit her lip, wishing she had not asked such a foolish question. She and her father ought to have taken turns with him keeping watch. Instead, tired from the day before, apparently they had slept through the entire night.

"Why didn't you wake us?" she demanded angrily. "We're more than willing to do our fair share on this journey."

"Had one of *you* taken the first watch, it would not have been necessary for you to awaken me." He picked up a strip of cooked meat and coolly held it out to her. "Here . . . I cooked the choicest meat during the night. The rest of the carcass I buried. I would dry the extra, but there isn't time. If you're coming with me, you'd better get moving."

Maura wanted to throw something at him. His smug superiority grated on her already lacerated nerves. But at least he had not tried to change their minds again—or worse yet, gone off without them. "Thank you for the meat, but I'm not hungry this morning."

"Then take it with you to eat on the way. You'll need your strength. We won't stop again before nightfall."

Rising to her feet, Maura snatched the cooked meat from his fingers and thrust it into her skirt pocket beside her pistol. Then she went looking for privacy behind the horses, the only place on the flat plain where Luke Cutter could not see her preparations to meet the new day. By the time she returned to the campsite, her father was awake and eating, and Luke was kicking dirt over the remnants of the fire.

"Good morning, Maura," Eben said. Maura only nodded. She did not trust herself to be civil in Luke Cutter's obnoxious presence. A cup of coffee would have helped immensely, but since Mr. Cutter had taken it upon himself to eliminate that possibility, she would have to make do with irritation to warm her chilled insides.

In strained silence, they mounted their horses and rode out. When Maura got hungry, she ate the cold meat in her pocket. When she grew thirsty, she drank from the canteen tied to her saddle. When she felt the need to relieve herself, she bore the discomfort in silence for mile after mile. Luke Cutter had said they would not stop before nightfall, and she would rather die than ask him to halt.

Fortunately, her father had no such foolish pride. Mid-afternoon, about the time Maura was squirming in the saddle from a combination of fatigue, hunger, and self-denial, Eben reined Greedy to a standstill and called out to Luke Cutter. "I'm stopping for a few moments, Mr. Cutter."

"Suit yourself." Luke Cutter reined his horse around and swung out of the saddle in one smooth motion.

Maura rode a short distance away, dismounted, and put Cinnamon and the two pack horses between herself and the two men. A few minutes later, much relieved, she led the three horses back to them. "Will we reach the Platte by nightfall, do you think?" she asked her father.

"By my calculations, we should be there within the hour. What is your opinion, Mr. Cutter?"

"Look there." Luke Cutter pointed to the western horizon. "Those are cottonwoods. They signal water."

Maura squinted and saw what *might* be trees in the far distance, though how Luke Cutter could be certain and how he could possibly identify the species astounded her. She doubted they would reach the trees by nightfall, let alone in another hour or two of riding.

"No more stops." Luke Cutter scowled at Maura as if she were responsible for this one.

"We won't have to stop on *my* account." Maura lifted her hem, placed her foot in the stirrup of her saddle, and sprang onto Cinnamon's back. She jerked the mare's head around so fast that the poor beast whinnied her surprise and displeasure.

"You can ruin a good horse's mouth doing that." Radiating disapproval, Luke Cutter mounted his own tall, rangy chestnut and spurred him into a canter.

Eben followed, and Maura came last, once again leading the pack horses. For some reason, she had gotten stuck with them. Yesterday, when there was only herself and her father, she had not minded. Today, she did. Today, she minded everything — particularly the tall, infuriating scout who turned every conversation into a verbal sparring match.

"Get along Zeke . . . get along Jack." She tugged hard on the horses' lead ropes. "Hurry up or I'll leave you behind to feed the buzzards."

The sun had set, and the moon was rising by the time they reached the grove of cottonwoods sprawled along the wide, sandy banks of the Platte River. Luke Cutter dismounted, unsaddled and hobbled his horse, then began setting up camp even faster than the Indians had the night before. Maura wearily crawled down from her horse and started to pick up fallen cottonwood branches to make a campfire.

Luke stopped her with a jerk of his head. "That won't be necessary. We can do without a fire tonight. The moon's as bright as daylight."

"I'd like some coffee," Maura said stiffly, thinking she would also like to bake skillet bread with the flour they had in their packs.

"And I'd like not to be tomahawked in my sleep."

"It's night. No one will see our smoke."

"They'll *smell* it. If you insist on making a fire, I'll cross to the other side of the river and bed down by myself."

I wish you would, Maura thought churlishly. Turning on her heel, she stalked back to the horses and did not return to the riverbank until her father and Luke Cutter were already sitting down, having chosen their spots for sleeping while she was gone. When he saw her, Luke motioned to a flat piece of stone forming a primitive table in front of him and Eben.

"Here's some more cooked meat. Better come get it before a coyote or a wolf jumps out of a bush and snatches it."

"If one does, we still have food supplies in our packs." The threat of coyotes and wolves did not bother Maura in the slightest. However, she did take the meat and retreat to her own bedroll before Luke could reconsider and eat it himself.

While she ate, her father made attempts at conversation. "I'll stand the first watch tonight, Mr. Cutter. Were you joking about the possibility of wild animals paying us a visit? I have never camped without making a fire before; my fires always kept them away."

"I doubt they'll bother us." Luke Cutter lay down with his head on the seat of his saddle. He had neither blanket nor oilskin. "Anyway, I'd much rather deal with four-footed critters than two-footed ones. The horses will nicker if any predators approach."

Maura debated whether or not to offer him the spare blanket they had brought with them. Grimly, she decided against it. Maybe the chill night air would make him ill — preferably *fatally*. She could not recall ever disliking anyone as much as she disliked Luke Cutter. He irritated her by his every word, his every glance . . . and what irritated her the most was that she could not help feeling faint whenever she remembered his mouth kissing hers, and his muscled body molding itself to her body.

"I'll stand the second watch, Father. Be sure and wake me." Willing herself to relax and forget Luke Cutter was even with them, Maura rolled herself in a blanket with her back to the two men. She ached in every muscle and bone, and expected to fall asleep immediately.

Just as she was sliding into oblivion, her father said, "Maura, did you remember to hobble the horses?"

"Of course," she answered sleepily, without giving the matter a second thought.

The next thing she knew, her father was shaking her and calling her name in a panic-edged tone. "Maura! Maura, wake up!"

As she opened her eyes, the morning sun blinded her. She rose on one elbow and lifted her hand to shade her face. "What is it? What's wrong? Have the Indians come back?"

"He's gone — the thieving scoundrel! Gone with all our horses!"

"What?" Instantly awake, Maura scrambled to her feet, her eyes discovering the truth: Luke Cutter's saddle was gone. So was his horse. So were *their* horses. She had left the animals grazing on the riverbank, plainly visible from the

grove of cottonwoods . . . oh, the blackguard! The rotten horse thief! She knew of no words vile enough to describe him. "We should have expected as much from *him*," she began, but her father stopped her with a wave of his hand.

"Forget it, my dear. We'll walk if we have to. But right now, we have to get out of here."

"Out of here?" Maura was still trying to assess the full extent of Luke Cutter's perfidy. "Did he leave us food—the canteens? What about our journals and my sketch book?"

Eben shook his head disparagingly. "None of that's important. We've got to cross the river if we can. Maybe they won't follow. If they do, we'll have to find some sort of barrier to keep between us."

"Father, what *are* you talking about?"

Beneath Maura's feet, the ground suddenly began shaking. A moment later, she heard a distant, rolling thunder, as if a storm was sweeping down upon them. But the sky was blue, and the sun was shining.

"There," Eben pointed. "On the other side of the trees. Buffalo. Thousands of them."

The trees were spread out, with plenty of room between them for horses to pass . . . or buffalo. On the other side of the trees, a great cloud of dust extended for miles in either direction. And inside the dust cloud were huge, shaggy animals, hundreds of them, tens of hundreds, charging toward them at breakneck speed.

"My God," she whispered. "They're heading straight for us."

"If we had the horses, we could outrun them," Eben hypothesized. "Since we don't, we'll have to swim the river. The water should slow them down somewhat. If we're lucky, it might stop them entirely. Come, let's hurry."

As they dashed through the encampment, Maura screamed at her father, "Your rifle! Don't forget your rifle!"

Eben bent down and scooped it off the ground next to his bedroll. Maura sprinted ahead to their packs, which were lying on the grass where she had unloaded them the night before. Tearing open the one containing her sketch book and journal, she grabbed the two items, plus her father's journal. Then she ran toward the river and waded in. Eben caught up to her just as the water reached her knees.

The river bottom was soft and sandy, sucking at their feet, but the current was weak, and they made good progress toward the opposite shore. Or at least, Maura thought they did. But when she looked back, she saw they had not gone nearly as far as she had hoped. Now, the pale brown water lapped at her waist, and her feet sank deeper into the muck. Each step was an effort. She held the precious books high above her head, while her father did the same with his rifle and powder horn.

The thunder of the approaching herd echoed all along the bank, the din punctuated by snorts, bellows, and the terrified bawling of calves. Something—Maura wondered what—had frightened the animals into stampeding. Fascinated as much as horrified, Maura could not keep from looking back over her shoulder. The first line of buffalo had nearly reached the trees. As she watched, a huge bull—dark brown in color, with a long, shaggy, black mane—crashed into a tree, snapping it in two as if it were a mere twig. Barely fazed, the bull kept coming, stumbling down the sandy river bank toward the water.

Paralyzed with fear, Maura stopped walking. She and Eben did not stand a chance. The animals seemed not to notice the river. On they came, hooves pounding, the whites of their eyes gleaming in the sunlight.

We're going to die here. We'll be trampled to death or drowned.

From the corner of her eye, Maura saw a flash of chestnut: Luke Cutter's horse—Luke astride—galloping along the river bank. Heedless of the approaching buffalo, Luke reined his horse to a skidding stop and shouted, "Come back here! I'll hold them off while you get out of the river."

Dropping his reins, Luke seized his rifle, aimed it at the

big bull, and fired. The animal leaped into the air. Blood poured from its shaggy head, and it collapsed in its tracks right at the prancing feet of the chestnut horse. Two buffalos coming immediately behind veered sharply—one to the right, one to the left—sidestepping their fallen comrad and avoiding Luke Cutter at the same time.

"I said get over here!" Luke wheeled his horse in place and again motioned for Maura and Eben to come to him.

Eben grabbed Maura about the waist and began dragging her toward Luke. The first buffalos reached the water and splashed into it. One passed close enough to Maura and her father to drench them with spray. Maura could smell the beast's thick, gamey odor. Luke Cutter's gun fired a second time, and another buffalo fell, its body crumpling atop the dead bull's and building the barrier higher. Luke had shot it just as it was going to jump the fallen animal.

"We're coming!" Trying to run in her water-laden skirt, Maura stumbled, and a sob burst from her throat.

They could not possibly make it; why didn't Luke Cutter save himself, instead of trying to rescue them? Maura felt her father's hand shoving her forward. Dropping the books, half-falling on her hands and knees, she broke free of the river. Another buffalo charged past, its huge head and curved horns missing her by inches.

"Take her!" She heard her father shout to Luke. Shoving his rifle back into its scabbard, Luke bent down and grabbed her arm.

Before she realized what was happening, Luke hoisted her onto the saddle in front of him. Suddenly, it dawned on her that he meant to leave her father to face the stampede alone.

"No, we can't go without him!" she screamed, struggling in Luke's arms. "Father! Papa!"

"Stop it! You'll get us all killed!"

Luke clamped one arm so tightly across Maura's breasts that her air was cut off. Wheeling his chestnut horse, he spurred it into a gallop along the riverbank. They zigzagged in and out between crazed buffalo, the horse sensing exactly when to run, swerve, stop, and turn. If Luke Cutter had not been holding her so tightly, Maura would have tumbled off. All around them, the great shaggy beasts surged, a torrent of brown, straining bodies.

The sights and sounds of the stampede, combined with the wild ride, simultaneously thrilled and terrified Maura, but her senses blocked out everything except the possibility — no, the *certainty* — that her abandoned father was being trampled to death on the riverbank. She twisted back and forth, vainly trying to see what had happened to him, but sky, river, and buffalo all blended into one.

This is a nightmare, she told herself. It has to be. I'm dreaming and soon I'll wake up and laugh at myself.

When the jolting and pounding stopped, she clung dazedly to the horse's mane. Her heart was still rattling in her chest, and a strange numbness had invaded her limbs.

"It's over," Luke Cutter growled in her ear. "You can relax now, it's over."

Over. What exactly did he mean by "over?" "My father . . . ," she began and faltered, fearing to ask the question.

"We'll go back and see," was all Luke said.

Chapter Six

Without speaking, they rode back across the trampled ground. Except for a few stragglers, the buffalo herd had reached the opposite side of the river and was disappearing into the western horizon. A thick cloud of dust hung over everything; Maura choked when she inhaled. Tears streamed from her eyes, and she could see little as they approached the cottonwood grove. Wiping her eyes with one hand, she frantically peered through the dust. Several of the smaller trees had been toppled and smashed into kindling, but the larger ones still stood.

Dread clutched at her heart. Would they even find her father's remains? It did not seem possible that he could have survived the onslaught of charging, brown bodies. They passed a dead buffalo calf lying on its back, feet stuck straight into the air. The calf had probably not run fast enough to avoid being trampled, or else it had been squeezed to death between larger animals. Maura willed herself to be strong. No matter what they found, she would not become hysterical in front of Luke Cutter. It was bad enough he had been right; if her father was dead, she was to blame. By now, they could have been back in Bellevue.

Luke Cutter directed his horse toward the two buffalo he had shot and killed. When he drew abreast of them, lying just as they had fallen, he reined in and shouted: "Magruder!"

Maura flung herself to the ground and ran toward the spot where she had last seen her father. Her eyes searched the sand for blood or bits of clothing—anything that might give a clue to his fate. She saw nothing but his smashed, broken rifle. Dropping to her knees, she picked up a piece of it.

"Maura? Are you all right?"

Hardly daring to believe her ears, Maura turned to see a dust-covered figure crawling out from between the stiffened forelegs of one of the dead buffalo. Shockingly blue eyes peered out of an incredibly dirty face.

"Father! Oh, Father, you're alive and safe!"

Maura lurched toward him. Rising and stumbling, he met her half way. They threw their arms about each other and pounded each other on the back. Laughing and crying, they clung together, their tears streaking jagged white paths down their dirt-rimmed cheeks.

"Oh, Maura . . . Maura . . . I don't know how many buffalo I counted jumping over me; there must have been a hundred at least. And everytime one jumped, I feared it wouldn't make it. I also feared *you* would be trampled."

"So did I! But Mr. Cutter's horse is a *wonderful* beast. How he dodged in and out among those buffalo I'll never know. No horse back home could have done it. Speaking of horses. . . ."

Maura spun on her heel and glared at Luke Cutter. Anger seared her breast as she remembered that *he* was the one who had taken their horses and placed them in such danger in the first place. "Where's Cinnamon? And Greedy, Jack, and Zeke? Why did you return, Mr. Cutter? Was your conscience bothering you too much? I didn't know horse thieves *had* consciences."

"Now, Maura," Eben demurred. "At least, give the man a chance to explain."

Luke kneed his horse nearer to Maura and returned her

glare with a disbelieving scowl. "What in hell are you talking about, Miss Magruder? I didn't *steal* your horses. I went *after* them after *you* forgot to hobble them."

"I did *not* forget to hobble them. I distinctly remember . . . that . . . is . . . I . . . I. . . ."

Maura paused, sputtering in confusion. She did remember unloading the pack horses and unsaddling Cinnamon so the mare could join Greedy in cropping the scant grass poking up from the sandy riverbank. She had been so tired, so thirsty and saddle sore, and it had been so dark. She had left the packs where they had fallen and gone to join her father and Luke under the trees.

"I reminded you about it last night," her father prompted. "And you said of course you had hobbled them."

"Of course, I did. I mean I certainly would have. I did it the night before. . . ." Maura trailed off uncertainly, unable to recall whether she had or not. Indeed, at this moment, she could not even remember her father questioning her about it.

"Well, they weren't wearing any hobbles this morning," Luke coldly informed her. "I found them a long way off, where the grass is richer and greener. Apparently, they didn't much care for this coarse stuff along the riverbank and decided to move elsewhere. I had just caught your mare when I looked back over my shoulder and saw the buffalos stampeding in your direction. I let her go and raced back here to try and rescue the two of you."

Maura's stomach plummeted. From the soles of her feet to the roots of her hair, her body flamed with chagrin. She must not have hobbled the horses. *She* was responsible for almost having killed herself, her father, and Luke Cutter.

"I . . . I . . . apologize. I was at fault, but it won't happen again."

"You're damn right, it won't. *I'll* hobble the horses tonight—on our way back to Belleview. And if you give me one word of argument, Miss Magruder, I'll lift your skirts and paddle you myself. Right in front of your father. It's long past time that *some* man took you in hand and made you behave yourself."

"How *dare* you!" Maura exploded. "If you lay a single finger on me I'll . . . I'll *shoot* you. That's what I'll do."

"With what?" Luke sneered. "Your weapons have all been trampled . . . and so have your belongings. Hell, lady, you don't even have a saddle. I hope your talents include riding bareback."

"I still have my pistol!" Maura declared, fumbling in her pocket.

"Would you kill a man who's saved your life not once, but twice?" Looking down at her from his horse, Luke Cutter dared her with his icy gray eyes. "Then go ahead and shoot. For if you don't, I promise you this: No matter what you say or do, no matter what your father says or does, the two of you are going back to Major Dougherty's—if I have to hog-tie you both and sling you over the backs of your pack horses."

"Maura, put down that pistol, please," Eben interrupted wearily. "Mr. Cutter is right. We have nothing left. Everything we brought has been ruined—except for the horses. We have no choice but to return to Bellevue."

Tears of disappointment and frustration stung Maura's eyes. With all her heart she wanted to protest and argue. But she knew it was useless. Until they could gather together more supplies—and replace their precious journals and her sketchbook, of which not even a single shred of paper remained—they could do nothing. All they had were the clothes on their backs and money in her father's money belt.

"Go down to the river and clean up while I go after your horses," Luke Cutter snapped. "The sooner we get back to Bellevue, the better."

"We could return by ourselves and you could continue on alone," Eben suggested. "The Pawnee still need to be warned about Shon-ka."

"That's true, but since we have only one rifle between us, we had better not split up. I'll take you back first and then ride out to warn the Pawnee."

"As you wish, Mr. Cutter. There will be no further arguments from either of us."

"First sensible thing you've said since I met you, Magruder."

Maura grimaced, but Luke Cutter did not see it. He was already riding away.

Eben tossed aside the last bones of the skinny rabbit Luke Cutter had snared for dinner and with a small sigh, lay down on the bare ground beside the tiny, discreet fire. He was cold and still hungry, but by tomorrow night, they would be back in Bellevue eating a decent meal with Major Dougherty. He was disappointed, but not nearly as much as his daughter. The comforts of civilization beckoned to a man growing old and soft. Only to Maura was the promise of plentiful food and a soft, warm bed apparently unappealing. She had scarcely said one word since they left the Platte.

Luke Cutter had been similarly incommunicative. Riding between the two of them was like being caught in a deadly crossfire of mutual hostility. The tense silence was far more potent than any harsh words either might have said. Whenever one or the other did say something, they said it to him—not to each other.

Despite their animosity, Eben sensed a certain electricity between them as well. Indeed, so charged was the air, he half expected lightning to crackle at any moment. In some ways, it amused Eben that his daughter had finally met a man who was more than a match for her silken ambition and honeyed strength of will. Not that their relationship would ever come to anything; they despised each other too much for that and would soon be parting anyway. But encountering a man like Luke Cutter might finally teach Maura that a man and woman *should* strike sparks off each other. Where there was no spark, there could be no fire, and Eben doubted that Maura had ever felt physically attracted to her fiancé, Nate Hibbert. Or he to her.

Eben supposed he was very broad-minded about such things. Women were not generally expected to feel passion and desire; certainly, their fathers never encouraged them along those lines. But Eben had known passion with Maura's mother, and he wanted their daughter to have the same joyful, satisfying experience. He wished he could stop thinking about Maura's future and just enjoy the present, but after almost losing her twice on this journey, he found himself thinking about her future more than ever.

Somehow, he must help his single-minded progeny to realize that one of life's grandest, most wonderful adventures was finding someone she could love with her whole being, body and soul. While there was satisfaction to be found in studying a remote band of Indians, true happiness consisted in sharing and giving of one's most intimate self. In Eben's experience, fame and fortune, even scholarship, were poor substitutes for the miracle of love; he had known them all, and love was the most valuable and irreplaceable. Without it, all other successes were hollow and meaningless.

He drifted off to sleep wondering how he could convince his stubborn daughter of anything. When Luke Cutter shook him awake, he sat up abruptly, rubbed his eyes, and discovered that the matter still lingered in his sleep-be-fuddled mind.

"Here's my rifle," Luke said. "It's time for your watch. I didn't wake your daughter to take a turn. Whether she'll admit it or not, she's exhausted from all those hours of riding bareback. She isn't fit for this kind of life, Magruder. Take her back east and make her stay there."

"I intend to, Mr. Cutter. What time of night is it?" Setting down the long gun beside him, Eben gazed up at the star-studded sky.

"Only an hour or two before dawn. I would not have awakened you at all, except I need some sleep. Wake me when the sun rises. I want to reach Bellevue by early afternoon."

"Don't worry, I'll wake you. I'm growing anxious to get there, too."

Luke Cutter lay his head down on his saddle and instantly fell asleep. Eben yawned and struggled to keep his eyes open. Beside him, Maura lay curled on her side, her silver-blond hair glinting in the starlight. The moon had already set, but the plain was only dim, not dark. He could see for miles in every direction across the still, flat grassland. He trained his eyes on the eastern horizon, yawned again, then drew up his knees and rested his arms on them.

A gentle breeze was blowing, but other than the riffle of the wind in the grass, nothing else stirred. He was alone beneath the vaulted night sky. Resting his head on his hands, he thought about Maura, only now his thoughts kept sliding away from him. How had Luke Cutter stayed awake all night? He closed his eyes and promised himself he would rest for only a moment. And it did seem only a moment later that he heard a long, bloodcurdling yell.

At the first sound of attack, Luke sprang to his feet and reached for his gun. His hand clutched air. Remembering that he had given the rifle to Magruder, he looked around for Eben and saw him lying on his back, struggling with two Indians for possession of the weapon. The gold ball of the sun had already risen high above the eastern horizon. Magruder must have fallen asleep—*damn him!*

A third Indian had wrapped one powerful, bronzed arm around Maura's white neck, while his other arm imprisoned her slender waist. She could not even scream, but her blue-gray eyes were wide and apprehensive. While his brain registered these details, Luke's hand flew to his waist and withdrew his knife. Where was the fourth Indian? Where was Shon-ka?

Hearing a twanging sound, Luke instinctively ducked. An arrow whizzed past. Then he heard a voice. "Do not move, Great Heart. My musket points at your back."

Slowly, Luke turned. Shon-ka sat astride Luke's own chestnut horse. A wide, triumphant grin split the big Indian's face. The Magruders' horses milled with the Indians' mounts—all of them tethered together and ready for traveling.

"You grow careless, Great Heart, sleeping in daylight while we steal your horses and the White-Eyes woman."

"It is you who are growing careless, Shon-ka. You're a fool to attack us this close to Bellevue."

Shon-ka's grin grew wider. "By time you reach Belle-vue, Shon-ka be far from here."

"Why don't you just kill us and be done with it?" Luke taunted, stalling for time as he tried to think of a way to stop Shon-ka.

"Too noisy," the Indian replied. "Someone come see. Track Shon-ka home to Sioux. Is more fun this way, humbling Great Heart, making him lose face."

Eben Magruder grunted and cried out. Looking behind him, Luke saw that the two Indians had subdued the older man and taken away the rifle. Now, Magruder was on his knees. One Indian stood behind him, twisting Eben's arm behind his back, while the other—the man Luke had wounded in their first confrontation—held a skinning knife to his throat.

A bloody strip of rawhide bound the wounded Indian's shoulder. Fresh blood was leaking through the bandage, but ignoring his wound, the Indian said something and looked expectantly at Shon-ka. Luke did not know the Sioux language as well as the Pawnee, but he understood enough to realize that the man was asking permission to kill Eben.

"No," Shon-ka said, shaking his head and responding rapidly in Sioux. His black eyes bored into Luke's. "I tell Walking Bear today is not good day for spilling blood. We have horses. We have White-Eyes woman. And we have shamed Great Heart, blood brother of Pitale-sharo. Is enough for one day."

"Don't expect to keep the White-Eyes woman. I'll come after her."

Shon-ka laughed arrogantly. "Is what I hope. Come north, Great Heart, to land of Shon-ka. I kill you there, far from Belle-vue. Is not good to kill you here. Make Major Dougherty angry, stop fur trade. Stir up soldiers and other White-Eyes."

"They'll be plenty stirred up when they hear you stole a white woman. They may kill the next Sioux they see."

"Then when I return, I kill them. Take many scalps. But I no give back Moe-ra. She belong to me now. When she see that I better man than any White-Eyes, she happy be Shon-ka's wife. She feel honored."

"I'll never be happy sharing your bed!" Maura suddenly screamed. "I spit on your name! Probably the only way you can *get* a woman is to steal her!"

Maura managed to wrench partially free of her captor, but the bronzed arm quickly encircled her neck, squeezing mercilessly, stopping further speech. Still, Maura struggled, her blue eyes fiery, her dismantled hair spilling about her shoulders like a silver-gold waterfall. Even disliking her as he did, Luke had to admit she was indeed magnificent. Little did she know that her defiance only made her more valuable. In the eyes of the Indians, she was proving herself to be a woman worth fighting for—spirited, courageous, and unafraid of her enemies.

"Don't do this," Luke cautioned, leveling a long look at Shon-ka. "It could lead to war between our peoples. It *will* lead to war. She's only a woman; she isn't worth it."

The sound of ripping fabric jerked Luke's attention back

to Maura; in her struggles, her dress had torn. The milk white flesh of her breast gleamed through her gaping bodice. The Indian holding her let go just long enough to cuff her smartly. Her head flew back from the force of the blow; she ceased struggling and collapsed in his arms.

"Maura!" Eben cried. "You swine—you've *hurt* her! By God, she's unconscious!"

Maura's father again scuffled with the two Indians. Helpless so long as Shon-ka held the musket aimed at his chest, Luke could only clench his fists. In a moment, the scuffles stopped, and Eben Magruder lay prostrate on the ground. Shon-ka laughed arrogantly. "I think she worth it," he opined.

In rapid Sioux, Shon-ka gave orders for his comrades to retreat, taking Maura with them, leaving Eben behind. Before galloping away, the big Indian saluted Luke. *"Na' wa!* I go now, Great Heart. Think of the White-Eyes woman sharing my buffalo robe, and rejoice in my good fortune."

Gritting his teeth, Luke watched Shon-ka wheel the chestnut around and join his friends. They slung Maura face down across the withers of her own little mare and lashed her hands and feet together beneath its belly. Within minutes, they were all astride their horses, ready to depart. Luke watched until they disappeared in a cloud of dust, racing for the north. Then he went to see if Eben Magruder's throat had been cut.

The silver-haired man was still alive when Luke turned him over, but his shoulder was dislocated, his wrist broken, and at least two ribs cracked. One eye was swelling shut, and his face was turning black and blue. Luke had no choice but to splash water in the unconscious man's face and then to try and get him up and moving.

"Come on, Magruder." Luke held his canteen to Magruder's split and bruised lips. "Drink. We've a long walk ahead of us.

"I . . . I don't know if I can make it."

"You'll make it . . . if I have to carry you."

"Oh God . . . ," Eben moaned, lurching to his feet.

Once he got up, however, Eben Magruder surprised Luke with a resurgence of strength and determination. Cradling his broken wrist against his battered ribs, he trudged uncomplainingly for mile after mile. When Luke suggested they sit down for a few moments to rest, Magruder stubbornly shook his head. "No, Mr. Cutter. It's my fault Maura was kidnapped, and I won't sit down again until we reach Bellevue. The sooner we get there, the sooner you can get a horse and some men to help you go after her. I don't care what it costs, I'll pay it. I just want her back safe and sound."

Luke conceived a grudging respect for Maura's father on that long, grueling walk. Despite his injuries, Eben never so much as whimpered, and they reached Bellevue shortly after midnight. Eben insisted on rousing Major Dougherty out of bed. "You can leave tonight yet, Mr. Cutter, as soon as the major can assemble some men and horses."

Luke was exhausted after the long walk and the little sleep he had had recently, but when he thought of Maura out on the plains beneath the bright moon with Shon-ka, he did not mention his own fatigue. He could understand how Eben must feel. What he did *not* understand was Major Dougherty's reaction—at least, not at first.

"I'm sorry this happened, Magruder." Dougherty motioned for them to sit down in the main room of his house. Still in his nightshirt, the major went to a cupboard, rummaged around inside it, and took out a bottle of whiskey. He poured shots into small tin mugs and passed them to Luke and Eben. "I sure hate to disappoint you, but I don't think raisin' an alarm and sendin' a passle of men out after your daughter is the best thing we could do right now."

"Why not, Major? The man intends to force my daughter to marry him. She won't do it, of course, but she *will* be forced to live with him and endure his . . . his assaults on her person. If the mood takes him, he may even kill or torture her. I know Maura; she'll never yield to him. She'd rather die first."

Luke wondered how Eben could be so sure of this, but remembering how Maura had fought her captors, he conceded that her father might know what he was talking about. Most white women would have succumbed to tears or swooning by then; Maura Magruder had been just plain *furious*. Nor had she shown the weakness he had expected on their journey toward the Platte or back toward Bellevue. Even when she was sagging with obvious weariness, she had kept on riding, her tender mouth set in a thin, unwavering line.

"Magruder's right, Major. We've got to go after her as soon as possible—before she goads Shon-ka too far. Any delays could prove disastrous. She . . . uh . . . may not even survive tonight."

Fearing he had been too blunt, Luke glanced sidelong at Maura's father, but the silver-haired man only nodded vigorously in agreement. "If there's someone here who can bind up my wrist, shoulder, and ribs, I'll accompany Mr. Cutter and whatever other men you can find. After I rest a few moments, I think I can ride again."

"No, you won't Magruder," Luke protested. "Frankly, you look like hell, and you must feel even worse."

He nodded at the older man's hand; it was shaking so hard that whiskey was slopping over the side of the tin mug. Luke waited expectantly for the major to suggest the only possible solution: rousing the entire settlement and asking for volunteers.

"I'm sorry, Magruder, I really am." Major Dougherty scrutinized the contents of his own whiskey mug. "I can understand how worried you are. In your place, I'd feel the same. But right now, if I announce what's happened, full scale war is gonna break out, a war we can't possibly win—

at least not at the moment."

"What's wrong? What's happened?" Luke queried. "On our way into town, I did notice more Indians camped around the post than there were when we rode out."

"Smallpox," Dougherty said. "Day before yesterday, a few more of Shon-ka's friends rode in with their winter furs and told how their whole village had nearly died of the pox after buyin' some blankets off a coupla white traders. This mornin', a band of *Chau-i* Pawnee arrived with near the same story, and this afternoon, a passle of Mandans brought news of the pox breakin' out down south of here. Naturally, the Indians are a bit riled up, but I soothed 'em down and gave 'em extra good deals on their furs, and I'm hopin' they'll go back home again without a fuss. But what do you think'll happen if word of Miss Magruder's capture gets around the post?"

"The whites will be up in arms," Luke said. "Add to that a bunch of already stirred-up Indians, and it would be lighting a fuse attached to a powder keg. We'd be fighting before we could even ride out."

"Exactly." Major Dougherty sighed. "I already had to stop a bunch of white trappers from callin' the Indians a pack of damn liars, and if those boys heard it was Sioux who stole Miss Magruder, why, they'd start shootin' Sioux Indians left and right. We'd lose every bit of ground we've gained these past few years establishin' Bellevue as neutral territory. And if we can't keep the peace here, then lots of other posts won't be able to keep it, either. The fightin'll spread fast — so fast that every white man west of the Missouri'll suddenly be in danger, and we've no way to even warn 'em. Do you understand what I'm sayin', Magruder?"

Impressing Luke with his calmness, Eben Magruder accepted the explanation with a slight shrug. "Well, Major, if that's the way it is, I'll ride out alone to rescue my daughter. I don't want this incident to touch off bloodshed all along the frontier, but I *do* want to save Maura."

"I can't stop you from doin' that, sir—hell, I'd do the same if it was *my* daughter. But you ought to know before you go that Shon-ka's a big man among his own people. Once, he reaches Sioux lands, a whole regiment of horse soldiers couldn't take her back too easily, even if we could get Fort Leavenworth t' send us one."

"Major," Luke held up his hand. "I've already said this, but now I'll say it again. Magruder isn't going anywhere. The man has suffered a severe beating; he isn't *fit* to go after his daughter."

"Then what do you suggest, Luke?" Dougherty turned guileless eyes on him. "*You* might be able to get her back, but even you will have a tough time against four of 'em."

"No tougher than some other battles I've fought and won. I'll want a keg of gunpowder though and a few other things that might come in handy. I'll also need the best horse you can lay hands on; I'll miss my gelding on this trip. That's another reason I'm going—to get back my buffalo-runner. Pitale-sharo helped me train him, and he's the best horse I ever had."

"Mr. Cutter . . . do you really think you can rescue my daughter?" Eben's pain-ravaged eyes held desperate hope.

"I can try, Magruder. But you may not see us for weeks— maybe months. Once I do get her, I can't just rush back to Bellevue. Shon-ka will be expecting that. We'll have to lose ourselves on the plains for awhile—maybe visit the Pawnee, after all. You'll have to trust my judgment as to when it's safe to return here."

Tears brimmed in the older man's eyes. He extended his good hand for a handshake. "She's all I have, Mr. Cutter. If any man can rescue her, I'm sure it's you. I place her entirely in your hands. Rest assured: You'll be handsomely rewarded."

"Yes . . . well . . . whatever you pay me, I'll do my best."

Luke shook hands with Eben Magruder, tossed down his whiskey, and crossed to the window to gaze out at the moon.

What had he gotten himself into, now? Somewhere out on the silvered plain, a beautiful young woman was in the hands of a ruthless, powerful, Sioux warrior. Was he kissing, fondling, raping her even now, as Luke pictured it?

No, Shon-ka would not be kissing Maura Magruder. The Indians did not kiss. But he might be touching and holding her, forcing her to submit to him. The very idea of it made Luke's gorge rise. He might not like the girl, but he *hated* to think of her screaming and squirming beneath a brute like Shon-ka. Maura Magruder was the sort of woman he associated with scented flowers and promises of marriage and eternal love. She belonged in a parlor, sipping tea from the finest porcelain, and gossiping about the latest fashions. Why hadn't her damn fiancé put his foot down and refused to let her leave the east?

When Luke found and rescued her, he would ask her that—just before he turned her over his knee and walloped the daylights out of her. *If* he found her . . . and if she was not a pathetic, broken creature, utterly destroyed by her experiences with Shon-ka, The Dog. Luke recalled the proud, haughty way she tilted her blond head to look up at him, and he rebelled at the image of her with slumped shoulders and shamed, defeated eyes, listlissly doing whatever Shon-ka demanded.

By God, he would kill the man and scatter his bones across the prairie so no one would ever find them! Let the wolves lick them clean! A hard knot of determination formed in Luke's stomach. Suddenly, he was glad he was taking no one else with him. This was the challenge and opportunity he had been awaiting; if he succeeded in rescuing Maura Magruder, he would earn a great deal of money, *honorable* money. More than that, he would be pitting his strength and cunning—everything he had learned in the past few years—against a worthy foe.

For the first time in months, he felt good about himself. Indeed, he felt stunningly alive, brimming with vitality, and eager to begin the chase.

Hang on, Maura. No matter what happens, don't despair. I'm coming for you. . . . Luke Cutter, your knight in shining armor, is on his way.

He laughed at himself, pleased with his sudden sense of humor. It had been a long time since he had found anything so amusing. The mental vision of himself garbed in clanking armor and clambering aboard a great white charger curved his mouth in a wry half-smile. A moment later, he was frowning again; the brave who had captured Maura Magruder was every bit as ruthless and cunning as a fire-breathing dragon. Rescuing the fair damsel in distress would be anything but a pleasant picnic.

Swinging back to face the major who had gotten dressed while he was contemplating the moon, Luke said: "Along with the gunpowder, I'd like the makings for it—saltpeter, sulphur, and charcoal, so I can vary the mixture to produce unusual results. I also want a sack of dried gourds. You might ask the Indians camped around town if they have some. I know Elk-Runner did—though she doesn't, anymore."

"Gourds, saltpeter, sulphur, and charcoal?" Major Dougherty's brows lifted incredulously. "You sure as hell don't want much, do you? How about if I throw in a half dozen Chinese firecrackers?"

"If you have them, I'll take them," Luke responded, in all seriousness.

"Don't get excited. I try to keep the post well-stocked, but not *that* well-stocked. We've just never had a call to put on a display of pyrotechnics."

"Fireworks—or illuminations, as the ladies call them back home—would *astound* the Indians," Luke observed, as much to himself as to Major Dougherty and Eben Magruder, both of whom were listening with unabashed curiosity. "Too bad there's no time to send for some. . . ."

"What exactly are you planning, Mr. Cutter?" Eben

asked.

"Just a few surprises, Magruder. Don't worry about it. If they work, I'll let you know. If they don't, you can forget you ever met me or had a daughter."

On that somber note, Luke took his leave and went to catch an hour of sleep before riding out to rescue Maura Magruder for what he hoped would be the last and final time.

Chapter Seven

By Maura's count, they had been four long days and
nights on the trail. Since they rarely stopped for more than
two or three hours at a time, day or night, it was hard to
keep track. During the brief rest spells, Maura collapsed in
an untidy heap and snatched what sleep she could before she
was rudely jerked awake, given something to eat, and then
set on her horse again, with the reins tightly held in one of
Shon-ka's big, powerful hands.

The days and nights were all running together, like a
series of dream-images, one piled upon the other. Whatever
Maura did, wherever she turned, she saw Shon-ka's smoldering eyes; they held the threat of what awaited her as soon
as she reached Sioux Territory. At least, she was permitted
to ride astride now — and had been ever since she had
become violently ill from being slung over her mare's back
and jolted and pounded for hours on end. Somewhere along
the way, she had lost her maidenly inhibitions and now
performed bodily functions in full view of her captors, who
in turn performed theirs in front of her. Without so much as
a hint of embarrassment, the Indians hawked phlegm, broke
wind, and scratched private parts. Nor was Maura any
longer the least embarrassed. The only thing that mattered
now was staying alive for one more day.

She knew she was dangerously close to complete collapse.

Even the threat of eventual rape and slavery did not seem to matter much, anymore. If they did not stop soon, rest, and eat properly, she would simply fall off her horse and be unable to get up again. When and if her father and Luke Cutter arrived to rescue her, it would be too late. She hoped Eben would not blame himself. For what had already happened—and for what lay ahead—*she* was to blame, no one else. She had been warned and had ignored the warnings. Luke Cutter had been right. She was a spoiled, manipulative, little brat. Yes, even a bitch. Though it had infuriated her to hear the truth, Luke had been right all along.

As she rode behind Shon-ka, clutching her mare's mane to remain upright, Maura thought about the tall Indian guide whose cold, gray eyes seemed to cut right through her, baring her darkest secrets. In her new clarity of vision, she was able to see that not only had he been right, but considering her inexcusable stubbornness and stupidity, he had been remarkably tolerant and forbearing. Repeatedly he had tried to save her and Eben from their own folly, when what he should have done was forget all about them the minute they rode out of Bellevue. If she ever saw him again, she would thank him—this time, honestly, humbly, and contritely, groveling upon her knees if that's what it took to convince him of her sincerity.

Swaying on her horse's back, Maura sniffed back a sob. Her tongue felt like a ball of woolen yarn in her mouth. Her eyelids were so heavy they might have been window sashes she was trying to keep raised by sheer willpower alone. Her feet were so raw, blistered, and swollen that she could no longer get off her boots. At the start of their journey, her father had insisted that she sleep in them, but Eben had never meant for her to wear them continuously for the rest of her life.

How long had they been riding since the last rest stop? Trying to guess the time of day, she peered at the sun illuminating the flat, empty plain. The huge golden ball was slowly sinking toward the western horizon. Soon, it would be night, but that did not mean they would stop. The Indians seemed to relish traveling by night even better than by day. They never got lost. While to her, the heavens seemed only a huge, diamond-studded dome, to Shon-ka and his cohorts, it was a carefully detailed map. In normal circumstances, these new discoveries would have fascinated Maura. But fatigue had so blunted her curiosity that she no longer cared if she *ever* understood the language of the stars.

Please, God, if only I could stop and lie down before I fall down.

When the Indians finally did stop, Shon-ka swung down from Luke's chestnut horse so swiftly that Maura did not at first realize what was happening. Landing soundlessly on his feet, the big Indian unceremoniously dragged her off the mare and propelled her toward a clump of brush lining a river. Maura was reminded of the Missouri; this river looked suspiciously like it. The sight of water after days upon the dry plain gave her a burst of energy. She tottered toward it, forcing her unsteady legs to do their duty one more time.

Stumbling down the sandy bank, she lay on her stomach at the water's edge and drank deeply of the coffee-colored, life-giving liquid. Much refreshed, she splashed water on her sun and wind-burned face. She suspected she would live—at least, for another night. Gingerly, she ran her fingers over the swelling on her left cheekbone. It marked the spot where the Indian had struck her on the day of her capture. Her face was still puffy and probably black and blue, but the throbbing had receded—or else she was just too tired to notice it.

"Tomorrow, we cross river," Shon-ka said behind her.

Crouching at the water's edge, Maura looked up at her captor. Despite the days and nights of relentless riding, the tall Sioux looked relaxed, almost cheerful. The only sign of the journey's hardship was the coating of dust on his turban-like hair and the streaks of dirt and dried sweat on his fine, elk-skin clothing. As he stood looking down at her, his black eyes gleamed with a passionate intensity that immediately made her wary.

"Tomorrow, we enter Sioux territory," he continued. "Ride more slowly. No longer need travel in darkness."

Maura's heart leaped with terror. Obviously, they had been riding north or northeast, and this was indeed the Missouri. According to Major Dougherty's maps, almost all of the land north of the great river belonged to the Sioux, while the area south, especially the land lying between the Platte and the upper Missouri, belonged to the Pawnee. And just as obviously, Shon-ka was no longer worried about Luke and her father catching up to them.

Shon-ka reached down and clumsily stroked her hair. "Prepare yourself, Moe-ra. Tonight, I send other braves downstream. You lie by my side. Become my woman." At her swift intake of breath, he flashed white teeth. "Shon-ka tired of waiting. Tonight, he enjoy his prize."

This was the moment Maura had been dreading. Slowly, trembling in all her limbs, she rose to her feet. "I won't lie with you willingly, Shon-ka."

As the boast left her mouth, Maura wondered how she could resist when she could scarcely stand on her own two feet. Shon-ka must have been wondering the same thing, for he grinned broadly, amused by her audacity. As if to mock her, his large hand closed over her right breast, half-revealed through her torn gown. Maura jerked backwards, but Shon-ka only laughed and caught her by the arm, one hand continuing to squeeze her breast.

"Fight, little yellow-hair. Your spirit pleases me. Is why I want you. You will breed strong sons. To find such spirit is big surprise. Shon-ka think White-Eyes women all weak, like White-Eyes men. But you are like Great Heart, different from other White-Eyes. He is worthy enemy. You are worthy mate. The more you fight, the more pleasure you give Shon-ka."

He drew her to him, his fingers tightening on her breast like an iron vise. Maura struggled but could not break free. The harder she fought, the wider Shon-ka grinned, and the harder he squeezed. Finally, she realized that if she kept on fighting, he might take her here and now, without waiting for nightfall. She stood still and glared at him.

"You said you would give me time to prepare myself. Does Shon-ka keep his word? Or does he lie—his honor having no more substance than a whisper of wind stirring the grasses?"

Immediately, Shon-ka let go of her and stepped back. His thick features twisted into a grimace. "Shon-ka not lie. His honor is sacred. If you hurry, you can bathe before darkness. I, too, will bathe. The Sioux are clean people. We must wash away stench of journey through land of Pawnee."

He turned and walked away, his swaggering, ambling gait reminding Maura of a bear or other large animal. She considered what he had said. Maybe a bath *would* revive her weary flesh and sluggish mind. If Shon-ka really had a sense of honor, maybe she could figure out a way to use it against him and protect herself.

Stepping behind the brush, she stripped off her clothing, yanked her swollen feet out of her boots, and limped into the icy water. Teeth chattering, she scrubbed herself with sand and rinsed her hair. Standing waist-deep in the river, she carefully rebraided her long wet tresses. By the time she finally emerged, she was nearly dry on the top half of her body. Heedless of the bottom half, she climbed back into her clothing and the torturous boots.

When she joined Shon-ka at his campfire, the sun had already set. She felt invigorated rather than chilled. Farther down the riverbank, a second fire burned. The smell of roasting meat wafted tantalizingly on the still evening air. Maura wondered what game had been shot that day. She remembered hearing a musket go off, but had not cared enough to look and see what animal had met its untimely end or who had killed it.

Shon-ka's eyes lifted from the roasting meat and roamed her body with scorching eagerness. "Sit down, Woman-With-Hair-Like-Moon-Beams. That is what Shon-ka call you from this night forward. The woman, Moe-ra, is dead. In her place stands new woman—not yet Sioux, but one who can earn place in Shon-ka's tribe."

Knowing she must eat to replenish her strength, Maura sat down cross-legged. "And what must I do to earn my place, Shon-ka?"

"Obey. Work hard. Please Shon-ka, your new master."

"I thought you admired my spirit. If I do as you command, I shall have no spirit to call my own. I will become a slave. And I will *hate* my master. Is that what you desire, Shon-ka—that I should hate you?"

Never taking his eyes from her, Shon-ka frowned. "No, Woman-With-Hair-Like-Moonbeams. I want you to look at Shon-ka with soft eyes and warm smile upon your lips. That is how wife looks at beloved husband. She sits at fire and sews his moccasins, and happiness dwells in her heart. She is proud to be his woman and bear his children."

"How can I be proud when my heart has not yet learned to love you? How can I be happy when you force me to your bed, instead of waiting until I come willingly? Is it the way of Sioux men to *force* their woman, instead of courting them? Among your people, how *does* a man win a woman's love?"

Shon-ka studied her thoughtfully. "There are many ways. One enjoyed by everyone is called Night Dance. It takes place in summer in large tepee set up for just that purpose. Sides are rolled up so all can see. Unmarried men sit on one side and women on the other. When drumming begins, a woman chooses her partner by walking over to him and kicking sole of his mocassin. Couples then form line and dance around fire. When dance is finished, all return to places, and men must then choose partners. Halfway through dancing feast is served—boiled puppy, great delicacy among my people."

"What happens afterward?" Intrigued despite herself and the loathsome ingredient of the main dish, Maura leaned forward. "Does choosing one partner over another mean that the couple will marry?"

"Sometimes." Shon-ka poked the roasting meat with the tip of his skinning knife. Satisfied it was not yet done, he lay down the knife on the ground beside him. "If two young people become interested in each other, girl invite young man to meet her in front of family tepee. Often, to find privacy, couple stand beneath blanket, so talk cannot be overheard. This only way they can be alone together because girl's virtue is well-guarded. Then, if couple decide to marry, young man bring gifts to her family—horses for her father and brothers."

"So you're saying that the man does not just take the girl and force her to his bed. There's some sort of agreement between them and then a ceremony."

Gravely, Shon-ka nodded. "Girl must agree to marriage, and so must family. New tepee must be raised. Wedding feast must be held."

"Yet you expect *me*—a woman you say you admire—to come to you with no courting, no agreement, no wedding feast, and no tepee to call her own."

Shon-ka's face darkened perceptibly. "You are White-Eyes woman, not Sioux. These are Sioux customs. Besides, I have stolen you. You have no choice."

Acting on impulse, Maura snatched the skinning knife he had just laid down and pressed the tip of it into her breast. In a shaking voice, she informed him: "You are wrong, Shon-ka. I have a choice. You may be able to force me to lie with you, but you cannot force me to give you my heart. If you take me tonight, without my consent, I will find some way to kill myself. I swear this to you. You cannot watch me all of the time. I will wait until you grow complacent, but one day you'll find me dead—your own skinning knife stuck

108

in my heart."

Shon-ka flung himself toward her and yanked the knife from her hand, but not before Maura succeeded in nicking the flesh above her breastbone. Sprawled beneath him, she felt hot blood seeping between her breasts. Glaring into the Indian's black eyes, she hissed, "If you don't respect me enough to court and wed me properly, I will kill myself, Shon-ka. Do you understand? My honor is as sacred as yours. I will not be shamed and meekly accept it."

"Moera, Moe-ra . . . ," the big Indian murmured. He tossed away his knife but kept her pinned to the ground beneath him. "Never have I known woman like you—brave like warrior, filled with courage like mountain lion, and proud like Sioux princess. If you wish to be courted, then I court you—first in White-Eyes way, then in Sioux way."

"What do you mean?" Maura wondered whether he really meant to wait before raping her or had some other terrible idea in mind.

"I have seen how White-Eyes men court White-Eyes women. Is how they court Indian women. Make them laugh and whisper behind hands."

"What do they *do?*" Maura demanded suspiciously.

"This." Shon-ka pressed his open mouth down upon hers.

Maura could not evade the kiss, so she had no choice but to endure it. The unwelcome intimacy reminded her of the last time she had been kissed—by Luke Cutter in the tepee in Bellevue. Luke's kiss had turned her insides to calf's-foot jelly, but Shon-ka's only disgusted and repulsed her. The Indian had obviously never kissed before; he held his lips rigid upon hers and mashed her lips into her teeth. Maura quivered with distaste.

At last, Shon-ka drew back, his big grin widening. "What you think? Shon-ka good at White-Eyes courting—yes?"

Maura had to swallow hard to resist the impulse to laugh in his face. "I—I'm much impressed. But the Sioux way of courting is what I want to learn about. I—I want to see if it's

109

better than the white man's way."

"It better," Shon-ka promised, pulling himself up and sitting beside her. "Soon, you forget White-Eyes you promise to marry."

"White-Eyes I promised to . . . oh, yes, Nate." Guiltily, Maura realized she had not thought of her fiancé for days. "I think I'm already forgetting him."

"Good," Shon-ka grunted. "Now, we eat. Then we sleep. Sleep all night. Tomorrow, cross river."

Relief flooded Maura; Shon-ka was *not* going to rape her tonight. She had succeeded in outmaneuvering him. But as they ate the dripping, delicious meat, the Sioux watched her with dark, impassioned eyes, and fear once again tiptoed across her shoulder blades. Yes, she had escaped *this* time, but they still had a long way to go. Shon-ka's patience might not last the entire journey, and if it did, there was no guarantee she would not be forced to marry him when they finally reached his village. One day, he would lose patience, and when she still refused, what then?

It was a foolish question. He would take her anyway. She had won a paltry skirmish, but defeat was inevitable.

With as much care as he had ever used to do anything, Luke faced away from the buffalo-chip fire and poured a thin stream of gunpowder from a large gourd into the mouth of a small one. Damn, but it was hard to see! It was also hard to keep his hands steady; what did he expect after not having had a proper night's sleep in over a week?

The precious black powder reached the top of the smaller gourd and cascaded over his fingers. He swore again and would have tossed the two gourds aside in frustration, except he needed them too badly. Annoyed with his own clumsiness, he poured some of the excess back into the larger gourd and then stoppered both containers with twists of rawhide. Gently, he lay the small gourd beside three others.

110

The crude, primitive bombs might not even explode at the proper time. Or they might explode in his saddle-packs. He wished he had paid more attention to that side of his father's business — the manufacture of explosives and "illuminations."

Cutter Munitions had produced both as a sideline to its main business of manufacturing weapons and gunpowder. Luke had been fascinated by the weapons aspect, especially the production of fine, light, well-balanced rifles, or "long guns," of the Pennsylvania and Kentucky type. They were the guns that had opened the frontiers of the Northwest Territory to white settlement. As a boy, he had spent the first half of his childhood dogging the footsteps of the gunsmiths employed by his father. Each had been a meticulous craftsman who labored countless hours to turn out a single rifle.

A properly made Kentucky rifle was a cherished masterpiece, meant to serve a man his entire lifetime and then be handed down to his son with pride. Luke's own rifle had belonged to his father and grandfather before being passed down to him, and he revered it as a precious possession, second only to his horse and his own scalp. The art of mixing sulphur, saltpeter, and charcoal to produce the black powder first invented by the Chinese and used in fireworks, had interested him less. Making gunpowder was a messy, dangerous undertaking, wherein a single stray spark could touch off a wicked explosion, resulting in loss of limb, life, and an entire factory.

Now, Luke was struggling to remember everything he had ever learned — albeit halfheartedly — in his youth. One thing he recalled was that by changing the amounts of the basic ingredients in gunpowder, one could achieve different sorts of explosions. Thus, if he added more sulphur or saltpeter, he could produce explosions with more or less concussion and sound. In order to scare the Indians without actually hurting them, he needed controlled explosions — much like fireworks — that would do minimal damage but achieve maximum light and noise.

Unfortunately, Luke could not remember the finer points of producing "illuminations." His father had manufactured a line of crude imitations of Chinese fireworks, using strong, heavy paper for the casings, and a mixture of gunpowder that allowed for considerable flash and noise. Color was as yet beyond the capabilities of most fireworks producers, though some were achieving success in creating ambers, coppers, and golds. Though his hopes had been high when he started, Luke now felt he would be lucky if he got something that simply blew up when he lit the fuse.

He hoped his idea of using dried gourds would work. The Chinese had first made fireworks by pouring gunpowder into lengths of the hollow bamboo plant and then sealing them. Luke had reasoned that gourds might serve the same purpose. If the gourds retained any dampness, however, the gunpowder would not ignite. And if he added too much or too little of any one ingredient, his "bombs" might do unpredictable things.

He was still trying to decide what to use for fuses. Fearing that the flint-and-steel strike-a-light method for starting a fire, currently in use and even adapted by the Indians, might fail him when he was nervous and in a hurry, he had taken the precaution of bringing along a small clay vessel just big enough to hold a live ember.

Elk-Runner had taught him that trick. In the days when only the firedrill had been available to the Indians, a provident squaw always carried her own burning coal as a quick, convenient method for lighting a fire out on the plains. For tapers, Luke had already braided several long strands of grass. Once the tapers dried, they would be ideal—they might even work as fuses.

Everytime he stopped to rest and allow the horses to graze, he spared a few moments to work on his gourd bombs. By now, he had decided *not* to kill Shon-ka outright. To do so would inflame Indian tempers all along the frontier, and would probably lead to the war Major Dougherty was trying so hard to avoid. As the major had pointed out, killing Indians over Maura Magruder's capture simply was not worth such a terrible risk. Setting aside his own turbulent emotions whenever he pictured the girl in Shon-ka's arms, Luke had finally realized that she *deserved* whatever cruel fate she was suffering.

She and her father had defied cooler, more rational minds such as his and Major Dougherty's, and now they were paying the price. He could not forget that. Nor could he forget that *he* was paying a heavy price, also. Here he was, in the middle of nowhere, and so exhausted he could hardly keep his eyes open or his hands from shaking. And once he "attacked" the Sioux using his homemade bombs, his only hope for survival lay in arousing the presumably superstitious natures of the Indians. Hopefully, they would bolt, forgetting all about Maura in their eagerness to flee whatever malevolent spirits were causing the bright explosions. The bombs had to create enough of a diversion so that Luke could free Maura and escape before the Sioux realized what was happening.

Yawning mightily, Luke put away his belongings and then allowed himself the luxury of dozing for several moments. He did not lie down, because if he did, he might not wake up for hours. Instead, he sat upright, cradling his head on his knees. Eventually, he fell over on his side, startling himself awake. Wearily, he rose and stretched, kicked dirt over the remnants of the fire, and broke camp.

Minutes later, he was once more in the saddle, leading his pack horse and heading north, knowing that sooner or later he must reach the upper Missouri. Once he did, he must find the spot where Shon-ka and his braves had crossed, ford the river, and pursue his quarry into Sioux territory. Originally, he had hoped to catch up to the Indians before they entered their own lands, but Shon-ka had maintained too fast a pace. Now, Luke would be satisfied to rescue Maura before the Indians arrived at their village.

Surely, they were as tired as he, and once they arrived at the Missouri would reason themselves safe and consequently slow down. If they did not, Luke must devise a plan for rescuing Maura from four hundred Indians, instead of four. The mere thought of it made him knee his tired mount into a gallop. He *had* to catch up with them before they reached Shon-ka's village.

Yanking on the pack horse's leadline, he threatened to do terrible things to the poor beast if it did not keep up. "Get along, you lazy hunk of wolf meat. If you hold me back, I'll slit your belly, crack all your bones, and feed your entrails to the crows. Better yet, I'll blow you up."

Talking kept him awake, so he kept at it, sounding to his own ears like a man who had eaten crazy weed for supper. For another three days and nights, he rode north, finally crossing the Missouri, and at long last spotted a small party of Indians and horses in the far distance.

Energy flooded his tired body. "Shon-ka," he breathed to himself. "At last, I've found you."

Chapter Eight

Maura was beginning to give up hope. By now, Luke and her father ought to have caught up with them. The Indians were no longer even making a pretense of hurrying. Yesterday, they had spent the better part of the day studying the movements of a herd of buffalo, and this morning, had killed two young bulls. Shon-ka had been much disappointed by her total ignorance of the proper way to skin and butcher the beasts. When she had refused to eat any of the bloody, raw liver the Indians were gleefully consuming, he had scolded her soundly, reminding her that for a white woman to become the wife of a Sioux chieftain, she must be willing to change her ways.

Maura was shocked and indignant. She had always intended to adopt Indian habits and customs while living among the Indians, but she had never *dreamed* that her immersion in Indian culture would include eating the still-steaming innards of a newly-killed buffalo. Nor had she imagined she might be forced to marry a man she barely knew, much less loved.

Tonight, they were having buffalo tongue for supper, and Maura's stomach rebelled at the mere thought of it. Angry with herself more than Shon-ka, she blamed her squeamishness on the fact that she had not freely chosen to experience these particular customs. What should have been an interesting, exciting adventure had turned into a nightmare.

As she sat turning the spit which held the huge tongue, she wondered if she dare ask Shon-ka about her father and Luke. All this time, she had been assuming the two were alive; what if they were not? After she had lost consciousness, Shon-ka might have killed them both and left their bodies to rot on the open plain. While she desperately wanted to know the truth, at the same time she feared knowing it. In her present state of near exhaustion, she was ill-equipped to deal with grief. The only thing that had kept her going this long was the hope of rescue.

Dismally, she contemplated the southern horizon, from whence help must come. The plain lay silent in a haze of late afternoon sunlight and stirred-up dust. The grass all around the campsite had been flattened by the buffalos—a smaller herd than the one that had almost trampled her father to death, but big enough to obliterate any evidence of human passing. If he were still alive, would Luke be able to track them this far?

Shon-ka had been careful to leave no telltale signs of campfires or bones from their meals. But these precautions might simply be the habits of all Plains Indians; she dare not interpret them as proof that Shon-ka was trying to keep Luke from discovering their whereabouts. Quite possibly, Luke and her father were dead, and she might as well abandon hope altogether.

Angrily, Maura dashed away a single, unbidden tear slipping down her cheek. If Luke and her father did not come soon, she must find a way to escape on her own. Escape should be easier now that the Sioux had relaxed their vigilance. Shon-ka still tied her up at night, but ever since they had crossed the Missouri in conveniently waiting bullboats, their horses swimming alongside, the Indians had been less wary, traveling only by day and sleeping all night. Now was the time to flee, but the prospect of surviving alone on the plains, hunting her own food, recrossing the turbulent river, and eluding an enraged Shon-ka daunted her. She was not yet ready. Despite the slower pace, she still ached with weariness. How long before time ran out? If she were ever going to escape, she must act soon.

Furtively, she studied her captors. The blood-spattered Indians lay sprawled where they had fallen after gorging themselves on the raw liver. Walking-Bear's mouth was open, his snores as loud as his namesake's. Shon-ka frowned while he slept, his head pillowed on the mass of his hair which had slipped to one side and was in danger of coming unraveled. The other two Indians lay as if dead.

Maura scolded herself for being a fool. Here, she sat— untied and unwatched; there could be no better opportunity. The Indians would probably sleep until nightfall, still several hours away. As she paused in turning the spit, the juices from the tongue sizzled and popped when they struck the flames of the buffalo-chip fire. Better to remove the spitted meat than to let it burn, she decided. The odor of burning meat might awaken Shon-ka. The tall Sioux always slept with his nose and one ear tuned to his surroundings.

Cautiously, Maura lifted the spit from the forked cottonwood branches which held it over the fire. Setting it on a flat stone, she debated whether to wrap the grisly meal in a piece of hide and take it with her. She must also steal one of the Indians' muskets and several other necessary items. Slipping quietly about the camp, she gathered together everything a horse could comfortably carry on the long journey back to Bellevue.

The decision of which horses to take was easy; Luke's chestnut was far and away the best for riding, and Cinnamon could be the pack horse. Stealthily, she loaded her hide-wrapped pack on the little mare and carefully fastened it in place. Then she crept among the horses and soundlessly removed their hobbles. The animals seemed content to remain where they were, munching the trampled grass. Maura hesitated to run them off before she herself was safely astride Luke's horse.

Mounting Luke's gelding proved more difficult than she had anticipated. Shon-ka always took a running leap and landed lightly on the animal's back. Maura had mastered the art of scrambling aboard her small mare without benefit of saddle, but Luke's tall chestnut would not stand still for her. His back was also too high to swing a leg over. She made several futile attempts and only succeeded in provoking the horse into a shrill whinny of protest as he danced around her.

Hooking an arm around his neck and grabbing a handful of mane for support, she heaved herself upward. No sooner had she straddled his hind quarters, when strong hands grabbed her and pulled her back.

"Let go of me!" Maura wriggled and squirmed, but her efforts were futile.

"Be still!" Shon-ka thundered, throwing her to the ground at his feet. Fury sparkled in the big Indian's eyes. "Why you try escape, Woman-With-Hair-Like-Moonbeams?"

Staring up into his flushed face, Maura hesitated. If she confessed she had no intention of marrying him no matter how well he courted her, he might rape and punish her on the spot. What could she say to explain her obvious intention of escaping? Her mind skittered over several possibilities and rejected them as being too farfetched. Somehow, she must make him think that *she* was the wronged party, the insulted one, and had merely been running away out of pique.

Sitting up and brushing off her already hopelessly stained garment, she said huffily, "Among my people, when a man scolds a woman in front of others, it means he has no respect for her. Today, you scolded me in front of Walking Bear and the others. Now, when I arrive in your village, your braves will tell everyone how little you think of me, and I will be shamed and laughed at, maybe even killed. . . . I *thought* you would give me time to learn your ways, Shon-ka. Since I don't even know how to skin a buffalo yet, how will I make a good impression on your people? I had rather die somewhere alone on the plains than meet your tribe so ill-prepared."

Shon-ka's face softened. He even started to grin. "Is good you care what Shon-ka's people think. Shon-ka happy to hear you run away out of pride, not because you despise him and have no wish to be his wife."

Maura demurely lowered her lashes. "I've already told you that I . . . I am willing to be courted. I did not mean to anger you today, but you must *teach* me how to skin buffalo and . . . and other things. There's too much I don't know. Your people will find me odd and . . . lacking."

Shon-ka surprised her by tilting back his head and barking with laughter. "Ah, Woman-With-Hair-Like-Moonbeams! Do not worry so. Shon-ka pleased you wish to learn squaw work. Tomorrow, I teach you how to skin and gut buffalo. When we arrive in my village, Ah-no-je-naje will teach you how to make buffalo robe."

"Ah-no-je." Maura could not get her tongue around the guttural Sioux syllables. "Who is she?"

"She-Who-Stands-On-Both-Sides, Shon-ka's first wife. Good woman. You be good friends."

"Your *first* wife?" If Maura had not already been sitting down, she would have collapsed in surprise. "Then you're already married? But . . . but, then how can you marry me?"

Shon-ka shrugged. "Why not? Ah-no-je-naje many time say she need help in tepee. Tell me take other wife. She old and fat now, not like work so hard. Shon-ka thinking of marrying her sister—until he see Woman-With-Hair-Like-Moonbeams."

"Oh . . . ," Maura murmured, at a loss for words.

Shon-ka reached down and pulled her upright. When she was on her feet, he did not let go. Instead, he drew her closer, sliding one arm about her waist and holding her tight against him. "When Shon-ka see beautiful White-Eyes woman, he not want wife's sister. He not want first wife. Woman-With-Hair-Like-Moonbeams open Shon-ka's eyes. Steal Shon-ka's heart. If Ah-no-je-naje not like new wife, Shon-ka beat her and send her away."

"You wouldn't!" Maura gasped, appalled at the man's callousness and savagery.

Shon-ka grinned. "Shon-ka is chief. He do what please him. When he speak, everyone listen. No one argue."

Maura bit her lower lip. No one back home would believe this—not any of it. Not that Shon-ka had stolen her when he had been unable to buy her. Not that he might make her his *second* wife or mistreat and discard his *first* wife because of her. Not that he ate the raw livers of newly killed buffalos. Not that he ruled like an absolute king . . . none of it. She herself had read and heard tales of Indian strangeness and cruelty. She had discarded them as being too farfetched and one-sided. Her own father had always defended the Indians against their detractors, and she had gone one step further, extolling the red man's virtues and lauding his simple, noble way of life.

Her disillusionment was chokingly bitter. How many more of her naive, idealistic misconceptions would become painfully apparent when she finally reached Shon-ka's village?

Before he let her go, Shon-ka kissed her again. Maura almost gagged on the salty taste of buffalo blood on his lips. The sound of a wolf's yipping in the distance gave her the opportunity to wrench away. "Shon-ka! The wolves are coming to steal our meat. We must build up the fire and scare them away."

Shon-ka gazed disinterestedly out at the plain. "Do not worry. If they come too close, we drive them off with torches. Wolves always follow buffalo. Wait for old ones to fall or young ones to stray. They not bother hunters. Besides, I see only one old white wolf. By himself, he can do nothing."

Maura followed his glance. After several moments of concentrated effort, she finally spotted a slow-moving shape creeping toward them on its belly. No others of its kind accompanied it, and the animal did indeed look decrepit or injured. If it did dare skulk into camp, one of the Indians could easily kill it.

"I'll put the buffalo tongue back on the fire." Now that Shon-ka was distracted from kissing her, she was eager to get away. "It will be dark soon; you must be getting hungry."

Making a great show of being busy, she left Shon-ka to hobble the horses.

Crawling on his hands and knees, Luke poked his head out from under the big wolf skin and inhaled a breath of fresh air. The gamey odor of long-dead wolf was nauseating. When he had conceived the idea of bringing along a wolf skin from the fur storehouse at Bellevue, it had seemed like a brilliant way of creeping up on Shon-ka undetected. Once he had participated in a Pawnee buffalo hunt in which everyone had donned a wolf skin to stalk the unsuspecting buffalo. Easily fooled, the big lumbering beasts had ignored the wolves until it was too late.

Luke expected Shon-ka to do the same. A lone white wolf, making slow progress due to some sickness or injury, would scarcely attract the attention of the Sioux, and certainly they would not bother to attack it. What Luke had not foreseen, however, was how tiring maintaining the disguise would prove.

He longed to stand up, throw off the skin, and commence hurling bombs at the Indians, but had to wait at least until darkness. For best results, he ought to wait until the hour before dawn, when his quarry would be most deeply asleep. That was the time when Indians believed that spirits walked the land, and humans were most vulnerable. The Indians themselves preferred attacking their enemies at that hour. When awakened unexpectedly, sleep-groggy, superstitious braves were far more likely to panic and flee, than to stand and fight.

Luke wondered if his aching muscles and itchy flesh could bear to wait that long. The wolf skin was flea infested, and the combination of his own sweat with countless fleabites had long since convinced him that enduring another fiendish tribal test to prove his courage and manhood could not be worse. Nettles in the crushed grass had scraped his hands and knees raw and bleeding, and the pack on his back was digging a hole between his shoulder blades.

He was also hungry and thirsty. The smell of roasting buffalo tongue wafting across the plain made his mouth water and his stomach cramp. The tongue was the most delectable portion of the entire buffalo. The Indians always ate the tongue, first — unless they were of a mind to eat the raw liver. When Luke had first donned the wolf skin and begun crawling toward his quarry, he had been too far away to see if they were eating the liver. But he had not had any difficulty identifying Maura by her pale blond hair.

At least, she was still alive, and if he succeeded in rescuing her, he would somehow make her pay for all this weariness, discomfort, and pain. Contrary to his expectations, she did not appear in the least broken-spirited or browbeaten into submission. Nor was she fighting her captivity. She had even permitted Shon-ka to kiss her! Luke had been watching intently, and if she had struggled, he had not seen it.

Maura Magruder had plenty for which to answer, Luke thought bitterly. It would serve her right if he *left* her with Shon-ka. She had probably sized up her situation and made whatever compromises were necessary in order to survive. Too bad. He had thought her a pluckier sort, one who would fight until the bitter end. What a disappointment to discover how easily she had bent to the will of her new master and accepted her lot as a slave!

Briefly, he wondered what she had been doing, messing with his horse. She could not have been meaning to escape; if so, she had waited a hell of a long time before trying. If escape *had* been her intent, why hadn't she fought harder when Shon-ka caught her at it? Her resistance had been cursory at best. Maybe Miss Magruder *enjoyed* being pawed and kissed by big, handsome Indians. This was a possibility Luke had never before considered, and the more he thought about it, the more enraged he became. Oh, the perfidy of women!

When he first came west, he had taken pity on an unknown female in St. Louis whose male companion was slapping her about in front of a sleazy tavern. Luke had challenged the brute and knocked him down, at which point the woman had attacked Luke. After scoring his face with her nails, she had then fallen to the ground beside the unconscious man and covered his face with kisses.

The incident had taught Luke a great deal about the illogical workings of the female mind. Women were totally unpredictable, possessed of odd compulsions, and when it came to men, their tastes were utterly incomprehensible. Never could he forgive or forget that his own Margaret had chosen an ugly lout of a corset manufacturer over *him*. If he had come all this way and endured all this discomfort only to discover that Maura Magruder relished her captivity, he just might kill them both her and Shon-ka.

Sprawled on his stomach, Luke lay still beneath the wolf skin and studied the scene before him. Maura was back at the campfire now, tending the meat. Shon-ka was busy with the horses. The remaining three Indians still slept. Buzzards were circling above the campsite, drawn by the possibility of stealing a meal from the carcasses of the freshly killed buffaloes.

A small drying rack, from which hung a few strips of meat, stood a short distance away from the sleeping Indians. A couple of experienced squaws would already have had both buffalos skinned, gutted, butchered, and all of the meat prepared for immediate consumption or further processing. Maura obviously had no idea where to start; from the looks of things, only the tongues, livers, and a few other choice parts had been removed from the two young bulls.

She's not a Sioux yet, Luke thought with savage satisfaction. She may be enjoying Shon-ka's amorous attention, but I wonder how she'll enjoy chopping up a dead buffalo.

He sighed and rested his head on his arms. Until it grew dark and he could move around undetected, he might as well relax and gather his strength. Maura and Shon-ka were not going anywhere, and he had a long night's work ahead. Dozing off, Luke did not awaken until a wolf howl echoed through his dreams. Startled, he peered out from under the skin and listened. A pack of wolves were yelping in the distance, loud enough to rouse him from sleep, but far enough away that he did not expect them to come nosing about, investigating his disguise.

Rising to his knees, he saw that Shon-ka's campfire had burned low. All but one man appeared to be sleeping. The lone guard had his back to Luke and was sitting in a hunched over position, as if dozing during his watch. There was no moon, but the position of the stars told

Luke that he had slept well into the middle of the night. Curse his exhaustion! Now, he must hurry, or he would not be ready; dawn might find him still trying to set his bombs in place, instead of already far from the scene of the explosions.

He eased off the wolf fur, rinsed his dry mouth with water from his leather canteen, and removed his pack. His neck and shoulders ached abominably, and he stretched and rubbed his aching muscles until the pain receded. Then he untied the pack, liberating his precious rifle which had been strapped to the outside. Inside the pack, the gourd bombs lay nestled in individual rabbit skins. A small pouch held gunpowder, and in another he had rolled his tapers and fuses. A small clay jar contained a single live ember slowly feeding upon itself and its bed of dried antelope dung.

If the bombs failed to ignite, he had only his rifle — though he did intend to keep back one or two bombs to hurl at his pursuers in mid-flight. He doubted these would explode; the fuses would probably fizzle and die out as the gourds flew through the air.

Bending over, he ran in zigzag motion toward the encampment. Halfway there, he paused and again studied it for signs of movement. There were none. The guard had fallen onto his side; his snores punctuated the silence. Luke had planned to sneak into the camp under his wolf skin. Now, he had no time to be extra cautious. Every moment counted.

First, he went to his chestnut gelding, Captain, and smothered its welcoming nicker with a hand over the horse's nose. The other horses regarded him curiously, but none gave the alarm. Luke walked among them, stroking flanks and velvet soft noses, accustoming the horses to his presence. He tested the hobbles on Captain and Cinnamon, Maura's mare, hoping they were strong enough to keep the beasts from galloping away when the bombs exploded. Now that Captain knew he was here, Luke had only to whistle, and the horse would come as fast as his hobbles permitted.

Removing two coiled rope halters from his belt, Luke slipped them over Captain's and Cinnamon's heads. He wished he had proper bridles with bits, but these would have to do until he reached the other two horses Major Dougherty had given him. They were hobbled near a small stream which meandered across the plain to the south, behind a slight rise in the land, out of sight of Shon-ka's camp.

Satisfied that he had done all he could to prepare the horses for a speedy escape, Luke stealthily skirted the camp and identified each of the sleeping forms. Maura lay curled in a ball some distance away from the Indians. Shon-ka slept on his stomach between her and the guard. Luke had expected the guard to be more vigilant, but perhaps the strenuous physical activity of the hunt followed by a bout of heavy eating had made it impossible for the man to keep his eyes open.

As Luke slipped past Shon-ka on his way to plant a bomb in the very center of the camp, he noticed a long tether stretching between the Sioux chieftain and Maura. The tether was tied to Shon-ka's wrist and Maura's ankle, so that if she stirred or moved too far away, the Indian would know it. Grinning, Luke unsheathed his knife, bent, and cut the tether in two. Had Maura really wanted to, she probably could have undone the knot and gotten away without awakening Shon-ka, but the fact that the big Sioux was still taking even this minimal precaution gladdened Luke's heart. It meant that Shon-ka, at least, still had his doubts that Maura was completely his.

Luke debated whether or not to awaken Maura and alert her to his arrival; even more tempting was the idea of trying to get her away without alarming the Indians. After a moment's thought, he discarded both ideas. If startled,

126

Maura might make some sound, and Luke would then be faced with fighting four Indians at the same time. His original plan was better. He wanted them confused and frightened, believing themselves under attack by superior forces, perhaps even by the gods.

After placing the largest of the gourds near the sleeping Indians but as far away as possible from Maura, he arranged the remainder around the camp's perimeter. Between the bombs, he trailed a thin line of gunpowder. He took his time inserting fuses and carefully positioning each gourd on its side so the fuse would catch fire from the line of burning powder.

Worries nagged at him. What if the grass started to burn, along with the gunpowder? What if he had put in too much of one thing or not enough of another to encourage the greatest amount of flash in the explosions? What if the trails of gunpowder ignited but the bombs did not? He had so little real control of the operation that he really could not be sure what would happen when he lit the long fuse of the first bomb.

At last, everything was ready. Hiding his rifle behind the carcass of one of the dead bulls, he crept to the largest bomb and bent over it. As he unstoppered the clay vessel containing the live ember, his hands were shaking. Quickly, he inserted a long grass taper into the vessel and held it near the ember until the twisted grass strands began to burn. When the taper was smoldering, he pulled it out and held it to the long wick protruding from the first gourd.

His nerve almost failed him then; he envisioned the bomb exploding with enough force to kill Shon-ka, Maura, and himself, as well as the other Indians. As the fuse crackled and ignited, he had no more time to think. Heedless of the noise he was making, he dashed for cover behind the buffalo carcass. Vaulting over the dead animal, he fell hard on his left shoulder and cracked his chin on his own rifle. With bated breath, he waited. Silence. He began to count, slowly and deliberately. One, two, three . . .

Chapter Nine

Maura was dreaming. In her dream, she stood at the entrance of a tall tepee decorated with brightly colored symbols. It was a Sioux tepee, inside which her Indian husband awaited her. She did not want to go in, but if she did not, Shon-ka would be angry. She belonged to him now; all her strategies had failed, and she was bound to him forever. Inside that tepee, he would make her his.

As she put out her hand to open the flap, her heart pounded with dread. Her breathing became labored. There was no longer any way of avoiding the inevitable. On this night, she would learn the mysteries of the marriage bed, what one did and felt within a husband's embrace. She was sorely afraid, but also drawn. How exactly was the act accomplished? The promise of satisfying her dark, secret curiosity was perversely tempting. At long last, she would discover what coupling was all about — why it attracted as much as repulsed. Why it sometimes kept her awake at night wondering what it felt like and how something so big could fit into something so small. Just how big *was* a man's . . . *thing?*

Tonight, she would find out. She stepped into the darkened tepee. There was just light enough to see by. At her feet stood a basket of gourds. In the center was a stone-ringed firepit. Fur-heaped platforms ringed the inside. A man stood before her—Shon-ka. Only he was *not* Shon-ka, after all. This man was slightly taller and leaner. He had clear gray eyes and a shock of unruly, dark hair, burnished with chestnut highlights. He wore tight-fitting buckskins with a quill design across the yoke, and his shoulders filled the tepee.

Barely had she entered and stood a moment, gaping at him, when he reached for her. "Wife," he said, pulling her into his arms. Conflicting emotions warred in her breast: elation, fear, desire, and protest. This man had kissed her before—a kiss that had shattered all her senses, obliterating all other kisses that had gone before. Ought she to resist? Or had resistance become impossible? Obeying its own instincts, her body melted against his, curved into him, rejoiced in the sensation of thigh pressing thigh, soft yielding to hard, heat spiraling upward.

He will consume me, she thought. I will splinter and explode into a million shiny fragments.

His mouth upon hers was hard and seeking—simultaneously demanding and promising. She shivered and let him have his way with her. How drugging and intoxicating was his kiss! How brash and bold his tongue! How could a kiss be this ennervating, robbing her of strength, while at the same time exciting and stimulating her beyond endurance?

Never taking his mouth from hers, he picked her up, cradled her in his arms, and carried her to the fur-heaped shelf. Then he lay her down and covered her with his own body, pressing her into the furs. Now, it comes, she thought—the knowledge, the pleasure, and, perhaps, the pain. She arched against him, throbbing deep within, aching to fill the hollowness in her belly with his magnificent warmth and strength.

A brilliant explosion shattered the air above her, jolting her awake. As the delicious dream faded, Maura opened her eyes to see stars shimmering in the blackness of the night. A burnt smell tickled her nose, and sparks swirled on the breeze, drifted and fell, dissolving like snowflakes before they touched the ground. The pretty sight reminded Maura of fireworks at a Fourth of July picnic, but in the next moment, panic engulfed the camp.

Men began shouting. Horses squealed and stamped, fighting their hobbles. Holding her bound wrists in front of her, Maura sat up. More amazed than afraid, she watched the Indians dash about the camp collecting weapons. They gathered together in the center, facing outward, their eyes searching the darkness for the enemy who had launched the attack.

A second blue-white bolt of light split the night. The ground quaked, and sparks rained down from the heavens. The Indians prostrated themselves on the ground, and Maura scooted backward to avoid the blazing shower. In the aftermath of this second explosion, an eerie silence ensued; even the horses seemed frozen with fear. Then Maura heard a faint, ominous, crackling sound.

As she raised her arms to shield her head, a third explosion ripped the sky, hurling clods of earth and clumps of grass in every direction. One struck her arm, and Maura rolled over on her side and curled herself into a protective ball. If the attackers were indeed her rescuers, she prayed they would soon desist, or they might kill *her* along with her captors.

Several seconds passed, during which a variety of sounds assaulted Maura's ringing ears. Cautiously, she lifted her head and saw the Indians fleeing for their horses. Another figure came rushing toward her. The white flash of quillwork on the man's chest was achingly familiar; Luke had come for her! Maura scrambled to her feet but was hampered by her bound wrists and the leather thong entangling her ankles.

Luke grabbed her elbow. "Hurry! To the horses! We must get away before they come to their senses and realize what's happening."

"Wait!" Maura tried to kick free of her restraints. "I'm tied to Shon-ka . . . at least, I was."

It suddenly dawned on her that Shon-ka had run first for his weapons and then for his horse, so she must *not* be bound to him anymore.

"I cut the thong," Luke confirmed in a rush. "Can't you go any faster? Oh, what the hell. . . ."

Barely pausing in his headlong flight, he picked her up and slung her over his shoulder as if she were a sack of beans or a bag of flour. She grazed her chin on the butt of his rifle, which was slung over his other shoulder. With her bound wrists, she could not even brace herself, and as Luke ran for the horses, the subsequent jouncing and bouncing made her gorge rise.

She heard the hoofbeats before she saw what caused them. Lifting her head, she caught sight of Shon-ka's black and white buffalo-runner thundering toward them. "Luke!" she screamed in warning.

Luke unceremoniously dumped her in the grass, seized his rifle, and swung it in a wide arc. Shon-ka leaned down from his pony's back, a dark blur brandishing a glinting tomahawk. Luke stepped back and brought the rifle butt down. A crunching sound signaled the impact of wood on bone. The horse rushed by, its hooves only inches from Maura's face. Shon-ka himself toppled and fell, landing heavily atop her.

Maura's bones crunched beneath the dead weight of the Indian; then Luke was pulling Shon-ka's inert body away. "For God's sake, can't you help at all?" he barked.

Catching her breath, she again tried to rise. Impatiently, he hauled her upward. "M—my hands . . . ," she started to explain, but past his shoulder, she saw the remaining Indians astride their milling horses. One of them was pointing at her and Luke. "Luke, now the rest of them see us!"

Hard on the heels of her exclamation came a nearby

132

sputtering sound. Luke leaped in her direction, slamming her to the ground, and shielding her with his body. The explosion rocked the earth beneath them, but all of Maura's senses shifted focus to the more intriguing reality of Luke's body pressing her into the grass. He was a sweet heaviness—all hard muscle and sturdy bone. She could feel his heart pounding against her own and his breath heaving in his chest. His thighs were supple young oak trees holding down her legs, his shoulders a protective bulwark.

He came for me, she thought. He came all this way to rescue me.

Except for a single, fleeting recollection, she scarcely thought of her father. Luke's stubbled jaw against her cheekbone commanded all of her attention. His cheek was as rough as bark and utterly masculine. He smelled masculine, too: sweaty, leathery, horsey, and divinely, wonderfully *male*. She inhaled him as if he were food and sustenance in the midst of famine—then he was gone, jumping to his feet, dragging her up after him, and propelling her toward the remaining horses.

"That last one did it!" he crowed jubilantly. "They've taken off like a flock of frightened sheep. Let's get out of here before Shon-ka wakes up."

"Where's my father?" Maura belatedly demanded, fumbling to get hold of Cinnamon's halter with her bound hands.

"Safe in Bellevue. He was injured and couldn't come with me."

Maura turned to face him. "When? How *badly* injured?"

"Save your questions for later, Miss Magruder, and get the hell on that mare while I grab the rest of these horses."

"I can't!" Maura shouted, incensed by his superior attitude. She shook her bound wrists in his face. "I'm tied tighter than a Christmas goose. And if you don't tell me what happened to my father, I won't go anywhere with you!"

Luke stared at her bound hands for several long seconds. Maura began to think it was too dark for him to see them. Then he whipped out his knife and briskly cut the thongs. "I'll tell you everything you want to know just as soon as we're safely away from here. Until then, your curiosity will have to wait. My first priority is making good this escape."

Not about to give in and meekly obey, Maura stole another moment to rub her tingling, half-numb wrists. "What about Shon-ka?"

"What about him?" Luke retorted. "Don't tell me you're missing his kisses already."

"Missing his k—kisses!" Maura stared at him in disbelief.

"Get on the damn horse! Or I swear I'll leave you here with that lovesick donkey of an Indian, and you'll never see your father again!"

"Oh, you . . . you are. . . ." Maura could think of no insult vile enough to express her opinion of him in that moment.

Whirling about, Maura hiked up her skirts and mounted Cinnamon without another word. Luke bent down and hacked at the mare's hobbles, and Cinnamon took off galloping as if all the devils in hell were in hot pursuit. By the time Maura got control of her, having nothing but the nearly useless rope halter, Cinnamon was lathered, trembling, and blowing, and Maura herself could barely stay astride. Her knees were shaking with a combination of relief and delayed reaction to the excitement of the bombs and the rescue.

Luke galloped up beside her, leading her father's big bay, Shon-ka's paint pony, Zeke, and Jack. "Haven't you learned to ride yet, either?" he bellowed. "You risked your mare's life letting her run like that at night. What if she had stepped in a prairie dog hole? She could have broken a leg or *your* neck."

"I couldn't *stop* her," Maura cried through chattering teeth. "She's only wearing a rope halter."

"You could have used your legs and your seat to stop her! Why in hell didn't you just lean back? Instead, you crouched on her neck like you were riding a damn race horse."

"I was hanging on for dear life! Or would you have preferred that I fell and got trampled?"

"I would have *preferred* that you use your head and your common sense! Or is it that you don't have any? I don't know why I should expect some now when you've never displayed any in the past."

Maura stopped her horse by doing exactly as he said, leaning back and digging in with her rear. "Forgive me if I haven't your riding skills—but you are hardly one to talk about common sense. You almost blew me up back there. You almost *killed* me trying to rescue me. How farsighted and intelligent is *that?*"

"Farsighted enough to have succeeded! Only now I'm beginning to wish I hadn't. Apparently, the only thanks I'll get is a lecture on what I did wrong. Would you care to part company here and now, Miss Magruder? I have two horses I still have to retrieve, but you need not delay your departure on *my* account. You're welcome to set off for Bellevue on your own."

Tears of frustration stung Maura's eyes. She *was* grateful to Luke Cutter for having rescued her again, but somehow he made her so angry that she could not see straight, much less say the right things. "Is it abject humility you want, Mr. Cutter? All right, then I'll admit it. I'm a complete fool. I *don't* belong here, just as you said. If I have to make my own way back to Bellevue, I'll die . . . or be recaptured. I can't ride worth a damn, I've no idea how to shoot a rifle, I've never skinned a buffalo in my entire life, and I can't eat raw liver. I'm . . . I'm just a silly worthless female who should have known better and stayed home."

Maura burst into tears and hid her face in her hands, unleashing all the pent-up emotions she had so stubbornly held in check since her capture. She wept and sobbed as she had not done for years, not since she was a child, not since her mother had died. Looking thunderstruck, Luke sat on his horse and stared at her, which made it all the worse, and she cried even harder. To have this man in particular witness her breakdown filled her with a bitter anguish that poured itself out in more tears, so that she felt she could never stop crying now that she had started.

"Stop it," Luke finally said, his voice low and curiously neutral.

"I *can't* stop it," Maura sobbed. "Isn't this what you wanted? Isn't it what you knew I would do all along?"

"You didn't cry when Shon-ka captured you. Or when you thought your father had been trampled by buffalo. Why start now?"

"I cried when I learned he was still alive. To you, crying is a weakness, and I guess you're right. If I weren't so weak, I wouldn't be crying, now."

"You're *not* weak," Luke calmly countered. He paused, then added softly, "In fact, you're one of the strongest women I've ever known."

"Then why *am* I crying?" Maura gurgled, choking on her tears.

"Beats me," Luke said, shaking his head. "You're also the *strangest* woman I've ever met. Come on. Quit bawling and let's go find my horses."

Maura sniffed loudly. Cold, infuriating, impossible man! Luke Cutter did not have the human decency and compassion to offer her a handkerchief, let alone a comforting shoulder. Why was he so cruel and hostile? Certainly, *he* was the strangest man *she* had ever met. He made no secret of despising her, yet still he had rescued her. And

136

when finally he had succeeded in reducing her to nothing-ness—in *forcing* her to admit defeat—he had then argued with her about it. And paid her a compliment.

The compliment confused and bewildered her most of all. Wiping her eyes with the palms of one hand, she turned Cinnamon around and followed Luke's broad-shouldered figure in absolute silence. This, she vowed, was the last time he would *ever* see her cry or grovel.

By mid-afternoon of the same day, Luke had managed to put many miles between Shon-ka and himself and Maura. To each of the horses they now had, he affixed old gunny sacks. As the animals dragged them flapping and bumping across the sometimes sandy ground, their hoof prints were obliterated. As another precaution, Luke also circled and rode ahead of the buffalo herd the Indians had attacked on the previous day. The herd was conveniently traveling south, trampling grass along the way. He was now satisfied that Shon-ka would have a difficult time trying to track them. The Indian would, however, be expecting Luke and Maura to return to Bellevue, as soon as possible, Luke intended to abandon the southerly route and head straight west.

As he had warned Maura's father, it might be months before they could safely return to Bellevue. To return too soon was to risk ambush and Maura's recapture. Shon-ka had enough warriors to patrol the entire area. He also had the hardheaded determination. His pride alone would de-mand that he regain Maura and punish Luke. If the Indian truly fancied himself in love with Maura, then nothing on earth would stop him from coming after her and even attacking Bellevue to get her back.

Luke and Maura rode in silence, with only minimal conversation. Upon retrieving his horses beside the stream, Luke had switched Maura to a fresher mount; they continued to change horses periodically. As soon as one horse tired, he and Maura dismounted, rearranged packs, and climbed aboard another, herding the spent animals ahead of them across the plain.

Minute by minute, the silence was growing longer and more awkward, but Luke had no idea what to say to Maura. His initial desire had been to see her cowed and beaten, but Luke had *hated* seeing her weep. Her tears had nearly undone him, wrenching his insides until he ached to take her in his arms and comfort her, the way he used to comfort his sister, Celina, after her childhood bumps and scrapes. No doubt if he offered sympathy to Maura Magruder, she would haul off and slug him. He already knew that she did not break down easily; other than the tears of joy that her father was still alive, she had never wept in front of him.

He was ashamed of himself for having driven her to it and embarrassed that he had witnessed it. Over and over, he rehearsed the argument preceding her weeping and could discover no logical reason for her to have suddenly burst into tears. He could not remember saying anything nastier than his usual barbs; why then had she begun blubbering and bawling her heart out?

Had Shon-ka made her cry like that, he would have killed him without a second thought. His fear that Shon-ka *would* elicit such a storm of defeated, brokenhearted sobbing had kept him going when he was almost too exhausted to stay in the saddle. The more he thought about it, the more angry he became—both at himself and at Maura. Now that she had recovered, she sat stiffly upright on her father's bay, her face distant and unreadable. Never mind that her blond hair hung in dusty disarray down her back, or that her face was dirty and her eyes red-rimmed; she still managed to look haughty and as regal as a queen. When their eyes accidentally met, she looked *through* him rather than at him, as if he were too far beneath her to be

138

counted important.

Luke felt torn. On the one hand, he wanted to scold and shout at her, possibly even wring her neck. On the other, he longed to kiss the color back into her pale cheeks. Most of all, he wanted to hold her in his arms and make her smile again. He had not forgotten her radiant smile, glimpsed on the first day they met. Unfortunately, that was the only time her dimples had ever flashed for his benefit. She bestowed her smile on others but never on him. And why should *he* care whether or not she ever smiled at him?

"Luke," Maura suddenly said.

Luke jerked his horse to a standstill, so he could give her his full attention. "What?" he asked cautiously.

"Are you sure this is the right direction? We *are* heading straight back to Bellevue, aren't we?"

Aware that his attention had been wandering, Luke eyed the sun peeking from behind huge, cumulous clouds. "Yes, we're going in the right direction, but no, we're *not* heading straight back to Bellevue."

"Why not? I want to see my father."

"Don't worry. He's being well taken care of. When he protested your capture, the Indians got a bit rough with him, but his injuries weren't all that bad. He just wasn't up to hard riding, so I came without him."

"Why didn't Major Dougherty accompany you — or some of the other men from the post?"

"It's too touchy right now for the major to leave. Smallpox has broken out, and the Indians are blaming the whites. So far, Dougherty's managed to keep a lid on things, but if word of what happened to you got out, we'd have a real mess on our hands. The whites would be furious, and we'd soon be at war."

Maura considered this for half a minute then demanded: "That still doesn't answer my question. If we aren't en route to Bellevue, then where are we going?"

Her peremptory tone irritated Luke. Since her fit of

weeping had finally subsided, she still had not thanked him, nor had she done anything but act cool and haughty. Inasmuch as they were going to be living in close proximity for an indefinite period of time, he thought he had better make clear who was boss.

"Well, now, Miss Magruder, I figure that decision is entirely up to me. I may decide to head west or maybe farther north. You might even get your damn wish to live among the Pawnee—at least, until I judge it's safe to return to Bellevue. At the moment, that's all I can tell you. We'll take each day as it comes. Just don't forget who's in charge, and we'll get along fine and dandy."

Her blue eyes flashed fire, but when she spoke, her tone was exaggeratedly subservient. "Of course, Mr. Cutter. I shall be obedient in every way. Thank you for rescuing me from Shon-ka. Once again, I am in your debt. My father will, I'm sure, pay you handsomely for your services. They have been . . . impeccable."

Impeccable. The word was ridiculously out of place in the context of what he had gone through to save her life. Her short, brusque speech annoyed Luke more than anything she had ever said or done.

"He'll have to pay me *damn* handsomely. Even then, it won't be enough, considering the hell I've suffered on your behalf."

"I'm sorry to have caused you so much bother, Mr. Cutter. If it's any consolation, in the last few weeks I've learned a thing or two about hell myself."

Luke jerked around to stare at her; what did she mean by *that?* Had Shon-ka had his way with her, after all? Had the kiss he witnessed been only the mildest of the intimacies the big Indian had stolen? Luke's glance fell to Maura's tender mouth, and jealousy rose hotly in his chest. He remembered kissing Maura in Elk-Runner's tepee; how soft and yielding her body had been!

He remembered her pink and white breasts, revealed

140

through the torn bodice of her gown when she was struggling to escape the Indians. Somehow, she had managed to arrange the ripped fabric to conceal what lay beneath, but Luke could see the outline of her feminine curves, and he knew that her flesh would be every bit as silky as he imagined. Had Shon-ka caressed her breasts? Touched her white thighs? Parted her legs and plundered the golden treasure between them?

Heat suffused Luke's face and ears. Even his hair seemed to sizzle and go up in smoke. His whole body grew tense and rigid, making it agony to be sitting astride a horse. What he needed was to ride a woman! And the only woman available was Maura Magruder. She was the cause of his acute discomfort, but she could *never* be the cure. Bedding her would mean marrying her—and a host of other problems, not the least of which was how in hell he could ever provide for her.

Good God, what was he thinking? Maura Magruder would never marry him. Nor did he want to marry her—or *bed* her. Clamping his thighs tight against Captain, Luke spurred the gelding into a faster pace. *Don't think about her as a woman. Don't think about her, period.*

Even as he sternly admonished himself, his ears were straining to capture the clop of hooves following behind him. He could not prevent himself from glancing over his shoulder to make certain she was still there. She was, and the sun chose just that moment to peek out from behind the clouds and bathe her blond hair in silver-gold radiance. Though dirty and tired, Maura Magruder was breathtakingly beautiful, and oh, how he wanted her . . . more than he had ever wanted any woman.

Chapter Ten

In the moonlight, the Missouri River glistened like a silver ribbon sewn onto a black velvet gown. From their encampment on a bluff overlooking the river, Maura could see for miles in any direction. The view awed and delighted her. To the east, a herd of antelope grazed on the grasslands over which they had been traveling the past several days. The graceful creatures paused now and then, lifted their heads, flicked their delicate ears, then returned to grazing.

A dense patch of forest lay to the south. To the north were more bluffs. Luke had chosen an excellent place to make camp. Tomorrow, they would ford the wide river and continue on their journey west, but tonight, they would simply rest and enjoy the moonlight. Thus far, there had been no sign of Shon-ka or anyone else. The plains belonged to them alone, and in the warmth of the early summer night, with the breeze soft upon her cheek, Maura was enchanted by the beauty of the landscape. Earlier, they had eaten, and Luke had already lain down to sleep, but for Maura, sleep was impossible.

Tonight, she felt full of life, as if the days of rigor and hardship had never been. Perhaps, her sense of renewed vigor was due to the bath in the river before dinner. She had waded into water deep enough for swimming, and had scrubbed her hair and body until she tingled from head to foot. Luke had been busy doctoring Greedy's lame forefoot; while he was occupied elsewhere, the idea of a bath had proven too tempting to ignore.

Afterward, as she sat in the sun drying her hair, Maura had glanced up and seen Luke standing on top of the bluff, looking down at her. How long he had been there, she had no idea. Their eyes met and held; then he turned away. Unaccountably, she felt rebuffed.

Thinking back on the incident, Maura wondered what Luke Cutter thought about all day. What went on behind those fathomless gray eyes? The man was every bit as difficult to read as an Indian. Unless he was angry — an apparently chronic condition — his face was inscrutable. He almost never smiled, and when he did, the smile did little to soften his harsh expression. Wariness and cynicism never left him. Such dark moodiness disturbed Maura; his brooding presence reminded her of a thundercloud cutting off the sun.

Normally, she herself possessed an optimisitc, ebullient disposition. She found it hard to understand how anyone could go through life enjoying it so little. Perhaps Luke was still angry and resentful that he must take so much time away from Bellevue to look after her. If so, he should be ashamed of his churlishness; her father *would* pay him well. The least the surly guide could do was endure their forced intimacy with better grace. He might not *like* being in her company day and night, but he did not have to be boorish about it.

Anyway, Maura told herself, she was not going to allow his hostile attitude to weigh her down and depress her. The land was beautiful, the journey fascinating, and she meant to take pleasure in it, if at all possible. Missing her father, she longed for the company of someone with whom she could share her discovery of this lovely land. Never in her life had she seen so many stars in the sky. Tilting back her head, she gazed at the sparkling display and wished, not for the first time, that she knew the names of all the constellations and could make some sense of what she was viewing.

"Studying the stars?" A voice said behind her, and Maura almost fell over backward.

Hastily, she straightened, and with one hand, brushed back her loose hair. "I thought you were sleeping."

Looking up, Maura discovered that Luke was bare-chested. Moonlight sculpted his chest muscles in burnished silver and gilded the curly hair that spread like a carpet across his ridged flesh. The carpet tapered in at the waist, she noticed, before disappearing below his belt buckle.

"It's too fine a night for sleeping. And too fine a view." He stood staring out across the landscape that had earlier won her admiration. "Now, you can see why the Indians love this land so much and will fight to the death before they ever give it up."

Pessimism, Maura thought. The man is consumed with pessimism. "Why should they have to give it up? There's land enough out here for everyone."

Luke dropped to his haunches, neatly balancing himself on the balls of his feet, as she had seen the Indians do. Moonlight softened his strong jaw and hawkish nose; silver sparks played hide and seek in his eyes. "Even the plains are finite; even the stars. First, we'll fight over the land—and someday, long after you and I are gone, mankind will probably fight over the stars. It's the nature of men to continually want more, to desire what belongs to their neighbors. Look long and well at these beautiful grasslands, Miss Magruder, because in your own lifetime, they'll be soaked with blood and despoiled of their riches."

"I don't believe that," Maura muttered disgustedly, overlooking her own deep-seated fear that this might happen. "Why do you choose to think the worst? The Indians have lived here for centuries, and they have not despoiled the land."

"The whites will despoil it," Luke responded with great certitude. "Eventually, they'll kill the Indians in order to get it."

Maura tore her eyes away from his handsome, brooding profile. His predictions frightened her; they were not what she wanted to hear in her present mood of contentment. A moment ago, she had felt at peace and pleased with her surroundings. Now, the night seemed sinister, seething with violent possibilities. She shivered and wrapped her arms around herself.

"Are you cold?"

Maura raised her eyes to meet Luke's. His question sounded casual enough, but the simmering intensity of his gaze startled her. As their eyes locked, she felt the heat of his body radiating toward her. It was almost as if he were touching her, stroking her cheek, running his finger down the inside of her neck. She saw that his hair was damp, indicating that he, too, had taken advantage of the river and bathed; why had she not seen him? Had he bathed naked in the cold water? What did he look like—naked and wet? She had asked herself this question more than once, picturing his nudity, wondering about the size of his . . .

Cheeks burning in embarrassment, she quickly looked away. "No, I'm not cold. I—I was just thinking of what you said. It frightens me. I know there are wicked, evil men killing the Plains Indians even now—men who sell them whiskey to get their furs, who give them gifts of tainted blankets that make the Indians sick. I've seen what's been done to the Indians back east, and I abhor it. I guess I still hope that sort of thing can be avoided here

. . . I think my father and I can help stop it, by *educating* people and telling them what the Indians are really like—that they're human beings like the rest of us."

Luke chuckled, a low, sarcastic sound. "If you do help stop the bloodbath I see coming—or even delay it—you will have worked a miracle. Of course, white men aren't the only bad folks around. Some of the Indians are wicked, too. I myself don't particularly care for Shon-ka."

"Nor do I," Maura hastened to say, glad they could agree on *something*.

"Then why did you permit him to kiss you?"

The accusation caught her off guard. Nonplussed, Maura picked at her skirt. "That's the second time you've mentioned him kissing me. Did it ever occur to you that I had no choice? Indeed, haven't you wondered why I'm still alive, why he didn't rape and kill me during the first few days?"

"You're saying you only *pretended* to enjoy his attentions in order to hold him at bay?" Bitterness and contempt edged his tone. "Maybe it wasn't pretense after all. Maybe you *did* enjoy his pawing you."

Maura could not have been more shocked and hurt if he had accused her of *seducing* Shon-ka. She jumped to her feet. "No, Mr. Cutter, I did *not* enjoy it. However, I did dangle the hope in front of him that someday I might willingly become his wife—*if* he treated me with respect, and courted and wooed me according to the customs of his people. Being marginally nice to him was the only way I could think of to prevent him from raping me on the journey to his village. As it's none of your concern, anyway, how *dare* you criticize my behavior! I don't owe you any explanations or apologies. I did what I had to in order to survive—and if he *had* raped me, or gone any further than a single kiss, I would have killed myself. I threatened him with that! And he understood how I felt. Despite being a mere savage, he proved to be far more understanding and gentlemanly than *you* have been tonight."

She would have run away from him, but he stood too swiftly and grabbed her arm. "Then you didn't lie with him willingly or suffer him to touch you intimately? You only kissed?"

His hand on her arm burned like fire. Fire emanated from his whole being. She had the sudden sensation of being scorched and bursting into flame. What business was it of his what she had or had not done with Shon-ka? He was not her father or her fiancé; he was only her rescuer, a *hired* one, at that.

"Let go of me, Mr. Cutter. You have no right to bully me like this."

She stared him down, which wasn't easy; his eyes were glinting pools of fury threatening to spill over and drench her in boiling liquid. When he finally let go, he sighed harshly. "You are quite correct, Miss Magruder. I have no right whatsoever. Please forget I ever dared ask such personal, embarrassing questions."

Maura knew she should walk away, but her feet were rooted to the spot. He recovered his aplomb before she did. Turning on his heel, he left her standing there, feeling like a fool. How long would it be, she wondered, before she *did* erupt into flames in his presence? Naïve she may be, but she did recognize that Luke Cutter affected her as no other man had ever done. She had recognized as much the first time she saw him in Bellevue. He had only to look at her, and her insides somersaulted. What if he took her in his arms and kissed her again? Would she fight him as she had the first time?

I *can't* feel this way about him, she argued with herself, thoroughly appalled. She did not even *know* Luke Cutter — certainly not the way she knew Nate. And what she did know, she didn't like. Luke was hostile, arrogant, difficult, aggressive, nosy, and critical — and those were just his good points.

When she was sure he had gone to bed and fallen asleep, Maura finally sought her own bed. But as she lay down and rolled herself in a thin blanket, she was more than ever acutely aware of Luke's physical presence. When he breathed, she breathed. She fancied she could hear his heart beating in unison with hers. Though he was twenty feet away, he seemed near enough to touch. They might have been the only two people on earth, alone together beneath the moon and stars.

A single thought hammered in her head: How could they spend weeks in each other's company and never think about . . . never be *tempted* . . . never weaken and give in to . . . ?"

Maura sighed deeply, afraid even to formulate the words for what she wanted to do with Luke. When at last she slept, she dreamed of him, the same dream she had been having for weeks. In her dream, they kissed and caressed, removed their clothing, and fondled each other until their excitement reached a point of mad feverishness. Then, she always woke up. Having never experienced a man's full possession, she could not relive it in her dreams. Her frustrated yearning grew and grew, flourishing like some wild, forbidden weed in the otherwise orderly flower garden of her soul.

Luke awoke early. He had not slept well. The tension that had kept him awake all night was every bit as strong this morning. He was ready to explode. Eben Magruder could be rich as a king, but he did not possess enough money to compensate Luke for the agony of being near a woman he wanted and had forbidden himself to touch.

Flat on his back, remembering the previous night, Luke

gazed up at the pink, magenta-streaked sky. First, he had tried to avoid Maura's company by going to bed. When that had not worked to put her out of his mind, he had then gone for a swim in the river. Finally, he had joined her as she sat on the bluff studying the stars. He had intended to engage her in congenial, unthreatening conversation. Somehow, as usually happened when he tried to talk to her, he had wound up behaving like a jealous lover and boorish lout.

The days were not so bad, but the nights had become painful ordeals in which all Luke could think about was removing Maura Magruder's stained traveling gown and caressing her naked body beneath the stars. In sunlight, the woman was lovely, but in moonlight, her beauty was unreal; she became a goddess with hair of spun silver and skin so fair and creamy that his hands itched to touch it. What would Maura do if he went over to her, lay down beside her, and awakened her with his kisses?

At the thought of sneaking up behind her, cuddling close, reaching around her slender body, and cupping her soft breasts in his hands, Luke broke out in a sweat. His heart started thudding like a Pawnee war drum. Knowing he must gain control of himself before he did something really stupid, he rose and swiftly, silently, made his way down to the riverbank. Another swim should make it possible for him to focus his mind on the day's challenges.

Seconds later, he was in the water searching for a shallow place to ford the river. Fortunately, the current was not as strong today as it had been yesterday. About a hundred yards downstream he found a place where the horses could cross easily, without becoming panicked by a long stretch of deep water. Taking his time, he swam back to where he had entered the river, got out, and began dressing. The sun had risen, and he was just tugging on his breeches and boots when he heard a scream.

Grabbing his rifle off a nearby rock, Luke scrambled back up the bluff. Maura was standing near a pile of rocks, her face twisted in terror, her eyes glued to the ground in front of her. With both hands, she was holding up her skirts. Less than a yard away from her bare feet and legs, a large gray and brown patterned snake lay coiled and ready to strike.

"Don't move. Don't make a sound."

As Luke approached, he could hear the ominous, warning rattle. Mouth open and fangs extended, the snake vibrated its tail and weaved its head back and forth. At the first provocation, it would sink its fangs either into Maura's calf or her thigh. Slowly lifting his rifle, Luke took careful, steady aim. As he shot, Maura screamed again. The rifle kicked hard against Luke's shoulder. When the smoke cleared, he saw that he had blown off the snake's head. But Maura continued to scream, uttering short bursts of incoherent sound.

Lowering the gun, he strode to her side and seized her arm. "Maura, it's dead now. It can't bite you. Do you hear me? The rattler's dead."

"Luke! Oh, Luke!" She stared down at the still twitching coils, her mouth working soundlessly as she grappled with her terror.

Thinking that if she could not see the snake, she would calm down, Luke pulled her a short distance away. "It was probably hiding in that pile of rocks. I should have thought to warn you to watch out for snakes around here. They like to sun themselves on the rocks. Why aren't you wearing your boots?"

Her wide blue eyes were dazed and uncomprehending. Luke realized she had not heard a word he was saying. "Maura, it's over now. *Over.*"

Setting down his rifle and placing both hands on her shoulders, he gently shook her. She gave a strangled cry and flung her arms around him, burrowing into his chest like a terror-stricken rabbit. The sunny scent of her assaulted his nostrils. Her blond, fragrant hair tickled his nose. He stood stock still and absorbed the sensation of her willing embrace. One part of him acknowledged that she was only hugging him because she was terrified. But the rest of him responded wholly as a man. With one hand, he cupped her bottom and pressed her body closer. With the other, he tilted up her chin.

Her blue eyes blinked. He knew the precise moment when terror left her, and awareness crept in. She did not move a muscle; indeed, she barely breathed. His fingers slid behind her head and worked themselves into her hair, doing what they had been yearning to do for so long. The texture of her hair was even silkier than he had imagined. He unwound a strand of it and held it up to the sunlight. Could anything be so gold and lustrous, so soft and shining?

He studied every detail of her face, drinking in the slightly flared nostrils, the high cheekbones, the delicate blond eyebrows arching over incredibly blue eyes. Constant exposure to the sun had darkened her skin to a rich golden color, and freckles shone faintly on her cheeks and forehead. Luke did not think he had ever looked into a face as beautiful as Maura's. Her mouth trembled slightly, the lips parting, the tongue shyly darting out to moisten the tender, pink lips.

The sight of her tongue was his undoing. Bending his head, he touched his own mouth gently to hers. She gasped, and the tiny, innocent sound was the spark that ignited his long-bottled passion. Crushing her to him, he fastened his mouth on hers and kissed her with the fervency of a thirst-crazed lunatic gulping water. She did not resist. Instead, her arms came up and encircled his head. She kissed him back, arched against him, pushed her breasts against his chest.

Luke lost his head. Bending her backward, he ate his way down the column of her throat. It wasn't enough to possess her mouth; he wanted her breasts, her slender waist, her gently flaring hips. He wanted all of her, naked and writhing, responding to him, *wanting* him as he wanted her. He tore at her bodice, freed her breasts, and claimed one beautiful, rosy nipple with his mouth, while he roughly squeezed the other between thumb and forefinger. God, she was so lovely, so pale and perfect . . . He wanted to touch and make love to her everywhere at once, but could not move his hands and mouth fast enough . . .

"Luke, stop! You're hurting me!"

Suddenly, Maura was no longer embracing him. Instead, she was pushing him away. In a far corner of his lust-inflamed mind, he realized that he *was* hurting her, practically chomping on her tender nipple, and squeezing her other breast much too hard. It was her own fault he could not control himself; she was too enticing, too sweet and tender. He had never touched anything so soft and warm as her flesh.

"Luke!" Futilely, Maura struggled against him.

Like a drowning man surfacing for air, Luke raised his head. Her dishevelment shocked him. So did the look of alarm on her face. The combination of the two had the effect of a bucketful of cold water dashed in his face. He could not believe what he had almost done—nearly stripped her naked and mounted her, with less care than a buffalo bull mounting a cow.

Withdrawing both hands, he regarded her sheepishly. "Damn. I don't know what got into me."

"It was my fault," she protested hastily. Averting her eyes, she clutched her torn bodice and stepped back from him. "I . . . I don't know what got into *me*."

"*I* almost did," he said crudely. "I apologize. It must be

152

the sun—or the excitement of killing the snake. Are you all right? Did I hurt you?"

She flushed a brilliant shade of scarlet and dropped her head even lower. "No . . . I'm not hurt. You just scared me."

"I think I scared myself," he admitted. "We better get moving. That rifle shot could have been heard miles from here."

All too eager to escape, Maura darted away. While she scampered about camp, picking up things and packing, Luke returned to the dead snake and poked at it with his toe. His friend, Pitale-sharo, would have skinned the reptile, taking its meat for food, its rattles for medicine, and its skin for ornamentation. Very likely, he even would have found a use for its venom.

Luke wished he had a more practical bent of mind; apparently, *his* mind was only capable of lusting after soft bodies and pretty faces. What *did* he feel for Maura Magruder? She stirred something in him that he had never felt for any woman. Certainly, she inflamed his senses—but Elk Runner and Margaret had done that. Though he hated to admit it, Maura compelled his grudging admiration. But he also admired Elk-Runner. The one thing Maura did more than any other woman he had ever known was to *irritate* him. And make him feel guilty.

He resented the conflict and confusion she aroused in him. Not since the day they'd met had they managed to have a simple, rational conversation. Their entire association had been fraught with explosive enmity, plagued by uncommon occurrences and the threat of danger. He wondered if he would have liked Maura if he had first met her back east, instead of here.

Instinctively, Luke realized he must resist whatever it was that he felt for Maura Magruder. Falling in love would be the worst thing that could happen to him. It would mean changes in his life that he did not want to think about, much less confront. He was less ready to take a wife now than he had been when he thought he loved Margaret.

Thought — a key word, he realized. Maybe what he felt for Margaret had not been love, after all. Margaret had never provoked him into tearing off her clothes. Though of course, he had *wanted* Margaret, he had been extremely protective of her virtue. His passion had been far more controllable, his motives above reproach. With Maura Magruder, he had no motives — honorable or otherwise. He reacted to her on a simple, physical level, wanting only to tumble her on her back.

They could not go on like this, spending day after day, night after night with each other, having nothing more on their minds than sex. *She* might not realize what was happening, but *he* did. He must find a way to distract them both, until returning to Bellevue was possible. But how? What? Luke kicked the dead snake off the top of the bluff and thought about it, but nothing came to mind.

"I'm ready," Maura suddenly said. Luke spun around. She was standing there watching him, her arms full of bundles. "I'm going down to find the horses and start loading them."

They had left the horses at the foot of the bluff, where the grass was better. Luke nodded, and she turned and walked away. His eyes clung to the single blond braid dangling between her shoulder blades. He preferred her hair loose and tumbling in silver-gold disarray down her back. It was on the tip of his tongue to say something, make some sarcastic comment about the braid — but he bit down instead, helplessly focusing on the gentle sway of her hips, an even worse distraction than the braid.

Think. Think of what you can do to get your mind off making love to her.

He followed Maura, his brain busily sorting possibilities, considering and discarding, until he finally hit upon something that was not perfect, but at least made sense. Starting this very day, he was going to teach Maura Magruder how to survive in this beautiful but harsh country. He would teach her to quick-load a rifle and shoot, to hunt and clean small game, and to properly ride a horse, just as Pitale-sharo had once taught him. He would exhaust them both with his daily lessons. As a pleasurable side effect, he would then not have to worry so damn much. When they finally parted, he could forget about her entirely, knowing he had done his best. He could put her out of his mind, purge himself of desire, and get on with the business of living.

Chapter Eleven

Maura rubbed Cinnamon's velvety nose and sighed. "What does he think I am—a circus performer?"

The mare whickered softly, lowered her head, and butted Maura's hip, searching for more of the fat, turnip-shaped tubers—prairie potatoes, Luke called them—hidden in Maura's pocket.

"Not yet," Maura whispered. "First, you have to earn them."

Thinking of what she and Cinnamon together would have to do, Maura grimaced. The mare must behave perfectly while Maura leaped aboard her bareback, galloped her through a maze of thorn bushes—without using reins, yet—turned her around, and galloped back again. For all Maura knew, she might even have to do a headstand on Cinnamon's back. As a reward for her obedient cooperation, Cinnamon would then receive a sliver of crunchy root that was otherwise practically tasteless . . . poor horse.

And poor me, Maura thought.

"Miss Magruder! Are you paying attention?" Luke pounded past, one leg hooked over Captain's neck, while he himself hung onto the horse sideways.

"I'm watching!" Maura shouted. "Cinnamon and I are

both watching!"

Blinking against the cloud of dust, Maura sighed as Luke executed several incredible stunts that rivaled anything she had seen back east in an occasional circus or traveling show. She did not know how he managed to keep his balance during these awesome feats, but he had assured her at the beginning of this lesson, that everything he would ask her to do today was something any Indian youngster could easily achieve.

That was his standard argument whenever she noted the difficulty of some particular act: loading and firing a rifle so she could crank off three to four shots per minute, remaining motionless for hours in the grass while waiting for an antelope to move within firing range, peeling the skin off a bloody jackrabbit so that its fur could be used to make a rabbit skin blanket, which she had no idea how to make, anyway.

Luke had been teaching her all this and more during the past several weeks while they lazily traveled west; now, he was determined to polish her riding skills, even if she broke her neck doing what he wanted. They had been hard at work since early morning, and it was now past noon—or so Maura guessed by studying the location of the hot yellow ball blazing down upon them.

Fortunately, a breeze was blowing, riffling the grass and rearranging the patches of sand in the flat stretch of ground Luke had chosen as a practice field. A movement at the corner of Maura's eye distracted her from watching Luke; a prairie dog was poking his head up from his nearby den. A prairie dog town stretched off to the right, and Luke had already cautioned Maura against riding too close to it, for fear that Cinnamon might step in a hole.

Brushing back a strand of hair blowing in her face, Maura smiled. Apparently, the creature's curiosity had finally gotten the better of it. Upon her and Luke's arrival, a cacophony of warnings had sounded across the plain, and all the prairie dogs had popped out of sight into their underground tunnels. While the opportunity presented itself, Maura wanted to observe the elusive beast. Luke had told her it was actually a type of squirrel, rather than a dog.

This one had bright button eyes, reddish brown fur, and a black-tipped tail. Its den was at the very edge of the town, which stretched for almost a mile over the gently rolling grassland. Maura was fascinated and amused by the little fellow's obvious interest in what was going on so near its home. The better to see it, she stood on tiptoe and peered over Cinnamon's ears. Obligingly, the mare bobbed her head and snatched a mouthful of grass.

"Maura! Watch this. You and Cinnamon are going to have to do it next!"

Luke sounded like a kid showing off in front of grownups, his deep voice causing a ripple of excitement down her spine. Maura could never ignore Luke for long—no matter how hot, tired, and in need of a rest she was, he somehow made her forget all her discomforts. Today was no exception, and when she saw what he was doing now, she snapped to attention. Luke was standing upright on Captain's back, his arms sticking straight out, his lean, muscular body silhouetted against the bright blue sky.

What a magnificent man he is, she thought to herself for what must have been the hundredth time. It was not just the sound and timbre of his voice that excited her; everytime she looked at him, he surprised her in some new, heart-stopping way. This time, it was his fluid grace. Despite his brawny strength, he had the suppleness of a blade of grass blowing in the wind.

He looked so wild, so free, more like an Indian than a *real* Indian. In the bright sunlight, his unruly dark hair gleamed with chestnut highlights. Gray eyes sparkling, sun-bronzed skin shining like wet copper, his handsome face wore a feral, delighted grin.

Lost in the beauty of the man, Maura watched Luke race the chestnut gelding dangerously close to the prairie dog town; had he forgotten it was there? Suddenly, Captain's right leg disappeared in a deep hole, and the horse fell, flipping head over heels in a somersault. Arms and legs outsprawled, Luke flew through the air and slammed headfirst into the sand. Maura could hear his bones cracking, could *feel* the impact of his fall within her own body.

Captain scrambled to his feet and shook himself, thoroughly amazed to find his rider gone and his big body still in working order. Luke lay deathly still, hands splayed on the sandy earth. With a strangled cry, Maura sprinted across the wind-flattened grass. Above her, the blue sky tilted, the sun wobbled. The sudden silence grew ominously deafening.

Falling to her knees beside Luke, Maura touched his shoulder. Lying face down, he did not move when she tapped him smartly. "Luke! For God's sake, answer me."

She ran her hands over his back and arms and down his long legs, finding no protruding bone shafts, nothing obviously broken. She managed to turn him over on his back and continued her examination. Again, there were no suspicious lumps, swellings, or protrusions. But Luke's face was ashen, his eyes tightly closed, his features twisted in a grimace of surprise and pain. He's badly hurt, Maura concluded, fighting a wave of panic. Somewhere on the inside where she could not see it, he had sustained life-threatening injury.

"Luke . . . please wake up." She leaned over him and gently slapped his face. "Can you hear me? Please, Luke. You must wake up."

Gradually, color crept back into his face, but Maura was too distraught to accept its appearance as a good sign. He was lying too still, as if he might never get up, might never again open those penetrating, gray eyes. She doubted he was even breathing.

"Luke!" she screamed, shaking him.

Her hysteria rose. Luke would die out here on the prairie, would die without ever awakening. Only a moment ago, he had been so vitally alive, so gloriously beautiful and strong. She had thought him the epitome of masculine grace and invincibility. Now, he was flat on his back, heeding nothing, not responding . . . no! No, *he could not die*. Could not leave her. She had never even told him how she felt about him.

"Why are you doing this?" she shouted at whatever deity might be listening.

Rocking back on her heels, she looked up into the vast blue vault of the sky, where a hawk or some other such bird was performing faultless acrobatics. Showing off, probably. Unaware of the fragility of life and the certainty of death. *Death*. It was obscene that Luke Cutter should die, not on a blue-gold day like today. Not when she had never lain in his arms and experienced all that she knew he could teach her, all that she *wanted* him to teach her. Oh, God . . . why had she denied herself—and *him*—what they both so desperately wanted? Why had she wasted a single precious moment in his company?

Tears flowed, hot and copious. They spilled in a torrent down her cheeks, her sorrow too poignant for words. Rocking back and forth on her heels, she soundlessly keened and mourned for Luke, believing him already lost to her. For the first time, she acknowledged her love for him. How it had happened—and when—seemed unimportant. Grief stripped away all her pretensions, exposing the startling truth: *she loved Luke Cutter*. Loved him hopelessly, helplessly, passionately. Now, when it was too late to do anything about it, she had finally found the courage to

160

admit it.

"Crying again, Miss Magruder? Dare I hope that this time your tears might be falling for *me?*"

Through a watery veil, Maura discerned Luke Cutter's eyes probing her face. *Dear God, he was conscious.* Wincing, he turned his head in her direction. "Well, Miss Magruder? I'm waiting for your answer."

Maura gulped but did not deny it. Her joy was too piercing, sweet, and triumphant. "Yes, I'm weeping for you," she confessed in a hushed, exultant whisper. "I thought you had finally killed yourself with your wild exploits."

Holding her eyes with his, he wonderingly touched her cheek. "I don't believe I've ever known a woman to cry over me . . . I think I like it."

The last time Maura had cried had been over Luke, too; she had wept because he confused her, frightened and belittled her, and made her doubt herself. Or maybe it was because she had loved him even then, but had feared facing the fact.

"Maura. . . ." His softly whispered utterance of her name sounded and felt like a caress.

"Are you hurt? Can you get up?" She started to help him, but he slid his hand around the back of her neck and pulled her head down, so her face was close to his.

"How I feel is unimportant. I'll probably have a hell of a headache when I do get up, but right now. . . ."

She did not have to ask what he wanted to do right now. Desire shimmered in his eyes. Gently, she lowered her mouth to his, brushed the soft firmness of his lips, and pressed her own lips down upon them. He kissed her long and thoroughly. She felt his hand on her breast but did not pull away, not even when he jerked at her bodice and impatiently tore it open. His fingers explored her naked flesh, caressing and fondling her, while he slipped his

161

tongue inside her mouth and stroked her tongue . . .

When he made a move to get up, she protested, "Your head—"

"Damn my head. This is what I need . . . what we both need."

She could not argue with such overwhelming logic. The sand was burning hot beneath her back as he rolled her beneath him, then stripped away the rest of her gown, exposing her body to the blazing sunlight. The sun's rays poured over her like warm honey. The hot, gritty sand burned her skin. Luke's hands and mouth were hotter, his eyes the hottest of all. Passion blazed in their gray depths; she opened herself to be immolated and consumed by it.

"You're so damn beautiful, Maura." He drew back a moment to look at her.

"So are you, Luke."

She lay naked and waiting, unashamed to be spread out for him in the sunlight under the brilliant blue sky. The moment felt so right, so good. She had come too close to losing him to back off now. At this point, false modesty would only be ridiculous. She touched his chest and boldly slid her hand inside his buckskin shirt.

With a low groan, he tore off his shirt and breeches and joined her naked in the sand. At sight of his revealed masculinity, she uttered a tiny gasp. Rather than frightening her, the size and beauty of him inspired a feeling of awe—and trembling desire. He gave her no time to admire his nakedness. Clasping her to him, he began to kiss her with frantic urgency. Maura surrendered to the maelstrom of emotion and physical sensation engulfing her.

Luke's hands roamed everywhere across her body, leaving no tender spot untouched and unexplored. His tongue traced fiery patterns upon her engorged nipples. His fingers dipped into hidden crevices. Maura moaned and writhed helplessly. The reality of their lovemaking was

162

better than any fantasy; Luke knew exactly what to do, where to touch, to make her body ache for his possession.

When he spread her thighs wide open, she was more than ready; she trembled with eagerness. As he rose above her and gently pierced her, she felt intense pressure and a single, sudden, sharp pain. While she recovered from the shock of it, he remained still, balancing himself on hands and knees, kissing her closed eyes and cheeks.

"Sweetheart, I'm sorry. I don't want to hurt you, but there's no escaping it the first time," he murmured into her hair.

"It's . . . not too bad," she lied. The pain of their joining had been more than she had expected, but it had not entirely obliterated the sweet, pulsing fullness in her lower regions.

"I want you so much, Maura . . . I've *got* to have you. If it hurts too much, tell me, and I'll stop."

Stop? He had better not stop or she would die of frustrated longing. As he began thrusting inside her, she had to grit her teeth to keep from crying out. Gradually, the soreness subsided, and a wonderful tension began to build. She tilted her hips and felt the burning length of him scrape a particularly tender, sensitive spot. Oh, God! It felt so wonderful. She caught the rhythm of his thrusting and, obeying her instincts, began to counter-thrust. The pressure grew, spiraling toward a grand conclusion.

"Maura! Maura!" Luke cried raggedly.

He lost whatever restraint he had been exercising and began to thrust harder—long, powerful thrusts that drove him into the very center of her being. Maura arched against him, receiving him in shuddering ecstasy and mounting excitement. She recalled the crackling, sizzling sound of flame racing along a fuse, signaling the explosion of one of Luke's bombs, and she, too, lost all restraint.

When her own explosion came, it blew her apart. Her

senses shattered, and her body convulsed. Spasms of pleasure rocked her from head to foot. With each one, she drew Luke Cutter more deeply within her, squeezing him tightly, possessing and being possessed. A moment later, he collapsed on top of her. They lay utterly still, too exhausted and spent to move.

Finally, Luke murmured, "You're hardly my first woman, Maura, but you are definitely the first to . . . to make me feel like *this*."

Reality crashed down in a cold, drenching wave. Had he actually said such a thing? Maura digested the comment with a growing sense of anger and embarrassment. For her, *he* was the first — and what they had just done together had been so wonderful, so beautiful and soul-shaking. Why did he have to spoil it by casually mentioning that he had done the same thing with *other* women?

All the dire warnings she had ever heard about men came flooding back. It was said that a man only wanted one thing, and once he had it, he lost all respect for the woman who had given it to him. Maura had just given Luke Cutter the gift of her virginity — supposedly the most valuable commodity a woman possessed — and he had had the audacity, the *gall*, to talk about *previous* sexual experiences.

A vision rose in her mind's eye: the pretty, petite moccasins in his tepee in Bellevue. "Luke. . . ." His name almost choked her. "You . . . you aren't married, are you?"

"Married?" He pushed himself up on his elbows and stared down at her in surprise. His eyes darkened. His mouth curved downward. "No, I'm not married — or planning to *get* married."

She saw that she had made a mistake. Her question sounded as if she now expected him to marry her — might indeed have been scheming to *trap* him into marriage. A horrible feeling of guilt and shame crept over her. Back home, surrendering one's virginity before marriage was the worst sin a woman could commit. Maura knew of girls who had given into pressure from potential husbands and gone to bed with them before the vows. In one case, the girl's betrothal was soon announced and the wedding date set. But in another, shortly after the girl confided in Maura that she was pregnant, she left on a visit to a mysterious aunt and was never again heard from. The man with whom she had had the affair subsequently married someone else.

Her cheeks reddening with acute embarrassment, Maura realized that she and Luke had never once discussed marriage. Or their feelings, beliefs, hopes, and dreams. They had especially not discussed their futures. If anything, they had gone out of their way to avoid intimate, potentially controversial topics. She was still engaged to Nathaniel Hibbert, and Luke had *some* kind of tie with an Indian woman. Why had she not remembered these things *before* she lay down in the sand with Luke Cutter?

In silence, Luke got up, collected his clothes, and began dressing. His coolness hurt and stunned Maura, swamping her with regret. She felt soiled and empty. The enormity of her actions loomed larger, weighing her down with unanswerable questions. What if she were now pregnant? What would her father say if he found out? What about Nate, the people back home, Major Dougherty, Luke himself? Did Luke now despise her as a woman of easy virtue? Had she lost his respect?

Quickly, she rose, shook the sand out of her garments, and struggled back into them. Afraid of what she might see in his eyes, she did not look at Luke. Nor did he look at her or say another word. As soon as he finished dressing, he strode away and called the horses, who now came to him on command, all seven of them, trotting obediently like well-trained dogs.

It would have been better if he *had* been injured, Maura thought with piercing bitterness. No, it would have been better if Captain had not stepped in the prairie dog hole, or if she herself had not fallen into Luke's arms like a shameless wanton.

Who was she fooling? What had happened was the inevitable result of proximity and opportunity, coupled with whatever had been building between the two of them since the unfortunate day they had met. If Luke came back this very minute, took her in his arms and started kissing her, it would probably happen again. Now that she had experienced passion, she would find it harder to resist the next time.

Maura clenched her fists determinedly: *There would be no next time.* One foolish fall from grace was clearly one fall too many. Closing her eyes, she uttered a silent prayer. *Please God, don't let me be pregnant, and I promise you I'll never sin again.*

There were no more lessons that day—or the next. Nor was there much in the way of conversation. Luke pointed Captain's nose toward the west and, trusting that Maura would follow, simply rode, hour after hour, without saying a single word. He did not know why it was so hard to talk to a woman with whom he had been physically intimate, but it was. What did she expect him to do? Agree to find the first preacher available and tie the knot?

He had nothing to offer her, damn it. She was no Indian squaw he could stick in a tepee, expect to hunt her own food and make no demands on him during his infrequent visits. Maura was a gently-bred white woman. She would expect a clapboard house with a picket fence, children, security, and some of the niceties of life. Surely she did not expect to grow old in the wilderness . . . no, of course not. She had a fiancé back east waiting for her. The east was where she belonged; Luke had known that from the beginning.

So why had he climbed all over her like a rutting bull? *He* knew what he was doing; she was too damned innocent to know, but he could have stopped their affair before it ever got started. Long, lingering glances always led to *something*, and despite all his good intentions, he had indulged in plenty of those. Damn! He positively disgusted himself.

You aren't married, are you? The only gentlemanly response to such a loaded question from a woman lying sprawled on her back beneath you was, "Not yet, but I'm willin' if you're willin'."

The problem was: he *wasn't* willing. Oh, yes, he wanted to roll around in the sand with Maura Magruder—an experience that had outstripped even his wildest dreams—but he did *not* want to marry her. How could he marry a woman who infuriated him as much as she did? And who understood him so little?

He could *never* go back east to live, never be hemmed in by the strictures of polite society and the dictates of one's employer. He had always known he could not work for anyone else. All his life, he had prepared for the day when *he* would be boss of the family business. When this had not happened, he had instantly realized he could not stay and lick someone else's boots. His mother had accused him of being too hardheaded and arrogant—well, so he was. He *preferred* poverty over swallowing his pride. If he could not get rich doing things his own way, following his own conscience and preserving his self-respect, than he would rather die poor. And his *wife*—whoever she turned out to be—would have to understand that.

Damn his soul for ever tumbling Maura Magruder! He had treated her like a common trollop—and had hurt her, besides. Beforehand, had he envisioned the look on her face when he told her he had no plans to marry, he never would have indulged his baser instincts. But now it was too late to start considering her feelings. Now, the best he could do was take her someplace safe, where he could keep an eye on her but not have to be alone with her. They would go where she had wanted to go in the first place: to the Pawnee village on the Loup. In the meantime, he would keep his hands off her and hope to God he had not made her pregnant.

Chapter Twelve

For three days, Luke and Maura had been following the Platte, the river that fur traders jokingly claimed was over a mile wide but only an inch deep. And so it seemed to Maura. The wide river snaked across the plains like a sluggish reptile. In places, she guessed it to be five or six feet deep, but for the most part, it was much shallower, and dotted with shoals and sand bars. She awoke each morning to the sound of sandhill cranes crying "Karoo! Karoo!"

When Maura exclaimed over the antics of the cranes in the water, Luke broke his silence long enough to explain that the plumed, red-crested birds were a common sight along the river, especially in the early spring, when hundreds of thousands of them visited the Platte. Headed north, they would stop to roost, feed, and court on the shoals and inlets, their bugling calls echoing across the plains.

Luke also talked about the Platte itself, warning Maura to watch out for quicksand when she bathed or fetched water. From year to year, the riverbed was constantly shifting and changing; new islands were being formed and old ones destroyed. This year, due to a lack of rain, the Platte was particularly sluggish and narrower than usual, but Maura was still impressed. To her, the Platte River valley held many wonders, not just sandhill cranes but great flocks of mallards, ruddies, pintails, and snow geese. Herds of bison stretched as far as the eye could see, and smaller herds of elk, antelope, and whitetail deer roamed the area, along with fox, beaver, and muskrat.

Clumps of cottonwoods along the river provided homes for bald and golden eagles, and always, despite the sun's searing heat, the wind blew constantly. Its hot breath chased great clumps of white clouds across the sky and flattened the grass below. To ride through the Platte River valley was to feel both humbled and exalted. And it was a good thing Maura had the scenery to occupy her mind; otherwise, she might have gone mad from the lack of human discourse and the strain of wondering what Luke was thinking as they rode along.

Sometimes, their eyes met, but both would quickly look away. For hours afterward, Maura's heart would pound as she agonized over what had happened between them and what she should or could do about it, which was clearly nothing. Now that he had bedded her, Luke had apparently lost all interest. No longer did his scorching eyes seem to follow her every move. Maura felt ashamed and humiliated. She still wanted him; if anything, she wanted him more than ever. How could he remain so cool and distant? How could he forget the rapture they had shared? Hadn't she pleased him, after all?

For the first time in her life, her self-confidence plummeted. Maybe the smallpox scars on her arms had repulsed him, or he had not liked her sun-bleached hair and darkly tanned skin. Maybe her breasts were too small—or too big. Maybe he did not enjoy the way she kissed—damn him! She could think of absolutely nothing about *him* that repulsed or revolted her in any way—unless it was his propensity to retreat into himself and deliberately shut her out.

Maura hoped they would soon reach the Loup River that emptied into the Platte. When Luke had told her they were no longer stopping until they found the Skidi Pawnee, she had been simultaneously relieved, triumphant, and disappointed. Finding the Pawnee was what she wanted, the reason she and her father had come west in the first place. But Maura knew very well that as soon as they reached the Pawnee, Luke would retreat from her even further. Why else was he suddenly in such a hurry to get there? Obviously, he intended to make certain there were no more opportunities for intimacy. He had decided to remain free and unencumbered; he did *not* want to be forced into marriage.

It would have been a kindness on Maura's part to inform him that he need not worry that she might be pregnant—if he ever *did* worry about it. That very morning she had received proof that no child was growing inside her. While she welcomed the cramping in her lower abdomen and the need to stuff dried grass in her undergarments as a sign that no one ever need learn of her indiscretion, she also resented it. Pregnancy would have been a terrible consequence—but it would have bound her more closely to Luke, pressuring them both to marry.

Now, she still had to decide if what she felt for Luke was love or mere physical attraction. She had to decide if he was indeed the right man for her, which she seriously doubted. Worst of all, she had to decide whether or not she ought to risk *telling* him that she cared for him. Never in her life had she known such uncertainty or felt so vulnerable. Enduring her monthly menses was far easier than suffering Luke's silence and withdrawal. If only he would *say* something about their relationship— *anything*—so that, at least, the suspense would end.

She could endure hearing him confess that her love-making had disappointed him and that she was the wrong sort of girl to become his wife. She could endure his scorn far better than his damn cold silence! Why, he even had her swearing as he did, damning anything and everything.

"Luke . . ." she finally burst out, kneeing Cinnamon closer to Captain. "About what happened the other day—"

"Hold it. We've got company." Squinting his eyes, Luke nodded toward the riverbank in front of them. "Up ahead. Indians."

"Indians?" Maura's throat constricted with sudden fear. Shading her own eyes and studying the two distant figures, she relaxed somewhat. "There's only two of them, following the river as we are."

"I'll ride ahead and find out who they are. You stay here with the horses."

"But . . . ," Maura started to protest.

"No buts! Just stay here and wait for me."

Without another word, Luke took off at a full gallop, leaving Maura with her hands full trying to keep the other five horses from bolting after him. The two Indians must have heard the commotion, because suddenly the taller one turned, saw Luke, wheeled his horse, and began galloping toward him.

Maura gaped in amazement as the two men raced for a head on collision. Both leaned forward and out to one side as if they meant to knock the other off his mount. That was precisely what they did. One minute the two men were astride, and the next they were on the ground,

172

rolling over and over. Luke's rifle was still in his scabbard on Captain's saddle, and Maura had no weapon. While she anxiously watched to see who would emerge the victor, the five horses milled restlessly about her.

The Indian was shorter than Luke, but possessed huge, bulging muscles. As he and Luke grappled and rolled in the sand, the Indian's wide, naked torso hid Luke's body from sight. The brave wore fringed buckskin pants and moccasins but little else besides several clacking necklaces. A shock of bushy, blood red hair stuck out from the top of his head. Maura surmised that it was false. The rest of the Indian's hair was black and pulled straight back from his temples, so that it hung down like a horse's tail. The base of the tail was braided and decorated with the shorter, bristling, red hair.

Luke struggled to pin down his opponent, but was unable to do so for longer than a few seconds before the Indian squirmed out from under him and leaped to his feet. Luke then swung his foot out and tripped him. The Indian sprawled on his back, and Luke burst out laughing, bent over the man, and stuck out his hand. "Enough!" he cried. "Here, old man, I'll help you up."

Grinning widely, the Indian grasped Luke's wrist, but instead of pulling himself up, he gave a quick jerk, whereupon Luke flew over the Indian's head and belly flopped onto the grass.

"Now, who is the old man?" the Indian cried, whooping with laughter.

To Maura's complete amazement, Luke rolled over, got up, and embraced the Indian, enthusiastically thumping him on the back. "Pitale-sharo, you sly old weasel! You haven't changed one bit. I *still* can't outfight or outfox you — and I probably still can't outride you, though God knows I've been trying."

"Why try, Great Heart? Why not admit defeat? Pitale-

173

sharo is a better warrior and always will be. He is the chief of all Pawnee, very strong, very smart, very wise."

"Very *conceited*, you mean!" Laughing, Luke again thumped the Indian on the back. "What are you doing out here anyway? And who's that pretty little Sioux you've got with you? When I first saw her, I thought you were both Sioux—until I caught sight of the dyed horsehair in your scalp lock. If you would shave your head like the rest of the braves in your tribe, I could tell at once who you are, or at least that you're Pawnee."

The man called Pitale-sharo responded in carefully enunciated English, the best Maura had ever heard an Indian speak. "*You* are the one responsible for my long hair. I do not pluck or shave my head because I wish to show friendship and respect for the ways of the White-Eyes, which you taught me. The girl I will explain about later. First, you must tell *me* what you are doing following the Platte. Are you coming to visit my people?"

Luke nodded, his smile fading. His glance flicked over Maura, and she realized that in all the time she had known Luke, she had never seen him smile, laugh, and converse with anyone as easily as he did with this Pitale-sharo. "Yes, we were coming to visit you. But that, too, is a long story which can wait. If you're going home, we'll travel with you. Unless, of course, you want to be alone with that pretty little Sioux."

Maura stifled the urge to weep; Luke had all but admitted he did not want to be alone with *her.*

"No! No!" Pitale-sharo protested. "I am delighted to see my friend, Great Heart. We will ride together, and we will talk. You will tell me what is happening in Bellevue, and I will tell you about my grandfather."

"And Bon-son-gee! Will you tell me about him? I presume he's still trying to take the chieftancy away from you. . . ."

"He still tries." Pitale-sharo's face darkened, then brightened as he looked at Luke. "Now that you are here, I will not waste time worrying about my rivals. I will think only of my friends. You have been gone from us too long, Great Heart. The Skidis have missed you — and I have missed you most of all."

"I am happy to see you again also, old friend."

The two men looked long into each other's eyes, their mutual respect and friendship apparent on their pleased faces. Maura's interest in the young Pawnee chieftan was mixed with jealousy. Luke had lain with her and possessed her body, but he had never looked at her, as he did at this Indian, with unspoken understanding, loyalty, and affection. One might almost think the two men were long-lost brothers.

"I see you still ride Captain," Pitale-sharo said, as Luke whistled for his horse.

"And you still ride Swift Arrow."

Nodding, Pitale-sharo also gave a short whistle, and his small, sturdy, brown and white pony came running. "Ah, and you have new horses . . . one or two good ones, I see."

He had noticed the horses even before *her*. Fuming, Maura nodded to the animals under discussion. "Luke, will you settle down these horses before one of them gets hurt or kicks Cinnamon?"

"This is your woman?" Pitale-sharo's black eyes lit up with admiration. "She is very beautiful. Her hair shines like the sun."

"No," Luke said. "She's not my woman. She belongs to another White-Eyes who lives back east."

"How strange that he should allow her to travel alone. You must explain this to me, Great Heart. Just when I think I understand your ways, I grow confused again."

They were talking about her as if she were not even there!

175

Vibrating with anger, Maura sat straight as a ramrod. Unaware of her agitation, Luke calmly mounted Captain and took charge of the horses, driving them away from Cinnamon.

"I *can't* explain it," he said. "In fact, I think the man's a damn fool. Be that as it may, Maura is here, and she's in danger. That's why we were coming to your village—to hide out until it's safe to return to Bellevue."

"Then let us leave at once. My village is still a journey of two full days from here. Tonight, when we camp, you will explain what has happened and who you are running from. Then I will tell you about the Sioux maiden I have stolen from my enemies."

Maura turned to look at the slender, graceful girl sitting erect on the white pony. During the men's conversation, she had ridden closer, and Maura could now see that she was very young and quite lovely, with enormous, velvet-brown eyes and long, shining braids, so black they were almost blue.

"What is her name?" Maura rudely demanded, tired of being ignored.

Pitale-sharo glanced at Maura in surprise; he seemed shocked that she expected to be politely introduced and treated as a fellow human being. "She-de-a," he said. "Her name means Wild Sage."

"She-de-a," Maura repeated. "That's a lovely name for a lovely girl."

As if he himself had never noticed, Pitale-sharo snorted and leaped aboard his horse. The girl's eyes followed his every move, lingering warmly upon his back. Maura thought she might have something in common with She-de-a. Pitale-sharo apparently treated the little Sioux with the same cool contempt as Luke treated *her*. Perhaps, they could become friends—two rejected unhappy females pining for men who would not even look at them.

Luke sat drinking coffee, and carefully studied Pitale-sharo, seated across the campfire from him. The young chief of the Skidi Pawnee had not changed much since the time he had dragged Luke out of the weed-choked ravine where he had fallen after being almost clawed to death by a grizzly. Pitale-sharo was a little heavier and older-looking but still reminded Luke of a good-natured cub. Though he had a rounded look about him — round face, round shoulders, rounded features and hands — most of his weight was muscle, not fat.

Pitale-sharo had none of Shon-ka's air of menace; he was an open, congenial man with few enemies, except for Bon-son-gee, his boyhood rival, and Shon-ka himself. Luke had always thought that Pitale-sharo was exactly the sort of Indian that whites should befriend. Not that he would not avenge insults to himself or his tribe, but by temperament, he was peace-loving, given to diplomacy rather than raiding or making war. In this, he greatly differed from his grandfather, Wetara-sharo. The old chief made no secret of despising the White-Eyes, though he himself had maintained the peace among the many Pawnee factions for years.

Luke was heartily glad to see his friend, not just because Pitale-sharo's presence discouraged any further intimacies with Maura, but also because Luke had missed him. Aside from Major Dougherty and Elk-Runner, Luke had few real friends. He simply could not abide the sort of men who dominated the plains — degenerate traders, trappers, whiskey sellers, and Indians of Shon-ka's shifty, warlike nature.

Luke darted a glance at the little Sioux maiden Pitale-sharo had captured. The girl was sitting back from the fire in the shadows, where Maura was attempting to engage her in conversation.

"My name is Maura," Luke could hear Maura saying. "Your name is She-de-a. Can you say Maura? I'd like to be your friend, if I may."

Luke wondered why Pitale-sharo had stolen the Sioux girl. She was a bit old for adoption into the tribe; still, if some Pawnee family had lost a beloved daughter, they might welcome the chance to replace her with another girl of similar age. The Indians frequently staged raids on enemy camps solely for the purpose of bringing back children to replace those lost to death or capture during raids. Such raids were an integral part of the Indian way of life. In his own good time, Pitale-sharo undoubtedly would explain why he had taken She-de-a.

"Tell me of Bon-son-gee," Luke urged his friend. "What tricks has he been playing on you now?"

Pitale-sharo frowned and poured out the remainder of the coffee in his tin mug. He wiped his mouth with the back of his hand, as though the coffee had an evil taste. But Luke knew it was not the coffee that bothered his friend; it was the mention of his rival's name.

"Bon-son-gee does as he has always done. He tries to make me look weak in front of my grandfather and the people of my tribe. He watches everything I do — follows me when I go out to hunt. If he discovers some cowardly act or lack of manners, he complains to others."

"He could never catch you in a cowardly act," Luke disputed. "And if he lied about you, no one would believe him."

"No?" Pitale-sharo lifted dark brows. "During our last buffalo hunt, he accused me of lacking courage when I rode into the herd. He rode like a demon and killed many choice young bulls. Among those *I* killed were several calfs, and these he claimed were of no account. Many agreed. I was shamed and did not learn until

178

many moons later that he had included another's man's carcasses among his own. When I confronted Bon-son-gee with this treachery, he denied it and called his accusor a liar. The next day, that man was found dead. It appeared he broke his neck in a fall from a horse, but I do not believe he suffered such an accident; the man was an excellent rider, and his horse very surefooted. I believe Bon-son-gee caused his death."

"You'll probably have to fight and kill him, Pitale-sharo. He'll give you no rest until you do."

"Much as I long to do so, I cannot kill him, Great Heart. He is a good warrior, a fine fighter. The Skidis need such men. If I *did* kill Bon-son-gee, people would say I did so out of jealousy."

"Then, you'll just have to wait until he discredits himself. You must watch him as closely as he watches you."

Pitale-sharo threw up his hands. "How can I watch him when I spend so little time in my own village? I left there in the Rose Moon; soon, it will be the Thunder Moon. Who knows what Bon-son-gee has been saying about me during my absence? Who knows what he has been plotting? While he has nothing to do but think of ways to harm me, I must tend to the tribe's business."

Luke knew that the Rose Moon meant June and the Thunder Moon, August. Had that much time really elapsed since he had first seen Maura Magruder standing on the deck of the *Yellow Stone*?

"Is that what you've been doing—tending to tribal business?" Luke's eyes sought the Sioux captive. Again, he wondered why his friend had stolen her and why she seemed so disinclined to run away and return to her own people. Pitale-sharo saw him looking at the girl, and a curiously guarded expression passed fleetingly across his friend's broad face.

"In a way . . . ," he said enigmatically. "My grandfather wishes me to marry and beget sons and daughters to strengthen our tribe. I do not like the woman he has chosen. So I have chosen my own."

"A Sioux?" Luke was incredulous. "You're bringing home a Sioux to marry?"

Pitale-sharo nodded. "If she pleases me and adapts well to our ways."

"Why didn't you just choose another woman from your own tribe? Why did you go out of your way to steal a maiden from the tribe of your worst enemies?"

Pitale-sharo dropped his gaze, his manner uneasy. "I did not go there to steal the girl. I went to . . . spy. The Pawnee have heard that the spotted sickness has attacked many villages and weakened many tribes. I went to see if the rumors were true. One day, while I lay hidden in the grass watching a Sioux village, I saw She-de-a. She walked a long way from the village, and I followed, thinking I might steal her and learn all I wished to know. She went to a burial place and stood for a long time looking up at a platform there. On the way home, she stopped to dig roots, and that is when I captured her. Afterward, when I saw how handsome she was, I thought to myself: Why shouldn't I marry this one? She is young, strong, and beautiful, surely a better wife for a chief than the fat old squaws my grandfather favors."

Fingering his coffee mug, Pitale-sharo added defiantly, "She-de-a herself favors the idea. The man on the burial platform was to be her husband, but the spotted sickness claimed him. It has claimed many from her village, including her mother and father. The disease has passed now, but those who survived are lonely and sad. She-de-a was glad to leave a place of mourning and sorrow; it held only unhappy memories."

Luke digested all this in silence and then offered his own opinion. "Your grandfather will be furious. I know the marriage customs of your people—how young men are first mated with old women, and young women with old men—so that they may learn what is expected of them in marriage. Only later, when the old spouse dies and they themselves are growing old, may they choose from among the young."

"My grandfather will be pleased that I have finally found someone I wish to marry. First, he recommended Pigeon Cooing, who has lost all her teeth. Now, lately, he has been pushing Heavy Basket at me. So far, I have refused to accept either of them. Once he grows accustomed to the idea, he will not mind if this girl is Sioux. Not if she learns our ways."

"What if she doesn't? What will happen to her, then?"

Still averting his eyes, Pitale-sharo shrugged. "I will give her to someone else—or take her back to her own people. Do not worry, Great Heart. While she lives among the Pawnee, we will be kind to her."

Luke stared hard at his friend; there was something wrong here, something strange. He had never known Pitale-sharo to lie; yet his friend's manner seemed almost furtive. After all the years of warring and hatred between the Sioux and the Pawnee, why would Pitale-sharo even think of marrying a Sioux? Why would he flout Pawnee customs and challenge his grandfather, whom he had always unquestioningly obeyed?

"Now, you must tell me about the golden-haired woman." Pitale-sharo's black eyes fastened upon Luke with the old eagerness he had always shown in Luke's affairs, and Luke began to doubt his dark suspicions. It did seem incredible that Pitale-sharo would ever permit subterfuge and dishonesty to drive a wedge between them and destroy their friendship.

"Oh, you mean Maura," he said casually, as if there were more than one golden-haired woman around. "I had

181

better begin at the beginning. . . ."

Luke launched into an explanation of how he had first met Maura and her father, how and why they had come west, and what had happened to separate them. As he talked, Luke was conscious of keeping his own secrets from Pitale-sharo. He never once mentioned how he felt about Maura—the raging, physical attraction that had drawn him to her from the very first, or the fierce protectiveness that had sprung up in him seemingly overnight, or how he lay awake nights pondering their relationship and trying to keep from reaching for her . . .

When he had finished, Pitale-sharo silently turned to look at Maura. Maura and She-de-a were still seated close together, absorbed in each other, and She-de-a was now patiently repeating English words. "Fin-ger," she said quite clearly, and then giggled.

"Yes, finger," Maura crowed delightedly. "You learn fast. In no time, we'll be able to talk about anything we want. I especially want to hear about Sioux customs . . . and what you are doing here with a Pawnee."

Luke groaned. This was obviously the opportunity Maura had been awaiting; now, there would be no stopping her. Once she reached the Skidi Pawnee, she would settle in and never leave until she had gotten what she came for. She certainly would not return to Bellevue at the snap of his fingers. He ought to have foreseen this and been far less anxious to finally link up with the Indians.

"That one is not bad looking—for a White-Eyes woman," Pitale-sharo said matter-of-factly.

"I never really noticed," Luke denied.

Pitale-sharo grinned, his black eyes dancing. "You cannot deceive me, old friend, It is too bad she belongs to a White-Eyes man in the east. I think she would make a perfect wife for you."

Luke jerked in denial. Every muscle quivered in protest. "No! Believe me: even if she did not already belong to another man, the *last* thing I need is a wife."

Chapter Thirteen

"Pitale-sharo, could I speak with you a moment?" Maura approached the Pawnee chieftan on the eve of their last night together before they reached his village on the Loup River.

Taking advantage of the waning light, Pitale-sharo was kneading one of his horse's hind legs; the animal had been favoring it, and Pitale-sharo looked worried.

"Of course," he said politely, never lifting his eyes from the task.

Maura knew he was not exactly eager to talk to her. She had been trying to engage him in conversation for two days. Not only had he been avoiding her, but he absolutely refused to translate any of her questions for She-de-a. Maura was deeply frustrated; Pitale-sharo spoke what sounded like fluent Sioux to his little captive, and what the girl did not understand, he filled in with sign language, the universal method of communication among the plains tribes. Since Maura knew neither Sioux nor sign language, she was at a great disadvantage. Though she had been diligently teaching English to She-de-a, she despaired of the girl learning it fast enough to satisfy Maura's burning curiosity regarding Indian customs.

"It's about She-de-a," Maura began, and then decided she must be more tactful. "From your discussions with Luke, you know that my father and I came west because we wish to live among your people and learn about your way of life."

Pitale-sharo grunted affirmatively.

"Well, one of the things that interests me most is your courtship and marriage customs."

"Women's concerns, not mine. It would be better for you to ask a woman about them."

"But that's just the point! I *can't* discuss them with a woman, because She-de-a cannot speak English, and I cannot speak Sioux."

"Wait until we reach village. Then Heavy Basket talk you. She know a little White-Eyes talk."

Tapping her foot in exasperation, Maura wondered why Pitale-sharo lapsed into a kind of broken, dim-witted English everytime he talked to her, but was able to converse almost flawlessly with Luke. And why did he not want her to ask many questions—or get answers for the ones she did ask?

"Pitale-sharo, I was hoping She-de-a could tell me about the Sioux. I also want to know how she feels about being your captive. Will she ever go back to her own people? Why did you capture her? What will you do with her?"

Pitale-sharo had been sitting on his haunches. Now, he stood and gravely regarded her, his black eyes piercing. "Maybe I marry her. Maybe not."

This information intrigued and startled Maura. Luke and Pitale-sharo had spent nearly every moment together in the last two days, avidly talking, but Maura had spent most of her time with She-de-a. She had not heard this before and was much surprised. While She-de-a gazed longingly after Pitale-sharo, the Pawnee chieftan paid little attention to the Indian girl. Was a romance brewing, after all?

"Why do you say maybe, Pitale-sharo? If the reason you stole her is because you *like* her, why not admit it and marry her right away?"

In response, Maura only got another grunt. Ignoring her questions, Pitale-sharo checked his horse's front legs.

"Is is normal for Indian men to *steal* women they find attractive?" Maura pursued, thinking of Shon-ka. "Or do they do that only if the girl is from another race or tribe, and they know they cannot possibly win the consent of her parents to marry? I *have* learned a little about Sioux customs, but I wonder if they are the same for the Pawnee."

Pitale-sharo stiffened; when he spoke, he sounded angry. "What is normal for Sioux is not normal for Pawnee. We different people — have different customs, ceremonies, gods. Everything different."

"Then will you *please* interpret some of my questions for She-de-a? I want so much to learn. Don't you see? Between the two of you, I can contrast and compare what each tribe does. It will make my study so much more meaningful, and it will help the whites who one day read it to understand and respect the Indians."

"No," Pitale-sharo said. "I no talk She-de-a for you. Is not good idea."

"But *why* not? What harm can it do?"

Sighing, Pitale-sharo picked up his horse's front foot and tapped its hoof with his knuckle. "Ask Pitale-sharo your questions. Ask now. If I can, I answer."

Gritting her teeth, Maura thought a moment. *All right, Pitale-sharo, if you insist on being difficult, I'll ask you some really difficult questions.*

"How do you feel about She-de-a, Pitale-sharo? Right now, this very minute. Are you glad you stole her? Do

186

you love her? Or do you secretly hate her because she is Sioux, one of your enemies?"

With great care, Pitale-sharo set down his horse's foot, straightened, and assumed an infuriatingly stoic expression. "Not love. Not hate. Only think she make better wife than many women of my tribe. But first, she must become Pawnee."

"Oh! Then she has to pass some kind of test to prove her worthiness and loyalty—is that it?" Pitale-sharo nodded, and Maura was ecstatic at having gleaned *something* from this uncooperative Indian. "What sort of test? When will it be?"

Pitale-sharo shrugged. "Is enough questions. Pitale-sharo hungry."

Maura saw that she would gain no more information from him tonight; for now, he had given her all she was going to get. Unless, of course, she persuaded Luke to ask him a few questions. With Luke, Pitale-sharo was willing to talk all night.

After they had eaten their evening meal, and Pitale-sharo had slipped off into the darkness—on a call of nature, Maura guessed—she said, "Luke, I have been trying to communicate with She-de-a, but Pitale-sharo refuses to translate for me. I am particularly curious about their relationship. Would you talk to him for me? Maybe if *you* asked him, he would be willing to cooperate."

Luke stared at her as if she had lost her wits. "Stay out of things that don't concern you, Maura. Pitale-sharo is my friend, but even I don't nose into his personal affairs. Nor do I suggest that you do so."

"My interest is purely for scholarship!" Maura huffed, affronted.

"I don't care what it is—I won't be a part of it. Among the Indians, women know their place. They don't

187

go around demanding to know what's on a man's mind. If he wants them to know, he tells them. If he doesn't, he doesn't."

"Then how will I ever *learn* anything?"

"That, Miss Magruder, is *your* problem, not mine. Here comes She-de-a, now. Maybe you had better just take the girl aside and continue teaching her English."

Glaring at him, infuriated by his continued coldness *and* arrogance *and* unkindness, Maura stalked to the opposite side of the campfire and joined the little Sioux captive, who was just returning from the river with an armful of newly washed cooking utensils.

"Come, She-de-a, let's practice our English. Better yet, why don't you teach me some of that sign language you use with Pitale-sharo?"

The girl set down the iron pot in which she had cooked antelope stew for supper. Straightening, she smiled sweetly at Maura. Across the fire from them, Luke sat idly watching. Maura could feel his eyes upon her. "Pi-ta-le-sharo . . . ," she repeated slowly. "You know who I mean, don't you?"

She-de-a's wide, velvet-brown eyes searched the darkness, and wistfulness stole across her lovely face. "Pitale-sharo," the girl said softly.

Maura sighed: How could the girl allow herself to fall in love with a man who was traditionally her enemy, a man who had kidnapped her from her own people? "You are Sioux," Maura began, trying to get a grip on her impatience. "What is the sign for Sioux?"

She-de-a gazed at her blankly.

"*Sioux*. I *know* you have a sign that stands for the name of your people." Maura smiled encouragingly.

Luke made a sudden gesture that Maura caught out of the corner of her eye. As She-de-a turned to look at him, he repeated it, lifting his right hand, palm flat to the ground, and passing it from left to right beneath his chin. "Sioux," he said. "Miss Magruder wants to know the sign for Sioux."

With a blinding smile, She-de-a eagerly made the sign. Maura did not know whether to be angry or pleased by Luke's interference after he had so pointedly refused his help. She herself made the sign; it was surprisingly easy to remember. "Now, *Pawnee* . . . will you show me the sign for Pawnee?"

"*Pa-ni*," Luke translated, pronouncing it differently.

Again, She-de-a's blinding smile appeared, followed by a gesture with both hands to indicate horns coming out of the head.

"Horns? Can that be right?" Maura asked Luke.

"*Pa-ni* is derived from *pa-ri-ki*, meaning horn, and it refers to the scalp lock worn by most men of the tribe," Luke explained. "Pawnee men usually pluck or shave their heads, except for the hair of the scalp lock, which sticks straight up like a horn, to taunt their enemies. A Sioux will do anything to bring home a Pawnee scalp lock. And a Pawnee will do anything to retain it."

"I don't need an entire lecture; I only asked a simple question," Maura said haughtily. "Not that your little discourse isn't fascinating, but I am *trying* to speak with She-de-a."

"Suit yourself," Luke responded, smirking. "I thought you wanted to learn something."

"Moccasin," Maura said, ignoring him as best she could. She touched She-de-a's soft, tan, leather footgear.

Catching on now, She-de-a swiftly made a motion of drawing on shoes.

"Why, that's easy." Maura repeated the motion, then plucked a blade of grass and held it up.

Obligingly, She-de-a made a new sign. Signs for kettle, sand, wooden bowl, and knife quickly followed. Flushed with success, Maura grabbed objects left and right, showing them to She-de-a, and exchanging information. She-de-a made the Indian sign for the object, and Maura taught her the English word. Maura learned the signs much faster than She-da-a could learn the words. Still, they were both elated by their successful efforts at communicating.

Suddenly, She-de-a pointed to Luke, now deep in conversation with Pitale-sharo. Since Pitale-sharo's return to the campfire some time ago, neither man had been paying any attention to Maura or She-de-a. With a questioning expression, She-de-a pointed first to Luke, then to Maura. She brought her two index fingers together, then pointed them outward in the same direction. Maura could not understand what the girl was trying to say.

"Luke, could you tell me the meaning of this sign?" Maura interrupted.

She-de-a displayed her fingers, and Pitale-sharo and Luke exchanged glances. "It means to marry." The corners of Luke's mouth thinned suspiciously. "May I ask what you two are discussing now?"

"No, you may not," Maura stiffly responded.

Only after the two men had resumed their conversation, did Maura point to herself and Luke, repeat the sign, and vigorously shake her head in denial. *No, she and Luke had no plans to marry.* Pointing to Pitale-sharo and She-de-a, she asked the same question. She-de-a's dark eyes glowed. A rosy blush crept up her cheeks. She neither affirmed nor denied, and Maura could only conclude that the poor girl *hoped* so.

Feeling sorry for her, Maura sympathetically touched her arm. In a swift, impulsive movement, She-de-a embraced her. It was a clear sign of friendship, and Maura's heart lurched. She had made her first real friend among

190

the Indians, and what a dear, guileless little thing she was!

"Friends . . . ," Maura said, pointing to herself and then to She-de-a.

"Friends . . . ," She-de-a repeated, teaching her the sign.

The next day, they arrived at Pitale-sharo's village on the Loup River. "It looks deserted," Luke said, as he and Pitale-sharo led the women and horses toward the circular, domed earthlodges, the peculiar permanent homes of the Pawnee that differed from all others of the Plains tribes.

Most of the Plains Indians lived in beautifully designed and ornamented skin tepees, which could be dismantled and readily packed as the Indians moved about the plains in an effort to remain near their main food source, the buffalo. The Pawnee, however, only used skin tepees when they went on a hunt. Being one of the few tribes engaged in agriculture, they built sturdy earth lodges for their permanent homes. Scattered between the lodges and on both riverbanks, parched-looking corn and squash plants sprouted from hillocks of mounted earth.

"I feared they would be gone by now," Pitale-sharo muttered. "It is the time of the summer hunt. But I had also hoped they might wait for my return."

He's worrying about Bon-son-gee, Luke thought. The bastard is sure to try and make trouble for him during the hunt.

"Shall we stop, or just keep going?"

"Keep going. My people have gone where they always go. You know the place. One can always find buffalo along the north fork of the Loup."

Luke nodded. It was where he would have gone to

look for the Pawnee had he and Maura been traveling alone. As if his thoughts had conjured the woman herself, Maura suddenly rode up beside Luke. "Where is everyone? Aren't we stopping? I can't wait to examine one of these strange-looking huts. I do remember reading that the Pawnee lived in houses made of dirt, but I had no idea they would be so large or sturdy-looking."

"They're built to withstand heavy storms, which can get quite fierce out here on the Plains," Luke commented, amazed by her never-flagging enthusiasm. "The reason they are all empty is because the tribe has left for the summer hunt. In another day or two we should catch up to them."

"Then we're *not* going to stop, are we?" Disappointment laced Maura's tone. "Why don't we just wait here for them? Maybe the Pawnee will return soon."

"It's too early for them to return—and Pitale-sharo is anxious to kill his share of buffalo. No, Miss Magruder, we're riding straight through. Look at it this way; now you get to see a full scale buffalo hunt. Should make wonderful material for your study."

"I suppose it will."

Luke darted a glance at her crestfallen face, still lovely as a prairie flower despite the long days of sun and wind. Craning her neck, Maura looked this way and that, truly curious about the earth lodges. She was the nosiest woman Luke had ever met—especially where the Indians were concerned. And the most determined. He had never known any white to tackle sign language with Maura's energy; all day long, she practiced with She-de-a. To almost every task, it seemed, Maura brought eager, wholehearted concentration.

Remembering their lovemaking, Luke recalled how she had returned thrust for thrust, learning by doing, and holding nothing back. *Careful, Luke, old boy. Don't start thinking about* that *or you're gonna have a long, uncomfortable ride ahead of you this afternoon.*

He urged Captain past Cinnamon and rejoined Pitale-sharo. Though he ignored Maura for the rest of the day, Luke could not keep stray images from leaping into his head: Maura naked upon the sand, her white breasts gleaming in the sunlight, the eye of her navel winking at him, the silky, curly, gold nest of pubic hair inviting him to burrow into its softness and never leave . . .

Desire burned in him like a fever, hotter than the summer sun, and the farther they rode, the hotter and drier the landscape became. When Pitale-sharo finally called his attention to the condition of the Plains, Luke knew he was not imagining the intense heat. He was relieved he could blame it on the weather, instead of on steamy recollections of Maura.

"It is very bad here, very dry." The young man shook his head, rattling his necklaces and ornamented scalp lock. "For many moons there has been no rain. See how narrow the river is, how short and dry the grass. I do not like it. This drought will cause much suffering before it ends."

"Don't worry," Luke attempted to ease his friend's concern. "Game is still plentiful. If the rains fall heavy next spring, everything will turn green again, and the buffalo will remain in the area."

Pitale-sharo frowned. "For the last three springs, the rains have not fallen hard enough or long enough. It will get worse before it gets better. Mark me well. The time of plenty is past. Soon, we will face a time of want."

Luke knew better than to argue; the Pawnee were excellent predictors of the weather. Long before white men realized a storm was coming, the Indians knew and took shelter. They were rarely caught unprepared. But in the case of drought, how *could* they prepare, except to dry and store as much meat as possible? Undoubtedly, this was why Pitale-sharo's tribe had not waited for him. They knew they must kill as many buffalo as they could before the huge herds swept farther north or west, in search of better forage. The herds never stayed long in one place; when they had grazed and trampled the grass in one region, they moved onward, heedless of the tribes who depended upon them for sustenance.

If the herds traveled too far out of their normal range, even the tribes who followed them would suffer. The Sioux, for example, wintered and summered in the same locations year after year, picking places where there was shelter from the fierce storms, ample water, and enough wood for cookfires and the fashioning of bows, tomahawk handles, and other implements. Life away from these familiar haunts would be hard, fraught with uncertainty.

Seized with a grim foreboding, Luke was glad to depart the silent village; suddenly, he longed for the noisy chatter of the squaws, the shrieks of Indian children, and the sly jocularity of the men. His time among the Pawnee had been a happy one, and he looked forward to seeing old friends, smoking the peace pipe with them, and arguing with Wetara-sharo.

Luke wondered how Maura would take to the buffalo hunt. A hunt was a severe test of anyone's strength and perseverance. This single experience might prove to be Maura's undoing, accomplishing what Luke himself had failed to do—get her to admit defeat. Not since the day she had wept had she said another word about quitting. Luke suspected that when the time came to return to Bellevue, she would refuse to leave the Indians—why else this unceasing effort to learn sign language?

Yes, the hunt should prove to her once and for all that she had no business out here in the wilderness, living like an Indian. Should he warn her, or just let her discover for herself how grueling, exhausting, stinking, and dirty a buffalo hunt could be? He decided to let her find out on her own. Smiling to himself, he also decided that this time, no matter what problems she encountered or what dangers threatened, he would *not* come to her rescue. Maura Magruder was entirely on her own.

Chapter Fourteen

Maura awoke with a start, looked up at the lodge poles supporting the conical ceiling of skins, and for a moment, could not remember where she was. Then it all came back in a rush. Yesterday afternoon, they had finally caught up with Pitale-sharo's tribe. While Luke had been welcomed into the tepee of Pitale-sharo's father, the most revered elder of the tribe, Maura and She-de-a had been assigned to the tepee of a plump, matronly squaw whose name, as nearly as Maura could tell from explanations in sign language, was Lizard Woman.

Yesterday morning before their arrival, the tribe had spotted a buffalo herd, and last night, every man, woman, and child had attended a religious ceremony conducted by the tribal shaman. The shaman, a skinny, painted, elaborately robed and feathered old man, had danced around with a pair of buffalo horns mounted on his head. After this, he and the other men of the tribe had sat around a blazing fire until late into the night, planning the best method of attack. Along with a dozen members of the tribe's special hunting society, Luke had been appointed as a guard to prevent overly ambitious individuals from frightening the herd prior to the communal assault. Following the hunt, Luke must then make certain that each man got his fair share of meat, meaning each carcass must be delivered into the eager hands of his wife and other dependent female relatives.

While the men had been sorting out jobs and responsibilities, the women did likewise, in between times hovering over Maura and She-de-a, exclaiming over their appearances, closely examining their hair and clothing, and overwhelming them with questions. Maura had gone to bed exhausted, her stomach upset and her head pounding from the combination of noise, excitement, and the strain of trying to communicate in Pawnee and sign language. She had been assigned to work with Lizard Woman today but had no idea of what her job would consist.

As all of this came back to her, Maura yawned and stretched, conscious of a lingering fatigue. Finally, she sat up and looked around the empty tepee. It was smaller and plainer than the one she had seen in Bellevue, but still orderly and comfortable, furnished with woven grass mats and buffalo robes, a shallow, stone-ringed fire pit for cooking in wet weather, and an assortment of parfleches, cookware, baskets, and other skin and woven grass containers.

Maura wondered where She-de-a and Lizard Woman had gone. Surely, the hunt had not already started, or if it had, the women would not have left for it without her. She jumped up and hurriedly jammed her feet into her sturdy, long-suffering, leather boots. Quickly, she ran a hand through her tangled hair and, without further ado, dashed from the tepee.

The temporary village of small, modest skin dwellings was deserted, but Maura could see women moving among the horses and affixing long poles to either side of each beast. Not a single man was in sight; apparently, the men had already ridden out. Maura spotted Cinnamon, Greedy, Zeke, and Jack. Shon-ka's paint and Luke's chestnut, Captain, were gone. So were the two horses he had brought with him when he rescued her from Shon-ka.

Angry with herself for oversleeping, Maura broke into a run. Here she was, attending her first buffalo hunt, probably the first white woman in all history to do so, and she had overslept! She ran as fast as she could and soon arrived among the women. Lizard Woman welcomed her with a delighted smile and a blast of Pawnee. Maura understood not a single word. Fortunately, She-de-a took her by the arm and showed her what they were doing: lashing poles together to form a travois, which Maura already knew was a conveyance used by the Indians for carrying heavy loads.

All around her, women were assembling travois, both for horses and dogs. Excited dogs were barking and romping about, dragging their travois behind them. Shrieking with laughter, children darted in and out of the chaos, while babies solemnly surveyed the animated scene from cradleboards slung between their mothers' shoulder blades. Horses stamped and whinnied. The women chattered ceaselessly.

Maura struggled to fasten together the various parts of a travois for Cinnamon, and the women took turns swooping down upon her, advising, demonstrating, and usually laughing outright at her clumsy efforts. The work was fun and interesting, but also frustrating. Maura knew *nothing* about properly joining the long, smooth poles and shorter sidepieces that made up a travois. She-de-a did most of the work for her, but while the women made a great show of admiring Maura's labors, they were sharply critical of She-de-a's.

One woman — a particularly plump, older squaw with a huge, jutting bosom and an exceedingly plain face —

shoved the pretty little Sioux out of the way and insisted upon retying the leather thongs holding Maura's travois poles together. Maura did not need to know the language to understand that She-de-a was being insulted, yet She-de-a endured the physical and verbal abuse with remarkable composure. Maura could scarcely see any difference between She-de-a's knots and those of the Pawnee, but She-de-a inclined her head in a grateful gesture, as if she had just learned something of great importance.

The contrast between the treatment accorded Maura and that given to She-de-a struck Maura as being quite rude and unfair; nothing She-de-a did was right, while everything Maura did was at least amusing and acceptable. Maura began to notice many differences between her little Sioux friend and these sturdy, gregarious women.

The Pawnee squaws were strong and buxom, with square shoulders, round faces, bright button eyes, and long, coarse-looking, black hair, parted in the middle, with two braids that fell behind their ears. They wore dressed-skin capes on their upper bodies, skirts reaching to the knees, fringed leggings underneath, and of course, moccasins. Many of the women had painted the center line parting their hair red, and several had tattooed round, black circles in the middle of their foreheads.

Maura would not have called any of the women beautiful, though the younger ones were passably pretty. None were as slender, graceful, delicate, and doe-eyed as She-de-a. Maura could not decide if the Pawnee women were merely jealous of She-de-a's beauty, or if their rude treatment was part of the ritual of testing to determine whether or not She-de-a was worthy to become a Pawnee.

When as many horses as there were women had been fitted out with travois, the women then clambered aboard and motioned for Maura to do the same. She mounted Cinnamon as Luke had taught her, with a running jump and a leap from the side that landed her upright in the middle of Cinnamon's back. The women all giggled and made gestures of admiration; for once, Maura was grateful that Luke had taken the trouble to teach her a better way of mounting bareback than an awkward scramble and tugging of the poor horse's mane.

As She-de-a started to mount her white pony, the large, heavy-set squaw grabbed the girl's streaming, black hair. When she had hold of it, she twisted her hand, throwing the little Sioux to the ground. Her eyes wide with bewilderment, She-de-a rolled over and sat up, whereupon all the women laughed. They then made it perfectly clear that She-de-a was to walk, not ride.

"Oh, surely, she can ride her own pony!" Maura protested. In sign language, she attempted to explain that the white horse belonged to She-de-a.

The fat squaw with the big bosom emphatically shook her head. At the same time, she extended her right hand, waist high, with the back facing upward and the fingers pointing to the left. Then she flipped her hand and pointed it outward.

The signal was one of the first Maura had learned; it meant *no*, in no uncertain terms. Emphasizing her point, the squaw rode nearer, seized the pony's lead rope, and led it away. Shocked and indignant, Maura invited She-de-a to climb up behind her on Cinnamon. Lizard Woman nodded approval, but several others glared at Maura. She wanted to be friends with all of them but could not condone cruelty to the little Sioux; after all, she herself knew what it was like to be a captive.

With children and toddlers perched upon the travois, the procession of women rode away from the tepees. Maura and She-de-a joined Lizard Woman, who was riding Zeke as if she now owned him. Looking around, Maura saw that another woman rode Greedy; Jack had also been appropriated. Greedy did not like the travois thumping along behind him over the rough ground. He tossed his head and sidestepped, whereupon the squaw riding him rapped him smartly on the head between his ears.

They did not find the men or the buffalo herd until noon, and the hunt was already in progress. Maura could hear it, feel it, and smell it long before she could decipher precisely what was going on in the huge cloud of dust that hung over the plain. There was the same sound of low, rumbling thunder that she had heard the day of the stampede when her father had almost been killed. Loud bellows, snorts, grunts, and human shouts punctuated the thunder of thousands of hooves.

The ground vibrated beneath Cinnamon's feet, and the mare danced nervously, ears pricked and nostrils flaring. Maura earnestly hoped that Cinnamon had attended a hunt before, and she clenched her knees a little tighter around the mare's belly. Already, the salty stench of blood filled the air, vying with the acrid odor of thick, shaggy bodies and the underlying, sulphurous scent of gunsmoke. Most of the Indians, Maura noticed, were not using guns.

On their backs, the hunters wore quivers filled with short arrows, which they withdrew as needed. Their bows were short and lightweight. The Indians rode galloping into the midst of the stampeding herd, separated the beasts they wanted, and then drove them away from their fellows. Having done this, each Indian then galloped along the right side of his victim, notched an arrow into his bow, and shot it into the great beast's heart.

Everywhere Maura looked, Indians were cutting, chasing, and shooting buffalo. As soon as one animal fell his attacker would wheel his horse around and take after another. The braves wore minimal clothing — usually only breechclouts and leggings — and used no saddles. Sturdy rope halters on the horses offered only limited means of control, yet the buffalo-runners seemed to know their business. They ran as if in a race, bodies extended, reddened nostrils distended. At the thrust of a horn, they twisted, leaped, and turned, never once losing their footing and relishing every challenging moment.

When the big-bosomed squaw stopped atop a slight rise overlooking the scene of battle, the women also stopped, and everyone, children included, sat astride their ponies and watched the drama of the hunt unfold below them. The huge, shaggy, black and tan bison milled in terror, undecided which direction to take to escape their attackers. Maura was amazed at the Indians' ability to bring down one of the monsters with a single short arrow. Sometimes, the beasts dropped dead in their tracks. Other times, they staggered and stumbled about for several minutes, bleating and bellowing, while blood poured from their mouths and nostrils. Whenever one crumpled to its knees and rolled over dead, the women and children cheered.

Numerous white dogs darted in and out of the fray, jaws snapping, tongues lolling, as they worried the dying behemoths. Finally, Maura realized that these were not dogs, but white wolves. Prodding her from behind, She-de-a called her attention to a pack of fifty or sixty of the ferocious animals surrounding a wounded bull. The broken shaft of an arrow protruded from the buffalo's shaggy chest. Blood streamed from his distended nostrils, but still, he stood squarely, facing his attackers and snorting his contempt. Red glinted in his eyes as he pawed the grass and roared an angry bellow.

Dashing in and out, dodging the bull's horns, the

wolves took turns biting at the big fellow's legs until flesh and sinew hung in long, bloody strings. The grizzle of the buffalo's nose was almost gone, and his tongue half eaten, but he would not give up. As Maura watched, he caught a wolf on one of his wicked curved horns, tossed his head, and threw the creature over his back. It landed in the dirt, its belly slit open and entrails spilling out.

Gagging behind her hand, Maura could not look away. As another wolf tore out one of the buffalo's eyes, she shuddered, wishing she had a gun to kill the wolves. She felt pity for the great, noble beast who was determined to fight until the bitter end. When the bull finally went down beneath the onslaught of gnashing teeth, Maura had to fight back tears. Why, she asked herself, should she mourn for this one single animal, when the plain was now littered with fallen buffalo, many of whom had died as bravely?

As if the bull's death had been a signal, the big-bosomed squaw raised her hand and urged the women forward. They rode, shouting, onto the plain, scattering the wolves and preventing them from devouring the bull. Splitting up, they drove the predators away from the carcasses, so that the meat and skins would not be wasted. She-de-a showed Maura which carcasses belonged to Pitale-sharo. Pointing to the arrow shafts protruding from the dead buffalos, the little Sioux indicated that the ones bearing yellow and white feathers were his.

Approaching a dead cow, Maura found herself sliding off Cinnamon's back and dashing, screaming, at a flock of vultures diving into the animal's stomach. Wolves, vultures, and blood-crazed dogs were everywhere, defying the women and children to chase them away. By now, the buffalo herd had moved to the west. As the animals fled, the Indians pursued and killed them, so that carcasses were spread across the prairie for a distance of over two miles. Maura wondered which ones belonged to Luke; should she be trying to protect his kills as well as Pitalesharo's? How could the women ever butcher and skin all these animals?

The enormity of the task made Maura feel faint. Remembering how displeased Shon-ka had been at her ineptitude, Maura determined that she would set aside her squeamishness and never let Luke or the Pawnee know how revolted or nauseated she felt. Somehow, she would cheerfully chop up tongues, livers, hearts, and guts. If necessary, she would even swallow hunks of raw, steaming liver, in order to prove Luke wrong about whether or not she *belonged* on the plains.

This was important research. One day, people back east would marvel at her hardiness and praise her courage and daring. With Shon-ka, it had been different, because he had kidnapped and held her against her will; but butchering buffalo among the Pawnee was exactly the sort of thing she had come to Nebraska to learn about.

That was how Luke finally found her, shoulder deep in the innards of a bull, scooping out intestines with her bare hands. Blood and guts slicked her face and arms, sweat had plastered her clothes to her body, and her hair hung down in her eyes so that she could barely see what she was doing.

"Maura, is that you?" a familiar voice growled.

Maura glanced up to discover a man who looked every inch a grime-covered Indian, except for the gray eyes peering out of the dirty face. If it were not for the chestnut horse he was riding, she might not have recognized Luke. "Of course, it's me," she snapped. "Who else around here has blond hair?"

White teeth flashed in the sun-darkened, dirt-caked face. "Why, Miss Magruder, I can hardly tell you apart from the other squaws. Your hair is so filthy it's almost

204

black."

"You don't look any too clean yourself, Mr. Cutter. Instead of gloating, why don't you dig in and help? I assure you, there's guts enough in here for both of us."

"Me?" Luke shook his head. "Sorry, but gutting, skinning, and butchering is woman's work. I've done my part by killing the beasts. You'll find there's at least a half dozen animals sporting my arrows—the ones with all black feathers."

"You mean you didn't use a gun?" Maura noticed that Luke was naked to the waist, and wore only a breech clout, fringed leggings, and moccasins. A beaded, leather band tied around his forehead kept his hair out of his eyes.

Luke grinned again. "When I live among the Pawnee, Miss Magruder, I *assimilate*—that is to say, I become one of them. Pitale-sharo is my blood brother. As you probably already know, my Indian name is Great Heart. It would not be fitting for a true Pawnee warrior to use a rifle, so I don't. I shoot with a bow and arrow. It's more sporting that way, also more challenging."

"Just *who* is going to clean all those buffalo?"

"Who do you think? We're guests here, and it's not really fair to expect the Pawnee to feed and clothe us. Later, we can divide the meat and robes between Wetara-sharo and Lizard Woman—to repay them for their hospitality. I've already given away a few horses, but sharing my meat will also be expected."

Maura's heart sank at the mere thought of six buffalo carcasses awaiting her in the hot sun. The one she was working on now belonged to Lizard Woman. Two blue feathers identified the arrow in its chest. Fortunately, the big-bosomed squaw had chased her and She-de-a away from Pitale-sharo's kills, though what claim the old squaw had on the young Pawnee chieftain Maura could not imagine.

"What should I do with all the meat?" she asked tremulously. "I only have one travois. Cinnamon's dragging it. Perhaps you should have thought of this problem before you gave away the rest of the horses."

"I still have Shon-ka's paint. I brought him with me to the hunt, in case Captain tired before I was ready to quit. Tonight, I'll fashion travois for him and Captain. Once the meat is cut into strips and dried, it will be much lighter. We'll just have to make as many trips as necessary to haul it all back to the village."

Thinking of the work ahead, Maura almost groaned.

"Don't let me detain you, Miss Magruder. I know how anxious you've been to *plunge* yourself into scholarship. . . ." When he said "plunge", he looked pointedly at her arms, plunged into the belly of the bull.

Maura wanted to throw something at him, but the intestines were too unwieldy and slippery. "Go ahead and laugh, Mr. Cutter. Enjoy yourself at my expense. But don't expect me to admit that this work is too difficult or disgusting for a white woman. I came here to learn how the Indians live, and I'm not afraid to get my hands dirty doing it. Did you kill only *six* buffalo? Pitale-sharo killed eleven, and Lizard Woman's husband killed eight."

"I could have killed more, but I saw no reason for it. We won't be here long enough to consume all the meat as it is. It's true that some whites—and some Indians— kill hundreds in a single day, just for their tongues, but the Pawnee are not so wasteful. They never kill more than they can use, and believe me, they use everything."

"I already know that, Mr. Cutter. Now, if you don't mind, I'll just continue as I was doing before you saw fit to ruin my day."

"Have a good afternoon, Miss Magruder." With one last mocking glance, Luke galloped away to rejoin Pitale-sharo.

Back aching, knees buckling, Maura worked until almost nightfall. Before it got too dark to see, she and the other women collected buffalo chips and lit small fires beside their carcasses. All night long, they would have to tend the fires to keep away the wolves. Since the big-bosomed squaw had claimed Pitale-sharo's kills, She-de-a helped Maura and Lizard Woman. By the light of the small fires, they continued stripping off the huge robes. At least five or six women were needed in order to remove the robes intact, so the women took turns helping each other. After all the carcasses had been stripped, the women went back to their own kills to finish gutting them before the stomach contents began to spoil the meat.

It was back-breaking, grueling labor, and Maura had not eaten since the night before. Hunger and exhaustion made her sway on her feet. However, food was the furthest thing from her mind. Not until She-de-a began cutting strips of tongue and laying them directly across the smoldering fire, did Maura even think of eating. Fearing collapse, she finally did sit down a moment, and the little Sioux, bothered not at all by the day's hard labor, brought her a water skin.

Gratefully, Maura drank from it and splashed water on her sticky, stinking hands and arms. Never had she felt so filthy or depleted in body, mind, and spirit. Maybe she *had* overestimated her personal resources. She glanced around at the other women, still slaving over their carcasses, while the men lolled on the ground, talking, laughing, and eating half-raw strips of tongue and liver. The female children had been put to work collecting buffalo chips to feed the fires, but the male children hung around their fathers, brothers, and uncles, reliving the excitement of the hunt.

207

What would she have done without She-de-a's help? Maura wondered. Reviewing the day's events from the point of view of a squaw, she could understand why an Indian woman might welcome the addition of another female to her household, even if it meant sharing her husband. To enjoy an exclusive, monogamous relationship, a woman must pay a heavy price in labor. Maura made a mental note to include this observation in her treatise on Indian life, especially as it involved women and marriage customs.

For a fleeting moment, she wished for writing materials so she could record the day's events while they were still fresh. Then she realized she was too tired to write anything—and she still had to keep her fires burning through the night. Not far away, the fat squaw with the big bosom was offering cooked meat to Wetara-sharo, Pitale-sharo, and Luke. Exending a huge portion to Pitale-sharo, she smiled coyly, and Maura wondered why the woman had not welcomed She-de-a's help. Who was she, anyway? And why was she so nasty to She-de-a and so possessive of Pitale-sharo?

The woman looked old enough to be Pitale-sharo's mother. Maura made a mental note to look into these things, tomorrow. Hopefully, by then she would have more energy. Tonight, she could barely keep her eyes open. Just as she was leaning over on her side, intending to lie down for a moment, Maura felt a hand on her shoulder. She-de-a gestured that the meat was done. With a sigh, Maura straightened and nodded, no longer caring if the meat was still raw; all she wanted to do was eat as fast as possible, then lie down and sleep.

Chapter Fifteen

The days following the hunt were long and fatiguing—
but also filled with satisfaction. Maura learned how to
efficiently butcher buffalo carcasses, build drying racks,
slice meat into long, thin strips to petrify in the sun, and
prepare every part of the animal for further use. Blad-
ders would eventually be made into water skins, sinew
into thread, hooves and horns into rattles, containers,
ornaments, musical instruments, and arrowheads. Robes
and skins were destined to become clothing, blankets,
shields, or lightweight bullboats for traversing the rivers.
Bones were set aside to be made into tools for cooking,
sewing, or hoeing corn, and so on . . . until nothing
remained of the original animal but a lingering, gamey
odor and a memory of its fierce, shaggy splendor.

Working side by side with the women, Maura gradually satisfied her curiosity regarding other matters. The
big-breasted squaw who displayed such possessiveness toward Pitale-sharo was appropriately named Heavy Basket. She was not mother, aunt, or otherwise related to
the young Pawnee chieftain. Instead, the fat squaw hoped
to become Pitale-sharo's *wife*—which accounted for her
jealousy and ill treatment of She-de-a. From Lizard
Woman, Maura elicited a rather confusing and garbled

explanation of how and why a marriage between Heavy Basket and Pitale-sharo would be far more satisfactory and desirable then one between Pitale-sharo and a younger, more attractive woman, such as She-de-a.

Heavy Basket was greatly respected in the tribe. She was a hard worker, highly skilled in basket weaving and skin-dressing, was known to be an excellent cook, a dispenser of sound advice, and most importantly, had proven her fertility. Once married to a much-revered older warrior and friend of Wetara-sharo, then chief of the tribe, she had borne three sons, of whom the first had married into another branch of the tribe, the second had died honorably in a skirmish with the Sioux, and the third still lived among the Skidi Pawnee.

Lizard Woman pointed him out to Maura. She was shocked to discover that he was even older than Pitale-sharo. Her shock deepened when Lizard Woman went on to explain that Pitale-sharo regularly sampled Heavy Basket's female charms, and that this was only to be expected given a young man's powerful mating urges. If Pitale-sharo married She-de-a, he would be giving up a mature, experienced woman in favor of a mere girl, whose fertility was unproven, wisdom untested, and housekeeping skills greatly in doubt. The time for a man to marry a beautiful young girl was when he himself had lost his first wife and was in need of a younger woman's youth and strength to offset his own advancing weakness and age. Then, he could guide and mold her into what he wanted, as well as train her to be an asset, not a liability, to the tribe.

After grappling with these amazing, unorthodox ideas, Maura furtively watched to see who sneaked into whose tepee at night, and soon concluded that, among the Pawnee, it was indeed the custom for the old men to marry young women and young men to marry old women. She even began to see a kind of logic in the arrangement; silly, giggling young girls needed to be taught responsibility, and conceited, arrogant young men needed to be mothered, corrected, and put in their places from time to time.

On her nightly watches, Maura often witnessed young, unmarried men sneaking into the skin tepees of aunts or other older, female relatives, some of whom were past childbearing age. Shocked by such promiscuity, she felt half-ashamed of her curiosity. Did she really want to know what went on in the darkened tepees, hidden from the moonlight? Did she want to understand all the sly jokes and teasing comments the older women made about the younger men? One night around the campfire, the women boisterously debated the sexual endowments of their various lovers, and Maura was both embarrassed and greatly intrigued. Apparently, Indian women had little shyness or reticence in discussing even the most intimate sexual matters.

But sex was not the only topic about which the women gossiped as they worked during the day or sat about the campfires at night. They bragged about the exploits and accomplishments of their sons, brothers, and husbands during the hunt or on horseback, during enemy attacks, or in trapping and hunting other animals besides buffalo. They praised those who could tell the best stories, fashion the best bows, arrows, spears, and shields, and most especially, capture the most horses and guns, and count the most coup.

Maura learned that Pitale-sharo was considered to be a distinguished warrior and a fine young chief, but he did have a serious rival: a short, powerfully built, plucked-headed young man named Bon-son-gee.

Bon-son-gee had killed thirteen buffalo to Pitale-sharo's eleven, and every night, when the men gambled and

211

played games by the fire, Bon-son-gee inevitably challenged Pitale-sharo to prove who was the better man. Both men and women were addicted to games of chances, and each night horses, weapons, robes, meat, grass mats, and other important articles changed hands on the fall of the dice.

Men and women played separately, and the game with which Maura became most familiar involved three large and three small plum stones tossed from a flat, twined basket. The smaller stones were burnt black, while the large ones were plain on one side and marked with a curved band and seven dots on the other. The player held her basket near the ground, tossed the stones in the air, and moved the basket smartly to catch them. Tallies were kept between opposing parties, and each woman laid bets on who would emerge the victor.

Maura herself never participated, mainly because she had so little with which to gamble—only her horse, Cinnamon, and the clothes on her back. For the same reason, She-de-a never played—also because she was not invited, though Maura was. However, both women eagerly followed the course of the exciting, unpredictable games. Maura noticed that Heavy Basket often won, and when she did, was merciless in her demands for immediate payment. Her round, plain face beaming, the fat squaw would gleefully appropriate the very buffalo robe upon which her luckless opponent was sitting.

Time passed quickly, and the days slid into a week, two weeks, and then three. In all that time, Maura saw Luke only from afar and conversed with him not at all. It was as if he had become a Pawnee and been utterly swallowed by the tribe. He rode out with the men everyday, competed with them in their endless games and competitions on horseback, hunted additional large and small game, dressed and ate like them, and slept as they did under the stars, disdaining the tepees where the women and children bedded down.

If Luke crept into some old squaw's tepee at night, Maura never caught him at it, though occasionally, in the interests of scholarship, she kept a lonely, nocturnal vigil, verifying and expanding on her previous discoveries. When a man wanted to sleep with his wife or merely visit her, he simply crept into her tepee. Otherwise, he practically ignored her, going about his daily duties as if she did not exist. Men and women did not work together or intrude upon each other's domains, except in the matter of courtship.

A man hunting for a wife would sometimes find an excuse to help a likely candidate perform a chore — collecting prairie potatoes or buffalo chips, for instance, that was normally strictly a female occupation. Or else he would sit quietly a short distance from her tepee after she had gone to bed and play a sad, mournful tune on a flageolet, a musical instrument resembling a flute. Flageolets were made of box elder wood with seven holes punctured into their stems.

She-de-a continued to gaze shyly and adoringly at Pitale-sharo, Heavy Basket never ceased scowling at the little Sioux and publicly berating her, and Maura often felt acutely lonely, even in the midst of the women and children. Everyone was unfailingly kind to her, always willing to show her the proper way to do a thing, but Maura's heightened awareness of the way the Indians lived, courted, and mated, made her realize that her own life was sadly lacking in tenderness or intimacy. She was exactly where she had always wanted to be, doing exactly what she had always wanted to do, but somehow, it was not enough.

She told herself that her moments of despondency were entirely due to the fact that she sorely missed her father, but in her heart, she knew that was not precisely true. She did miss Eben, and wished he were there to share her discoveries, but she wished even more that she felt free to discuss them with Luke. If he wanted to, Luke could explain so much to her. She had absolutely no doubt that Luke, totally accepted by the Pawnee and completely comfortable with the way they did things, could answer any question she had about them.

He not only held his own in any and every Indian pursuit, he actually beat the Indians at most of their own games. Only Pitale-sharo and Bon-son-gee gave him any real competition. Maura did not want to admire him half as much as she did, but in this wild, raw setting, Luke Cutter stood head and shoulders above other men, even the men who had been born and raised here. He could shoot, ride, Indian wrestle, hunt, break and train horses as well as or better than his Pawnee friends. Yet, amazingly, he did not seem to rouse anyone's jealousy. If anything, the men respected him and treasured his friendship, and the women often ducked their heads, stole admiring glances, and whispered among themselves whenever he walked past.

Maura was certain Luke was a better lover than all of the Indian braves put together. With all the women's talk about sex, she had heard very little mention of female pleasure. Did the old women *enjoy* lovemaking with their young lovers? Did young girls shiver in anticipation at the thought of mating with old men? Did any of these Indian women ever feel as she had felt that day in the sand with Luke?

She wanted to forget that day altogether, just as Luke had obviously forgotten it. But she had only to see him walk by — with that smooth, gliding, arrogant walk of his — and her heart started to pound erratically. A hot blush would creep up her cheeks, and quickly, she would

214

glance away, hoping no one had noticed, most of all Luke.

One morning, anxious to escape the women's endless chatter, Maura walked down by the Loup River, washed, combed and braided her hair, then decided to collect buffalo chips for the cookfire later that day. Absorbed in searching the grass for dried piles of dung, she did not realize she had company until a horse suddenly snorted nearby.

Looking up, she saw Luke riding Captain bareback, using nothing but a rope halter to control the gelding. Luke himself more closely resembled an Indian than at anytime since Maura had met him. Wearing nothing but a breechcut and moccasins, his hair now sweeping his shoulders, and his legs and body darkened by the sun, he sat straight and still on his horse, so incredibly masculine and heart-stoppingly handsome that Maura could only stare in admiration.

Only his sparkling gray eyes reminded her that he was *not* Indian, and only a slight softening of the lines at the corners of his mouth suggested he was glad to see her, alone for once, beneath the dazzling, blue morning sky.

His greeting took her by surprise. "Except for the color of your hair, you could be mistaken for an Indian, Miss Magruder. What are you doing out here all alone?"

Maura glanced down at herself in sudden amusement; she supposed she *did* look like a Pawnee squaw. Lizard Woman had given her a soft, doeskin garment that fell to the level of her knees and was fringed around the bottom. In addition, she was wearing fringed moccasins and a soft leather band around her forehead to hold back stray wisps of hair that might escape her long braids. Her skin was more of a golden hue than brown, but undoubtedly, she did look more Indian than he had ever seen her. They had both assimilated themselves into the tribe.

Venturing a tiny smile, she said, "I'm collecting buffalo chips—a proper job for a proper squaw, wouldn't you agree?"

Luke's gray eyes skewered her. "I hope you are not forgetting that you are a white woman. We'll soon be returning to the Pawnee village, and when we do, you and I are leaving for Bellevue. By then, it should be safe."

Angered by this reminder that he thought her unfit to live among the Indians, Maura tossed her head. "I am forgetting nothing, Mr. Cutter. However, while I'm here, I have a job to do, and I intend to do it as well I am able."

Luke carelessly jumped down from Captain and tossed aside the rope halter, allowing the animal to graze on the short dry grass. Coming toward her, he scowled. "Aren't you ready to quit yet, Miss Magruder? How much longer are you going to go on pretending to *love* this sort of life, which most white women would find altogether too harsh and impossible?"

"I am *not* pretending!" Maura hotly denied. "I do love it. This life is exactly what I expected, I am adjusting to it just fine, and if only I had my journal, I'd be as happy as I could be! Is that what's bothering you, Mr. Cutter? You can't *stand* the thought of being wrong about me?"

Less than a foot away from her, Luke's near-nakedness screamed at Maura to be noticed. She stared at his chest, which differed greatly from an Indian's in that Luke had a pelt of fine, curly hair that narrowed where it disappeared into his breechclout. He had hair on his legs, too . . . and fine dark hair on the backs of his hands and on his forearms. There were scars on his chest—scars she had never before noticed, not even dur-

216

ing their lovemaking that day on the open plain. Two identical scars, as if the flesh had purposely been slit, marred his flesh on either side.

Startled, she reached out and touched one. "Where did you get these?"

As her fingertips traced the raised ridges, dark pink against his brown skin, he flinched and half-groaned. Wondering if the scars were still sensitive, Maura raised her eyes to his.

"Damn you, Maura," he gritted. "Why did you have to *touch* me?"

The vibrations in the air between them changed from hostility to expectancy. Like two dancers drawn together in a dance that each remembered perfectly, they moved toward each other. Luke bent his head. Maura tilted her face to meet his. They stared long into each other's eyes. Maura felt his breath caress her mouth and unthinkingly moistened her lips with the tip of her tongue. At the exact same moment he reached for her, she reached for him. Their bodies surged together, her arms around his neck, his around her waist, and their mouths greedily sought each other's.

His hands spanned the curve of her buttocks and pressed her to him. She entwined her fingers in his dark, silky hair and kissed him with all the yearning she had tried so futilely to subdue. Passion boiled in the pit of her stomach. Drowning in need, she would not have protested had he lowered her to the grass then and there; she *wanted* him to do it, did not care *who* might see them. The taste of his lips and tongue were honey-sweet; the feel of his strong, hard body was both torture and ecstasy.

Her breasts throbbed with the sweet, aching desire to once again feel his mouth upon them. The empty hollow between her thighs begged to be filled with his hot, slick rigidity. She wanted him as she had never before wanted anything—to be touched, kissed, loved, suckled, probed, and possessed. This was Luke, *her* Luke, and it had been an eternity since last they had held each other.

Suddenly, he thrust her away from him. "No, damn it! Not *again!* I swore I'd not touch you again, and by all that's holy, I will *not!*"

"*Why* not?" Maura demanded, incensed and frustrated. "You need hardly worry anymore about taking my virginity! You've already taken it! Why do you scorn me, now?"

"Is that what you think—that I *scorn* you? Don't you realize what a torture it is to see you everyday and not be able to touch you?"

"I never said you *couldn't* touch me! I thought you didn't *want* to touch me, anymore. I thought I had displeased you in some way—that somehow I didn't measure up to your *previous* women!"

"*What* women? What in hell are you talking about? Do you think I go around tumbling women in the sand every chance I get?"

"You *said* I wasn't your first woman," Maura furiously reminded him.

"You weren't my first woman. But if you think I'm going to marry you just because *I* was your first man, you had better think twice. *You* are the one engaged to someone else, *you* are the one who doesn't belong out here, *you* are the one who's stubborn, spoiled, headstrong, impulsive—"

"And in love with *you,* you stupid, vile, crude-talking oaf!"

"*What* did you say?" Caught in the midst of his tirade, stunned and incredulous, Luke gaped at her.

"I *said* I'm in love with you. Somehow, for reasons I can't understand much less explain, I have stupidly man-

218

aged to fall in love with you!"

"You're damn right, it's stupid. . . . No way in hell should you be in love with me. A man like me isn't good enough for a woman like you. I can't give you *any* of the things you'll eventually want. Or *should* want, if you have half a brain in your head."

"Well, I'm sorry!" Maura shouted, desperately trying to hold back tears. "I had no intention of falling in love with you, and now that I have, I don't *want* to love you. *No* woman could want to love a callous, cruel bastard like you. You hold me, touch me, caress me, make me feel things I've never felt before, and then you don't even talk to me for three and half weeks, except to make nasty, snide remarks. And just when I think I'm getting over you, you kiss me again and bring it all back—all the wanting, the hoping, the—"

With a muttered oath, he crushed her to him, holding her so tightly against his body that she could scarcely breathe. The thumping in her breast might have been *his* heart, instead of hers. "Do you mean that, Maura? You love me; you *want* me? Do you really mean it?" he rumbled into her hair. "Damn it, *do* you?"

Like a flower seeking the sun, she lifted her face to his. The naked longing in his eyes echoed her own longing and inner tumult. "I love and want you so much that I sometimes think I'll go mad if I can't have you," she admitted honestly.

His mouth swooped down upon hers. Lifting her off her feet, he held and clasped her to him, grinding his hips into her hips, flattening her breasts against his bare chest, bending her backward as he kissed her into a mindless frenzy of desire. Abruptly and unexpectedly, he broke away again. "Not here," he growled. "I won't take you where someone may come along and see us. Come on . . . I know a place we can be alone together."

He took her hand and pulled her roughly toward his horse. Unresisting, lost in a haze of tingling nerves and throbbing need, she followed, He mounted first, then reached down, pulled her up, and set her on the horse in front of him. One bronzed arm encircled her waist, simultaneously anchoring her to the horse and to his body. As they rode swiftly along the riverbank, leaving the camp behind, his hand moved upward to cup her left breast, and his fingers teased her nipple through the soft doeskin.

The sensations he evoked with his skillful, knowing fingers radiated outward, suffusing her body with pleasure. Maura leaned back against him, closed her eyes against the sun's glare, and gave herself up to the flood of warmth and spiraling rapture. By the time he finally stopped the gelding in a copse of cottonwoods well away from the Indian camp, Maura felt as if her bones had melted and were oozing out through the pores of her skin. Luke's hand dropped to her spread thighs, opened wide to accomodate Captain's girth. Her doeskin dress was bunched around her hips, her legs bared to the sunshine. Underneath, she wore nothing; Indian women eschewed undergarments. Fleetingly, Maura wondered if ease of sexual access had anything to do with their preference for being half-undressed.

Nuzzling her neck, Luke pressed a finger into the sensitive flesh of her crotch and began a slow, rubbing motion. "Luke!" Maura gave a strangled cry, but Luke did not stop. Instead, he encircled her waist with his other arm and began fingering her right breast, while his right hand continued exploring the tender area between her legs.

"I'll give you what you want," he whispered huskily into her ear. "Did your fiancé ever touch you like this? Did *he* ever make you feel this way?"

220

"No!" Maura gasped, unable to even think of Nate at a time like this. In a dim corner of her mind, she asked herself why Luke should even mention her fiancé, and the answer came in his low, triumphant chuckle.

"No one but me had better ever touch you, Maura Magruder, or I think I'd be so jealous I'd have to kill the poor bastard."

Removing her hands, he slid down from the horse. Then he lifted her into his arms and carried her toward the peaceful, placid shallows of the river, where sandhill cranes were wading and feeding. "Where are we going?" Maura whispered, clinging to his neck.

"You'll see."

Just short of the water, Luke halted, set Maura on her feet, and impatiently tore away his breechclout and moccasins. Maura simply stood and stared; she had forgotten how magnificent Luke was in his nakedness. No majestic buffalo bull sported grander equipment for pleasing a lady buffalo.

He reached for the fringed hem of her dress and tugged it over her head and arms in one swift motion. She kicked off her moccasins and took his outstretched hand. He led her into the sandy shallows, stooped and splashed water on her stomach, and then, grinning, drew her into his arms.

"How about a bath? I'll wash you, then you wash me. First, let's undo your hair from those damn braids."

Unable to speak for the wild fluttering in her chest, Maura fumbled with the thongs binding her braids, still damp from the bath she had taken earlier. When she removed the thongs, Luke raked his fingers through her long, flowing hair, fluffing it about her shoulders and back. "That's better," he sighed. "Silver-gold goddess, more beautiful than the sun or moon. That's what you are — a goddess."

221

He led her deeper into the water, until it rippled about her thighs, gently lapping the golden triangle of hair between her legs. He scooped a handful of water and dribbled it across her breasts. "Now, you do the same thing to me," he directed huskily.

She did. Droplets glistened on his chest hair, and she touched them lightly, brushing the dark, curly hair with the palm of her hand. Next, he scooped water on her belly, knelt down suddenly, and then licked the droplets out of her navel. His tongue was feather-light and teasing. Maura moaned softly. Still on his knees, he began to kiss and lick her stomach, brushing his rough-smooth jaw back and forth across her sensitive skin.

His mouth moved lower, until his chin grazed the water. He kissed the golden triangle of hair, buried his nose there, and inhaled deeply. Maura's first impulse was to move away, but Luke's hands held her buttocks and prevented escape. Her second impulse was to spread her legs slightly and let him do whatever he wanted; with Luke, she never felt shame. Somehow, whatever he wanted, always turned how to be what *she* wanted . . .

Chapter Sixteen

To Luke, Maura's body was a gleaming gold treasure finally to be enjoyed at his leisure. Despite the clamoring needs of his own body, he wanted to cherish every single moment, to prolong the joyous ecstasy of making love to her for as long as possible. He had no delusions that what they were doing might lead to a permanent union; Maura might think she loved him, but when she finally came to her senses, when her passion waned, she would realize the truth. She must leave, and he must stay.

They belonged to two incompatible worlds. She might be able to survive for a time in this one, even to succeed, but eventually, when the novelty and excitement paled and danger alone remained, she would have no choice but to return home, where he could not, *would* not, follow. He cursed himself for wanting her so much. Desire made him willing to risk breaking her heart, getting her pregnant, incurring the wrath of her father, and whatever else might happen. Fighting his own wants and needs was suddenly impossible; in the face of her willing and eager capitulation, he *had* to have her again.

Maura's thighs were smooth as satin, her thatch of

silver-gold hair as soft as swan's down. Exploring the source of her female mystery and pleasure was the rarest of exotic delights. He probed her with his tongue, teased her to honey-making preparedness, then stood, sliding his body the length of hers until he felt her thighs close upon him.

He grasped her breasts—one in each hand. She was womanly, full, her rose-colored nipples engorged from his earlier attentions. He rubbed his thumbs back and forth across her nipples, at the same time undulating his hips. Though she was warm, wet, and ready for him, he did not want to end it. He could never get enough of Maura Magruder.

She clung to him, gasping. "Luke, my dearest Luke . . . let me *see* you . . . *look* at you, *touch* you."

Indulging her, he stepped back, and was totally unprepared for what happened next. She dropped to her knees, her golden hair swirling about his hips and trailing in the brown water. He could not see what she was doing, but he could *feel* it—and his control vanished in one ragged intake of breath. "Oh, God, Maura. . . ."

He thought he would explode. Grabbing her shoulders, he hauled her upright. She gazed at him through heavy-lidded eyes, her cheeks glowing, her face radiant. "You're so beautiful down there, Luke. So strong. So powerful."

"Men aren't beautiful, *women* are—at least, *you* are," he amended hastily.

"So are you," she retorted. Moving out of reach, she playfully splashed him. "You are the most beautiful thing I've ever laid eyes on."

He grabbed for her, but she eluded him, laughing, giggling, and running away. A light breeze tugged at her tresses. One moment, her breasts and body were alluringly revealed, and the next, her long golden hair floated around her like a concealing cloak. Maura was all tempting,

224

ACCEPT YOUR **FREE GIFT** AND EXPERIENCE MORE OF THE PASSION AND ADVENTURE YOU LIKE IN A HISTORICAL ROMANCE

Zebra Romances are the finest novels of their kind and are written with the adult woman in mind. All of our books are written by authors who really know how to weave tales of romantic adventure in the historical settings you love.

Because our readers tell us these books sell out very fast in the stores, Zebra has made arrangements for you to receive at home the four newest titles published each month. You'll never miss a title and home delivery is so convenient. With your first shipment we'll even send you a **FREE** Zebra Historical Romance as our gift just for trying our home subscription service. No obligation.

BIG SAVINGS AND **FREE** HOME DELIVERY

Each month, the Zebra Home Subscription Service will send you the four newest titles as soon as they are published. (We ship these books to our subscribers even before we send them to the stores.) You may preview them *Free* for 10 days. If you like them as much as we think you will, you'll pay just $3.50 each and *save $1.80 each month* off the cover price. *AND you'll also get FREE HOME DELIVERY.* There is never a charge for shipping, handling or postage and there is no minimum you must buy. If you decide not to keep any shipment, simply return it within 10 days, no questions asked, and owe nothing.

Get a Free
Zebra
Historical
Romance

*a $3.95
value*

ZEBRA HOME SUBSCRIPTION SERVICES, INC.
P.O. BOX 5214
120 BRIGHTON ROAD
CLIFTON, NEW JERSEY 07015-5214

taunting, "female," playing a seductive game as ancient as the river itself. Luke eagerly embraced his role of aggressive, pursuing male. He chased her out of the water and back up the riverbank. He dove, caught, and carried her down with him into the sand.

Once again, they had the blue sky above, the hot sand below, and nothing but bare, tantalizing flesh in between. Luke made love to Maura in earnest then, caressing, kissing, and stroking every inch of her golden skin. When he had her moaning and tossing her head, he finally mounted her, plunging home to a glorious reward. She arched her body, drawing him further into her hot, honeyed depths, and he reared and plunged like a bull gone wild.

When release came—unbearably sweet, explosive, and fulfilling, sweeter than he had ever known with any woman—he was not sated. Still, he wanted more of Maura Magruder, wanted to possess not just the body but the very soul of the woman beneath him. Resting atop her, murmuring her name, he quietly asked the question that had been nagging at him since the day he had first met her.

"What is he like? Your fiancé back east. Tell me about him."

She stiffened. There was a silence and a long pause, and then she asked: "What is *she* like? The Indian woman whose moccasins were in your lodge in Bellevue. Tell me about *her.*"

He drew back and looked down into her blue-gray eyes, now wide and hurt. "You know this will never work out between us, don't you?" he gently queried.

She half smiled, pathetically eager, a child about to beg for a treat. "You could come back east with us when my father and I finally go home, when our work here is done. Surely, you could find a way to earn a living in the east."

Hating himself, hating what he was doing to her, he slowly, emphatically shook his head. "I can't live in the east, Maura. When I left there, I left for good. Actually, I was going to make my fortune in the fur trade and then return in triumph to claim a woman who was already married to someone else. During my first year out here, I learned I could not do what I would have to do to become a rich man; so I decided *not* to get rich. The woman was only a foolish dream anyway. She never *did* care as much as I did. . . . In any case, all of value I really own is my rifle and my horse, not enough for her, not enough for *you*. The tepee in Bellevue doesn't even belong to me. It belongs to . . . a friend. A very understanding, undemanding friend."

"I could stay out here in Nebraska," Maura said hopefully. "I *do* love it here. . . ."

"No." Luke rolled away from her and sat up, turning his back to her so he did not have to witness her disappointment. "That's the one thing you *won't* do. You still don't realize what it's like out here. You won't accept what I've told you. One day soon, the Plains will explode in violence and bloodshed. Major Dougherty is doing his best to forestall that day; I help him the best I can. But it's only a matter of time, Maura. What you have been studying is a way of life that is dying, a primitive civilization that cannot last. I repeat: the day is fast approaching when there will be no more buffalo roaming the Plains, no more Indians chasing them astride their ponies, no more herds of antelope or white-tailed deer. The White-Eyes—your people and mine—will destroy it all. They'll kill the animals and drive off the Indians. You can't stop it from happening, Maura, and you sure as hell can't stay here in the middle of it and get yourself killed."

226

"Luke. . . ." He felt her hand on his arm. "It *doesn't* have to be that way! We could stop it from happening! My father and I can *tell* people back east what it's like out here. We could even go to the president and Congress and convince them to make laws forbidding whites to sell whiskey to the Indians, to take their land, or to kill large numbers of buffalo."

Luke turned back to her, exasperated and angry because she was no naive. "How can you be so blind, Maura? Do you think for one minute that President Jackson or a bunch of senators will *care* what's happening out here or be able to understand it? I respect and admire my friend, Pitale-sharo, but I recognize that at best, he can only be a curiosity to people back east. Even if easterners try, they can never comprehend, much less accept, what the Indian does and thinks. How can you justify or explain someone who wears human hair he took from his enemies as a decoration on his clothing — what little clothing he even wears? He lives by a code of honor that most whites have no way of understanding and will refuse to accept, if you do try and explain it to them. To them, the red man can never be anything but an illiterate savage whose culture *should* be stamped out and replaced by a better one. To explain it is impossible."

"*I* could explain it! *I* could make people understand how wise and educated the Indians really are. Why, just look at what they're able to do with the parts of a buffalo; they make food, shelter, clothing, weapons, musical instruments, tools —"

"You don't have to convince *me*, Maura. I know the Indians better than most white men — hell, I've practically *become* one of them. But even I don't take scalps, worship strange gods, believe in their spirits, torture my enemies, or do any of a dozen other things that are perfectly acceptable to Indians but alien and unacceptable to

227

whites. When I know that my Indian friends are going to be doing something I can't approve—such as torturing an enemy—I leave. I *flee*, so I won't have to watch."

"Nobody's torturing She-de-a! She's an enemy of the Pawnee, but they have been treating her remarkably well. Maybe not accepting her totally, but that will follow in time. I myself was not really mistreated while I was among the Sioux . . ."

"Oh, no!" Luke scoffed. "They just kidnapped you and threatened to rape and kill you because you refused to marry one of them—and probably would have raped and killed you eventually, anyway."

"Maybe not," Maura said stubbornly, reaching for her clothes.

Luke caught her hand. "Maura . . . listen to me. You can't stay here. You can't change the way things are just because you want them some other way. Though I think it's hopeless, I *am* going to stay here and fight to avert destruction and bloodshed. But *you* have got to go back east. Go ahead and write your letters and treatises. They certainly can't hurt. But don't . . . don't count on too much."

Maura's lovely, blue-gray eyes were luminous with un-shed tears. "I think perhaps I've already counted on too much, Luke . . . and I don't mean about the Indians."

Hungrily, Luke devoured her naked beauty: the shimmering, windblown, silver-blond hair, the firm, full breasts with their rosy pink nipples, the wonderful, lush curves and indentations, the naive, guiless, altogether too trusting face . . .

"Yes," he finally said. "You've counted on too much, Maura. Forgive me for taking advantage of what you feel for me. Maybe the experience will teach you not to trust so easily. I relish making love to you, Maura, but I don't *love* you. Go back home where you belong, where someone *does* care enough to want to marry you."

To her credit, Maura did not weep. She simply gazed at him as if he had thrust a knife into her heart—but it was in his own heart that Luke felt the blade twisting and turning, cutting the vital organ to shreds.

"If you don't mind . . . ," she whispered at long last. "Instead of riding back to camp with you, I would prefer walking."

Having no intention of leaving her alone so far from camp, he nonetheless nodded. He would ride out, double back, and follow, making certain she came to no harm— no *physical* harm. As for her emotional injuries, he deeply regretted having inflicted them, but it had to be done. It was for her own good. He must tell himself that everyday, and from now on, he must stay as far away from her as possible.

Two days after Maura gave herself to Luke for the second time out on the plain, the Pawnee began hauling their meat back to the village of dome-shaped lodges on the Loup River. Some of the women stayed in camp to guard the meat that could not be packed on the first trip. She-de-a and Lizard Woman were among them. When Maura rode away on Cinnamon, dragging the loaded travois behind her, She-de-a waved a smiling good-bye.

Without her two friends, Maura was forced to keep company with Heavy Basket and some of the other women whom she did not know as well. Fortunately, it suited her bleak mood not to have to make more than minimal conversation. The last two days had been a terrible strain. On the same day that Luke had rejected Maura's love, Pitale-sharo had exchanged a few kind words with She-de-a. Now, the girl positively glowed, certain she was winning her captor's approval and affection. For two days, She-de-a had dogged Maura's footsteps, chattering in a marginally comprehensible combination of English, Sioux, Pawnee, and sign language that really needed little translation. Every other word she spoke was Pitale-sharo's name. But whenever the young chief came within ten feet of the little Sioux, she fell silent, flushed a becoming shade of dusky rose, and averted her eyes.

Because she was not accepted or welcomed into the gossip sessions of the other women, She-de-a had no one but Maura with whom she could share her happiness. Lizard Woman was kind to the girl, but the others continued to treat her with contemptuous disdain. Maura would not have minded She-de-a's ebullience half so much had she herself been happier—or at least less miserable because of Luke. Sadly, She-de-a's joy was salt rubbed into Maura's wounds. So Maura was glad to be riding alone, free of the need to smile, nod, and feign a mood she did not feel.

The women left in the early morning, spent the night on the trail, and reached the village at mid-afternoon of the following day. Heavy Basket pointed out Lizard Woman's lodge, and Maura went by herself to explore it and find empty containers in which to store the sun-dried meat until it could be made into pemmican. The lodge itself was impressive, exceeding Maura's expectations. From the outside, it could be seen as a large, circular, dome-shaped structure roofed with earth and entered by a covered passageway.

Inside, the structure was surprisingly spacious; it had been built over an excavation that allowed for a bench encircling the entire outer circumference. Four sturdy central posts supported the immense weight of the earthen roof, while lesser posts held up the walls. Connecting beams ran between them, forming slender rafters which extended from the outer to the inner ceiling. The walls and roof were covered with successive layers of willow branches, grass thatching, a shingling of sod, and finally, earth.

The entrance was similarly built, eight-feet long, and had a skin curtain at either end. At first, Maura found it difficult to see, but then her eyes adjusted to the semi-darkness. As she reached the lodge's center, sunlight poured through the smoke hole, illuminating even the dimmest corners. Apparently, Lizard Woman had not expected rain, and so had not positioned a rain shield, or wooden, skin-covered frame, across the generous opening. Before entering, Maura had spotted the shield lying atop the roof and had guessed that the lodge had a central fire pit, which it did. Now, she discovered that it also had a palisade of short stakes ringing the pit, acting as a fire screen.

Maura estimated the ceiling to be about thirteen-feet high, and the distance from one wall to the opposite about forty to forty-five feet. In addition to the earthen bench, there were platforms for beds and food storage, a stall big enough to hold a favorite horse, bullboats hung up on the walls, and special places for storage. Maura walked around the lodge examining everything: the box-like structures with corner posts, skin canopies, and enough elbow room to sleep a half dozen people; the wood or grass thatched partitions dividing the lodge into specific sections; the backrests, cooking implements and tools hanging from the walls; the storage pit for meat and vegetables that Lizard Woman had told her about; the Sacred Place at one end of the lodge where women were not permitted to trespass, for fear of contaminating it; the low, covered, sweat lodge — just big enough for one person to sit huddled not far from the fire . . .

She was examining a collection of hammers hung on the wall near the Sacred Place when she heard Luke's voice. "What are you doing over there? Don't you know better than to go snooping around a holy place?"

Maura quickly moved away from the section of the lodge where she had already been warned not to venture. "I wasn't where I shouldn't be. Even if I was, there's no one here to see me."

"Anyone could have come in and found you over there. You were so busy snooping you never heard me come in."

"I was just *looking* at things, not snooping. I've waited a long time to get inside a Pawnee earth lodge, and now that I'm finally here, I want to *see* it."

Luke came closer, his face and eyes determinedly neutral. "There's not that much to see, actually. Only the usual assortment of necessities for everyday living. Some of those tools may be made of skin and bone, instead of iron, but they do the job just as well, perhaps better. What do you find so interesting?"

"Just what you said—about the tools. It's what I'm going to say when I write about them."

Luke studied her across the lodge. "Now, don't start that again, Maura."

"I'm not starting anything. Why did you follow me in here? Other than trivial conversation, we have nothing more to say to each other."

"I just *thought*, with Lizard Woman and She-de-a still at camp, you could use some help unloading and storing meat."

Maura summoned every ounce of strength she possessed to keep her voice steady. "Thank you, no. I can manage fine by myself."

"Then I guess I'll go help Heavy Basket." Luke's voice was equally steady; his gray eyes registered no disappointment or dismay—*none* of the turbulent emotions *she* was feeling.

"Wait . . . ," Maura croaked in a whisper.

For two days, she had been forcing herself not to watch for him. Though achingly aware of his presence in the camp and on the trail back to the village, she had purposely ignored him. Now, her eyes greedily devoured him, particle by particle. The thought of him leaving so quickly devastated her. Frantically, she cast about for an excuse to keep him with her, if only for a few moments of inane and pointless discussion.

"Do you think Pitale-sharo will succumb to pressure from his grandfather and marry Heavy Basket?"

Luke scowled at the question. "How in hell should I know?"

He paused, seemed on the verge of saying something, then apparently reconsidered. "Wetara-sharo thinks highly of Heavy Basket . . . so does the rest of the tribe. She is well-respected. She-de-a, on the other hand, is young and beautiful. Pitale-sharo captured her on impulse and apparently doesn't quite know what to do with her. Everyone *expected* him to marry Heavy Basket. That puts him in a difficult position."

Maura thought about her own difficult position, loving a man who did not love her. "Yes, I imagine it does. Sometimes, I . . . I wish I could ask you things about the Pawnee. You know so much. You could explain so much."

"I could," Luke admitted. "But I won't because I've no desire to encourage you. Actually, I didn't come in here just to help you unload buffalo meat. I came to tell you that it should be safe, now, to return to Bellevue. I want to wait a few days yet, until all the meat is stored and everyone has returned from the hunt. The Pawnee will celebrate for a couple days, which I know you won't want to miss. But after that, if there is still no sign of the Sioux, we'll leave. Pitale-sharo wants to take a few robes to the post to trade; he and several other braves will accompany us."

"I see," said Maura, resenting how well he had planned, insuring they would have no time alone together. "As usual, you are making plans without consulting me."

"There's nothing to consult about. You're going back when I say so."

"What if I refuse?"

A muscle twitched warningly in Luke's jaw. "We won't discuss that possibility, because it won't happen. I won't accept your refusal."

Maura had the urge to run at him screaming, to bang her fists on his chest and call him vile names. How *dare* he think he could make her do whatever he wanted! How *dare* he make love to her, then tell her he did not love her! How *dare* he tear her heart to shreds and behave so coolly, as if his own heart were quite invulnerable!

In that moment, she hated him, hated his arrogance and insufferable conceit. Hated his handsomeness. Hated his masculinity and the heady allure that made her still love him, even after he had rejected her. In that stunning, hate-filled moment, she knew she would not go. If for no other reason than because *he* was determined to make her go.

"You've told my why you came in here," she said icily, matching him chill for chill. "Now, I suggest you get out and let me get my work done."

He nodded. "Of course. Just be ready, Miss Magruder."

She spun on her heel and did not reply. Oh, she would be ready, all right — ready to send him straight to hell! But before she dispatched him on the journey, she had to make certain she was welcome to stay among the Pawnee. If it was the last thing she ever did, when he left, *she* would remain.

Chapter Seventeen

Luke waved away a fourth helping of boiled tongue and leaned against the backrest Heavy Basket had provided for his comfort. Everyone had finally returned to the village, the meat was all stored, and already the women were talking about making pemmican. Tomorrow, after recovering from tonight's feast, they would go looking for chokecherries, which should now be ripe. When they had enough of these, they would pound the dried buffalo meat into thin, fine strips, then mix it with a paste of melted fat, bone marrow, and chokecherries, crushed pits and all, resulting in pemmican, the food staple of the Plains Indians.

On the opposite side of the fire from Luke sat Maura. He watched her out of the corner of his eye; she would, of course, want to stay to master the fine art of pemmican-making. And after the pemmican was made, it would then be time for the corn harvest, and after that, there would be the annual fall hunt to secure the thick, woolly, winter robes of the buffalo. The longer Maura stayed, the longer she would *want* to stay, and the more firmly entrenched she would become in the life of the tribe.

Luke himself had gone through the same process several years before; somehow, this austere, challenging, busy, fulfilling life had a way of seducing one into thinking that he—or she—could live it forever and be perfectly content. It was only after he had lived it long enough to encounter the less idyllic moments, the alien, dangerous, life-threatening ones, that he had finally realized he could not *truly* embrace this life.

So far, Maura had been lucky. She had not personally witnessed the dark, violent underside of the Indian mentality. Her experiences with Shon-ka had actually been sheltered and unusual. She-de-a had not been treated like a normal captive, either. For a shorter time than he had lived among the Pawnee, Luke had also lived among the Sioux, not Shon-ka's tribe, but another. He had gone there on behalf of Major Dougherty to try and win the confidence of the Indians by giving them gifts from the trading post. It had been an exploratory, peacemaking mission but it had begun with a brutal lesson on Indian moral values. Luke had arrived just in time to witness the torture of a young Hidatsa brave unlucky enough to have been caught in the act of stealing Sioux horses.

Luke had pleaded and bargained for the young man's life, finally gaining permission to take him back to Bellevue. But when the squaws cut the thongs holding the brave's arms and legs in a spread-eagle position on the ground, he was unable to rise. All his fingers and toes had been cut off, other parts of his body were badly mutilated, and a fire was still smoldering on his belly. Several hours later, he died in silent agony, a look or triumphant hatred in his glazed black eyes.

His death had been a powerful addition to the steadily growing list of reasons why Luke knew that he could not completely assimilate into any tribe, however much he might occasionally delude himself otherwise. Once, his delusions had caused him to undergo the Sun Dance ritual, whereby a brave engaged in rigorous self-denial and torture in order to prove his manhood. Though not practiced by the Pawnee, Omaha, or Wichita, the religious ceremony was quite popular among at least twenty other Plains tribes. By willingly participating in it, Luke had won the respect of all the tribes. This made him particularly good at helping keep the peace between traders and Indians. Knowing the price he had paid for his effectiveness, as evidenced by his scars, Luke was not about to abandon his position in order to follow Maura Magruder back east, like some docile, obedient lapdog.

Watching her across the fire as she ate, conversed, and carefully mimicked the Indian women surrounding her, Luke knew it was time to take Maura back to her own people. She had been here too long already—long enough to slip on the Indian culture as if it were a gown or cloak that could keep her warm and happy—but *not* long enough to realize that the woman underneath was still the same woman, basically unchanged except for the outer trappings. For reasons he did not care to examine too closely, he wanted to protect and preserve her wide-eyed innocence as long as possible. All the time that he had been mocking it, in his own peculiar way he had also been trying to shelter it. He dreaded the day when she finally discovered that the generally quiet, placid, agreeable Skidi Pawnee were as capable of violence as any other tribe of Indians.

Sighing to himself, Luke glanced at his hosts. Pitalesharo was doggedly watching She-de-a with a wrapt expression on his broad, attractive features, and the wrinkled old chieftan, Wetara-sharo, was watching Pitale-sharo in deeply scowling disapproval. For several moments, the older man studied the younger one, measuring and assessing him, as if worried he would not compare favorably with some other image in the old man's mind.

Luke just hoped that image was not Bon-son-gee's. The short, squarely built Bon-son-gee sat some distance away,

238

magnanimously sharing a jug of forbidden firewater with his friends. All evening, Bon-son-gee had been boasting of his bravery and skill during the hunt, while Pitale-sharo had been noticeably subdued and quiet. The introduction of a jug of whiskey to the feast blatantly challenged the long-established rules of good conduct among the Pawnee, yet Pitale-sharo had thus far chosen to take no notice.

Either that or he had indeed not noticed what was happening, being far too bemused by She-de-a's radiant loveliness, which shone like a beacon in the midst of the plainer Pawnee women. Seated next to Maura, She-de-a was trying very hard to maintain a shy, disinterested demeanor, but her long lashes kept sweeping upward to reveal luminous, velvet-brown eyes that could not keep from returning Pitale-sharo's enraptured gaze.

The two stared at each other with unabashed longing, and Luke realized that his friend was badly smitten, much to his grandfathers' disapproval. The old chief availed himself of every opportunity to prove that Heavy Basket was a far more suitable candidate to become Pitale-sharo's wife. Heavy Basket regularly cooked for them, processed the meat and hides from the hunt, mended torn clothing, and performed other wifely tasks. But each day, Pitale-sharo's feelings became more apparent. He was enamored of the beautiful, captive, Sioux maiden.

Luke did not blame Pitale-sharo for preferring She-de-a over Heavy Basket, but he realized that if Pitale-sharo married the girl, he would alienate not only his own grandfather but the rest of the tribe, increasing Bon-son-gee's chances of gaining the chieftancy. In the midst of feasting and rejoicing, tension hung like a cloud over the gathering; the older, loyal braves sat near Pitale-sharo and his grandfather, but the young bucks sat with Bon-son-gee. Even the women gravitated toward the brash young brave, who never seemed to tire of spinning exciting tales of

239

bravery and triumph.

The Indians of almost every Plains tribe prized storytelling ability in their leaders and placed no value on humility. Most of their dances, stories, and religious ceremonies were reenactments of moments of personal triumph. Over and over, they relived the excitement of the hunt, of battle, and of victory. Indian boys grew up dreaming of the day when their own exploits would be re-told at feasts and celebrations.

If Pitale-sharo did not start defending his claim to leadership, and did not thrill and excite his followers, he could easily lose his position. One day, Bon-son-gee would disagree with some order of Pitale-sharo's, and the people would simply obey him rather than Pitale-sharo. Or else Pitale-sharo would be forced to fight Bon-son-gee in hand-to-hand combat, and whoever emerged the victor would then rule the tribe. Luke hoped it never came to this, because Bon-son-gee was strong and capable, and the fight would probably be to the death.

Luke touched Pitale-sharo's arm. With a start, his friend turned to him. "Is it permissible for the Pawnee to get drunk on firewater at their feasts these days?" he quietly asked. "I thought you and your grandfather had forbidden the stuff to be brought into your village."

Luke nodded toward Bon-son-gee and the handful of glassy-eyed braves; their speech was slurred, and they could hardly sit upright, but they were still passing the jug and taking hearty swigs. As he saw what was going on, Pitale-sharo's mouth tightened. "I had not even noticed the jug being passed around," he confessed. "I will stop it at once."

Pitale-sharo moved as if to rise, but Wetara-sharo's thin, bony hand shot past Luke had grabbed the younger man's shoulder.

"No, my son. You will do nothing. It is too late now to

stop the drinking. They will only turn on you. . . . The firewater has already gone to their heads and made them forget who they are. While they are in its clutches, they will only act foolishly, and someone will be needlessly hurt."

"They *know* they should not be doing this," Pitale-sharo gritted between clenched teeth. "It is Bon-son-gee who brought out the jug; no one else would have had the nerve."

"The time to have stopped him was before, when first he brought it out. But you were too busy watching the Sioux and did not notice."

"Why did you not tell me?" Pitale-sharo's face flushed as red as the dyed horse hair decorating his scalp lock.

"Why did you not see it?" his grandfather countered. "If you take no care to protect your hunting grounds, you will be driven off them. When the panther comes, the fox does not protect the wolf; so I shall not protect you. Look to your own territory, and guard it well—or else you will one day go hungry."

After his grandfather's rebuke, Pitale-sharo sat still and silent, radiating fury. His eyes did not stray to She-de-a. Instead, they fastened upon Bon-son-gee, and Luke knew that somehow, some way, Pitale-sharo would exact revenge. Time and again, Luke had watched Bon-son-gee push Pitale-sharo to the limits of his patience; this time, the brave had gone too far. Pitale-sharo was normally a congenial, forgiving man, slow to take offense or be goaded into violence. But tonight, Pitale-sharo's anger flourished like a voracious weed.

By waiting so long to speak, Wetara-sharo had added insult to injury; Pitale-sharo would have been much less shamed and embarrassed if the old chief had called his attention to Bon-son-gee's actions earlier in the evening. Luke squirmed inwardly for his friend, understanding completely how Pitale-sharo felt, being scolded like a child in a public place, in front of a White-Eyes to boot.

The evening wore on—with more eating, drinking, boasting, storytelling, and later, dancing. Depressed, Luke enjoyed none of it. Nor, it seemed, did Maura. Once she yawned and rubbed her eyes as if anxious for sleep. A short time later, she said something to She-de-a and Lizard Woman, then rose and left the semi-circle of women. When she did not return in a few moments, Luke concluded that she had gone to bed. He debated whether or not to go after her, then stood abruptly, his mind made up.

Now, was as good a time as any to tell her that they would be leaving first thing in the morning. Maura would need time to gather any last minute items she needed for the journey and to say her good-byes. He and Pitale-sharo had earlier discussed the matter and decided that regardless of tonight's feast, which might last until the wee hours of the morning, they would leave at daybreak for Bellevue. The only one who had not yet been told was Maura, a deliberate oversight which Luke intended to remedy, here and now.

Nodding to Wetara-sharo and Pitale-sharo, Luke wended his way through the clustered, sweat-slicked celebrants toward Lizard Woman's lodge.

Maura was warm and uncomfortably full. As she approached Lizard Woman's lodge, she decided not to go to bed immediately, after all. The thought of lying in the still, airless lodge, listening to the sounds of revelry still going on outside, made her feel lonely and moody. Instead of turning into the lodge's entranceway, she walked past it and through the village to where the plain began, stretching out beneath the star-studded sky.

It was cooler here, with a fresh breeze blowing. The breeze rippled the dry grass, producing a soft shush-shush sound that was oddly comforting. Maura inhaled deeply of the earth-scented air and tilted back her head to gaze up at the sparkling panoply of start.

A night such as this was made for lovers, for moonlit embraces and declarations of undying love. It was hard not to think of loving when one was forced to spend the entire evening watching another man and woman exchange tender, searching glances. She-de-a had not said two words during the feast; she was totally preoccupied with Pitale-sharo, and Maura no longer had any doubts that the young chief was equally attracted to the little Sioux. Pitale-sharo may pretend not to notice She-de-a, may even at times treat her rudely, but his desire for her was as plain on his face as the stars in the sky. Would that Luke might reveal his feelings as honestly and easily.

Not once had Maura been able to catch his eye that evening—not that she had been trying; in truth, she had been trying *not* to. Unlike She-de-a, Maura had her pride. The worst thing she could imagine would be for Luke to know the depth of her pain over his rejection. He had told her he did not love her, so she would pretend it did not matter. She was "over" him, and nothing he did or said could hurt her anymore.

Any day now, she expected him to come and tell her he was ready to leave. She would not go. He could not force her. Not when Heavy Basket, the most respected and influential woman in the tribe, wanted her to stay. That very afternoon, Maura had approached the big squaw, and with a combination of outrageous flattery and abject humility, had begged the conceited woman to teach her how to make pemmican the *right* way.

This, of course, would take a long time. Maura had also insisted that she *must* learn how to cure hides properly, as only Heavy Basket could do it, and that she considered herself the most fortunate of white women, having gained the opportunity of living in close proximity with such a talented, remarkable squaw as Heavy Basket.

If she could just stay among the Pawnee for a while longer, she had lamented, she could learn so much and could one day *prove* to white people, women in particular, how clever and superior Indian women were. If she just had someone to champion her cause, she could resist Luke Cutter's efforts to force her to go back to her own people. At this point in their conversation, Heavy Basket had then invited Maura to live in *her* lodge, if Lizard Woman no longer wanted her, and had assured Maura that she was welcome to remain among the Pawnee for as long as she wished to stay — or at least, for the winter. For some reason, Heavy Basket had seemed to think Maura would not want to stay any longer than that, although Maura had already made up her mind to stay at least until midway through the following summer, so that she could experience the complete, seasonal life cycle of the Pawnee.

At any rate, Maura was now ready for Luke to tell her it was time to return to Bellevue. When he did, she would not only refuse, but suggest that he return to Bellevue without her and fetch her father. Eben could then come and stay for the winter; Lizard Woman and her husband were eagerly anticipating his arrival. If he brought supplies with him, so that he could write and Maura could sketch, everything would turn out exactly as they had planned in the beginning.

If Luke pursuaded Pitale-sharo or Wetara-sharo to order her and Eben away, Maura had powerful friends and allies ready to plead her cause. With Heavy Basket to fight for her, she felt certain of victory in the coming battle. Indeed, she could hardly *wait* to see the look on Luke's face when he realized he had lost.

"Maura?" said a voice behind her. Maura did not have to turn around to know who stood there. As usual, Luke was sneaking up on her unexpectedly. Only this time, she was ready for him.

"Good evening, Mr. Cutter," she responded coolly. "Lovely night, isn't it?"

As he came up beside her, he ignored the merits of the weather. "I thought you had gone to bed."

"I wasn't ready to sleep. I just needed to get away from the feast and thought I would take a walk."

"I hope it won't be a long walk. You really should go to bed and get some rest. We're leaving for Bellevue in the morning."

"Maybe you are. I'm not." Maura disinterestedly strolled away from Luke. "I have been invited to stay."

"Damn it, Maura, you *can't* stay!"

His hands encircled her waist, jerking her around to face him. "Well, I'm going to!" she spat. "And you can tell my father that he, too, is welcome to come and stay the winter. We are *both* welcome. This is what we both want—why we came. And I'll not be forced to leave just because you say so."

"Damn it, I knew you were going to try something like this! What's your excuse—you want to learn to make pemmican?"

His accusation caught her by surprise; how had he known what argument she was going to use? "Pemmican is only part of it, as you very well know, Luke Cutter. I want to learn much more than that."

"And I've already told you why you can't stay. We've already *had* this argument. I don't intend to have it again."

"Then *don't*. Just tell my father to bring along supplies—writing materials, if nothing else. And gifts. I want gifts for She-de-a, Lizard Woman and her husband, Heavy Basket, Wetaro-sharo, and Pitale-sharo."

"So you've lined them all up on *your* side, have you?"

Maura did not answer; she simply glared, allowing him to make whatever assumptions he wanted.

"I can force you, you know," he growled, pulling her close to him so that her breasts grazed his chest.

Heart pounding, Maura said nothing. She stared into his eyes, darkly shadowed and unreadable. Moonlight made a silvery aureole of his hair. She was almost glad she could not seem him clearly; fury would be stamped on his face.

"Shall I prove to you that I can force you?" He pressed against her, the bulge of his breechclout adding yet another dimension to his threat. Unwittingly, Maura felt the stirrings of her own body, treacherously responding to his nearness and desire.

"If you do force me, then you are no better than Shonka. Indeed, you are worse. You keep warning me how violent the Indians are, but you never mention your own violence."

He uttered a long-drawn sigh of defeat. "Sometimes I think I hate you, Maura. Hate you for what you do to me—for the power you have over me. For how well you know me." Removing his hands from her waist, he cupped her face between them. "Damn it all, Maura, I want to stop wanting you, but I can't."

With a throaty growl, he pressed his lips down on hers, thrust his tongue inside her mouth, and kissed her long and deeply. Maura sagged against him. She could not stop wanting him, either, even though he did not love her and would never marry her.

He was the first to break away. "So have it *your* way, Maura Magruder. Stay here and get yourself killed. I wash my hands of you. I'll bring your father back—and your damn supplies. But then I'll leave you both to whatever fate has in store for you. I've got my own life to live, my own problems to solve, my own questions to answer. . . . You aren't part of my plans, and I can't spend any more time worrying about you, wanting you, desiring you. You *deserve* whatever happens to you out here. Good-bye, and be damned to you."

With that, he turned on his heel and left, striding resolutely back to the village and the feast still in progress. Maura stood and watched until he was out of sight. She had won, but felt she had lost and would never know happiness or contentment again. Luke Cutter was taking her hope and happiness with him.

Chapter Eighteen

Luke was gone by the time Maura arose the next morning. To her surprise, neither Pitale-sharo nor anyone else accompanied him. She-de-a had seen him riding out alone. Later, as they carried water vessels down to the river to fetch water for Lizard Woman, they saw Pitale-sharo stalking through the village, his face dark as a thundercloud. She-de-a stopped in her tracks and peeped at him from beneath her lashes, but the young chief never so much as glanced at her.

Glowering ferociously, he headed straight for the lodge where Bon-son-gee lived with his thin, stringy-haired, tight-lipped wife who got along with no one. Heavy Basket, in particular, despised the woman. Arriving at the covered entranceway of the lodge, Pitale-sharo did not pause or clap his hands to request permission to enter. Instead, he jerked aside the hide curtain and stalked inside.

A moment later, Maura heard a loud, indignant bellow, and Bon-son-gee stumbled through the hide curtain, closely followed by Pitale-sharo. The short, squarely-built Bon-son-gee turned and swung at Pitale-sharo, but was so drunk and bleary-eyed that instead of hitting his target, he staggered and fell. Snorting derisively, Pitale-sharo stepped behind Bon-son-gee and grabbed him around the chest, holding him upright as he struggled weakly and ineffectively, like a beached, dying fish.

"Is *this* the man who wants to be chief of the Skidi Pawnee?" Pitale-sharo shouted in a ringing voice. Maura congratulated herself on understanding every word of the tribal dialect. She listened avidly for some response.

The villagers had celebrated into the wee hours of the morning, but many were already astir. Two or three women en route to the river along with Maura and She-de-a stopped to stare, and several children darted inside lodges to alert their elders. While Pitale-sharo shouted insults and shook the drunken Bon-son-gee, the people gathered, huddling in doorways and whispering behind hands.

"Do you want this man to be your chief?" Pitale-sharo demanded of everyone in general and no one in particular. "He cannot fight. He cannot hunt. If the Sioux come today, he cannot defend you."

Pitale-sharo's insults struck the helpless Bon-son-gee like a lash. Some of what the young chief said escaped Maura, but his actions spoke louder than words. Bon-son-gee's futile struggles were both comical and pathetic. Unaccustomed to whiskey, the normally strong, powerful warrior-hunter could neither coordinate his limbs nor gather his wits to answer his accuser. He reminded Maura of a wooden puppet whose strings were cut; had Pitale-sharo not been holding him, Bon-son-gee would have collapsed on the ground.

A silvery skein of spittle drooled from Bon-son-gee's slack mouth, prompting one woman to laugh. Pointing to Bon-son-gee, she called him a derisive name, comparing him to a toothless old crone who should be sent to keep company with his ancestors rather than be elevated to the status of chief. Her comments provoked more laughter, and the merriment enticed others out of doorways to join the fun.

Soon, almost everyone in the village had gathered and were laughing, pointing, and calling names. When Pitale-sharo let go of Bon-son-gee, the drunken man fell like a stone and lay unmoving on the ground.

"See what happens when you drink firewater?" Pitale-sharo bellowed. A strained silence ensued. In a slow, deliberate voice, the young chief drove home his point. "Strong men become weak. This is what our enemies want. This is why they sell us firewater. If you want me to step aside, tell me now, and I will. Bon-son-gee can be your chief, and you can join him in drinking all the firewater you desire."

The only sound was the breeze rustling the cottonwoods along the river. A woman jostled past Maura; it was Heavy Basket. The big squaw walked ponderously toward the fallen man and kicked at him contemptuously. "We do not want this one . . . He is a fool. He does not even know we are laughing at him. When I kick him, he does not feel it. He is unworthy to be chief."

She gazed adoringly at Pitale-sharo, standing rigid and angry behind Bon-son-gee. Heavy Basket's plain, round face glowed and became almost pretty as she studied the young man she so obviously wanted. She licked her thick lips, and with a pudgy hand, tossed one heavy, greasy braid over her shoulder. "Pitale-sharo is a *real* man . . . a true chief of the Pawnee. Come, beloved . . . I have prepared food for you. Come to my lodge, and I will serve you well."

She extended her hand to Pitale-sharo, and half-reluctantly, he took it. With great dignity, as if she herself had proven something today, Heavy Basket led Pitale-sharo away. When he had gone, Bon-son-gee's wife hurried out of the lodge, trailed by her young son, a thin, glaring boy with stringy black hair. Together, they struggled to get Bon-son-gee on his feet and back into the lodge. Staggering beneath her husband's weight, the woman shot an angry glance at the onlookers.

"Do not forget!" she screamed. "My husband killed thirteen buffalo and Pitale-sharo only eleven. *I* will eat better this winter than Heavy Basket." Dragging her heavy burden, she disappeared into the shadowy depths of the entranceway.

As the crowd dispersed, Maura and She-de-a continued toward the river. Bending to dip her water skin in the shallow water, Maura caught sight of her little friend's troubled face. Straightening, she summoned her faltering, uncertain Sioux to point out the positive aspects of the incident.

"Today was a day of victory for Pitale-sharo." She hooked the still-empty waterskin over her arm and made the sign for victory. "Victory," she repeated in English.

She-de-a nodded, dark eyes brimming with tears. "Yes, a victory also for Heavy Basket. She called him beloved."

"Don't worry so. You are far more beautiful than Heavy Basket. I'm certain he will choose you over her."

She-de-a signaled emphatic denial. "No! He will choose what is best for his people. And I am not best."

"You must remember why he captured you. Why he brought you here. If he loved you enough to steal you and brave the wrath of his people to bring you home, he must love you enough to marry you."

Again, She-de-a denied this, her beautiful eyes downcast in misery. "He has many chances to find me alone. If he asked, I would willingly lie with him and give him my love. . . . But he does not ask. Instead, he goes to Heavy Basket's lodge. He eats her food. He allows *her* to repair his moccasins. He will do as his grandfather wishes and marry her, not me."

"But *you* are the one he looks at! You are the one he *wants*."

"He will marry Heavy Basket," She-de-a insisted, tears spilling down her cheeks. "And I do not know what will become of me. Perhaps, I shall be given to an old man who will beat me. Or perhaps, I shall even be tortured and killed."

Maura's chest constricted. Anger almost suffocated her. *It was unfair.* Pitale-sharo had no right to capture the girl and then break her heart. Wetara-sharo had no right to pressure his grandson into marrying a woman he did not love. She-de-a was far better suited to become Pitale-sharo's wife than that fat cow, Heavy Basket; any fool could see the attraction between the two attractive, young people. While the Pawnee were not physically abusing She-da-a, they were certainly making her miserable. Someone should confront the old chief and ask him why he was ruining other people's lives. Why shouldn't *she*—Maura Magruder—be that someone?

Considering the idea, Maura debated how best to go about it. She did not need Luke to tell her that Pawnee women did not lecture and scold the men of the tribe, especially not revered elders. And she did not want to offend Wetara-sharo at a time when he might retaliate by ordering her to leave the village or forbidding her father to visit. Despite what Luke had thought, she had confined all her friendship-making efforts to the women, the most important of whom was Heavy Basket. Unless Luke had mentioned it to them, neither Pitale-sharo nor his grandfather even knew that Eben might be coming.

Upon realizing these facts, Maura's impulse cooled. She simply could *not* barge into Wetara-sharo's lodge and demand that he rethink his position concerning his grandson's marital obligations. However, if she contrived to befriend the old man, or if her father befriended him, the right word at the right time could make a difference. Maura wondered just how much time she had before Pitale-sharo would be forced to choose.

Maura slung her water skin into the water, filled it, then turned to her friend. "She-de-a, has Lizard Woman or anyone else ever told you when Pitale-sharo's marriage will take place?"

She-de-a raised her eyebrows questioningly, and Maura realized that she had spoken in English instead of Sioux. She tried again—groping for the right words, saying them slowly, employing all the little tricks she and She-de-a had devised to achieve better communication.

Finally, She-de-a understood. "Yes," the girl responded. "I have heard that among the Pawnee, it is the custom for a chief to marry during the—."

She-de-a used a word Maura did not understand. The girl then pointed to the sun tracking its way across the sky, and with several gestures indicated a time of year when the hours of daylight were longest.

"During the summer solstice?" Maura questioned. She-de-a gazed at her uncomprehendingly. "Is it during the Rose-Blooming moon?"

She-de-a nodded. That meant the month of June. What time could it be other than the summer solstice, which usually fell on or about the twenty-second day of June? Maura was relieved. If Pitale-sharo did not have to make up his mind until next summer, then there was plenty of time to try and influence Wetara-sharo to give his blessing to the young couple. At least, Pitale-sharo was not being *rushed* into marriage with Heavy Basket; during the long fall, winter, and spring, She-de-a's continued efforts to please must surely result in her acceptance, both by the old chief and the rest of the tribe. Perhaps, that was what Pitale-sharo himself was hoping.

"Don't give up, She-de-a," Maura consoled her friend. "Instead, why don't we see if Lizard Woman will let us trade a buffalo robe for some of those doeskins she has stored in the lodge? Then you can make Pitale-sharo some fine new leggings and moccasins. Haven't you noticed how shabby and worn his are becoming? I'll help you—you can show me how, and we will both have something interesting to occupy us over the long winter."

Excitement blazed in She-de-a's velvet brown eyes. She started to speak in a rapid, staccato tone, then slowed down and repeated herself, augmenting her words with gestures. "I will make Pitale-sharo the most beautiful breechclout, leggings, shirt, and moccasins he has ever worn. I will work the skins until they are as soft as fawn skin. *Then* he will know what a good wife I can be to him."

"And he can show the garments to his grandfather and to everyone else," Maura added. "You do know how to make them better than Heavy Basket could, don't you, She-de-a?"

She-de-a nodded, smiling through her tears. "No one tans softer skins or fashions finer garments than a Sioux," she assured Maura. "Have you ever seen the skin tepees of the Sioux? They are *much* better than those of the Pawnee."

Maura thought of the tall, beautiful tepees in Bellevue. She never had found out who made Luke's; the woman could have been a Sioux. Obviously, she was not Pawnee. None of the Pawnee tepees used during the buffalo hunt could begin to compare with those at the trading post.

"Let's get started," Maura said. "As soon as we finish making pemmican, our next project will be Pitale-sharo's new clothes."

The days passed busily, and Maura began to suspect that Pawnee women *always* kept busy. When she was not making pemmican or participating in whatever other communal task was in progress, she helped She-de-a dress the doeskins Lizard Woman had traded for one of Luke's buffalo robes. The first step was to remove the hair from the skins. This they did by throwing a skin over a log and painstakingly rubbing it with a rib or leg bone from the deer itself.

Lizard Woman had already removed the flesh from the

skins with an implement made from the foot bones of a large elk. Not only must all the fat, muscle, connective tissue, and hair be removed, but the skin must also be worked with a special antler adze to a uniform thickness.

She-de-a had decided that if she planned carefully, she would have enough skins to make a ceremonial parfleche or container, which she intended to elaborately fringe and decorate so that Pitale-sharo could keep religious objects in it. Lizard Woman must have suspected that all this work was being done for Pitale-sharo, but she never said a word about it; she acted as if the project was solely for Maura's benefit, so she could learn more about the Indian ways. Long after Lizard Woman pronounced the skins suitably prepared for any purpose imaginable, She-de-a kept working and rubbing them, reducing them to a thinner, finer rawhide than had been used to make anything else in the lodge.

At last the day came when She-de-a declared that it was time to tan the stiff, thin product of all the back-breaking hours of work. Shaking her head because it had taken so long to reach this point, Lizard Woman produced a clay jar of the most obnoxious mixture Maura had ever seen, smelled, or touched. Following instructions, she scooped out a mass of the oily thick substance, which She-de-a explained was made of buffalo fat and crushed brains. Maura was to smear the obnoxious mixture over the surface of the rawhide and work it in, first with her fingers and then with a smooth stone.

Maura gulped, holding her breath to avoid the fumes, and set to work. After an entire morning spent at this task, She-de-a and Maura rolled the now pliable rawhides into individual bundles and set them out to dry in the sun. Then She-de-a got a hoe made from the shoulder bone of a buffalo, fetched another for Maura, and the two joined the other women in hoeing the parched, stunted corn.

As Maura toiled in the hot sun, she could not help

wondering what was taking Luke so long to return with her father. Already, it was September. Though the days were still warm, the nights were cooling. Occasionally, heavy, dark clouds gathered in the northwest and hung immoble for several days, but it almost never rained, and the grass was so dry it crackled when you walked on it. The horses had to range far and wide in order to find enough green forage to fill their bellies.

Everyone said the corn harvest would hardly be worth the effort. Fortunately, the buffalo hunt had yielded plenty of dried meat, and the fall hunt should provide enough of a reserve to feed the Pawnee over the winter and early spring, and add to the stockpile of robes to keep them warm and dry. Lizard Woman was now working on some winter clothes for Maura; already she had turned one of Luke's buffalo robes into a cape, with the fur side turned in, to protect her from the howling winds and snow.

Hacking at the stubborn weeds threatening to choke the sparse corn, Maura thought about the dry weather, her father and Luke, and her secret, garment-making project with She-de-a. As usual, her mind buzzed with questions. Why was the corn so fragile, while the weeds were strong and tenacious? Why had Luke and Eben not yet arrived? Why did Pitale-sharo spend most of his time with Heavy Basket when he could scarcely keep his eyes off She-de-a? Why was everyone except Lizard Woman and her tall, taciturn husband, still so distant and unfriendly to the little Sioux?

With Maura, the women were kind, helpful, and curious, but they almost never spoke to She-de-a, and when they did, they were rude. Even Lizard Woman, who willingly shared her home, tools, food, and bedding, often spent hours ignoring She-de-a, and then guiltily made up for it by giving her some small gift or showing her how the Pawnee performed a particular task. Maura could not understand the undercurrents of tension battering her shy,

256

sweet friend; it was almost as if the Pawnee were *afraid* of liking She-de-a or becoming fond of her.

Pausing a moment to push her damp hair out of her eyes, Maura stretched to relieve the stiffness in her back and shoulders. In her zeal to rout enemy weeds, she had knocked over a corn plant. She stood the plant up again and patted the dry, sandy soil into place around it. If the winter snows were scant, by next year, the corn would not sprout at all. Already the water from the river had a sandy, brackish taste; fresh rain and snow were badly needed to replenish it. Stretching again, Maura searched the horizon for storm clouds; instead of clouds, she spotted two distant figures on horseback, coming from the east.

Her heart skipped a beat. Could it be Luke and her father? Squinting, Maura saw that two men were accompanied by a heavily laden pack horse. Afraid of being disappointed, she resisted the impulse to drop her hoe and run toward them. Instead, she gripped it tightly and silently watched as the figures came closer.

At last, Maura recognized the glossy chestnut coat of Captain, Luke's horse, and her father's windblown silver hair. With a glad cry, Maura flung her hoe to the ground and dashed through the corn plants. Reaching even ground, she broke into a run.

"Father! Luke!" she shouted joyously, completely forgetting that she had no reason to be glad to see Luke.

Her moccasins and Indian dress allowed freedom of movement, and she sped across the uneven ground as lightly as a gazelle. Catching sight of her, Eben kneed his horse into a lope, and when he drew within fifty feet, swung out of the saddle and hit the ground running. Arms outstretched, he raced toward her. Then she was in his arms, laughing and crying at the same time, poignantly reminded of their joyous reunion following the buffalo stampede. "Oh, father, how *good* you look! You're as hale and hearty as I remember."

"Wait a minute—let me look at you!" Holding her at arm's length, Eben studied her with a pleased grin on his deeply bronzed face and a twinkle in his bright, blue eyes. "Mr. Cutter said you had become half Indian, but I think he was wrong. You are one hundred percent Indian, my dear. I scarcely recognize you."

"I don't know why you should be so surprised," Maura retorted, laughing. Seeing Luke's scowl, she swallowed hard and laced her fingers through her father's. "I always knew that when I finally got here, I would have no difficulty fitting in, Father. That's why I did not return to Bellevue with Mr. Cutter. I'm doing marvelously well; the only thing I lacked was *you*—and pen and paper. Now that you've finally arrived with all those lovely supplies, I lack for *nothing*."

She darted a pointed look at Luke, but he ignored it. "Come on, Magruder. We had better pay our respects to Wetara-sharo. He'll be the one who decides where you stay. Lizard Woman and her husband are fairly low in rank. Their lodge is fine for a captured Sioux and a White-Eyes woman, but I doubt the old chief will think it's good enough for a famous anthropologist."

This was the first time Maura had heard that she was living in the lodge of lowly-ranked people and was herself lowly ranked; with the exception of She-de-a, the Indians seemed to treat everyone equally. Now that she thought about it, she realized that many gradations in rank existed: men and their coveted hunting societies and "moities"—which Maura was still trying to figure out—while women took their status from their husbands and their maternal lineage. Heavy Basket's mother and first husband had been people of importance, therefore *she* was important.

"Perhaps my father will be invited to live with Wetara-sharo himself." Playfully, Maura struck a haughty pose, sticking her nose in the air. "When everyone realizes *his*

258

importance, they'll also recognize mine, and I shall be invited to live there, too."

"Perhaps," Luke conceded darkly. "In any case, your father must be properly introduced."

Maura bristled. She could not remember having been "properly introduced." Why did Luke have to spoil her reunion with her father by being so . . . so arrogant and difficult, as usual?

"Where's your smile, Maura?" her father gently chided. "After all this time, I thought you would be overjoyed to see me."

"I *am* overjoyed," Maura insisted, hugging Eben. "I hope you were not angry or disappointed that I did not come back with Luke — Mr. Cutter — but I knew you would understand how anxious I was to finally start our work, here."

"Yes, I understood." Eben sighed, a gentle censure. "And I've brought all the items you requested — as well as some that you didn't."

"Wonderful! Then let's go and see Wetara-sharo. I want you to become good friends with him, Father."

"I intend to. Obviously, I am going to have to work very hard to catch up with you, though. Luke tells me you've already won over the tribe and all its leaders."

"Well, not exactly," Maura hedged. "But I have made many new friends, and I'm learning Pawnee, Sioux, and sign language. Soon I should be able to understand everything the Indians say."

"Excellent!" Eben proudly patted her arm. "Perhaps I wasn't mistaken in bringing you out here after all. After such a bad beginning, I was having my doubts."

"You ought *still* to have them," Luke rudely interjected. "Just because no one here or in Bellevue has heard from Shon-ka doesn't mean the man has given up."

"Ah, but the next time we encounter him, we'll be ready for him, won't we, Maura?"

Maura smiled and nodded, overjoyed that her father sounded like his old confident self, again. "Just how badly were you hurt, Father?" she asked, changing the subject as they walked toward the village.

"A broken wrist, a couple cracked ribs, some bruises . . . nothing serious."

"Your wrist was broken?" Maura seized his hands, turning them this way and that, examining them.

"Easy, there!" Eben cautioned, wincing and withdrawing his left one. "It's healed now, but still tender. Luckily, it was my left, not my right. I have a bit of stiffness in the joint, but if I wrap it well, it doesn't bother me."

Maura saw that his wrist was indeed tightly wrapped with a narrow length of homespun. "Had I known you were not completely well, I would have returned to Bellevue, after all. I had not realized you broke any bones. . . . Mr. Cutter slighted your injuries. Did your wrist bother you on the journey? Was the trip exhausting?"

She tossed an angry glare over her shoulder at Luke. Returning it, he snapped, "Sorry, I tried to soothe you rather than worry you. At the time, I didn't think anything would change your mind about staying, unless I lied and claimed your father was half dead."

"The trip was not difficult, just long," Eben reassured Maura. "Mr. Cutter was right not to make an issue out of my injuries. A week after he left me in Bellevue, I was feeling better and wishing I had gone with him. I was so worried about you, Maura. . . . You don't know how glad I am to see you well and happy. Major Dougherty kept telling me to relax and trust in God and Mr. Cutter—but I have been suffering the tortures of the damned since I saw you being carried away by Shon-ka's warriors."

Studying her father's familiar, dearly loved features, Maura noticed that his eyes did have a faintly haunted look. The grooves around his mouth were much deeper, but otherwise he was still handsome and distinguished-looking. She linked her arm through his and squeezed it. "Well, the nightmare is now over, Father. We can go on with our work exactly as planned. I can't wait for you to meet my friend, She-de-a! We do everything together. She is teaching me so much. . . ."

Halfway back to the village, the villagers overtook them, pointing and chattering, and bombarding Luke and Maura with questions. Between answers, Maura regaled her father with her experiences living among the Pawnee. Her happiness at being reunited with Eben almost blotted out the pain of seeing Luke again, knowing it was over between them. Despite the finality of their last meeting, Maura had hoped for a new beginning, had imagined Luke sweeping her into his arms and declaring what a fool he had been to ever leave her. She had prayed that, somehow, his lust would turn into love — but alas, one look at his face had told her it was not to be.

Luke was still angry, still thought she was wrong, still believed she did not belong here. And he still made her feel more alive — and therefore, more vulnerable — than any man she had ever known.

Just knowing he was near — scowling as usual — made her heart beat faster and her knees quake. Why did she have to love him so much? And how long would it be before he left again, this time, probably, for good?

Chapter Nineteen

Luke filled his lungs with the fragrant smoke from a ceremonial wooden pipe with a stone bowl, carefully exhaled, and then passed the pipe to Maura's father. A small circle of men — the most influential in the tribe — sat in Wetara-sharo's smoky, dimly lit lodge, waited upon by Heavy Basket and two other squaws. Having eaten, they were now circulating the pipe as a gesture of good will and friendship, but Luke sensed that not everyone was as pleased by Eben's presence in the village as Eben himself and, of course, Maura.

Luke was surprised that Wetara-sharo had even permitted the smoking of the pipe tonight. Among the Pawnee, pipe smoking was restricted; only on special occasions were a select few tribal members allowed to smoke. Pipe smoking, it was believed, slowed a man down, so that he could not run or think as fast. The latter was certainly true, Luke reflected, trying hard to stay awake and concentrate on his surroundings. The combined smoke from the pipe, the cookfire, and several small clay saucers containing burning buffalo fat, made breathing difficult. Luke badly needed a breath of fresh air, but leaving too soon would be impolite; they had not even begun serious conversation, yet.

Stifling a yawn, Luke took note of who was present for

this special occasion. Besides Wetara-sharo and Pitale-sharo, there was Bon-son-gee and a half-dozen other men, eleven in all, including himself and Eben. All of the Indians but Pitale-sharo had the smooth, plucked heads so distinctive of the Pawnee, and the erect, ornamented scalp locks resembling buffalo horns. Some were dressed in breechclouts and moccasins, while others wore clothing they had obtained from traders. Wolf Laughing, the man across from Luke, wore brown homespun trousers, a calico shirt, a red vest, and tall black boots that obviously pinched his feet. His White-Eyes attire amused Luke, especially since he himself preferred the soft, comfortable Indian clothing made for him by Elk-Runner.

The circle of men sat at one end of the lodge, near the Sacred Place, where a small stone altar held various food offerings for the spirits. The lodge itself was neat and well-kept, though not as neat as it had been when Wetara-sharo's wife still lived. After the death of his third wife, a young girl with hips too small for childbearing, the old man had not remarried, declaring that he was too old to train another wife. The housekeeping chores had thus fallen to Heavy Basket and several other squaws. Being as yet unmarried, Pitale-sharo slept in the lodge, as did Luke when he was in the village. It was also used for ceremonial, religious, and business meetings of the council.

Keeping two lodges must have been difficult for Heavy Basket, but the stalwart squaw proudly managed. From where he sat, Luke could see her efficiently directing the cleanup of the meal and the precise arrangement of the cooking implements in their proper places. In no time, she had everything put back where it belonged, and then, without a word to anyone, ushered her helpers ahead of her out of the lodge, leaving Luke to ponder her unusual role in the tribe.

Though currently unmarried, Heavy Basket merited her own lodge because she was a respected medicine woman, second in prestige only to the shaman. In payment for driving out evil spirits, the source of earaches, nosebleeds, and rheumatism, Heavy Basket accepted meat and skins, and was thus able to live independently until such time as a younger man—Pitale-sharo, for instance—fancied marrying her.

In a matrilineal tribe such the Pawnee, the big earth lodges customarily belonged to the women and were passed down from mother to daughter. Often several families shared a single lodge. As daughters of a particular family married, their husbands simply moved in and helped to support all the females living there.

Luke wondered if Maura had yet discovered these facts. If she had not, she would be most interested, but she'd never hear them from him. Anything Maura was going to learn about the Indians, she would have to learn on her own. Dragging his thoughts away from Maura, a topic too dangerous to dwell on for long, Luke made an effort to prepare himself for the tedious task of translating.

Eben would need help in understanding what was being said and in saying whatever he wanted to say. Most of the Indians understood a smattering of English—Pitale-sharo being the only fluent one—but good manners required that Luke make certain there was no misinterpretation on either side. He passed a hand over his smoke-reddened, watery eyes and peered at Bon-son-gee, who looked no more enthusiastic about being here than Luke himself.

There had not been time to catch up on the news with Pitale-sharo before the meal, no time to find out what, if anything, had been done to punish Bon-son-gee for getting drunk at the buffalo feast. Pitale-sharo had been deeply upset over Bon-son-gee's behavior, so upset that the young chief had decided not to accompany Luke to Bellevue, after all. When he backed out of the trip, the other braves did also, leaving Luke to return alone.

No, all was not well with the Pawnee. Abruptly, Luke

recalled something he had forgotten in the excitement of their arrival that afternoon: Pitale-sharo had not been pleased to hear that Maura was remaining in the village. And he had not looked happy to see Eben. Maura must have been lying when she said that both she and Eben had been guaranteed welcome for an extended visit. Either that, or Pitale-sharo's preoccupation with She-de-a and his continuing problems with Bon-son-gee had made him forgetful and displeased about everything. There was also the possibility that Maura had gone only to Wetara-sharo, bypassing the younger man altogether.

Luke watched with mounting interest as Wetara-sharo leaned forward, his ancient face and body more shriveled and weakened than Luke remembered from just a month ago. "Among the Pawnee, you will be known as Silver-Hair," he said to Eben in measured Pawnee.

Luke translated, and Eben responded with a self-deprecating frown. "That is what Shon-ka called me. I guess, because of my hair, it's the obvious name for me."

The old chief also frowned. "We are not one with Shon-ka. If the name displeases you, we will give you another."

"No . . . Silver-Hair will be fine. What name have you given my daughter?"

Luke repeated the question. Wetara-sharo and Pitale-sharo exchanged glances, then Wetara-sharo said something under his breath.

"What is he saying?" Eben whispered.

"He says that because Maura is only a woman, they have not yet given her a special name. Everyone just calls her the White-Eyes woman."

Eben looked surprised and slightly insulted. "Shon-ka called her the Woman-With-Hair-Like-Moonbeams."

Wetara-sharo inclined his head graciously. "If you want, we can call her that."

"No," Eben protested. "Since there is no other White-Eyes woman in the village, the name at least explains who

265

she is."

"How long will you and your daughter remain here?" Wetara-sharo suddenly, rudely demanded.

"Why, I don't yet know . . . ," Eben glanced questioningly at Luke. "My daughter said we were welcome here. I hope she was not mistaken or making a foolish assumption."

"You *are* welcome. The Skidi Pawnee always welcome those who come in friendship—but how long will you stay?" Wetara-sharo persisted.

Reddening slightly in embarrassment, Eben weighed his answer. While he did so, Luke noticed Bon-son-gee muttering behind his hand to Wolf Laughing. Beside Luke, Pitale-sharo stiffened. To speak while others were speaking was considered a shocking breach of good manners.

"I'm sure my daughter has explained to you why she and I wish to live among your people," Eben delicately began.

"I have never spoken to her," Wetara-sharo denied. "But I have heard that the White-Eyes woman came here because Great Heart wished to keep her safe from Shon-ka."

"That's true," Luke broke in. So Maura *had* lied to him. Obviously, she had not spoken to Wetara-sharo *or* Pitale-sharo about her real mission. "But the Magruders were coming here to begin with. I had agreed to guide them—until I discovered that one of their party was a woman, and then I refused. I *knew* there would be trouble, if not with Shon-ka, then with other Indians or the traders themselves. White women are too much of a curiosity out here for there *not* to be trouble."

"But *why* did they come?" Wetara-sharo demanded. "No one has yet told me that."

"Yes, I have, Grandfather. Surely you remember." Speaking in rapid Pawnee, Pitale-sharo reminded the old chief that he had already explained about Eben being an important man among the whites, a teacher akin to a

266

shaman or medicine man, and a respected orator whose purpose in visiting the Indians was to study their way of life so he could tell the whites back east about the people who lived in the Land of the Shallow Rivers.

"Is that not so, Great Heart?" Pitale-sharo's glance sought confirmation.

"That is so," Luke confirmed. "His daughter, Maura, helps in his work. I understand she draws pictures of the things her father writes about and copies his writings so everyone can read them easily."

"Ah, yes . . . now I remember." Wetara-sharo closed his eyes a moment, as if recalling everything he had been told about the Magruders. When he opened them, his expression was shrewd and calculating. "But for what reason does Silver-Hair and his daughter now wish to remain among the Pawnee? The White-Eyes woman has already lived among us for two or three moons, time enough to learn about the Pawnee. With winter coming, it would be better for them both to return to Belle-vue."

Luke could scarcely control his elation; the old chief did *not* want the Magruders underfoot. Either he didn't want the responsibility of protecting them from Shon-ka, or he was simply maintaining his traditional position of mistrusting whites.

"I must disagree, sir. It is *not* time enough to learn about you," Eben stated emphatically. He paused to allow Luke to translate and then continued with fervor. "My daughter and I wish to learn *everything* there is to know about the Skidi Pawnee. We will write it all down so that the whole world will realize what a fine tribe you are. The Great White Father in Washington wishes to learn what you are like, how you think, what gods you worship, what you eat, drink, and wear. . . . He very much admires you. *He* is the one who can prevent the whites from coming here and killing your buffalo, stealing your lands, and selling firewater and tainted blankets. You must understand how important it is for us to tell our people the *good* things about you. From the traders, they hear only the *bad* — things they do not understand, because no one has ever explained them. In the east, most whites believe that all Indians are wicked and evil. Some claim that you eat your captives and drink their blood . . . and when you have no captives, you kill your own children to slake your appetites."

As Luke translated, the Indians muttered among themselves, exchanging glances of anger and outrage. Eben had presented powerful arguments; only Luke knew that most whites *wanted* to believe the worst of the Indians, and thus would probably reject facts or opinions to the contrary. Where greed was involved, people were likely to be damn stubborn. In an effort to justify their own despicable behavior, they would willingly embrace all kinds of ridiculous lies and slander.

"Silver-Hair speaks the truth, Grandfather," Pitale-sharo finally said. "The whites hate and fear us because they do not know or understand us — and we do not understand them. This man comes to us in friendship to try and remedy the problem; we ought not to send him and his daughter away before they have finished what they came to do."

Wetara-sharo gazed long and hard at his grandson. "I want to believe that whites are anxious to learn the truth about us, and that the truth will not shock them as much as the lies. But I am an old man who has seen too much, *suffered* too much. The wolf and the hawk can never be friends, my son, not while they hunt the same rabbit. We have argued this before, and my opinion remains unchanged."

"It cannot hurt for them to stay the winter, Grandfather. Nothing happens in winter except snow and wind. During the long, cold nights, we can entertain each other."

The old man looked down at the floor mats. Then he lifted burning black eyes to study his grandson for several uncomfortable moments. Finally, he shrugged his thin shoulders in defeat. "All right, my son. If you are certain no harm will result, then yes, you may give them permission to stay for the winter . . . but after that, when spring comes . . . ," the old chief trailed off warningly.

Luke wracked his brain to guess what controversial events might be happening in the spring and summer— events the old chief apparently did not want the Magruders to know about. He could think of no ceremonies or rituals that he himself had not already witnessed. Were the Pawnee planning to attack the Sioux or some other such violent act that would engender white disapproval? Was Pitale-sharo finally bending to pressure to become more aggressive and warlike?

Luke searched his friend's face; Pitale-sharo refused to meet his eyes. His uncharacteristically furtive manner convinced Luke that the Pawnee *were* planning some secret, violent act. Luke's stomach plummeted into his moccasins. He had thought he and Pitale-sharo were close enough that if plans were afoot to go to war, raid an enemy tribe, or even to attack the whites, Pitale-sharo would at least warn him and give him a chance to resolve the problem peacefully. In the past, their friendship had prevented several potential bloodbaths, involving not just the Skidis, but other tribes as well. Pitale-sharo had warned Luke ahead of time, and he had been able to avert disaster and keep things under control.

Clearing this throat, Bon-son-gee suddenly leaned forward. "Wait," he growled. "Before you give permission for Silver-Hair and the White-eyes woman to learn all our secrets, I wish to speak."

Everyone looked at Bon-son-gee. Their faces registered surprise, consternation, and expectation. "Then speak," Wetara-sharo commanded. "You are a member of the tribal council and entitled to give your opinion on any matter that comes before us."

Luke translated for Eben. Then silence fell while Bon-son-gee gathered his thoughts. When he finally spoke, his voice was quiet and menacing. "I do not approve of allowing White-Eyes to live among us. I have never approved of the friendship between our chief, Pitale-sharo, and Great Heart. Too often in the past, Pitale-sharo has not given us leadership because he is worrying what the White-Eyes will think."

Pitale-sharo made a sudden movement of protest, but Wetara-sharo calmed him with a restraining hand. "Let him speak, my son. Before you state your own case, you must allow him to finish."

"Yes, let me finish, Pitale-sharo. For far too long, I have been silent, watching as you made terrible mistakes. Now, I will tell my brothers *my* thoughts, and you may then agree or disagree, as you choose."

Bon-son-gee squared his shoulders and set his jaw. "Brothers," he intoned sonorously, as if he had waited a long time for this moment and was going to make every word count. "The White-Eyes are our enemies. No man among us can any longer deny this. We trade with them, sell them furs, and welcome them into our villages. In return, they bring sickness, cheat us by giving us tools and glass beads that break, guns that blow up, and firewater that makes fools of us. I myself have sometimes allowed the White-Eyes to make a fool of me. . . . You have seen it; Pitale-sharo himself has mocked me for it. But I at least recognize that all whites must be regarded as enemies, while Pitale-sharo continues to act the fool and embrace those who mean to harm us."

"All whites are *not* our enemies!" Pitale-sharo nostrils flared; his mouth quivered.

"Patience," counseled Wetara-sharo. "Let him make his point."

At the old chief's reprimand, Bon-son-gee flashed a wolfish grin, then scowlingly continued. "I do not think the

White-Eyes will come to love us when they learn more about us. Rather, they will use that knowledge to defeat us and drive us off our lands. Does the rabbit teach the wolf the ways of rabbits? No, he guards himself against his enemies in hopes that he may live and prosper. Already the White-Eyes know too much they could use against us. Great Heart knows all our hunting places; he knows when we are gone from the village and when we will return. If he gave that information to the Sioux, they could come and destroy the village in our absence."

Luke stopped translating for Eben long enough to point out that if he had wanted to destroy the Pawnee, he could have done so long ago.

"You might *still* do it," Bon-son-gee accused. "If I kill Silver-Hair tonight while he sleeps, what is to prevent you from gathering many White-Eyes and returning to destroy our homes and murder all who live here?"

"The knowledge that you alone did the killing. If Silver-Hair or his daughter come to harm, I will kill *you*, Bon-son-gee," Luke threatened. "Only you. So you had better make certain they come to no harm."

"I have not said I *would* harm them—*yet*," Bon-son-gee responded unblinkingly. "What I am trying to show is how weak and vulnerable Pitale-sharo has made us—and how much weaker we will become if this Silver-Hair and his daughter, and you, too, are permitted to live among us."

"I will not be staying," Luke informed him.

"No, but if *they* stay, even for the winter, they will learn too much—especially during *this* winter, when we prepare for—"

"Enough!" Wetara-sharo barked. "Guard your tongue, Bon-son-gee, lest secrets you accuse others of divulging slip unnoticed through your own mouth."

Red-faced, Bon-son-gee clamped his jaws shut. Luke wondered what the brave had been going to say. What *were* the Pawnee preparing for?

271

As if wondering the same thing, Eben whispered, "What was just said?"

Luke related his exchange with Bon-son-gee but did not mention the brave's slip of tongue. Then Pitale-sharo said, "Are you finished now, Bon-son-gee? May I defend myself against your accusations of weakness and poor leadership?"

"No," Bon-son-gee replied, rapidly recovering his aplomb. "I wish to say one more thing. *All* the White-Eyes should be expelled from our village, and if they dare return, they should then be killed. No longer should we trade with them, meet, or talk with them, not even with Major Dougherty. It is not enough to ban firewater from the village; in the end, that will accomplish little. Since the White-Eyes have proven themselves to be our enemies, we must now *treat* them as such. I challenge all of you to decide tonight—shall we go on allowing them to weaken us? Shall we expose our secrets to our enemies? Or shall we return to the ways of our ancestors, and once more become proud, independent, and strong?"

As he finished his speech, Bon-son-gee locked glances with Pitale-sharo, who glared at him in return, knowing he had been outmaneuvered and more seriously challenged than ever before. It was so quiet in the earth lodge that Luke's own breathing sounded loud in his ears. How ironic, he thought. He wanted Pitale-sharo to send Maura back to Bellevue, but he did *not* want him to do it as a demonstration of a new—and hostile—policy toward whites. Bon-son-gee was demanding that Pitale-sharo end *all* contact and friendly commerce, the first step toward all-out war. With bated breath, Luke waited to see what his friend would do now.

Chapter Twenty

Pitale-sharo took his time before answering. The grim slash of his mouth revealed his determination to remain calm and not allow his hatred of Bon-son-gee to provoke him into rash speech or action. The young chief's forbearance was what made him such a good leader; he *thought* before he acted—but to some, his hesitancy signified weakness. And so it was now, Luke realized, when Wolf Laughing began to mutter loud enough for all to hear.

"Does the mighty Pitale-sharo have no response? Does he fear to cast out the White-Eyes? I agree with Bon-son-gee; let us send these strangers away and kill them if they dare come again. They must not be allowed to discover our weaknesses as well as our strengths."

Pitale-sharo gazed intently at the brave who had sided with Bon-son-gee. As his glance flicked across each of the other Indians in turn, the silence grew oppressive. "My brothers . . . do not think I have never considered the questions raised here, tonight. Or that I sleep well in this lodge, with no worries for the future and no doubts . . . My doubts are greater now than they have ever been. So also is my commitment to peace. Have you forgotten what it was like in the old days, before Great Heart and Major

Dougherty came to Belle-vue? We warred constantly among ourselves, tribe against tribe, Indian fighting Indian. . . . My own father died in one of these endless skirmishes. Only for the past few summers have we known peace—and then only because of Major Dougherty and Great Heart."

Pitale-sharo mournfully shook his head. "Now, you are demanding that we spit in the faces of our loyal, proven friends. Instead of peace, your hearts seek war. But I tell you this: If we return to our warring ways, not only will we anger the whites, we will give our old enemies—the Sioux—an excuse to raid us, and we cannot expect help to stop them. Now, at least, if they attack our village, they will suffer harsh consequences. No one will buy their furs or sell them the goods they desire. Major Dougherty knows how to punish without bloodshed."

"Pah!" Bon-son-gee spat. "I had rather punish them myself—*with* bloodshed."

"You will not be so anxious for war, Bon-son-gee, when it is your own loved ones whose blood is spilled. I have killed, and I have also lost loved ones. The satisfaction of killing can never compensate for the pain of loss. Why are you so afraid of Silver-Hair? He is an old man, and his daughter is not worthy of your notice. She tries hard but cannot perform even half the work of a healthy Pawnee squaw. We have nothing to fear from either of them, but we do have much to gain, if we permit them to remain for the winter. When they return to Belle-vue, they will tell everyone of our hospitality, and perhaps what Silver-Hair says will come true: The White-Eyes will learn to respect us."

"They will *never* respect us!" Bon-son-gee snorted. "Can you not see the danger? Or are you so blinded by your friendship with Great Heart that you—"

"Be still! This is *my* time to speak, and I am not yet fin—"

274

"I know what *else* has weakened you!" Bon-son-gee goaded him, scenting blood. "Your heart is so filled with lust for the little Sioux captive that you—"

"Silence!" Pitale-sharo roared, leaping to his feet.

In a flash, Bon-son-gee also rose. The two men eyed each other across the fire. Glaring and red-faced, they stood with clenched fists. Then, Bon-son-gee began to laugh. "So it's true!" he crowed triumphantly. "You actually fancy her, a maiden who belongs to—"

Pitale-sharo flung himself across the cookfire and rammed Bon-son-gee in the mid-section, toppling him to the ground. The two men rolled across the floor mats, each trying to choke the other. Luke, Wolf Laughing, and Eben scrambled to their feet and tried to separate them. Fighting in the tribal council was unheard of; on the rare occasions when disagreements flared, they were settled some other way, either through diplomacy or by allowing the opponents to meet later and battle it out. Luke finally got hold of Pitale-sharo, and Wolf Laughing grabbed Bon-son-gee. Realizing what they had done, the two men ceased struggling. Like guilty children, they stood shame-facedly before Wetaro-sharo. The old chieftain lost no time in scolding them.

"See how you disgrace us before the very strangers you argue about. Sit down both of you. We have heard enough. Now, the council will vote. Pitale-sharo, fetch the stones."

Pitale-sharo disengaged himself from Luke and, scowling ferociously, retrieved a small woven container from the Sacred Place. While waiting for the vote, Luke returned to his seat beside Eben Magruder. Everything had happened too fast for translations, and now Maura's father leaned close to Luke and whispered in his ear. "Am I right in assuming that they are fighting over whether or not my daughter and I shall be permitted to remain in the village?"

"Yes," Luke muttered. "But other issues have been raised as well. I'll explain them later—assuming I myself figure out exactly what's going on. Right now, the council is going to vote. Just sit still and look confident. If more white stones than black are cast, you and Maura can stay. But if the majority of the stones are black, we're both in big trouble."

Eben nodded and watched quietly as Pitale-sharo presented the woven container to his grandfather. Wetara-sharo removed the lid and took out two small, round stones, one white, one black. He then passed the basket around, and each Indian took out two stones, a white and a black. Only Eben and Luke received no stones. This was a tribal matter; they were not entitled to vote.

When each man had been served, the basket was returned to Wetara-sharo, who emptied out the remaining stones on the mat in front of him. "You have heard the arguments," he said. "Now cast your stones."

In silence, the Indians voted. The stones clacked as they fell atop each other in the basket. When everyone except Wetara-sharo and Pitale-sharo had voted, Luke saw that there were three white and four black stones in the basket. Wetara-sharo passed the basket to his grandson, holding it low enough so that all could see the tally. As expected, Pitale-sharo dropped in a white stone. Now there was an equal number of black and white, which meant that Wetara-sharo would cast the deciding vote.

The old man set the basket down in front of him. All eyes watched as he tossed in his stone. It was white. Luke exhaled in relief. He had not really expected the old man to desert his grandson, but Wetara-sharo's animosity toward whites ran deep. Luke would never take his friendship for granted. Once, years ago, Luke had brought Wetara-sharo's young wife a looking glass, which pleased her mightily. The old chief had smashed the harmless thing to pieces, saying he would not allow "White-Eyes magic" to contaminate his lodge.

"Silver-Hair and his daughter may stay through the winter," Pitale-sharo announced triumphantly. "Remember whose choice it was—not mine, but *yours*. Though I am chief, I am only your servant and would have abided by your decision no matter how you voted this night. It is not I who command you, but you who command me."

"Hah! You say that only because you won—*this* time," Bon-son-gee growled.

"I say it because it is the truth."

"Excuse me," Eben broke in awkwardly. "I want to thank those who voted to allow my daughter and me to remain. Truly, it was the right decision. I do believe I can help the White-Eyes to better understand the Pawnee, and that peace between our peoples will be the result. I assure you, we will do nothing to interfere in any of your tribal ceremonies or decisions. We are here as observers only."

Eben nodded to Luke, and he translated, his mind replaying what had happened, what had been said . . . and *not* said. Twice, Bon-son-gee had made reference to things Luke did not understand: first, when he let slip that the Pawnee would be preparing for something this winter, and second, when he mentioned She-de-a. Matters involving females were rarely discussed in the men's council. And Pitale-sharo's response had been so violent—as if more were at stake than tribal displeasure if Pitale-sharo married She-de-a instead of the woman his grandfather favored. But what could be at stake? What had Bon-son-gee been going to say before Pitale-sharo attacked him?

After Eben's conciliatory speech, the council adjourned. Bon-son-gee and his followers were the first to leave, underscoring the grim reality that Pitale-sharo's liberal views had lost favor. The vote had been too close for comfort. After Bon-son-gee's departure, an uncomfortable silence descended. Those remaining sat still and thoughtful, the lodge unnaturally quiet.

Several long moments passed, and then, one by one, the others left, leaving only Pitale-sharo, Wetaro-sharo, Luke, and Eben. Luke yawned and pretended to act sleepy so that he might be urged to go to bed. He and Eben had been invited to sleep on the big platform linked with skins in Luke's usual curtained alcove, but he did not want to be rude and retire if his presence was still needed. What he really wanted was to go to bed and eavesdrop in the hopes of hearing Pitale-sharo and Wetara-sharo discuss what had happened tonight.

Noticing his yawn, Pitale-sharo waved his hand. "The hour is late, Great Heart. Go now, and sleep. Take Silver-Hair with you. My grandfather and I will sit awhile and ask the spirits for guidance."

Luke accepted the dismissal with a slight nod, but Eben seemed ready to say something. To forestall him, Luke grabbed his arm. "Come to bed, Magruder. Whatever you have to say can wait until morning."

"No, it can't." Surprisingly, Eben wrenched his arm away. "I've been through this sort of thing before, Mr. Cutter. It never hurts to show a few courtesies."

Turning to Wetara-sharo, Eben said, "Good night, and thank you again for allowing my daughter and me to stay. You honor me, and I shall not forget it. Nor will I allow my people to forget your kindness."

Before Luke could overcome his reluctance and translate, Pitale-sharo did so. In an astounding gesture of friendliness, Wetara-sharo lifted his head and grinned at Eben. "It is the old and wise who understand the importance of small acts of kindness and good manners. I look forward to talking with you during the long, cold nights, Silver-Hair. Since Great Heart is leaving, it is fortunate my grandson speaks your language—or perhaps your daughter can translate. I understand that already she speaks our language."

"My daughter and I have admired your people for a

278

very long time. It would give her great pleasure to translate, though I'm sure she's not yet as good as Great Heart or your grandson."

She had better not be, Luke thought jealously. It had taken years for him and Pitale-sharo to reach their present state of fluency in each other's language. "Good night," he muttered, heading for bed.

Moments later, Eben followed. Luke made certain the older man got the side of the platform closest to the wall, while he himself claimed the side that opened toward the lodge's center. Eben fell asleep shortly after he removed his boots and shirt and climbed onto the wide bed of furs. But Luke stayed awake a long time, mimicking the deep, even breathing of sleep, while at the same time listening for Pitale-sharo and Wetara-sharo to speak.

Just as he began to doze off, convinced that the two were not going to discuss the night's happenings, he heard Wetara-sharo say, "It is true, my son, is it not? You lust after the Sioux captive. I myself have seen how you look at her."

Luke strained to catch Pitale-sharo's response. "I have not touched the maid."

"If you do, you will ruin her. And for what good reason? Heavy Basket will gladly ease your lust. So will other women in the tribe. Go to one of them."

"They are not young and beautiful."

"If youth and beauty are more important to you than goodness and wisdom, then I will consider giving you one of the younger women—only do not touch the Sioux."

Pitale-sharo's voice rose angrily. "You do not have to tell me these things, Grandfather. I already know them—better than you. I have seen all the signs; I have noted the warnings. There is no question to whom She-de-a belongs. What you and Bon-son-gee have noted is not so much *my* desire, but She-de-a's. The girl *yearns* to become my wife."

"That is good," Wetara-sharo said softly. "That is as it

should be. So long as you understand your duty, it will not be necessary for me to mention this matter again, especially while the White-Eyes are among us."

" 'Twas not I who introduced the matter, Grandfather. Why do you harass me? Have I not suffered enough insult for one night? One day, I shall have to kill Bon-son-gee; even Great Heart says as much. If you wish to worry, worry that one day I shall kill the man. This tribe is not big enough to contain us both. And I will not be the one who leaves—or the one who drives us into war with the White-Eyes."

"Let us not argue," his grandfather said wearily. "I have not the faith that you have in the White-Eyes, but still I stood by you tonight. For as long as I can, I shall stand by you, my son. Only do not betray me in the matter of the little Sioux, and all will be well. Now, more than ever, the girl is the future of our tribe."

"I will not betray you, Grandfather. All I have done is look at her. I swear to you I have not touched her—nor will I. But it is hard, so very hard, when she looks at *me* with such longing."

"So have all the maidens looked at their captors. . . . Remember that, my son. I felt your pain; so did your father. It is the pain that binds us, one to the other. It is the pain that gives the offering value. It is the pain that will save us all."

After Wetara-sharo's last comment, there was only a deep silence. Luke kept hoping one or the other of them would speak again. But they did not. Frustration overwhelmed him. What in hell was going on? Lying in the musty darkness behind the skin curtain, Luke mulled difficult, perplexing questions. Why couldn't Pitale-sharo marry the little Sioux? What did he intend to do with her? Why was she the tribe's 'future'?

Only one thing was certain; She-de-a was *not* just a pretty female who had captured Pitale-sharo's fancy and was now tormenting him because he couldn't have her. Perhaps she was the sister or daughter of an important Sioux, such as Shon-ka. Was she a hostage? Was that why Pitale-sharo dare not marry her? Did he intend to trade her back to her people in exchange for a peace settlement or something else the tribe badly needed? Why would she be "ruined" if Pitale-sharo bedded her?

Heretofore, Luke had never known the Pawnee to place any great importance upon a female's virginity. It just wasn't an issue; as soon as a maiden reached puberty and caught the eye of an older, widowed brave, he would begin negotiating with her parents. Virgins were soon married and placed under the protection of powerful, respected warriors. From then on, until her first husband died, a young girl was expected to be faithful and take no notice of attractive younger men. Though strange and incomprehensible to whites, the system had many advantages, not the least of which was the fact that both men and women had plenty of time to look around and make their choices for a second mate. In the meantime, they still had an outlet for their sexual energies.

Whatever was going on among the Pawnee was not his business. Though disappointed that his friend had not confided in him, Luke doubted that Pitale-sharo would allow any harm to come to the girl. He had confidence in his friend's basically gentle, peace-loving nature. Tonight had proven once again that Pitale-sharo craved peace and order, and would uphold his present policy of friendship toward whites.

Bon-son-gee remained a worry, but so long as Pitale-sharo had his grandfather's support, there should be no trouble. Spring would be time enough to return to the tribe and discover what, if any, dangerous plans were in the making. Luke would have to return in the springtime anyway, to escort Maura and her father back to Bellevue. In the meantime, Luke decided, nothing much could be done except to warn Maura and her father to keep their eyes and ears open, but on no condition to interfere. Eben seemed to be committed to a course of noninterference; the one who needed the warning was Maura . . .

Thinking about Maura reminded Luke that he himself had had no release for his own sexual energies in a very long time, not since the day he had made love to her on the riverbank. Tiredly closing his eyes, he pictured her exactly as she had looked standing naked in the brown, eddying water, with her silver-blond hair swirling about her shoulders and hips, her blue-gray eyes misty with desire, and her beautiful body so ready and eager for his possession.

He remembered how soft and silky her skin had felt beneath his fingertips, how tender and full were her breasts. He recalled the sweet roundness of her bottom that always made him want to cup it in his two hands while he rubbed against her. His first impulse when he had seen her earlier that afternoon had been to grab her, sling her across his lap, and ride away somewhere they could be alone, where he could make love to her. Having been unable to do that, he had then gone out of his way to be curt and hostile. Because of Maura and the spell she had cast over him, he had avoided Elk-Runner while in Bellevue. He had seen her tepee on the fringes of the little settlement but had not gone there to sleep or eat, because he knew that if he did, Elk-Runner would expect him to resume intimacies. *That* he could not handle.

In time, he might be able to banish Maura's golden beauty from his mind, but for now the thought of being intimate with another woman turned his stomach. Maura was a burning fever eating at his gut, but she was a fever he intended to conquer, once and for all. Tomorrow, he would leave again, return to Bellevue, and concentrate on forgetting that he had ever met the Magruders.

But tonight, he would enjoy his erotic images: Maura

with her head tilted back and eyes closed, leaning into him while he kissed her white throat. Maura arching her back in the sand and writhing beneath him as he drove into her. Maura touching and caressing him—driving him wild with desire.

Beside him, Eben Magruder coughed and turned over, reminding Luke that he was lying in the same bed as Maura's father. Thoughts of Maura's nudity and passion were obscene occurring in such close proximity to someone who had every right to shoot Luke for having done what he had done to innocent, virginal Maura Magruder.

Luke rolled over on his side and willed himself to stop thinking about Maura lying naked and willing in his arms. For a brief time he succeeded, but as soon as he fell asleep and began to dream, his dreams were of Maura. All night long, he made love to her, and when he awoke in an agony of frustrated desire, Maura's name was on his lips. He could not be sure he had not spoken it aloud. Fortunately, Eben was still deeply asleep, snoring loudly, and Luke was able to get up and leave the lodge without awakening him.

Once outside in the dew-fresh morning, he headed for the river and a cold bath downstream behind a clump of cottonwoods. Stripping to bare flesh, he threw his buckskins on the ground and was startled when they landed beside another pile of clothing. There, on the ground, was a neatly folded buckskin garment and a small pair of fringed moccasins.

They belong to a squaw, Luke tried to convince himself, all the while knowing that squaws usually bathed in groups, amidst a crowd of chattering children, while washing cooking utensils at the same time. Only one woman in the entire village would be stupid enough to risk bathing alone in the river at this early hour. It had to be Maura.

Luke wrestled with himself only a moment, then gave up pretending he did not want to come upon her naked, bathing in the river, alone. Desire rose in him like a fountain. Parting the concealing, scruffy bushes, he stepped out of the grove of cottonwoods and proceeded down to the water's edge. There, naked and every bit as lovely as he remembered, stood Maura . . .

Chapter Twenty-one

The snapping of a dry twig alerted Maura to the presence of another person. Protectively tugging her hair around her to shield her nakedness, she turned and saw Luke, splendid in his tall, broad-shouldered masculinity, and fully ready to prove to any woman what a fool she had been to think she could ever forget him.

Staring at him, drinking in his rugged beauty, she could think of nothing whatever to say. She had come here this morning expressly for the purpose of washing away yesterday's grime and making herself beautiful, in the hopes of arousing Luke's notice. However, now that she had his undivided attention, she did not know what to do with it. Nothing had changed between them; they had parted on a hostile note and greeted each other in the same fashion, as if neither of them cared. But Maura knew that she cared very much. For the price of a kind word she might fall into his arms again and do anything he wanted.

"Is the water cold?" he finally asked, seeming not the least embarrassed that they should both be naked in the early morning sunlight.

"No," Maura said tremulously, desperately trying to quell the hammering of her heart. "The water's quite tepid. I'm finished now, so I'll leave the river to you. I hope you enjoy your bath."

She started to walk past him, but he stepped into the river shallows beside her and grasped her arm. Quivering with anticipation, Maura gazed into his eyes. A shaft of yellow light illuminated his handsome face, turning his steel-gray eyes a molten gold and making the chestnut highlights in his hair flame red as fire. Never had he looked so vividly alive, so compelling; his awesome, bronzed strength took her breath away.

"Don't go yet," he pleaded in a raw, hungry whisper.

There was no mistaking his desire. Even had she not seen his body below the waist, she would have known he wanted her from his tone of voice and the expression on his face. Looking past him, she searched the cottonwood grove for signs of possible intruders. "Where's my father?" she asked, her voice barely audible.

"Still sleeping. There's no one here but us."

He drew her into his arms. Though she wanted to resist—knew that she *should*—she could not. It would be refusing sustenance when she was starving, rejecting water when she was parched. She allowed him to put his hands on her lower back and press her body into his. Gently, he rubbed his curly chest hair across her breasts. The friction made her nipples contract into small, tight buds that throbbed and quickened with intense feeling—a marvelous sensation that quickly spread to engulf her entire body.

Never doubting that she welcomed his attentions, he instructed her in a gravelly voice, "Put your arms around my neck and hold on."

As if in a dream, she did so. His hands clamped tightly onto her bottom and lifted her, so that the apex of her thighs was level with his. She felt the probing of his stiff, slickened member and obediently opened her legs, wrapping them around his waist. In one burning thrust, he was inside her. She clung to him while he buried his face in her hair, growling incomprehensible endearments.

"Squeeze me," he begged.

Gladly, she complied. He spread his legs slightly, finding more secure purchase on the sandy river bottom, and then began to move his hips, thrusting into her gently but fully. She sighed from the depths of her being and surrendered herself to spiraling pleasure. What they were doing was shameless—but oh, so sweet, wondrous, and exciting. Her body contracted, drawing him more deeply within her, squeezing him, rejoicing in his eager thrusts.

Rhythmic waves of pleasure radiated from her inner core. At the crest of the largest wave, Luke groaned deeply and held her still while he thrust into her one final, glorious time. Maura felt as if she had somehow escaped her body and was floating on a warm sea of rapture. When she finally slid her legs down and tried to stand, her knees buckled. Luke had to hold her to keep her from falling.

He tilted her face toward his and gently kissed her lips. Drawing slightly back, he said, "I'm sorry, Maura, but this time I could not resist you. You're lucky *I* found you bathing and not one of the Pawnee."

"I bathe here every morning. No one ever bothers me."

With one finger, he traced her mouth. "You must be more careful, sweet, not only about bathing by yourself but also about other things. . . . You lied when you said you and your father were welcome, here; last night, the tribal council almost went to war over the issue."

"I did *not* lie!" A guilty flush consumed Maura's cheeks. "Heavy Basket said I could stay, and Lizard Woman, too. I have made friends here, and—"

"And enemies," Luke finished for her. "Some in the village think that you, your father, and I should be driven out and scalped if we dare come again. If you don't believe me, ask your father. Something strange involving She-de-a is also going on."

"She-de-a?" Maura stepped back from Luke, the better to see his face. "What do you mean? It's true that everyone still criticizes or else ignores her, but I don't think their rejection will last forever. How can anyone hate such a lovely, sweet girl, even if she is Sioux?"

"I don't know, Maura, but if I were you, I'd keep my eyes and ears open and my mouth shut. I know it's futile to try and convince you and your father to return with me to Bellevue, so I'm not going to try. However, I'll be coming back in the spring to get you both. That's how long you're permitted to stay."

Two things competed for Maura's attention: that Luke was already thinking of leaving, and that if she and her father left in the spring, they would miss Pitale-sharo's wedding on the summer solstice.

"When are you going?" she blurted, mentioning the worry uppermost in her mind.

"As soon as I get dressed."

An icy chill descended on Maura. Goose bumps erupted on her bare flesh. "So . . . what we just did . . . it still means nothing to you."

"I said I was sorry . . . and I am. You're a beautiful woman, Maura. When I look at you, I get carried away . . . as you already know."

Maura's eyes stung. Grimly, she refused to cry in front of him. "I have the exact same problem when I look at you . . . only where I come from, they call it love." She choked back a sob and glared at him. "It's too bad we don't speak the same language."

"Yes, it is," he retorted evenly. "In my book, it's called lust. I would feel the same way about any ravishing, young woman I found standing naked in a river."

Maura did not know what to say. She could not imagine responding to *any* man the way she had just responded to Luke. This morning, he had not even kissed or caressed her beforehand; he had simply picked her up and joined their bodies with a single, eloquent thrust that spoke volumes about his feelings—feelings which he, now, would not admit. Lust, he called it; such a dirty, crass word for something so beautiful!

"If you're going, why don't you just *go?*" She flung at him. "And don't come back! Not in the spring or at any other time. We're not your responsibility anymore, Mr. Cutter. By now, I'm sure my father and I can find the way back to Bellevue without your help."

"I'm going, Miss Magruder. Just remember to be careful in what you say and do. Guard against the unexpected. Something is brewing here, but I don't yet know what it is. I don't anticipate trouble before spring, but when spring does come, you and your father may well be in danger. I don't advise you to set off for Bellevue on your own."

"Just *go!*" she screamed at him. "And stop giving me your damn advice!"

Turning from him, she splashed through the shallows until the river water was waist deep. Then she stooped down in the water to her shoulders and washed away the odor of their lovemaking. When she had finished and turned around again, Luke was already gone. She saw his tall figure—fully clothed, now—striding through the trees toward the village. The darkest despair she had ever known seared her soul. Why did they keep having the same arguments over and over? Why did their lovemaking drive them further apart, instead of closer together? Why ever had she given herself to Luke Cutter in the first place?

Splashing water on her face, she scrubbed it violently. Then she scrubbed the scars on her forearms, and lastly, she again scrubbed her body. It was no use. All the scrubbing in the world would not rid her of Luke's lingering presence. In possessing her body, he had somehow come to possess her mind, soul, and spirit. If he *did* return in the spring, she would not go with him, no matter what anyone said. She planned to remain among the Pawnee at least until the summer solstice. Only after that would she consider going home to Nate Hibbert. If Nate *never* made her feel the way Luke did, he would be doing her a great favor. Never again did she want to experience love or lust or whatever one called it; it was far too painful. In the future, she would gladly settle for friendship and mutual respect, which Luke Cutter was totally incapable of providing and probably did not even understand. Sobbing soundlessly, Maura left the water and got dressed.

After Luke's departure, life went on. First, there was the corn harvest, then the fall hunt, and finally, the winter. Eben lived in Wetara-sharo's lodge and Maura lived in Lizard Woman's, but saw her father everyday. They always shared the evening meal, either with Wetara-sharo, Pitale-sharo, and Heavy Basket, or with Lizard Woman, She-de-a, and Lizard Woman's husband, Small Hand.

It became a time of conversation about the happenings of the day and a comparison of notes jotted in their journals. Maura did a little sketching on the few precious scraps of foolscap her father had managed to purchase in Bellevue, but mostly she recorded her own observations of Indian life and customs. While Eben concentrated on the lives and habits of the men, Maura focused on the women and children. There was so much to learn—too much, actually—and all of it had to filter through the thorny barrier of language and cultural difference. Maura quickly learned that she ought not to draw inferences without checking them several times. She could not *assume* anything. Often, there was a religious reason behind the way a thing was done, but sometimes there wasn't. She always had to ask.

The discovery of pictographs drove her to near ecstasy. The little stick drawings were one more way to communicate. Cut or burned into the hide coverings of shields, weapon cases, parfleches, and pottery, the drawings were not just decorations. They told stories of things that had happened to the Pawnee. Using sharp, pointed sticks, She-de-a and Lizard Woman made drawings on the dirt floor near the cookfire in Lizard Woman's lodge, thereby demonstrating the facility of both the Pawnee and the Sioux to tell stories by means of the easily understood symbols. Maura was delighted and eagerly studied every drawing she saw in hopes of learning more about the customs, habits, and past experiences of the Indians.

When the snows came, and the winds piles huge drifts around the circumference of Lizard Woman's lodge, Maura spent a good deal of time helping She-de-a complete Pitale-sharo's new clothing. After the deerskins had been rubbed down with buffalo fat, rolled up, and dried, they had shrunk, and She-de-a had stretched them out again. Next, she had rubbed the surface of the skins with a rough-edged stone and had run them back and forth through a loop of sinew attached to a pole. This processing made the skins soft and pliable, after which She-de-a went to the additional trouble of smoking them over a smoldering fire set in a small pit. The smoking turned the skins a warm brown color, and Maura was much impressed by the results. The skins would now remain soft and flexible even after exposure to moisture and rainwater.

Similarly impressed, Lizard Woman produced a substantial quantity of porcupine quills, sorted according to size, and neatly packed into bladder bags. She-de-a selected large quills to embroider onto the parfleche and shirt, and smaller quills for the extra-fine ornamentation of the moccasins. Not happy unless everything was perfect, She-de-a dyed the quills before using them. Thus Maura learned that yellow was produced from the roots of a certain vine, or from early cottonwood buds when available, while black was made by roasting yellow earth and tallow, constantly stirring the mixture, and then adding it to boiling maple bast and leaves. Before doing anything with the quills, the women first had to flatten them. They put the quills into their mouths, sucked on them, and then mashed them down with their fingertips.

Through snow and ice storms, Maura and She-de-a cut, sewed, and embroidered, using awls made from splinters of horn and thread made from sinew. Maura conceived a great respect for Indian women during these long winter work sessions. The women were solely responsible for clothing their families in whatever skins were available, and each item of apparel involved hours and hours of backbreaking, eye-straining labor. As the garments slowly began to take shape, Maura grew every bit as excited as She-de-a. She could not wait to see what they looked like on Pitale-sharo. Only Lizard Woman seemed displeased by the emerging beauty of the garments. Maura was sure her disapproval stemmed from jealousy that a Sioux and a white woman had managed to produce anything so fine.

Finally, the day arrived when the last quill was sewn into place, the last seam inspected, the last fringe applied. Lizard Woman had gone to visit friends, and Maura and She-de-a were alone in the lodge. She-de-a held up the soft, buckskin shirt, leggings, and moccasins, and proudly announced, "They are finished, Moe-ra. Do you think them worthy of a Pawnee chieftain?"

Flooded with admiration, Maura sat back on her haunches. "There's nothing finer in the village, She-de-a. The garments are even softer and nicer than the ones Luke Cutter wears."

She-de-a peeked mischievously from behind the shirt. "And how do you know how soft his garments are?"

Maura felt her cheeks reddening. "I . . . I just know."

She-de-a giggled, then grew serious. "Great Heart's Indian clothing was made by a Blackfoot woman. I can tell by the manner in which the quills are sewn onto the shirt."

Maura skirted the painful subject with another question.

"Each tribe does it differently?"

She-de-a nodded and launched into an explanation of how to determine the tribal identification of a particular piece of embroidery. Maura had no trouble understanding; by now, both she and She-de-a were conversing more or less freely in Pawnee, with only minimal lapses into Sioux, English, or sign language. When the little Sioux had finished, Maura introduced another topic—one far more important than the identity of Luke's female friend.

"When are you going to give Pitale-sharo your gift?"

A frown marred She-de-a's lovely face. "I do not know. I should like to give it to him when he is alone—away from prying eyes. But I never see him alone. When I do see him, we never speak. He does not yet know that I have mastered his language."

"I have an idea. Why don't you give it to him right now, here in Lizard Woman's lodge, while everyone is gone for the afternoon?"

"How would I get him to come here?" She-de-a wailed. "I dare not go to his lodge and invite him. That would be considered bold and ill-mannered."

"*I'll* go and invite him," Maura impulsively volunteered. "I was going to visit my father this afternoon, anyway. While I'm there, I'll think of some reason to persuade Pitale-sharo to come here—I know! I'll tell him Small Hand is looking for him. When he comes and finds you alone, all you have to do is tell him I was mistaken, give him your gift, and wait for his reaction. I just know he'll love the new garments!"

"Do you really think so?" She-de-a's brown eyes were shining. "Oh, I must wash my face and re-braid my hair, first. How I wish I myself had a new garment to wear!"

Setting down the clothing, She-de-a jumped up and began straightening the lodge, smoothing down her doeskin, and fussing with her hair—all at the same time. "Slow down!" Maura cautioned, laughing at her friend's frantic preparations. "There's no need to rush. I'll walk slowly to Wetara-sharo's lodge."

Taking her time, Maura fetched her warm, buffalo cape and wrapped it around herself, preparatory to facing the snow and howling wind. She pulled it snugly around her ears. Without its warmth and weight she would have frozen to death long ago. She walked slowly through the dark, tunnel-like entranceway to the lodge and paused before stepping outside. The cold and wind eddied around the skin curtain, and Maura mentally prepared herself for the blast awaiting her outside the warm lodge.

When she stepped outside, the wind nearly knocked her down. She had to examine her surroundings carefully. Everytime she left the warmth and security of the lodge, she found a new world awaiting her; the wind carved the snow drifts into constantly changing shapes. It bullied her as she hurried along, head down against the gale, toward Wetara-sharo's lodge. Once there, she darted inside the entranceway and paused to catch her breath and allow her eyes to adjust to the gloom after the blinding whiteness.

She heard voices—her father's and Wetara-sharo's—and stumbled through the darkness toward the sound. When she came into the spacious interior, she saw her father and the old chief engaged in animated conversation. Eben, too, had made great progress in conquering the language. He spent part of everyday quizzing Wetara-sharo about the days before the coming of the White-Eyes to the Plains. The topic fascinated the old chief as much as it did her father; the two often spent hours together, hardly noticing who came or went from the lodge.

In a corner, Pitale-sharo sat fashioning arrowheads, half listening, half lost in his own daydreams. He looked up when Maura entered, but did not otherwise acknowledge her. Eben only nodded in her direction; as was his custom, Wetara-sharo completely ignored her.

Good, Maura thought, they are all preoccupied.

Brushing snow from her cape, she crossed the lodge and knelt down beside Pitale-sharo. "Pitale-sharo, you must come at once to Lizard Woman's lodge," she said quietly but urgently.

Pitale-sharo shot her a startled glance. "Why?" he inquired coolly. He resented taking orders from women, especially from her.

"Small Hand wishes to see you. He would have come himself, but he . . . he is ill," Maura lied, hoping She-de-a could explain away these falsehoods.

With one hand, Pitale-sharo held an arrowhead steady on a flat board, while with the other, using a tool made of stone, he carefully chipped away a sliver of flint. Never having witnessed the procedure for making arrowheads, Maura watched with interest.

"If Small Hand is ill, why does he not call for the shaman or Heavy Basket? They will know better than I how to make him well again."

"*You* are the one he wants to see," Maura insisted. "Please . . . it will not take long." She kept her voice low so as not to disturb her father or Wetara-sharo.

Pitale-sharo chipped away two more splinters of flint before he sighed and set down his tools. "I suppose if I do not come you will only sit there the rest of the afternoon watching me, and the work will be spoiled, anyway."

"Small Hand told me I must do whatever was necessary to convince you to come." Maura smiled inwardly, careful not to betray her amusement which she knew would only fuel the young chieftain's anger.

"Wait until I get my robe," he said resignedly.

A few moments later, Pitale-sharo was enroute to Lizard Woman's lodge. When they came to the entranceway, Maura turned to him. "You go ahead inside. Small Hand awaits you within. I'm going back to visit with my father."

Grunting his irritation, Pitale-sharo disappeared behind the skin door. Maura waited several seconds. When she was certain Pitale-sharo must have passed through the tunnel into the main room of the lodge, she ducked in the dark passageway and tiptoed along its length. Having spent so many months helping to make the surprise gift, Maura fully intended to witness Pitale-sharo's reaction. The first thing she heard was Pitale-sharo asking where Small Hand was.

"I do not know," came She-de-a's soft, parplexed reply. "He left here this morning and has not returned."

"Is this a trick?" Pitale-sharo demanded angrily. "The White-Eyes woman said he was ill and wished to see me."

"That . . . that was just an excuse to get you here," She-de-a admitted in a trembling voice.

Expecting Pitale-sharo to come stalking through the entrance tunnel at any moment, Maura flattened herself against the earth wall. There was a moment of tense silence, and then Pitale-sharo said gently, "I see that you have learned to speak Pawnee at long last."

"Yes . . . I . . . I wanted to please you, to make you smile at me . . . and I . . . I have also made you a gift."

Another brief silence followed. Maura could not resist going to the very end of the tunnel and turning back a corner of the skin concealing the main room. She had an excellent view; Pitale-sharo stood facing She-de-a, who was holding up the new shirt she had made for him. The girl's face glowed with love, longing, and fear of rejection. A tiny piece of her heart had gone into each stitch of the shirt. If Pitale-sharo found her efforts wanting, he would be trampling her fondest hopes.

"It . . . it is unworthy of you," She-de-a said, crumpling the shirt in her hands and hiding it behind her back. "I should not have had you come here. I should never have made these things."

"Wait a minute . . . let me see it." Advancing toward the cowering girl, Pitale-sharo held out his hand. "Give it to me."

She-de-a's eyes filled with tears. She shook her head. "No . . . the work isn't good enough for a Pawnee chieftain."

Behind She-de-a, laid out on the floor mats, were the leggings, moccasins, and perfleche. Spotting them, Pitale-sharo reached down and picked up the moccasins. Holding them awkwardly, he ran his hands over them, fingering the quillwork and the leather fringe.

"I've never seen work as fine as this. No moccasins I have ever owned are as soft as these—not even the ones my own mother made for me."

"Do you really think so?" She-de-a's eyes shone. "My mother taught me. She was the best in our tribe. People used to come to her and offer all sorts of presents if she would just sew them a pair of moccasins like these."

"I shall treasure them always," Pitale-sharo whispered. He moved closer to She-de-a and held out his hand. "Now, let me see the shirt."

As She-de-a surrendered the shirt, her face beamed with radiance. "I hope it fits. I hope you like the colors."

Pitale-sharo set down the moccasins and held up the shirt, openly admiring the perfection of the embroidery. Shrugging out of his buffalo robe, he let it fall to the mats while he measured the shirt against his wide chest. "It will fit perfectly. How did you manage it?"

She-de-a lowered her eyes. "I have watched you many times," she murmured, blushing. "I had only to measure the skins against your image in my mind, and I knew how big to make the shirt."

"She-de-a . . . ," Pitale-sharo lowered the shirt and reached for the girl. She came shyly but willingly into his arms. "Your gift pleases me very much. Indeed, it shames me, for I have not treated you with the kindness you deserve."

"It does not matter!" She-de-a objected, raising her velvet-brown eyes to his. "I understand. I am Sioux—your

297

enemy. It is right that I must prove my worthiness."

"She-de-a, no . . . you do not understand."

Pitale-sharo pulled the girl close, wrapped his arms around her, and rested his chin on her hair. His eyes were closed, his features contorted into a mask of sorrow and regret. "If I could," he said, "I would marry you this very day and spend my life sheltering and protecting you."

"I know why you cannot." She-de-a burrowed closer to him, her slender arms encircling his waist. "It is Heavy Basket. You must marry her. She is your grandfather's choice, and the tribe expects it."

"You know nothing, Little One."

An agonized groan burst from Pitale-sharo. He clasped the girl to him, as if he could possess her with a single embrace. Maura dropped the skin covering, suddenly ashamed to be eavesdropping on such an intimate scene. Whatever the problem, they would have to work it out between themselves. She had done all she could to bring the two young lovers together. Tiptoing back down the tunnel, Maura headed toward Wetara-sharo's lodge and the visit with her father.

Chapter Twenty-two

On another cold afternoon two days later, Maura and She-de-a were once again alone in Lizard Woman's lodge. This time, they were working on a shirt for Small Hand. Lizard Woman had asked She-de-a to embroider it with quills. Maura was flattening the quills, while She-de-a sat hunched over the shirt, deciding on a design. The atmosphere was heavy with disappointment, devoid of the happy anticipation characterizing earlier work sessions.

According to She-de-a, nothing much had happened after Maura left She-de-a and Pitale-sharo alone in the lodge. Shortly thereafter, Pitale-sharo had also left, taking the new clothing with him. He had made no commitments, nor had he given any explanations or encouragement. He had simply held her a few moments and then departed without another word. Neither Maura nor She-de-a had seen him since. She-de-a was deeply depressed, wondering what more she could do to win the favor of Pitale-sharo and his people. Maura thought the young chief's behavior was very strange and coldhearted. Having experienced unrequited love herself, she felt great sympathy for her friend. Why were men so difficult to understand, so callous of a woman's feelings?

Hearing a sound in the entranceway, Maura glanced up in time to catch She-de-a's expression of wistfulness and hope as she, too, waited to see who was entering. When Heavy Basket waddled into the main room, She-de-a's eyes registered alarm. The big squaw looked angry, her mouth set in a grim line, her eyes flashing contempt. Stomping snow from her mocassins, Heavy Basket strode toward them, stopping just short of She-de-a. From beneath her buffalo robe, she withdrew a wad of rolled up buckskins and flung them on the floor mats in front of the girl.

"Did you think these poorly made garments would please a Pawnee chieftain? Did you think I would not discover what you are up to?" Heavy Basket kicked the clothes and sent them flying. "Even should you entice him into marriage, I will win him in the end. One day you will learn the truth of these words. While you are suffering, I shall laugh at you."

She spat at She-de-a, and a wad of spittle landed on the girl's smooth cheek. She-de-a's eyes widened, and she leaned back, gaping in horrified astonishment. "That is what I think of you, little Sioux bitch!" Heavy Basket shrieked. "That is what we all think of you! Hereafter, do not think to bribe the great Pitale-sharo with crude examples of inferior Sioux stitchery. Your fate is already decided. None can change it—not even Pitale-sharo himself!"

As Heavy Basket turned and stomped out of the lodge, Maura quickly retrieved the fallen garments and unrolled them, only to discover that the shirt, leggings, and parfleche had been slashed to pieces with a knife or some other sharp object.

"What did she mean?" She-de-a sobbed, bending over and clasping her arms around herself in an agony of despair. "What are they going to do to me?"

Maura hurried to the girl, wiped the spittle from her cheek, and tenderly embraced her. "I don't know, my dear—oh, do not cry so! Surely, she is just mean and jealous. No one else has seen fit to threaten you. In any case, Pitale-sharo will not allow you to be harmed."

She-de-a stopped sobbing long enough to gather the slashed clothing into her arms. "Where are the moccasins? I do not see the moccasins."

Together, they searched the ruined items, but the moccasins were not there. Later that night, Maura went to visit her father in Wetara-sharo's lodge. Walking in, she spotted Pitale-sharo's moccasins; he was wearing them. The sight of the exquisitely made footgear on the young chief's feet made her so happy that she dashed back to Lizard Woman's lodge to tell She-de-a, who was lying on a sleeping platform and staring listlessly into space.

Lizard Woman and Small Hand looked up questioningly from their evening meal, but Maura went hurriedly to She-de-a and said in a low voice, "Don't worry anymore, She-de-a! Don't be afraid of that jealous old hag, Heavy Basket! She could not destroy the moccasins because they are safely on Pitale-sharo's feet . . . and why would he be wearing them if he didn't care for you?"

A hesitant smile spread across the girl's sad features. "Do you really think he cares for me?"

"If it isn't love he feels for you, it's something very close," Maura assured her. Unwittingly, she remembered her own problems with Luke. Maybe it was only lust that Pitale-sharo felt for She-de-a—but whatever it was, it should be enough to ensure the girl's safety among the Pawnee.

"I still have until summer to win him," She-de-a remembered, a fact she had apparently forgotten during the past several hours. "And somehow, before then, I will find a way to make him love me."

If such a thing is possible, Maura thought, hoping it was true but doubting it.

Gradually, the dark, short days of winter lengthened, challenging the cold and wind. Then, one sunny morning, Maura stepped outside the lodge and discovered icicles dripping from the roof. A warm breeze kissed her cheek, and the air smelled fresh and spring-like. Despite her determination to spend as little time as possible thinking about Luke, Maura could not keep from walking through the village and out onto the slushy plain, where she had a clear view of the eastern horizon.

When Luke returned he would come from the east. The mere thought of seeing him again caused a wild fluttering in her breast, as if a thousand moths were trapped inside, trying to get out. She told herself that she did not want to see him, did not want to face the confrontation over whether they would really have to leave the village. But in her heart, she knew she was aching for the sight and sound of him. Her body yearned for the *feel* of him. The searing memory of their lovemaking haunted her; all that had been necessary for her to abandon decency and propriety was for him to look at her with his penetrating gray eyes, and she had shamelessly embraced him and eagerly joined her body with his.

The power he had over her was unfair. Like She-de-a, she was incapable of denying her attraction to a man who, for obscure, ridiculous reasons of his own, was stubbornly resisting her. Maura stood and gazed at the eastern horizon for a long time, then dispiritedly went looking for her father. She found him on the other side of the village, among the horses, brushing crusted mud and dirt out of Greedy's long-haired winter coat. He was using a brush made of porcupine bristles tied to a stick with rawhide thongs, the same sort of brush favored by Lizard Woman and She-de-a for their own hair.

"I hope you aren't doing that in order to prepare for a journey," Maura said by way of greeting him.

Winter-pale but spry and hearty even after the hard winter, he turned and grinned. "As a matter of fact, I am. Pitale-sharo is going to visit one of the Pawnee villages on the Platte. I have been invited to accompany him."

302

"Wonderful!" Maura responded, brightening. "Then I presume nothing has been said about our having to leave the village soon."

"No, nothing has been said yet." Eben stopped brushing long enough to pluck several burrs from Greedy's tangled black mane. "I keep telling the old chief that I am particularly anxious to attend the summer buffalo hunt, as you did last year, to get a male point of view. He never says I can't, so I'm hoping he's forgotten we were only invited to spend the winter."

"When Luke returns, he'll remember. And so will Bonson-gee."

Eben shot her a wry look. "You don't have much faith in your father's charm, do you, my dear?"

"Your charm? Well, I know it persuades wealthy members of the Anthropological Society to help underwrite your expeditions, but I don't know if it works as well on Indians."

"I think it does. Wetara-sharo and I have become good friends. After all, we're two old men who like nothing better than to philosophize about life. I've been acquainting him with Aristotle and Homer, and he thinks the Greeks and the Pawnee have much in common."

Maura smiled. "Perhaps they do. Luke has many times pointed out to me that the Indians are a dying civilization. The Greeks are already dead, so maybe the similarity lies in an inability to survive."

"I hope not." Suddenly serious, Eben brushed so vigorously at Greedy's tail that the leggy bay cocked a hind leg in warning. "Whoa, boy. Stand still. I want you to look good when we go for our visit."

"How long will you be gone?" Maura asked.

"I've no idea. We're going to travel down the Loup to its juncture with the Platte, and then up the Platte 'til we get to the other villages. There's more than one. Pitale-sharo wants to see how they wintered and catch up on the latest tribal news. Maybe Mr. Cutter will come while we're gone and just turn around and go back again. I don't guess that I have to worry about you going back to Bellevue without me."

Eben glanced over his shoulder at Maura. At the mention of Luke—and the possibility of traveling alone with him—she blushed furiously. "Hardly, Father. You know I want to stay here at least through the early part of summer. Pitale-sharo's marriage is supposed to take place during the summer solstice. I'm hoping She-de-a will win him yet."

"Now, Maura, keep out of the Pawnee's domestic affairs." Eben paused and pointed the brush at her. "The surest way to induce Wetara-sharo to send us packing is for you to interfere with whatever plans he has for his grandson. We *observe;* we do *not* interfere. Remember that, and maybe we'll be invited to stay."

"Yes, Father," Maura said quiescently, though inwardly, she was rebelling.

They talked a bit longer about the weather and other inconsequential topics. Then Maura kissed him good-bye and returned to the lodge to see what She-de-a was up to that day.

The warm spell continued, melting the snow and ice, and Maura began to feel that any day now she would suddenly see Luke riding into the village. She hoped he would come while her father was gone. One week passed, then two. One night there was sleet and a howling wind, but the next day, the sun shone, warmer than ever, and tiny buds erupted on the cottonwoods by the river.

Eben and Pitale-sharo had been gone over three weeks when Luke finally rode into the village. Maura was brushing her little mare, Cinnamon, pulling out handfuls of thick brown hair. She caught a glimpse of chestnut from the corner of her eye and knew without looking that Luke had come, at long last.

Pretending not to see him, she carried on a conversation with the mare instead. "There, now, doesn't that feel better? Soon, all this ugly, heavy hair will be completely gone. Your new coat will be so pretty. . . ."

"Good afternoon, Miss Magruder. You're looking well, I see — a bit thinner, but then everyone looks thinner after a long winter."

Maura hotly blushed. She shivered with cold, then grew hot again. Already, he was noticing her body. To give herself time to think, she kept brushing as if she had not heard him. When she finally finished the job, she looked up to see Luke laughing at her — silently, but laughing just the same — as if he *knew* just how desperately she was trying to get a grip on herself.

"Trying hard to ignore me, aren't you, Miss Magruder? Sorry, but it won't work. I'm actually here, and I expect you know why I've come."

Yes, you're here, Maura thought, taking in the tall, lean figure, the icy, gray eyes, the dark, windblown hair. He was wearing the same carefully made buckskins with the quill design on the yoke, and no coat or cape; chest hair protruded from the carelessly laced front neck-opening. As he sat at ease on Captain, he was, in every respect, noticeably masculine, exuding the peculiar aura of poise, grace, strength, and danger that made her shiver every time she saw him.

"You could have saved yourself the trip, Mr. Cutter. My father and I aren't going back with you. My father isn't even here. He and Pitale-sharo left almost a month ago to visit some of the other Pawnee villages."

"Which bands? The *Chau-i*, *Kit-ke-hahki*, or the *Pita-hau-erat?*"

"I . . . I don't know. Whichever ones are living on the Platte." Maura realized only then that she had never thought to ask. She knew that the Loup River Pawnee were known as the Skidis, but she had not as yet sorted

305

out the other tribes or bands. The Pawnee confederation sprawled all over the Nebraska Territory and included tribes living on three different rivers.

"Never mind. Wetara-sharo or Bon-son-gee will know." A worried frown crossed Luke's handsome face. Distracted, he glanced toward the village.

"What is it?" Maura asked, her instincts humming. "What's wrong?"

Luke's eyes came back to her, skewering her as they always did. "I didn't come here just to fetch you and your father back to Bellevue," he quietly informed her, all trace of mockery gone. "The weather's still too chancy for that. I only risked the spring ice storms because I have bad news for Pitale-sharo."

"What news?" Maura inquired breathlessly.

The old, familiar scowl twisted Luke's handsome features. "Major Dougherty has recently received word that Shon-ka's on the warpath. And the Skidi Pawnee are the ones he's mad at."

"But why? How does he even know for certain that I'm here?" Maura burst out, certain *she* was the reason for the Sioux's anger at the Skidis.

"It has nothing to do with you. I doubt Shon-ka's had much time to think about you. Apparently, after we escaped and ran off his horses, he went home to nurse his injured pride. He walked right into the middle of a smallpox epidemic. The pox raged among the Sioux villages all last August and continued through the fall. The snows ended it, but hundreds still died. The Sioux couldn't hunt or follow the buffalo or store meat for the winter. During the heavy snows, many died from hunger."

"How awful!" Maura exclaimed, genuinely horrified. She tried to imagine the devastation and hardship the Sioux must have suffered. Tears welled in her eyes; She-de-a had more than once described how terrible an outbreak of smallpox could be in a village.

306

"Shon-ka is blaming the Skidis," Luke said matter-of-factly.

"The Skidis! But how can he? If anything it's the whites he should blame! Probably, white traders are responsible. . . ."

"You know that, and I know that. Shon-ka probably also knows it. But if he attacks the whites, he can't trade furs with them anymore. He'll make too many enemies and provoke retaliation from soldiers at the nearest forts. Apparently, he's decided it would be much better to wreak revenge on his *old* enemies, the Skidi Pawnee. It's a pack of lies, of course, but he's been telling any able-bodied Indian who will listen that the Skidis — Pitale-sharo, in particular — are in league with the evil White-Eyes who first sold tainted blankets to the Sioux. He claims Pitale-sharo put the traders up to it, hoping to gain vengeance for the death of his father, Massish-sharo."

"Good lord! And the Indians believe this nonsense?"

"Enough of them believe it for Shon-ka to have managed to assemble a good-sized army to wipe out this village. Major Dougherty and I have been doing such a good job of keeping the peace these past few years that there haven't been any opportunities for the young-bloods to earn coups, take scalps, or steal horses. That also has something to do with Shon-ka's success; the young-bloods are spoiling for a chance to show how courageous they are, and Shon-ka has given it to them."

"I can't believe this! It's all so . . . so—"

"*Primitive* and *violent*, Miss Magruder? Are those the words you're searching for? Well, what did you expect? I've been telling you all along that Indians aren't as gentle and noble as you and your father make them out to be. But I expect you still won't believe me until you see it with your own eyes."

"But what can we do to stop such an attack? Surely, Major Dougherty is—"

"Is doing everything he can to counteract Shon-ka's lies. Unfortunately, he's making little headway. That's why he sent me — to warn Pitale-sharo and help him prepare for an attack. If I can get you and your father out of here ahead of time, I will."

"You think we would just turn tail and run when death and destruction threaten our friends?" Maura demanded, incensed.

"What are your plans, Miss Magruder? Will you *shoot* the man you let kiss and paw you?"

"Yes!" Maura shouted. "Thanks to you, I *have* learned a thing or two about firing a rifle. When and if Shon-ka does show up, I'll be only too happy to blister his backside if I can hit it!"

"Blister his backside?" Luke's raised eyebrows conveyed his scorn. "More likely you'll just load the damn thing wrong and have it blow up in your face."

"I'll *practice* ahead of time!"

Luke sighed wearily. "You'd better practice. I doubt there's going to *be* time to get you someplace safe — especially if your father and Pitale-sharo aren't even here. For now, why don't you just go back to brushing your horse? I can't waste any more time sparring with you; I've got to see Wetara-sharo and give him the bad news."

"Gladly," Maura snapped, spinning and employing the brush with great vigor to her startled mare. Cinnamon had stood all this time with her head down, hopefully nosing the earth for the first blades of grass. Frightened by the unexpected attack, she danced in circles around Maura.

Maura did not even watch as Luke rode toward the village. Ten minutes of conversation with him had made her so angry she could scarcely see straight. Cinnamon's spooked behavior further enraged her. Maura smacked the mare *hard*, and she bolted, galloping for the open plain.

Knowing the cost of that single moment of impatience,

Maura groaned. It would take hours, if not days, to convince Cinnamon to trust her again and stand still for grooming—and all because of Luke Cutter. He had not been back for an hour, but already he had destroyed her contentment and peace of mind.

Chapter Twenty-three

"This very day I will send someone to inform Pitale-sharo," Wetara-sharo said when he heard Luke's news. "In the meantime, we prepare for battle. Bon-son-gee will act as chief."

"Bon-son-gee?" Luke was well aware of how Pitale-sharo would feel about having his rival lead the tribe during this time of crisis.

"I am too old and tired to direct the preparations, and you are not Pawnee," Wetara-sharo pointed out. "In the absence of my grandson, Bon-son-gee is the best we have."

The old chief coughed and moved closer to the tiny fire smoldering in the center of the lodge. The day was not cold, yet Wetara-sharo hovered near the fire, his deep, racking cough warning that he might not live to see another winter.

"If your mind is set on Bon-son-gee, then will you at least assign some men to me? I have a few ideas for mounting a defense against such a large army, but I need help in carrying them out."

Wetara-sharo's sunken eyes sought Luke's face. Sadly, he shook his head. "It will be for Bon-son-gee to say if you may have braves to help you. Even then, the braves may refuse. Though you are Pitale-sharo's friend, you are still a White-Eyes. They will not want to follow your orders."

"Then assign me some squaws. They can do the work as well as mighty warriors; perhaps, they can even do it better."

Wetara-sharo grinned, flashing broken teeth in the same sly smile Luke remembered from years gone by. Luke's jibe amused him. "I shall ask Heavy Basket to assist you. But only until the battle begins. As soon as the Sioux are spotted, all the women and children must flee to safety. That is our way. Usually they hide in the rocky clefts of the big bluff overlooking the village."

"That will suit me fine. If everything is set up properly, I won't need them during the battle itself."

"Good." Wetara-sharo tugged his buffalo robe more closely around his thin, bony shoulders. "Go now, and send Bon-son-gee to me. From what you have told me, I think it would be wise to begin preparations at once."

Luke nodded and exited the lodge. His head throbbed with thoughts of all that must be done. Coming out of the lodge, he almost ran into Heavy Basket. He delegated the task of finding Bon-son-gee to her, and after that, went for a long walk around the village, studying it from every angle. There were only two directions from which an attack could come—from the east and from the north. Nestled between the river and the high, rocky bluff, the earth lodges were shielded on the remaining two sides, unless the attackers somehow came across the river or over the bluff itself.

Luke decided to concentrate his efforts on protecting the most exposed sides, though he would, for the sake of prudence, plant a few gourd bombs at the foot of the bluff and near the river's edge. If attack came from more than one quarter, he would be hard put to cover the entire area. He pondered the dilemma and finally concluded that if time permitted, he would assign the squaws and children to digging trenches at intervals around the entire village. With the dirt from the diggings, they could make ram-

311

parts to protect the braves as they fired rifles, bows, and arrows. The trenches themselves could be hidden beneath mats and scrub grass, so that when the Sioux galloped toward the village, their horses would fall into them, throwing the Indians. Remembering his own fall when his horse had stepped in a prairie dog hole, Luke realized it would be a good idea to pepper the nearby plain with small, deep holes which afterwards could be filled in again.

He spent most of the afternoon deciding where to place his gourd bombs to achieve the maximum effect in frightening and wounding the attackers. The only problem he could foresee with using bombs again was that, this time, Shon-ka would not be surprised. He might even have warned his comrades to expect the unexpected. Luke wished he had the fireworks he and Major Dougherty had ordered. A partial shipment of them were due to arrive in Bellevue via the first steamship of the season on the Missouri River. The fireworks would then be stored where only Luke and the major knew of their existence.

None of the Indians had ever witnessed anything resembling a pyrotechnical display—unless it was an electrical storm over the Plains. It was for just such an occasion as this that Luke had hoped to first employ fireworks. Shon-ka and his braves had been terrified by the little homemade bombs; Luke guessed they would be stunned speechless by the sight of rockets and pinwheels exploding overhead in a black, pre-dawn sky, the usual hour of Indian attacks. Their horses would not stop running until they got back to wherever they had come from.

But it was no use wishing for what he did not have. His primitive gourd bombs would, once again, have to do the trick. If they did not, then the Skidi Pawnee were as good as dead. While the whites in Bellevue gloated over the amusing prospect of Indians killing Indians—except for Major Dougherty, of course, who had thus far been unable to muster any support whatsoever to stop the potential slaughter—Shon-ka's army would destroy them.

Luke was overwhelmingly disappointed in his own race. After this was over, assuming he lived through it, he might just move on—go farther west, maybe to California or up into Canada. He was weary of the whole mess. Before things improved, they would only get worse. The prevailing white sentiment was that the best thing that could happen would be for the Indians to kill each other. Few fur traders felt pangs of conscience about the smallpox epidemic; no one but Luke and the major mourned all those needless deaths. As one man had put it, "The Indians're just a goddamn nuisance. Without them t' dispute us, we could move in and help ourselves t' all the damn furs 'n land we wanted."

The urge to escape and find a better life grew stronger in Luke every day. Still, he could not picture himself ever returning to the east. If he were to leave, he would follow the sun as it tracked its way across the Nebraska sky, and hopefully, one day he would come to a less violent land. Despite what he had told Maura, he wondered why he should stay and witness the destruction of the Indian in the Land of the Shallow Rivers. He did not want to be a part of it, and yet he would be, if he remained, whether he wanted to or not. When red man and white finally started fighting over the land itself, he would have to side with the whites—might even be forced to fight his own blood brother, Pitale-sharo.

Sunk in sorrow and self-pity, Luke finally went looking for Heavy Basket to tell her what he wanted the women to do. He found her in Wetara-sharo's lodge, listening to Bon-son-gee make plans with the old chief. To Luke's disgust, Bon-son-gee's plans consisted of holding a tribal feast, wherein the warriors would paint themselves, dance around the fire, and relive past glories in preparation for meeting their enemies anew on the field of battle.

Luke took Heavy Basket aside and explained about the

313

trenches around the village and the deep holes he wanted dug on the nearby prairie. The squaw's eyes lit at the possibility of watching Sioux horses stumble and throw their riders. Heavy Basket promised to organize the whole thing. But when he also asked her to gather gourds from among the women, she frowned and stared at him as if he had suddenly started foaming at the mouth.

"For what purpose?" she demanded. When he tried to explain about the bombs he intended to make with gunpowder, she simply frowned all the harder.

Such a thing was beyond her powers of imagination. She said it would be a waste of perfectly good gourds that could otherwise be used for more practical things, such as the fashioning of drinking containers, rattles, and ladles. Luke managed to persuade her to gather a small number for his use, but he knew he would get no help in making the bombs themselves. Perhaps Maura could be entrusted with some of the tricky, dangerous work—that is, if she could spare time from her target practice. With all he had to do, he would not be able to get her out of the village, anyway.

In the days that followed, Luke worked feverishly from dawn until dusk, and found himself wishing that Eben and Pitale-sharo would hurry and return to the village. He needed help in digging trenches; it was difficult, demanding work ill-suited to the few women who finally consented to cooperate. Despite Heavy Basket's enthusiasm, the big squaw was unable to obtain many workers. Luke realized that the women had other vital concerns. Most were busy burying and hiding precious stores of food and household goods—but he could not help being impatient with them for failing to see the great potential of the trenches.

Most of the squaws and children saw trench-digging as a slight to their male relatives, whose job it was to protect them from raids by their enemies. Again and again, Luke had to remind himself that the Pawnee were an agricultural people with more placid natures than most of the Plains tribes. The women were perfectly willing to haul supplies up to the top of the steep, rocky bluff, in case the battle proved to be a long, drawn out affair, and to dig storage pits, concoct war paint, and do other attack-related tasks, but they were *not* willing to shame their men by behaving as if they did not trust them to overcome the Sioux by sheer bravery and courage alone.

When Bon-son-gee learned of Luke's efforts, he and other respected warriors were openly scornful of what they regarded as unorthodox and cowardly methods to trick and defeat the Sioux. They preferred to spend their time cleaning and repairing weapons, fashioning shields, and boosting their confidence by bragging of past victories. Occasionally they staged mock battles among themselves, and they passed many hours in wrestling and hand-to-hand combat in order to toughen their bodies for the real thing. Had Pitale-sharo been in the village, Luke knew that his friend would not have allowed Bon-son-gee's arrogance and conceit to defeat such a good idea as the trenches, but as it was, Luke wound up digging most of them by himself.

Only three people gave him any real, substantial help: Heavy Basket, She-de-a, and Maura. Hampered by the lack of a decent spade in the entire village, Luke first had to break up the hard, unyielding ground with a digging stick, and then employ the thigh bone of a buffalo to scrape the loosened dirt aside. The three women then scooped the soil into baskets and carried it away. Heavy Basket actually seemed to enjoy the hard labor—or perhaps she just enjoyed proving who among the three females was the strongest. Her baskets of dirt were always heaped the highest. As she trudged back and forth with the heavy loads, she kept up a constant stream of insults directed at the Sioux in general and She-de-a, in particular.

Though She-de-a kept pace, basket for basket, with Maura, Heavy Basket accused her of being the weakest and laziest of females. Luke grew weary of hearing the insults, but nothing he said seemed to penetrate Heavy Basket's consciousness.

"See how the little Sioux allows even a white woman to outwork her," Heavy Basket would announce to anyone within hearing distance.

All the while the trenches were being dug, the big squaw never seemed to recognize or take into account She-de-a's willingness to work against the best interests of her own tribe. If the trenches did what they were supposed to, it would be Sioux who suffered, yet She-de-a seemed willing to work until she dropped of exhaustion. Sometimes, Luke noticed, it was Maura and Heavy Basket who stopped to catch their breaths, not She-de-a. Ignoring Heavy Basket's taunts, the girl doggedly kept working, as if by labor alone she could prove to everyone where her loyalties lay.

At night, while Heavy Basket caught up on domestic duties, Maura and She-de-a helped Luke fashion his bombs. The women braided the grass fuses, while Luke measured and poured the ingredients, varying the amounts as he had done before, in order to produce different effects. He and Maura spoke little; there didn't seem to be much to say. He wanted to thank her for helping him and for working so hard, without complaint. He also wanted to tell her how much he admired her stamina and perseverance, but the words stuck in his throat. To compliment her in any way might give her the idea that he had changed his mind about not wanting her to be here in the first place.

But even though he rarely spoke to her, Luke was always conscious of Maura's presence. Sometimes he would look up, notice the way the sunlight or firelight was glinting in her blond hair, and his breath would catch in his throat. Maura was losing weight; everyday, she looked thinner. Often, she had bluish smudges under her eyes from exhaustion. Still, her beauty did not diminish. If anything, as her delicate bone structure became more apparent, she radiated an ethereal quality. Measured against the darkness of the Indian women, Maura's fairness made her appear almost angelic. Her air of fragility caused a tightness in Luke's chest, as if a band of iron had clamped itself around him and was slowly, inexorably squeezing him to death.

It would be so easy for her to die; indeed, it seemed a miracle she had survived the winter and living among the Indians for as long as she had. Luke could not look at her without thinking that she ought to be wearing a gauzy, white dress and snipping roses in an English garden, instead of hauling huge basket-loads of dirt or twisting strands of grass into bomb wicks. At night, rampant desire kept him from badly needed sleep. Even during the day, he had to resist the impulse to drag her off somewhere so they could be alone.

In her eyes, he often saw hurt and bewilderment. Knowing he could have her if he really wanted her only made him feel all the more miserable and guilty in her company. He *did* want her, but seeing her work like a drudge day after day only served to remind him that this sort of life would eventually destroy her. If they married, his need for wide open spaces, the vast blue sky overhead, and the challenges of living in a harsh, inhospitable land would destroy her.

"Luke," she said one day while they were digging little holes in the prairie. "Do you really think all this work will help? How big is the Sioux army going to be?"

He paused in digging to look at her. She-de-a and Heavy Basket were out of hearing, each of them employing their own digging sticks to tunnel the surface of the plain with small holes just big enough to trip an unwary horse.

"I wouldn't be surprised if three or four times the number of warriors in this village show up," he said.

"Goodness! Then we had better dig faster."

For several moments, she stabbed at the hard earth with her digging stick. Watching her, Luke was overcome with fear for her safety. He ought to have taken her back to Bellevue and left the Pawnee to their own devices.

"Maura," he said, dropping his own stick and crossing to her. Grabbing her wrist, he stopped the stabbing motion. Her eyes locked with his. Avoiding her questioning look, he studied the tender white skin stretched over the high, pale cheek bones. "Promise me that when the Sioux come, you'll stay with Heavy Basket up on the bluff. She's a capable woman; she'll look after you."

A crimson stain spread across the white skin. "I'll promise no such thing! *I* am a capable woman, too, and I don't intend to run off and leave you to set off those bombs by yourself."

Startled, Luke stepped backward. "I don't need you to help me set off the bombs," he protested, though it suddenly occurred to him that her help was *exactly* what he needed.

"Yes, you do. You can't be everywhere at once, Luke. If some Indian starts grappling with you, there will be no one to set off the bombs. The Pawnee don't really understand them."

"And you do?" he queried mockingly.

"Of course I do! By now, I could make them myself. I can slip about the village as easily as you and light them. I can probably do it better. Even if the Sioux should spot me, they'd never expect a white woman to be doing anything that might actually harm them. In that, they are probably as conceited as you and Bon-son-gee."

"I won't have you in the thick of the fighting!" Luke roared. "I won't have you *any*where where Shon-ka can see you!"

"I don't have to obey *you!*" Maura shot back. "I can be anywhere I damn well want to be!"

"I'll tie you hand and foot and carry you up the bluff myself! You *won't* stay down in the village."

Maura glared at him, but when she answered, her voice was soft and chillingly determined, causing hairs to prickle on the back of his neck.

"Luke Cutter, since the day we met, you've been underestimating me. I've been taking it as long as I care to. By now, I should think you would have learned something—that I'm much stronger and more competent than I look. I never took you for a stupid man, but it would seem I've been *over*estimating your intelligence. Don't you *ever* dare threaten me again, or I promise you, one night while you're sleeping, I'll creep up on you and . . . and *cut off* those family jewels you're so damn proud of! When the basic difference between us no longer exists, we'll just *see* how arrogant you are!"

Shock rendered Luke momentarily incapable of speech. He could not believe that Maura had just said such a thing, had actually threatened to *geld* him. Snatching the digging stick from her hand, he turned, drew back his arm, and threw the stick like a spear. It arced high into the air—almost flying out of sight. When it fell to earth it pierced the hard, dry ground with a thwanging sound and then split down the middle from the impact.

Maura stared at the broken tool for several moments, gave him a cool, measured look, and stalked away without another word. Thinking their work must be finished, Heavy Basket and She-de-a soon joined her, and the three women headed back toward the village, leaving Luke alone on the plain beneath a gray, glowering sky.

Chapter Twenty-four

On the day Eben and Pitale-sharo returned to the village, Maura was helping Lizard Woman strip the last of the valuables from the lodge. "Now we are ready for the Sioux," Lizard Woman said, patting earth over the pit they had dug in the floor, wherein food, extra clothing, and tools were hidden. "If they burn the roofs off the lodges and pull the walls down, we shall not go hungry or be without shelter. In a day, we can put up our skin tepees, and the food in our pits will sustain us until we can hunt fresh meat again."

"I never dreamed that your people were so resourceful," Maura said.

The compliment drew a pleased smile. "Ah, well," Lizard Woman sighed disparagingly, resting her dirty hands on her wide hips. "You know how the Pawnee love to eat. It is why we plant corn, because we like fat bellies. Don't *your* people enjoy their food? The only White-Eyes I have ever seen are thin. Just look at you, your father, and Great Heart!"

"Maura, are you in there?" Eben called from the entranceway, and that was how Maura learned of his arrival.

"Father, you're back!" she cried, whirling to greet him as he came into the main room.

Their tender reunion made Lizard Woman laugh. She

was especially amused by the kissing. Maura wondered what the plump little woman would think of the way Luke had sometimes kissed her.

"Where's Pitale-sharo?" Maura asked, after the kissing and hugging had ended.

Eben kept one arm around her shoulders. "With his grandfather and Mr. Cutter, reviewing the preparations for Shon-ka's attack. I wish Luke had taken you away from here, my dear. I don't like the thought of you being in the middle of a battle. It's more dangerous than I care to think about."

"*Life* is dangerous," Maura snapped irritably. "Why do men always assume that women are useless then it comes to a fight—and most everything else, except cooking and having children?"

Eben's silver eyebrows shot up. "My, my. You've obviously been arguing with Mr. Cutter, again. I recognize that particular wrinkle between your pretty eyes."

"Let's not discuss Mr. Cutter, Father. Where I am concerned, he has the most infuriating opinions imaginable. I work every bit as hard as he does, speak Pawnee as fluently, and have mastered everything I set out to do here, but still, he holds me in contempt—because I'm a woman, and therefore inferior."

"I doubt it is contempt he feels for you, my dear. And I doubt he thinks you are inferior." Eben studied her flushed face with speculative eyes. "The question is—what do you feel for him?"

Before Maura could formulate a bland, deceptive answer, She-de-a burst into the lodge. "The Sioux! Their army has just been spotted by the scouts."

"Where? How close?" Maura raced for the old musket Luke had given her to use as a weapon; he had wanted her to take it with her to the top of the bluff, not stay in the village, firing at the enemy.

"Only a half-day's ride. By nightfall, they should be

here, though I don't think they will attack until morning, before dawn. I have never known them to attack at night."

"Have you told Bon-son-gee or Wetara-sharo what you think they will do? Since you are Sioux, you should know better than anybody."

"I tried, but neither would listen." She-de-a's expression was downcast. "They still don't trust me enough to take my word."

"Nor do they think you know anything, because you're female." Maura glanced bitterly at her father, as if to say I told you so. "Go and tell Pitale-sharo. Maybe he will listen, though I doubt it."

The rest of that long, nerve-wracking day passed in frantic, last minute preparations. As scouts came and went, they reported that the Sioux army was indeed huge, numbering more than twice the inhabitants of the village. If it had swept down upon the Skidis without warning, undoubtedly everyone in the tribe would have been slaughtered.

By late afternoon most of the women, children, and old folks had climbed the bluff to hide in the rocky clefts. Lizard Woman pleaded with Maura to accompany her to a cave-like depression near the bluff's summit, a hiding place impossible to discover if one did not know of its existence. "Once I crawl inside and pull brush across the opening, I can stay there for days, and no one will find me. I have plenty of food and water. You must come now, or you will not be able to find it alone."

"I am staying," Maura said softly, so her father could not hear. He was busy anyway, helping Luke build one of the ramparts higher. Maura could see the two of them digging a trench at the base of the rampart and throwing the dirt they removed on top of it. "Take She-de-a, but don't worry about me."

"She-de-a has already gone up the bluff. She told me to tell you to be sure and join her. Fighting is men's work, not women's."

"She's gone already?" Maura was surprised. "I thought she would accompany you. The last I saw of her she was filling water skins for the men, in case they get thirsty during battle."

"She has gone," Lizard Woman confirmed with a nod. "But it would have been better if she waited for us and hid in my special place. Some of the others—I am thinking of Heavy Basket, in particular—may treat her badly if they look down from the bluff and see the battle going badly."

"That's true." Maura was suddenly worried for her little friend. "I wonder why she went off by herself."

Lizard Woman shrugged. "Maybe she has found her own hiding place where neither Sioux nor Pawnee can find her. That would be wise—to hide and wait until the battle is over, and she knows who has won."

"I think She-de-a will be loyal to the Pawnee no matter who wins the battle. She loves Pitale-sharo," Maura reminded Lizard Woman in a biting tone.

Embarassed, Lizard Woman dropped her eyes. "I am going now, Moe-ra. May Tirawa watch over you."

It was the first time Lizard Woman had ever called Maura by her name; only She-de-a used it. Everyone else still called her the White-Eyes woman. Swamped with emotion, Maura hugged the plump little Pawnee. "May Tirawa watch over you, Lizard Woman."

After Lizard Woman left, Maura entered the silent, dark lodge, made a fire, and cooked a pot of stew with the last of the fresh antelope Small Hand had killed a few days before. She intended to feed her father, Small Hand, Luke, and whoever else was hungry. After that, she would return to the lodge and stay out of sight until morning—or until the attack started, whichever came first.

The aroma of the bubbling stew made Maura's mouth water; she could hardly wait until it was done. When it was, she filled three gourd bowls and took them to the men. Luke and her father were now working by torchlight to deepen the trenches, but every other man, including Small Hand and Pitale-sharo, had gathered around a large bonfire. Maura could see the warriors sitting on their haunches, chanting, and applying war paint.

Eben was startled when he looked up from his digging and saw her. "Maura, why are you still here? I thought you had gone to hide with Lizard Woman and Heavy Basket."

Maura thrust a streaming gourd shell at him. "Food to give you strength tomorrow. I have extras if Pitale-sharo or any of the others would like some."

Luke shook his head. "They won't eat before a battle—but I will." He put down his digging stick and reached for a gourd.

Laying down his own tool, Eben took his hesitantly. "Maura, don't ignore me; I'm deeply concerned. Why did you stay? I had assumed you left this afternoon with the other women."

Maura shot him a wry look as she blew on the remaining bowl of stew to cool it. "Would I have left without saying good-bye? Really, Father . . . I thought you knew me better than that."

Luke was already starting to eat, but Eben clutched his bowl, frowning. "Sometimes, Maura, I wonder if I know you at all. Have you always been this headstrong and stubborn, or am I just noticing it more? Since we arrived in Nebraska, these qualities seem to have grown in you."

"I'd say she's always been like this." Luke calmly sipped his broth. He fished inside the gourd shell with his fingers, withdrew a chunk of meat, and popped it into his mouth. "Beats me how you've put up with it all these years, Magruder."

"If the two of you want to discuss me in private, I can always return to the lodge." Maura was greatly tempted to fling the contents of her bowl in Luke's face.

"No, sit down," Luke invited, sitting down himself on the shoulder of the trench. "If this is going to be our last night alive, I think we should share it and be nice to each other. By tomorrow night, we'll either all be dead, *wishing* we were dead, or, possibly, victorious."

"What do you mean—*wishing* we were dead?" Maura perched near her father and glared at Luke.

"I mean that if we *aren't* victorious tomorrow, and if we aren't already dead, the Sioux will make a slow, painful work of killing us. With you, they'll start with rape. But they won't stop there. . . . By this time tomorrow night, Miss Magruder, you may be wishing you had gone up on top of the bluff with the women, like you were told."

"You're just trying to scare me." Maura tossed her head in a show of bravado she did not really feel. "Only I don't scare easily. Instead of dwelling on unpleasantries, you would do better to tell me where you want the bombs to go off. You never have explained that."

"I never expected you to be around to help," Luke countered. "Now that your father is here, I don't really need your help."

"Fine. Then I'll jump into this trench tomorrow morning and fire my musket at every passing Sioux. I might even hit one of them."

"Maura!" Eben cried. "For once in your life, I'm taking a stand. In the morning, as soon as it's light, I want you to leave at once to join the women and children."

"I won't," Maura said quietly. "And there isn't a damn thing you can do to make me."

"Maura! This . . . this is outrageous!" Eben sputtered, spilling his stew in his agitation. "Why, I . . . I've never even heard you use language like that before!"

"I'm afraid she learned it from me," Luke interrupted. "And at this point, there's no sense arguing about where she ought to be. It's too dark for her to climb the bluff tonight or before dawn in the morning. At first light, the

Sioux will be swarming all over us."

"But where can she go to be safe?" Eben's blue eyes were wild with worry. Despite her determination not to be banished like a useless child, Maura felt a twinge of conscience for hurting her father so much.

"I'll be careful, Father—" she began, but Luke again interrupted.

"She can stay near the river, down in the cottonwoods. I'll give her a few bombs to use in case the Sioux split up and some of them come at the village from that direction. There's a bullboat or two down there on the bank. If she sees the battle going badly, she can always keep one and destroy the others, so no one can follow her downriver. . . . If you do have to flee, Maura, slash the rest of the boats with a knife, first. And for God's sake, lie down in the bottom of the boat, and pretend you're dead. Though the river is shallow, the current will soon carry you away."

"Not a bad idea," Maura grudgingly conceded.

As Maura already knew, a bullboat was a small, round, lightweight vessel made from the stretched hide of a buffalo bull. One was just big enough for two or three people crowded close together. If she lay down in one and floated downstream, the Sioux might not realize the boat was even occupied. But of course, she did *not* plan on having to do that—and would not do it unless defeat was inevitable, and both her father and Luke were already dead.

"Don't you dare stay around to see if I'm still alive!" her father warned, guessing the direction of her thoughts. "If victory looks at all uncertain, do as Luke says. Promise me, Maura!"

Maura peeked at her silver-haired father through her lashes. In the flickering light from the torches, Eben suddenly looked old. Fear and annoyance had etched deep grooves in his face. He looked almost as old as Wetarasharo.

326

Maura was ashamed of herself for defying him. "All right, Father . . . I promise."

"Good," he rasped. "Now, let's eat this good stew before it goes to waste."

They ate in silence, and then Maura took the dirty bowls and returned to the lodge. She had just started to clean up when she noticed something strange. She had left three empty bowls on the hearthstone beside the stew pot. Now, there were only two, but she had seen no one enter the lodge while she was outside, talking to Luke and her father, and no one had been *inside* when she left the lodge.

Slowly turning, expecting at any moment to hear a wild yell and see a Sioux warrior jump out at her, she searched every dark nook and cranny with her eyes. The lodge was less cluttered now; little remained except for the sleeping platforms with their skin curtains for privacy. If someone *was* here, the intruder had to be hiding behind one of the drawn skins.

The worst fear Maura had ever known crept over her. Perspiration dripped between her shoulder blades, and her legs felt too shaky to walk. She forced them to carry her to the nearest platform, where Lizard Woman and Small Hand slept. Grabbing the curtain, she tore it open, revealing the bare, plain platform. There remained not a single skin to cover it; Lizard Woman had either buried the bed coverings or taken them with her.

Breathing deeply, Maura approached the second platform with equal dread. This was the bed where she and She-de-a usually slept—where she intended to lie down, tonight. Now, it was a sinister place, filling her with horror. Maura could barely keep from running out of the lodge, screaming. Again, she grasped the curtain and tore it aside. There *was* someone sitting on the platform. With her knees drawn up, She-de-a was eating stew from a gourd bowl.

"*You!*" Maura gasped.

She-de-a looked up, startled. "Moe-ra!"

"What are you doing here?" they chorused in unison.

Setting down the gourd shell, She-de-a climbed off the platform. "Moe-ra, you look so frightened. What is it? Have the Sioux come already?"

"I'm frightened because I didn't know you were here! Lizard Woman told me you had gone. Do you want Bonson-gee and all the rest to think you stayed behind in order to greet the Sioux—to have them *free* you?"

She-de-a's eyes widened. Plainly, the girl had never realized the misinterpretation her odd behavior might engender, yet the first thing that leapt into Maura's mind was that maybe She-de-a *did* see the attack as an opportunity to go back to her own people. Knowing how much She-de-a cared for Pitale-sharo, Maura found it hard to believe, but still, the thought *had* occurred.

"No. Oh, no!" She-de-a wailed. "I did not stay so I could betray the Pawnee. I stayed so I could *fight* the Sioux. I . . . I thought if Pitale-sharo saw me fighting my own tribesmen—if his grandfather also saw me—they would realize that my loyalty now lies with my *new* people. It . . . it is my last chance to prove myself, Moe-ra! Nothing else I have done has worked!" She-de-a's velvet-brown eyes swam with tears, and Maura threw her arms about her little friend.

"Oh, my poor She-da-a! I should have known you would try something like this."

"Can't I help touch fire to the bombs? If not that, then I can surely wield a club or a knife. If I had a bow and arrows, I could hide in a pit and shoot my tribesmen as they ride toward us. I am not the best, but I *can* shoot. Please, Moe-ra, tell me what to do! You are my friend. You are strong and wise."

"She-de-a, thank you for your faith in me, but it's a mistake for you to be here. If anyone sees you—Pawnee *or* Sioux—they may not understand why you didn't join the

328

women and children in escaping to a place of safety. Either way, your life is in danger. My own father was furious that I remained behind. I had to promise to flee in a bullboat at the first sign of defeat."

"I will never flee," She-de-a insisted, wiping away the wetness on her cheeks with the flat of her hand. "Tomorrow, when Pitale-sharo meets the Sioux, I will stand beside him and fight—with my bare hands if I have to. If he dies, I will die, also. We will journey together to the Happy Hunting Grounds."

The little Sioux squared her shoulders. Her mouth trembled slightly, but her eyes glowed with dark determination. "I am not afraid to die. Not if it means that Pitale-sharo and I will be together."

Maura recoiled from the force of the young girl's love; it was too pure, too strong and certain, whereas Maura's feelings for Luke had always been fraught with doubt and sullied with carnal desire. She wondered if she would be prepared to die if it meant she could be with Luke. A love such as She-de-a's was noble and awe-inspiring. By contrast, Maura's love for Luke was cheap, shallow, and unworthy.

"I don't see why you have to die in order to be with the man you love," she responded pettishly. "But maybe your plan will work after all, She-de-a. What you need is a weapon. Then, in the morning, you should go straight to Pitale-sharo and let him *see* that you are ready and willing to fight. If it does look like defeat is inevitable, I'll leave a bullboat intact by the river for you. Don't be foolish and refuse to use it. Pitale-sharo himself would not want you to die for his sake."

"I won't use it," She-de-a insisted stubbornly. "But I thank you, Moe-ra, for suggesting it. You are the best friend I have ever had; no matter what happens tomorrow, I will never forget you."

Determined not to be maudlin, Maura began looking

for a weapon She-de-a might use. She-de-a helped her. Finding only a sharp skinning knife left in the lodge, they fastened it to a digging stick with leather thongs to make a spear. It was not much, but it was better than nothing. They then decided that She-de-a should sleep on Lizard Woman's platform, in case Eben joined Maura in the lodge for this, their last night before battle.

Sometime later, her father did join her, but Luke remained outside, where the first sounds of Shon-ka's approach could better be heard. Maura lay down beside her father, but neither could sleep. Eben reached out and patted her shoulder. "Remember, dear daughter, how very much I have loved you all these years."

"My fondest memories are of your love, Papa," Maura whispered. "I'm sorry if I've hurt you. I will treasure your love always."

In the darkness, she blinked back tears. If only she had memories of Luke's love to treasure! If only he had ever *said* he loved her. What was he thinking, all alone out there in the dark? She wanted to go to him, but felt it was not appropriate. *He* should be coming to her. If he did love her, he would come. But she waited for him all night, and he never came—not until morning when it was time for battle.

Chapter Twenty-five

Maura awoke to find Luke shaking her father's shoulder. "Get up, Eben. It's time."

She rose on one elbow and strained to listen, but heard nothing but the crackle of flame from the torch Luke held in one hand. "Has the battle started?" she asked. "Are the Sioux here, yet?"

"Not yet," Luke answered. "But they will be, soon. Dawn is only an hour away. The warriors are all taking their places, and I think we should, too. Stoke up the cookfire, Maura, so that smoke will be coming out of the smoke-hole, and everything will look as normal as possible when they do come. We want the Sioux to think they've surprised us."

Eben rolled off the platform, and Maura followed close behind. Almost immediately, Luke thrust three gourd bombs and a small clay jar into Eben's hands. "Put the bombs at the base of the bluff where I showed you yesterday, and leave the ember jar somewhere safe nearby," he instructed. "In the meantime, as soon as Maura gets the cookfire going, I'll have her fix a few more jars."

"I'll be back as soon as these are placed," Eben promised.

As Maura started a fire in the previous night's ashes, she noticed that Luke had all the bombs lined up like soldiers in one corner, while beside the firepit, an assortment of small clay jars stood ready and waiting to receive live coals from the fire. Nearby, in easy grabbing distance of the lodge entrance, were Luke's rifle, shot bag, and powder horn. He must have been busy in the lodge for some time.

Maura fed buffalo chips to the licking flames and tried hard not to look at Luke. She was desperate for reassurance — rather, she yearned for some sign of affection, intimacy, or at least some personal notice. What she got was an angry bark that startled her into scattering chips left and right.

"What in hell are *you* doing here?" Luke demanded in Pawnee.

Darting a quick glance over her shoulder, Maura saw She-de-a climbing down from her sleeping platform. Unruffled by Luke's astonishment, the girl reached for her spear leaning against the wall in the dark shadows. "I am going now to help Pitale-sharo defeat my people," she said evenly. "Do not try to stop me, Great Heart. If Pitale-sharo dies today, I shall also die." She paused, smiling a wry little smile. "As my people say when they ride off to battle, it is a good day to die."

"Both of you women are moonstruck!" Luke exploded, pacing up and down the lodge. He paused and forked the air with an outstretched finger. "There's not another female in this village except the two of you. You may think you're braver and stronger than all the rest, but I don't. Now my worries are *doubled*. I've half a mind to tie up both of you and leave you here in the lodge, where you can't get into trouble — only a flaming roof might cave in on top of you."

She-de-a calmly pointed her spear at Luke. "Do not try it, Great Heart. I will fight you to the death, if you do. My place is beside Pitale-sharo — just as Moe-ra's place is beside you."

Maura gulped in surprise. So did Luke. He looked from

332

one to the other as if they utterly amazed and stupefied him.

"Good-bye, Moe-ra." The little Sioux nodded in Maura's direction. "After the battle, I'll come back here to look for you."

"I'll be waiting," Maura said, tossing another chip on the fire.

After She-de-a departed, Maura dared not look at Luke again. Taking a long wooden spoon, she began to fill the ember jars with smoldering lumps of dried buffalo dung. Suddenly, Luke grabbed her long, braided hair and hauled her up to face him. Dropping the spoon, she gave a loud screech. *"What* are you doing?"

Her scalp stung, and tears smarted in her eyes, but when she saw Luke's eyes, the discomfort faded. Emotion contorted his bronzed, handsome face; his eyes burned like live coals. "Damn you, woman. This isn't the first time you've made me curse you, and it probably won't be the last." His dark brows crashed downward over the fiery eyes; he seemed to be in pain and wrestling with himself.

"All night long, I wanted to come to you," he grated. "I wanted to take you in my arms and hold you close — so close that we became one body. I wanted to kiss and make love to you all through the night."

"Then why didn't you?" Maura challenged. "I was here — waiting for you, *wanting* you."

He sighed raggedly. "Maura, Maura . . . I've fought my feelings for you so long that it's almost become a habit I can't break. Over and over, I've argued with my conscience — telling myself I shouldn't care for you, because my caring would only keep you here and one day kill you. But you're here anyway, aren't you? On a day of death, you're right here beside me, and I still haven't told you that I love you. . . . Damn you, I love you more than my life, more than I thought I could ever love any woman! I love you with my very blood and bones, with every breath, thought, heartbeat. . . ."

Each word fueled the joy which surged through Maura; she thought she might drown in happiness. "Oh, Luke! I love you, too! And I've waited so long to hear you say it — a lifetime, at least."

He slanted his mouth across hers. They clung together, sharing a kiss that rocketed Maura into a state of quivering passion. She raked her fingers through his dark, tousled hair and ground her breasts into his leather-clad chest. She thrust her hips into him, reveling in the feel of his rising desire. It scarcely mattered that her father might return at any moment and find them locked in a wanton embrace — or that the Sioux might attack and pelt the lodge roof with flaming arrows.

All that mattered was that Luke had at long last admitted his love. *I love you more than my life.* The glorious words exploded in her brain, ripped through her belly, thundered along her veins. He was hers, now, and always would be. Never in her life would there be a more wonderful moment than this. Suddenly, she was standing on the pinnacle of a mountaintop, glimpsing the meaning of life and the source of all joy, triumph, and fulfillment: it was to love and be loved in return.

The crack of gunfire close to the lodge brought her crashing down to earth. Luke thrust her away, holding her at arm's length while he tilted his head and listened. War whoops followed; then came the muffled thud of horses' hooves.

"Take as many bombs as you can carry, and an ember jar, and get down by the river." Luke was all business; the preceding moment of tender revelation might never have taken place. "Don't set off the bombs until the Sioux are overrunning the village. Then fire them one after the other. As soon as you've finished, don't stay around to judge their effectiveness. Get in a bullboat, and shove off."

Maura nodded assent and watched breathlessly as Luke

334

slung his rifle, powder horn, and shot bag over one shoulder, snatched an ember jar, and filled his arms with bombs. Barely had he done so, when he was out into the entranceway and gone from sight. They had not even had time to say good-bye. For several moments, Maura stood in stunned silence. Stirring to life again, she calmly and methodically got her musket and the rest of the things she needed.

She could not carry all of the remaining bombs; there were too many. Yet she feared abandoning them. If the roof and interior partitions of the lodge caught fire, the bombs might explode, destroying the dwelling. She pushed the remaining gourds against the earth wall where Luke could see them if he came back for them, but where they would be out of the way of any falling debris. It was the best she could do. Finally, she was ready to face the din outside.

The sounds of raging battle, though muffled, filled the entranceway with shouts, screams, explosions, horse whinnies, and the continual *pop-pop-pop* of gunfire. Dreading what she might see, Maura parted the skins at the outer doorway and peeked out at a scene resembling her worst imaginings of hell. Several lodge roofs were already aflame, illuminating the darkness. Brandishing torches, a handful of braves on horseback were tearing through the village lighting every flammable thing in sight, while other braves—identifiable as Pawnee by the erect horns on their scalp locks—flung themselves over ramparts and out of doorways to try and stop the intruders.

The air was heavy with smoke and the acrid odor of burning. Everywhere she looked, Maura saw Indians fighting. Some had hidden themselves behind the ramparts and were firing rifles or arrows at the mounted attackers. The Sioux had already broken through, leaping their horses right over the trenches, most of which were now exposed. Hand-to-hand combat raged on either side of Lizard

Woman's lodge. A knot of fear tightened, then expanded in Maura's stomach. The fighting was too thick; she would never make it down to the river.

Setting down the bombs and the clay ember jar, Maura loaded the old musket and crouched in the doorway, waiting for a clear shot. It was impossible to be sure of hitting a Sioux and not a Pawnee. She crouched in the doorway for what seemed like hours before she dared take a shot. Then she saw Small Hand, Lizard Woman's husband, wrestling a big Sioux over a tomahawk. In their frantic grappling, the two combatants moved almost close enough for her to touch one of them.

Aiming at the Sioux's broad back, Maura waited until the man had knocked Small Hand down and was lifting his tomahawk to deliver the death blow. Knowing she could not miss at such close range, she sighted down the barrel of the heavy old gun and squeezed the trigger. The retort knocked her flat on her back in the entrance tunnel. When she caught her breath, got up, and peered out to see what harm had been done, she saw the headless body of the Indian sprawled on top of Small Hand.

Blinking dazedly, Small Hand crawled out from underneath it and glanced around, searching for his savior. He never spotted Maura hiding in the doorway, nor did she call out to gain his attention. Her eyes clung to the headless torso of the dead man; it was twitching and jumping, the feet still kicking, while blood poured out of the ragged stump where the head had been. Unable to look away, Maura watched in horrified facination until the body quit moving entirely. By then, Small Hand had run off to find another opponent. In a momentary lull in the battle, Maura stepped outside and vomited the meager contents of her stomach.

Afterward, she felt better but had an overwhelming urge to relieve herself. She went around the side of the lodge, found a sheltered spot, and did so. Somewhat refreshed, she was then able to concentrate on what her ears were telling her. The battle had moved to the north end of the village. Darting back to the entranceway, she picked up the bombs and the ember jar, then debated whether or not to reload the musket and take it with her. No, she decided. One killing was enough; though she had saved Small Hand's life, the thought of blowing off another man's head made her stomach churn with nausea.

Keeping to the dark shadows of the lodges still intact, she moved toward the sounds of battle. Why had she heard only two or three explosions? What was Luke waiting for? Why didn't he use the bombs they had labored so hard to make? Hearing the thunder of horse's hooves, she turned her head and saw a fearsome sight: On the other side of the trench, a line of mounted Sioux was galloping toward the village.

Behind that line, there was another in the far off distance: warriors sitting calmly astride their horses, awaiting the command to attack. Against the paling eastern sky, their silhouettes resembled statues.

So that's Shon-ka's plan, Maura thought despairingly. He's sending them in one wave at a time.

With the Sioux riding down upon her, Maura knew she had little time to act. Quickly, she set down the ember jar and all the bombs but one. Removing the lid from the jar, she dipped the long grass fuse into it. A flame lit and began eating its way toward the gourd. Fearing the flame might go out, she waited until the last possible moment to throw the bomb. When she finally drew back her arm and let the missile fly, some of the Sioux were already jumping the trench. The bomb arced toward the advancing horsemen, landed at the feet of an oncoming horse, and did nothing but lie there and sputter.

Alarmed, Maura lit another bomb, set it down on the ground, and raced toward a nearby lodge. Barely had she reached the shelter of an entranceway, when the second bomb exploded. One wall of the tunnel collapsed, showering dirt on Maura's head and blocking her exit. Choking and gasping, Maura fell to her knees and scrabbled in the rubble, trying to push enough of it away so she could see outside. Determined digging soon cleared an escape route, and crawling out of the lodge on her hands and knees, she was amazed to discover at least a half dozen men and horses flopping about on the ground, unable to rise. At least two men were dead, and parts of a horse were scattered all around.

But past these gruesome sights, she saw a most satisfying one: retreating Indians struggling to stay astride panicked, fleeing mounts. This time, instead of feeling sickened by the carnage, she felt victorious. Maura raced back into Lizard Woman's lodge, retrieved her musket, loaded it, and went outside again. Picking her way among the dead and dying, she dispatched squealing horses, too wounded to survive. The fallen Indians she ignored, telling herself they were not her concern. The truth was that she could not bring herself to kill wounded men face-to-face yet, though she did manage to shoot one who tried to sneak up on her while she was reloading the musket.

When the man died almost at her feet, she looked down at him and felt nothing; a curious detachment had taken hold. Her brain seemed to be functioning without any conscious direction. It simply gave orders; she obeyed. *Pick up the bombs you set down in order to fire the first one. Go find Luke and your father. See if Pitale-sharo and She-de-a are still alive.*

Half-dazed, Maura gathered what she needed and continued walking toward the sounds of concentrated fighting. Twice, she saw another wave of Sioux sweeping down on the village. Twice, she injured some and scared away others by setting off bombs. It was actually rather amusing to terrify grown men, though she regretted scaring and maiming poor horses. The number of dead and wounded

338

would have been much higher, but most of the bombs did not explode when she lit their grass fuses. Long before she arrived at the scene of the worst, hand-to-hand fighting, she had used all the bombs she had brought with her.

Reloading the musket, she crouched beside Heavy Basket's lodge. Its roof had fallen in, and smoke was pouring out of the top, but the walls still stood. To avoid the fighting all around her, Maura crept inside the doorway. Once again, she watched for a clear shot at one of the enemy. Sighting down the musket, she aimed at two men crashing into lodges and rolling over and over on the ground. One of them looked familiar, but not until she saw the gray eyes in the smoke-blackened face did she recognize Luke.

Instantly, her head cleared, and the curious feeling of lethargy fled. In an agony of dread, she balanced the musket and watched the drama being played out. The Indian had a tomahawk, but Luke had a skinning knife — the one he usually wore in a sheath at his waist. It was now full daylight, and every detail of straining muscle, clenched jaw, and dripping sweat jumped out at Maura. First, Luke was on top, and then the Indian, then Luke again, and lastly, the Indian. Maura stepped out of the lodge and aimed the musket dead-center in the Indian's back. Her hands were shaking so badly that she feared she could not pull the trigger.

Suddenly, Luke arched his body and threw the Indian off. The brave fell to one side. Quickly, Luke rolled over on top of him and plunged the knife to its hilt in the man's heart. The man jerked and flailed. Blood bubbled out of his mouth. Within seconds after he died, Luke yanked out the knife, wiped it in the trampled grass, and was on his feet again, looking around for the next villain.

"Luke!" Maura screamed. Terror suddenly poured fourth in a torrent, as if unleashed from a crumbling dam.

"God almighty, Maura!" Luke swung around like a

madman. "I thought you'd be halfway down the river by now!"

"I—I've been fighting. I couldn't get to the river. I've been shooting Indians with the musket and blowing up men and horses, and . . . and. . . ." Nausea gripped her, and she swallowed hard. "I bet I've killed as many Sioux as you have, Luke—maybe more."

He grabbed and steadied her, then propelled her backward into the lodge doorway. "You stubborn, willful, disobedient, little fool! Who gave you permission to fight? I *told* you what I wanted you to do!"

"And I just told you why I couldn't do it! Do you realize how many Indians are out there?" Her voice spiraled hysterically. "They'll kill us all before they're through! Half the time, your stupid bombs don't even work."

"I *know* that! Why in hell do you think you haven't heard more of 'em exploding? The gourds must have been damp inside, or else the powder was bad—probably purchased from Cutter Munitions."

"Cutter Munitions?" Maura did not know what he was talking about.

"Did you use all of the bombs?" Luke rattled her arm to get her attention.

"No, there are still some left back at Lizard Woman's lodge, if it's still standing."

"Then here's what I want you to do. Go get them and bring them here. We're losing this damn battle. Every wave of Sioux leaves fewer Pawnee to defend the village. Soon, Shon-ka will be able to *walk* in and take it."

"But what if the bombs won't go off?" Maura quavered, trembling in her moccasins.

"Then we all die." Searching her features, Luke's gray eyes were bright and piercing in his dirty face. "Just remember what I said this morning, Maura. I love you, and if we get out of this alive, I'll marry you, though I haven't the faintest idea how in hell I'll provide for you as

340

a husband should."

"It's not important," she started to say, meaning that *money* was not important, but he cut her short by yanking her out of the doorway.

"Get going! Run!" he ordered, spinning her around and swatting her bottom.

Startled by the blow, Maura dashed off in the direction from which she had just come. Only as she dodged past smoking lodges and clusters of grappling warriors did she realize that she had completely forgotten to ask about her father—or Pitale-sharo and She-de-a. Were any of them still alive?

Chapter Twenty-six

Before Maura even returned with the bombs, Luke knew it was too late to use them. Shon-ka was preparing for the final attack. Squinting his eyes, he could see the big Indian astride a huge white horse, gathering his braves for one last, devastating assault. The fighting in the village had virtually stopped, the remaining Sioux having slunk off to rejoin their fellows. After the recent din, the silence was oddly deafening.

Blood-smeared and soot-streaked, Pitale-sharo dashed up to Luke and Eben, who had just come up beside Luke. "He's coming. At last, the coward dares show his own face. I've ordered everyone to go out and meet him. We won't die like dogs, cowering between our lodges. We shall die like *men*, bravely meeting our enemies on the plain beneath the blue sky."

"No!" Luke protested. "We don't stand a chance out there. At least in the trenches we still have cover. Don't forget the holes in the plain; as the Sioux horses tumble and throw their riders, we stand a good chance of killing the bastards. So far, the holes have been doing a fine job of unseating warriors. Riding close-packed as they are, they can't avoid them."

Pitale-sharo's forehead puckered doubtfully. "If I am going to die today, I want to die honorably. Hiding in a ditch is not honorable."

"Who says you have to die? You always claimed one Pawnee was equal to ten Sioux. All any of us have to do is bring down ten men, and we'll have won the battle. Don't you agree, Eben?"

Nearly unrecognizable with his soot-caked hair and clothing, Maura's father was still gripping a smoking rifle. His energy was remarkable in a man his age, especially after such a wearying morning. "I think we could win if the odds were a little better. Those temperamental bombs of yours made me lose hope this morning, Luke. The sight of Shon-ka getting ready to wipe us out hasn't made me any more optimistic."

"Maura's gone back to get the rest of the bombs," Luke said, hating to let her father know that she had not escaped in a bullboat, after all, though defeat now seemed inevitable.

Eben stiffened in surprise, but otherwise said nothing. His tight-lipped bravery made Luke proud to think of becoming his son-in-law—if such a miracle ever occurred. Quickly, Luke changed the subject. "Where's She-de-a, Pitale-sharo?"

The question distracted his friend from the rows of Sioux now sitting silently astride their horses, awaiting the signal to attack. "With my grandfather in his lodge. She-de-a stayed to fight her own people, but I would not permit it. In the darkness, my grandfather fell this morning, and now he can scarcely walk. So I commanded her to watch over him during the battle."

"She's as stubborn as Maura," Luke muttered.

Intense emotions engulfed him. In Pitale-sharo's eyes, he saw the same fear for She-de-a that he himself felt for Maura. He and Pitale-sharo had both waited too long to acknowledge their deepest, most precious feelings. For all Luke knew, Pitale-sharo might still be denying his.

"Come," Pitale-sharo said. "Let us go to your big hole in

the ground. Anything is better than dying where we stand. Bon-son-gee may not join us, but I think I can convince the rest that one Pawnee is worth ten Sioux. If we fight wisely, perhaps we can still win."

Dodging the dead and dying, the three strode purposefully toward the trenches. As soon as the remaining Pawnee saw Pitale-sharo climbing into a ditch, they joined him. Even Bon-son-gee, who did not look nearly as arrogant usual, climbed down into one of the waist-deep holes. Then everyone silently began counting their remaining arrows, rifle, and musket shots. When Shon-ka did not attack immediately, Luke suspected that the big Sioux was savoring the moment—or else, he hoped to rob the Pawnee of courage in this final, threatening hour.

Into the bleak silence, a voice suddenly spoke: "Brothers . . . hear me."

Everyone turned. Behind the trenches, stood Wetara-sharo, leaning heavily upon She-de-a's arm and gripping the spear she had fashioned from a digging stick. The beautiful young girl assisted the old chief as he hobbled slowly, painfully toward them. Pitale-sharo climbed out of the trench and hurried to his grandfather's side. Spotting Maura returning with the bombs, Luke motioned for her to wait until the old chief had said his piece.

"Grandfather, what is it?" Pitale-sharo inquired politely, with a touch of impatience. "The Sioux are coming. Look there, across the plain."

Luke jerked around and saw that, indeed, the Sioux *were* coming. With Shon-ka leading them, they were crossing the plain at a careful walk, not a trot or gallop, as he had expected. Luke's stomach sank into his moccasins. Now, the faulty homemade gourd bombs in Maura's arms were the only hope for a Pawnee victory. He beckoned to Maura. She reached him just as Wetara-sharo's sad, trembling voice floated over the trenches.

"Brothers . . . I have come here to die with you. Tirawa

344

has deserted us. Fight bravely and die proudly. That is all you can do, now. Fetch me a *real* spear, Pitale-sharo; I can't face our enemies with *this* poor excuse for a weapon." Wetara-sharo shook the walking stick with the knife still bound to it.

"Grandfather, we shall *not* die. We are Pawnee, and we will fight bravely and *live!*"

Luke could see that no one believed the bold, brave boast. There were too many on the plain and too few in the trenches. An idea born of desperation came to him, and he climbed out of the trench and stood beside Maura.

"Pitale-sharo, wait. . . . Why don't you walk out on the plain and challenge Shon-ka to fight you—just *you*—and if you win, then his army must spare the village and all who live here."

"No!" She-de-a screamed. "He *must* not fight him! Shon-ka is too strong, too powerful. He will—"

"Silence!" Wetara-sharo barked. He dug claw-like fingers into the young girl's arm and pulled her back. "Your suggestion is good, Great Heart. It is a chance, where before there was none."

"It's more than a chance, Grandfather. It's certain victory!" Pitale-sharo's eyes gleamed. His face shone with hope. "I will *shame* him into fighting me. He must fight or else lose face. When we fight, my thirst for vengeance will give me strength to overcome him."

"I will walk out with you," Wetara-sharo said. "I fought Shon-ka's grandfather and his father. He in turn killed your father, Massish-sharo. Our destinies are intertwined; it is right we should walk out together."

"Then come, Grandfather."

Pitale-sharo passed the makeshift spear to She-de-a. Trembling but subdued now, She-de-a accepted it. She offered her arm to support Wetara-sharo. With She-de-a on one side and Pitale-sharo on the other, the old chieftain walked around the trenches and out onto the plain. When

345

Shon-ka saw them coming, he kicked his horse into a trot, rode out ahead of his army, and came across the plain to meet them.

Hoping to use the delay to good advantage, Luke whispered urgently to Maura and Eben. "Listen. Each of you take a couple bombs and spread out. When I want you to set them off, I'll signal with a nod. Do you both have an ember jar?"

"Mine's nearby," Eben said. "Is there anything else we can do? Even if the bombs explode, I doubt the Indians will be much impressed. In the daylight, the explosions will lose their impact."

"They'll scare the hell out of the horses," Luke reminded him. "That's all I care about. If Shon-ka doesn't accept the deal, or if he wins the fight with Pitale-sharo, the bombs are our last chance."

"I've got my jar right here." Maura held it out. "Where's yours, Luke? Do you still have it?"

"Don't worry about me. I can lay hands on mine in a hurry. Good luck . . . and watch for my nod."

Maura and Eben nodded agreement. Maura divided up the bombs, and she and Eben moved away—one to the right, one to the left. Watching them sneak off while everyone's attention was focused on Shon-ka, Luke was glad he had such brave, dependable assistants, even if one of them *was* a helpless, weak female and the other an old man filled with doubts.

He stooped down in the trench and retrieved his own ember jar. It was right where he had left it, jammed into the earthen wall. Then he stood up again. Though he had not prayed in years, he bowed his head a moment and closed his eyes. *Please let Shon-ka agree to fight. Give Pitale-sharo the strength to win. If he doesn't win or something goes wrong, then please make these damn bombs explode.*

Reaching a small, empty trench, Maura climbed down into it and carefully set her bombs and ember jar in front of her, where she could easily grab them. Craning her neck, she saw her father still walking down the line of trenches to Luke's left. Eben selected one inhabited by Small Hand, still alive and gripping his tomahawk, ready to fight.

Small Hand's tomahawk would not be much use against all the fierce, painted Sioux, Maura thought. Looking down at the two gourd bombs in front of her, she noted that they were slightly larger and heavier than the ones she had set off earlier. So were the bombs she had given to Luke and her father. She had used the smaller, lighter ones first, because they were easier to carry. If only these large, unwieldy ones would work properly! If only they would explode bigger, higher, and louder than all the rest of the bombs put together!

She darted a glance at Luke—loving him, wanting him, feeling a swell of joy in her breast at his declaration of love and his promise to marry her. This new beginning, this precious commitment, could *not* end in bloody tragedy. They had come so far, gone through so much; Maura could no longer remember a time when she did not love Luke Cutter. But she could recall only too well the misery of believing he did not love her in return.

No matter what happened, she must be brave and make Luke proud of her. This was her chance to prove to him— once and for all—that she was fashioned of the same stern, strong stuff as the Indians and Luke himself. She and Luke were made for each other and for this harsh, unrelenting land; it must not defeat them. Spotting She-de-a, Maura drew strength from the sight of her slight friend accompanying Pitale-sharo and his grandfather into the presence of their enemies. If the little Sioux could face death without flinching, so could *she*. Of all of them, She-de-a was perhaps the bravest, the least afraid.

As Maura watched, Shon-ka stopped his huge, white horse several paces from the trio walking out to meet him. The big Sioux was nearly naked except for his breechclout and distinctive shell necklace. Slashes of yellow, black, and white crisscrossed his body. The very image of a fierce, noble, arrogant Indian, Shon-ka towered over Pitale-sharo and Wetara-sharo. Even had he not been mounted, he would have dwarfed them both; he was far taller than the short, muscular, square-bodied Pitale-sharo. Assailed with doubts, Maura wondered what had ever prompted Luke to match his friend against such a strong, formidable foe.

Shon-ka held out his feathered spear in greeting, the tip pointing at the ground. Maura shivered, knowing he could easily throw it, and neither Wetara-sharo nor Pitale-sharo could stop him. Other than She-de-a's makeshift spear, they had no weapons, except for the skinning knife strapped to Pitale-sharo's waist.

"So . . . my old enemies. We meet again," Shon-ka said in perfect Pawnee.

"I see you dare not face me alone this time," Pitale-sharo taunted, nodding at the army. "Why did you bring so many when this fight is between you and me, Shon-ka?"

Shon-ka's eyes glittered. "Because you conspire with evil white men to defeat the Sioux with sickness, instead of facing us honorably in battle."

"That's a base lie!" Pitale-sharo's shout echoed across the plain to the waiting army. "The Pawnee are always ready to battle the Sioux. Summer after summer, we have raided and fought back and forth. It is you who have lost your honor, Shon-ka. Not only do you lie, but you fear to fight me alone, here and now, where all can witness it."

"Shon-ka fears no one!" Shon-ka retorted angrily. "Especially not *you*, Pitale-sharo!"

"Then prove it. Get down from your horse, and let us fight as equals. If you win, then you have earned the right to destroy my village and slaughter my people. But if *I* win, then you must withdraw and go home. And you must give me your word that you will never again come here seeking vengeance under false pretenses."

"I have spoken no lies or falsehoods. Hundreds of my people—braves, squaws, and children—died of the spotted sickness this autumn past."

"I grieve for your people, Shon-ka. The spotted sickness is a terrible thing. One day, it may destroy us all. But I did not cause it, nor did I or any of my people conspire with evil White-Eyes to spread it among your people."

"How many Skidi Pawnee have died from it?" Shon-ka demanded. "Tell me who had died, and then perhaps I can believe you."

"Not for many seasons have we suffered from pox," Pitale-sharo admitted, more quietly now. "But surely you must know that my own mother died of the terrible sickness, when I was a cub of a dozen summers. My younger sister also died of it."

From Shon-ka's shocked expression, Maura knew that the big Sioux had *not* known, nor had she. How strange that she and Pitale-sharo should share nearly the exact same tragedy and loss! Maura rubbed the telltale marks on her forearms; they had faded to pale, sickle moons against the golden tan of her skin, but the scars she bore on her heart would last until the day she died.

"Will you fight me?" Pitale-sharo asked. "Or will you show yourself for a coward before your mighty army? As you can see, the Skidi Pawnee are a pitiful tribe compared to the Sioux; what honor will there be in killing us?"

Shon-ka's brows plunged downward. His black eyes snapped. "I will fight you," he growled. "You have left me no choice."

With a single quick motion, he jabbed his spear into the ground and dismounted. Then he motioned to his army. The waiting braves carefully skirted the holes Maura, Luke, and Heavy Basket had dug. Except for the hammering of Maura's heart, the clop of hooves, snorts of horses, and jingle of necklaces was the only sound on all the vast, wide plain.

"We will fight with our hands, Shon-ka. There will be no weapons. Agreed?"

Shon-ka's brows shot skyward. "Not to the death? What will that prove?"

"Who is the strongest and wisest like the fox. . . . The victor will be the one who can pin the other down and hold him there until—"

"Until nothing!" Shon-ka yanked the knife from the sheath at his waist. "The victor must be the one who first takes the other's hair. Until your proud, Pawnee horn hangs beside that of your father on my center lodge pole, I will not rest, Pitale-sharo."

Pitale-sharo reached for his own knife. "A worthy challenge, Dog. For more than half my lifetime, I have coveted your long, Sioux hair. You wear no horn, but the length of your hair is as much a symbol of Sioux pride as my horn is to me, a Pawnee. Before we begin, tell your braves the conditions of this fight. If I win, they must turn round and go home."

"They will not need to turn round," Shon-ka boasted. Nevertheless, he told them.

Maura suspected they already knew. The army had stopped a respectful distance away, and the warriors sat quietly on their horses, watching everything with dark, inscrutable eyes. Knives drawn, bodies crouched, Pitale-sharo and Shon-ka warily circled each other. Shon-ka feinted attack, but Pitale-sharo nimbly leaped away. The hatred in the big Sioux's eyes convinced Maura that Shon-ka would not be satisfied with merely hacking off Pitale-sharo's scalp-lock. He wanted blood—Pitale-sharo's and everyone else's.

Shon-ka feinted a second time. His blade knicked Pitale-sharo's arm. Crimson droplets splattered the trampled grass. Grinning widely, Shon-ka flung himself at Pitale-sharo, knocking him to the ground. They rolled over and over, each grabbing for the other's hair. Shon-ka's elaborate turban came undone, and his magnificent, ankle-length, black hair flew in every direction. A cry of elation went up as Pitale-sharo seized a hunk of it and began sawing away with his knife.

Shon-ka fought to free himself, again stabbing Pitale-sharo in the fleshy upper arm. Blood spurted, and She-de-a screamed, but Wetara-sharo held her back. He uttered a command Maura could not hear. Tightly gripping her spear, She-de-a anxiously watched the two combatants roll on the ground, each seeking to pin the other down. Shon-ka used his superior strength to gain the advantage, but each time he did so, Pitale-sharo managed to grab a hunk of his hair, and Shon-ka had to give way in order to save himself.

Once, Pitale-sharo wriggled right out from under the bigger man, and another time, gouged his eyes so he could not see. Small and light on his feet, the Pawnee chieftain was quick and wily—more than a fair match for the big Sioux. But Pitale-sharo was fast losing blood, while Shon-ka still had not a mark on him. Once again, Shon-ka toppled Pitale-sharo. Pitale-sharo twisted and turned, knocking the knife from Shon-ka's hand. The weapon spun into the air. With a triumphant cry, Pitale-sharo seized it and flung it toward the trenches, out of Shon-ka's reach.

Luke and Bon-son-gee both vaulted out of their respective ditches. Bon-son-gee got there first and gleefully claimed the knife. Shon-ka was furious. "Give me back my knife!" he screamed. Shaking their heads, agreeing for once, Bon-son-gee and Luke retreated.

"Come and take mine!" Pitale-sharo invited.

Shon-ka ran to his spear, still implanted in the ground where he had left it when he dismounted. Yanking the weapon free, Shon-ka stalked Pitale-sharo. "Now, you will die, Pawnee coward. First, I will plunge my spear into your heart. Then I will cut off your horn, and strip away your scalp. After that, I will kill your grandfather and all your people."

A blur of sudden movement caught Maura's eyes. She-de-a stepped away from Wetara-sharo, lifted her makeshift spear, and took careful aim. Just as Shon-ka aimed for Pitale-sharo's chest, She-de-a flung the spear with all her might. The digging stick wobbled as it cleft the air. Maura expected the knife blade to miss the Sioux altogether, but it sliced Shon-ka's back and hung there a second, quivering, before the unbalanced weight of the digging stick pulled it out again.

Shon-ka half-turned. Maura had a clear view of his startled, enraged face. The superficial wound only spurred his determination to kill everyone, beginning with Pitale-sharo. Turning back and grunting deep in his throat, he hurled his spear. Screaming his name, She-de-a dove toward Pitale-sharo. The long spear arced high into the air, whizzing toward its human target. With a crunching sound, it impaled She-de-a, drove completely through her body, and exited the other side. As she fell, Pitale-sharo caught the girl.

A second later, a hail of gunfire pelted Shon-ka from the trenches. Luke and Eben stood upright, shouldering smoking rifles, while Indians on both sides watched in stunned silence. The silence lasted only the space of a heartbeat. Screeching war cries, the army of Sioux leaped forward. Panicked, Maura gripped her bombs and stared at the oncoming Indians.

"Maura! Maura! Light the bombs and throw them!"

Was it Luke's voice or her father's? Maura could not concentrate, could not recall what Luke had told her to do in the event of attack by the watching Sioux. Death was thundering toward her, riding on the backs of the galloping horses. She saw Pitale-sharo frantically trying to remove the spear from She-de-a's broken body. The girl was probably already dead. She saw one of the oncoming horses stumble and go down, tossing its rider over its head. The man rolled to a stop and did not get up again.

At least, the holes we dug are working, she thought.

"Damn it, Maura, light the bombs!"

The sound of Luke's voice finally pierced the fog in her brain. Forcing her stiffened fingers to open, Maura set down the bombs and reached for the ember jar. Inside, the tiny ember still glowed; it had not gone out. Heartened by the discovery, she clambered out of the trench, and lit first one bomb, then the other. A bomb in each hand, she ran toward the advancing army.

Lowering the bombs to the grass, she checked the fuses; they were still burning. Tiny licks of flame traveled inexorably toward the gunpowder in the gourds. Spreading her hands, she shielded them from the breeze until the last possible second. Then she sprinted back to the trench, jumped in, and huddled in the dirt. Her breath came in painful gasps as she waited . . . and waited . . . and waited . . .

Chapter Twenty-seven

Luke paused between cranking off shots and reloading his rifle; Maura had jumped into the trench, but the bombs she had lit were not exploding. Neither had his. Neither had Eben's. Furious with himself for failing to concoct a proper explosive, he trained his rifle on the largest of the useless gourd bombs and sighted down the barrel. Shooting one would be a waste of badly needed ammunition, but he figured what the hell—it was all over now, anyway. They were all going to die. He himself had only a half-dozen shots left, not enough to kill his ten Indians even if he made every shot count.

Slowly squeezing the trigger, he hit the bomb dead center. The resulting huge blast knocked him head over heels into the bottom of the trench. For several stunned moments, he lay gasping, wondering what had hit him. Then a wave of elation flowed over him; one of his lousy, damn bombs had finally exploded! Spitting out dirt, he scrambled to his feet and peered over the trench's edge. Chaos greeted him. The explosion had killed or maimed a dozen or more of the attackers. Crazed horses were stampeding in every direction. Dazed Indians were lying on the ground, holding their heads and blinking in astonishment and terror. The effect was precisely what Luke had envisioned all along.

"Eben!" Luke shouted, waving his rifle to catch the older man's attention. "Shoot your bombs! Don't light 'em, *shoot* 'em with your rifle!"

Deciding Eben could not possibly hear him over the din of noise, Luke demonstrated. Quickly, he reloaded and sighted another bomb. The second explosion was greater than the first. Pawnee cowering inside the trenches scrambled out in panic and fled for the protection of the thick-walled earth lodges in the village. By the time Luke himself had recovered from the blast, Maura's father was carefully aiming at his own dud bombs lying out on the plain.

With no trouble at all, Eben picked off the first, causing a fiery blast that knocked Luke back into the trench, again. Sprawled in the dirt on his back, he began to laugh. Laughter welled up in him like a rain-swollen river leaping its embankments. The sight of Shon-ka's fierce army fleeing in mindless terror so tickled him that he guffawed like a braying mule. Even knowing that so many were dead or injured, he had to laugh; he couldn't help himself. Maybe the powder in this batch of bombs had *not* been bad; maybe it was the fuses. Whatever it was, Luke soon began to blame himself for not having thought of shooting the bombs much sooner. If he had, many lives might have been saved.

On that sobering thought, Luke got a firm grip on his hilarity. Crawling to his feet, he climbed out of the trench, and once again looked around. Clearly, the battle was over. With their leader dead and their self-confidence shattered, the demoralized Sioux were fleeing for the safety of the villages they had left, only too anxious to put this day of infamy behind them.

A thick pall of smoke drifted over the trenches; in places, the dry grass was burning. Luke squinted but could not see much except the carnage lying nearest him: an unconscious Indian with his arm blown off, another with no face, a dead horse with three legs sticking straight up.

His gorge rose, and he turned away. No matter how many times he witnessed senseless, violent death, he could not accustom himself to it. Depression descended; how many lives had been lost today? How many good men and horses were now lying silent upon the plain?

"Luke! Luke!" Maura was running toward him, arms outstretched, eyes jewel-bright in her sooty face.

He opened his arms and caught her, hugging and kissing her, smoothing back the dirty blond hair that fell in long tangles across her cheeks and down her back. She was so filthy as to be almost unrecognizable, but she was the most beautiful sight he had ever seen.

"Oh, Maura . . . Maura . . . thank God you survived. If anything had happened to you. . . ."

"The bombs, Luke! They finally worked! That first blast knocked me right off my feet!"

"Me, too. If only I'd thought of shooting them sooner. . . ."

"You couldn't have known. How *could* you? What ever gave you the idea in the first place?"

"I was riled," Luke told her. "So riled I couldn't see straight."

"But you *shot* straight! And you *did* it! Oh, Luke, I'm so proud of you!"

In the midst of Maura's wildly enthusiastic embrace, Eben came up. "Does this unrestrained behavior in broad daylight mean what I think it means?" he archly inquired.

Maura's dirty face was radiant. "Oh, yes, Father!" Luke has asked me to marry him, and I'm going to, as soon as possible. I don't want to give him a chance to change his mind. Maybe She-de-a and Pitale-sharo will marry, now, too. . . . Oh, my God, *She-de-a!*" The joy in Maura's eyes turned to horror. "Here we are celebrating,

356

and we don't even know if she's still alive! Or what happened to Pitale-sharo and his grandfather!"

Her face mirrored Luke's feelings; he had been so pleased about the victory he had completely forgotten about his friends. "Stay here with your father, Maura. I'll go see what's happened to the three of them."

"No, I'm coming with you," Maura insisted, stubborn as ever. "Whatever's happened, we'll face it together." Shyly, she touched Luke's arm. "From now on, we'll face everything together—*won't* we?"

The old fear for her nibbled at his heart. Doubt reared its ugly head. He could scarcely believe she had not been killed, today. "We'll try, Maura. I should say *I'll* try—but treating you as an equal is going to take some practice before I get it perfect. My first instinct is still to protect you from harm, both physical and emotional, and also to protect you from yourself."

"Don't push him too hard, Maura." Eben slanted his daughter a warning glance. "I may have failed in my duty to keep you safely out of trouble, but I don't want your future husband to fail. You're the equal of any man in courage and strength of character, but no matter how you protest, you're still a woman and therefore vulnerable. No, don't argue." He raised a hand to forestall the objection Maura was about to make. "I've spent this entire, awful morning berating myself for raising you the way I have; it's a miracle you survived all this."

Maura's mouth tightened. Her eyes flashed fire. "It's a miracle *any* of us survived," she retorted in a small, tight voice. "I am no more precious than She-de-a or any of the others, yet neither of you lecture them. Frankly, I'm *sick* of lectures. Why don't both of you just get out of my way while I go see what happened to my friends?"

Stepping past Luke, Maura stalked off toward the spot where they had last seen Pitale-sharo, She-de-a, Wetara-sharo, and Shon-ka. Thick smoke still wreathed the plain, and Maura soon disappeared in a cloud of the choking stuff. Luke and Eben exchanged long, worried glances.

"You have my heartiest congratulations on winning my daughter's affections," the older man said. "You also have my sympathy. She will not be easy to tame, Luke, not even after all that's happened."

Luke tried to sort through his conflicting emotions, an almost impossible task at the moment. "I think, sir," he said respectfully, struggling to be honest and not mislead Eben, "that Maura's wild, free spirit is the main reason I have come to love her. It may also be the thing that tears us apart. She will not, as you said, be easily tamed. Though I want to marry her, I . . . I have many doubts, many questions that as yet have no answers."

"I understand." Eben laid a fatherly hand on Luke's shoulder. "Whatever you decide, you have my blessing. I know your intentions are sincere and honorable. Don't let her rush you into anything—or you will both be miserable."

"I won't," Luke assured him. "Maura's happiness is the thing I want most, not just now but in the future."

"Well, then . . . ," Eben smiled ruefully. "Shall we follow our little standard-bearer and see what she's gotten herself into this time?"

Luke gestured for Eben to lead the way. "After you. I believe she stomped off in this direction. . . ."

Maura did not have to go far to find Pitale-sharo and She-de-a. As she exited the cloud of dust and lingering gunsmoke, she met Pitale-sharo carrying She-de-a back toward the village. Running to them, she peered down at her friend. "Is she dead?" she blurted anxiously.

"No. Not yet."

While Pitale-sharo paused to adjust his tender burden,

Maura examined the pale, silent figure in his muscular arms. She-de-a's eyes were closed, her head cushioned against Pitale-sharo's chest. Maura found it hard to believe the girl still lived; blood soaked her doeskin and Pitale-sharo's arms. It oozed through a strip of rawhide tied tightly around her shoulder. The magnitude of the injury overwhelmed Maura.

"Such a terrible wound! Can the shaman save her?"

"I will send someone to fetch Heavy Basket. She is better than the shaman at curing spear wounds."

Maura gulped to think of She-de-a's worst enemy being assigned the responsibility of healing her. "I'll help Heavy Basket," she offered. "Day and night, I'll nurse She-de-a."

Pitale-sharo ignored the offer. "Where is Great Heart? Someone must go and help my grandfather."

"Is he injured?" Maura's eyes searched the billows of smoke, but did not locate the old chieftain.

"No worse than he was. But he cannot walk unaided. When the Sioux came, he lay down beside Shon-ka, using the Sioux's body as a shield."

"What did *you* do? You and She-de-a?"

"When the first horse dropped dead, I carried She-de-a to its side, and we lay together on the ground near it. I removed the spear and bound the wound with a strip of rawhide. It was all I could do. I pray it was enough."

Pitale-sharo's rigid control suddenly broke, and he hid his face in She-de-a's blue-black hair. "If she dies . . . I cannot go on. I cannot be chief, anymore. Even if she lives, I no longer desire to be chief. Bon-son-gee can have what he has always wanted. I will take her away from here — or her bones if that is all that's left. We will never return."

"What are you saying? Bon-son-gee would not make a good chief! And you have *won* today! She-de-a *will* survive, and the two of you can marry, beget children, and live happily until a ripe old age—"

Pitale-sharo raised his head, his face hard, his eyes empty. "Leave me alone, White-Eyes Woman. You know nothing of me or my people. You should never have come here, trespassing where you don't belong, spying on our ancient ways. I do not want you here. Do you understand? Keep away from me. *I do not want you!*"

Shocked and hurt, Maura stumbled backward, colliding with Luke and Eben. Neither man seemed to have heard Pitale-sharo's vehement rejection of her help; they calmly asked the same questions she had asked and received the same stoic responses. Then they went looking for Wetara-sharo, while Pitale-sharo jostled Maura aside and continued on his way toward the village.

Not knowing what else to do, Maura followed at a discreet distance. She could not believe that Pitale-sharo had actually spoken to her like that. Why had he been so nasty? What had she done? She pondered his hostile attitude all the way back to the village. The only conclusion she could draw was that Pitale-sharo must be half-crazed with guilt, grief, and worry over She-de-a.

Well, no wonder, she thought angrily. He deserves to suffer, considering how he's treated She-de-a. She can't help being a Sioux.

Maura decided to ingored Pitale-sharo's churlishness. It was far more important to protect She-de-a from Heavy Basket and make certain the big squaw *healed* instead of harmed her little friend. When Pitale-sharo turned into one of the few lodges that still stood intact, its roof unburned and its entranceway passable, Maura marched in behind him and rushed ahead to draw back a skin from one of the sleeping platforms.

"Set her down here," she instructed, "I'll see if I can find some furs to make her more comfortable."

Pitale-sharo stiffened. His jaw clamped down hard in anger. "I said I do not want you near me—or She-de-a.

You have not been a good influence on her."

The accusation was absurd; Maura had to catch her breath before refuting it. "I have been her *friend* — far more than anyone else in this village, including *you*, Pitale-sharo. Were it not for you, she would be with the other women on top of the bluff."

"You *encouraged* her to love me. You even helped her sew the clothes she made, and the moccasins I am wearing."

"What is so wrong with *that?* I did help her sew the clothing and moccasins, but loving you was *her* idea. I myself could not understand how she could care so much for a man who first abducted and then ignored her. If you feel guilty for the callous way you have treated her, Pitale-sharo, do not blame *me*. I am the only true friend she has in this village."

Pitale-sharo's shoulders sagged; the fight suddenly left him. "You are right, White-Eyes Woman. You have been her only true friend."

Quickly, he deposited She-de-a on the sleeping platform and stepped back. "Look after her. I myself will climb the bluff and fetch Heavy Basket and the shaman. After that, I must see to burying the dead and sheltering the wounded. . . . Do not let her die, White-Eyes Woman."

Tears shone in Pitale-sharo's eyes, the first humble, tender emotion Maura had ever seen him display. "If I can keep her alive, I will, Pitale-sharo. Is there no one beside Heavy Basket who can tend her wound? Heavy Basket despises her."

"That is true. But if I order it, no matter what she feels, Heavy Basket will use all her knowledge and power to save She-de-a. The women of my tribe are accustomed to obeying orders; in this they are not like White-Eyes women who argue all the time."

"Not all White-Eyes women are like me, Pitale-sharo.

If you doubt it, ask Great Heart and my father. My refusal to obey orders is the one thing about me that greatly irritates both my father and Great Heart." Maura ventured a tiny smile at the departing Pawnee chieftain and then worriedly bent over She-de-a.

No one thought She-de-a would survive the night. Despite Heavy Basket's ministrations and the chants and rituals of the shaman, the little Sioux did not open her eyes. Heavy Basket cleaned the terrible wound, stitched it shut on both sides, and applied foul-smelling, herbal poultices. She then forced an equally disgusting brew down the girl's throat and declared she had done all she could; the rest was up to Tirawa. Since others among the wounded stood a better chance of survival, Heavy Basket departed to minister to them, leaving Maura alone to keep the vigil over the dying girl.

From time to time, Eben came to see how She-de-a was doing and to bring food that Lizard Woman had prepared. Luke also came and went frequently. In the aftermath of the battle, much work remained to be done. The dead had to be prepared for burial, the wounded bandaged, lodges cleaned up, and food supplies unearthed. After organizing the initial efforts, Pitale-sharo joined Maura in her lonely vigil, so Luke assumed the task of directing work parties to help Wetara-sharo and Bon-son-gee bring order to the chaos.

The first time Luke tried to solicit Pitale-sharo's opinion, if not his labor, Pitale-sharo would not respond. She-de-a had been moved from the chilly, sleeping platform to a warm pallet of furs near the firepit, and the Pawnee chieftain sat beside her, holding her hand, staring down at her face, and neither listening nor speaking to anyone.

"I never realized Pitale-sharo felt so strongly about She-de-a," Luke whispered to Maura on his way out of the lodge after the futile effort.

"Neither did he. Men never seem to realize what they want until they're about to lose it."

Luke's brows arched questioningly. "I suppose that applies to me, too. Is that what you're trying to say?"

"I would never presume to warn *you* against potential losses." But she *was* warning him, and he knew it.

"Remember what your father said, Maura. Don't push too hard."

"Does that mean you *don't* want to marry me, after all?" Maura shamelessly sought confirmation that he had really meant what he had said earlier that day. Since then, Luke had had many opportunities, but had not uttered a single, tender, intimate word to her. "Away from the heat of battle, have you reconsidered?"

Dark shadows made Luke's face look lean and cruel; when he spoke, he sounded impatient. "We're both tired tonight, Maura. This is not the time or place to discuss our future. I'm not thinking clearly, and I doubt that you are, either."

Maura felt as if he had stabbed her. Either he loved her and wanted to marry her, or he did *not*. Why did he need to be fresh and well-rested to know how he really felt about her? Was he regretting today's declaration, made impulsively and under great strain?

"You're quite right, Luke," she retorted icily. "If you want to take back what you said this morning, go right ahead. I'll pretend you never said it. Undoubtedly, you weren't thinking clearly then, either."

"Damn it, Maura! Quit twisting everything I say or don't say! I do love you and want to marry you, but—"

"But *what?*"

"But it isn't as simple as you want it to be! We're still a hell of a long way from an altar and a preacher—and that's part of the whole damn problem that you just don't want to face!"

"I've already told you, Luke. I can face anything as long as I have you beside me. What I won't do is trail *behind* you, the way squaws mince after their husbands. Haven't you noticed, yet? I'm not that kind of woman; I don't need that kind of protections—if protection is what it really is."

"For God sake, Maura." Luke wearily raked his fingers through his hair. "I'm not even sure what the hell we're arguing about, or what it is you want. All I know is I'm scared half out of my wits. Whenever I think of marrying you, I get a sinking feeling in my gut and break out in a sweat. I'm just so damned fearful of losing you—of having to sit helplessly like Pitale-sharo, watching you die and not being able to do a damn thing to stop it."

"Luke . . . oh, Luke. . . . It doesn't have to be that way for *us!*" Maura reached for him, but just as she did so, Wetara-sharo came into the lodge, leaning heavily on Lizard Woman's arm.

"I've got to go now, Maura. We'll continue this discussion another time."

Before she could even ask when, Luke escaped, darting past the old chieftain without even acknowledging him or saying good-bye.

Chapter Twenty-eight

Three days passed, and She-de-a tenaciously clung to life. On the fourth day, fever set in, accompanied by bouts of delirium, during which she uttered snatches of what sounded like a chant.

"What is she saying?" Maura asked Pitale-sharo as the two of them bathed She-de-a's forehead, neck, and arms with a cool, damp cloth.

"It's a Sioux mourning chant. And she has been calling names. I think they are the names of her family, who died from the spotted sickness. Her village must have been the one where the sickness first started, before it spread to the other Sioux villages, last summer."

Maura had forgotten the circumstances of She-de-a's capture. No wonder the girl had been so willing! And how incredible that all three of them had lost family members to smallpox. Perhaps that was why she felt such a sense of oneness with these people; mutual suffering had bound them together. Over the last few days, Maura had come to regard Pitale-sharo with the same affection she felt for She-de-a. He had begun to seem almost like a brother to Maura.

The thing that pleased her most was Pitale-sharo's unfailing devotion to the little Sioux; whatever doubts or misgivings he had had about expressing his feelings seemed to have vanished. Love and caring underscored every small act he performed for She-de-a. Maura wished she could say the same about Luke, but Luke had been avoiding her, sending others to inquire after She-de-a's health. What really hurt was that her own father made excuses for Luke, citing how busy he was. Maura did not believe the excuses; she now had the same sinking feeling of which Luke had complained. Things would probably never work out between them. Their love would die of neglect before it ever had a chance to flourish.

A sound at the entranceway distracted her from these dismal thoughts. Wetara-sharo had come for his daily visit, this time accompanied by Bon-son-gee. Darting a glance at their two unfriendly faces, Maura knew that something was very wrong. She was not surprised when Wetara-sharo pointed a bony finger at her and rasped, "Leave us, White-Eyes Woman. I wish to speak to my grandson in privacy."

She nodded and immediately got up to leave. "When I come back, I will bring you something to eat, Pitale-sharo." She handed him her damp cloth. "I will also bring broth for She-de-a. We must keep trying to get some food into her."

"Do that, Moe-ra. And do not be gone long."

Upon hearing Pitale-sharo's request for her speedy return, Wetara-sharo and Bon-son-gee glowered with displeasure. Maura hurried down the dark tunnel leading to the fresh air outside, but when she got to the end of it, paused and waited to see if Bon-son-gee would join her. Why should Pitale-sharo's truculent rival be permitted to stay for a private conversation, while she was sent away?

Poking her head outside, Maura inhaled deeply of the sweet, earth-scented air. No longer was there any doubt that spring had arrived. The tight buds on the cottonwood trees by the river were erupting into pale green leaves, and the winds blew warm and welcoming from the south. The last two days had been unseasonably warm, causing Lizard Woman and Heavy Basket to complain because the heavy spring rains had likely bypassed them. Maybe the rains would still come. Maura hoped so; like everyone else, she dreaded the idea of what drought would do to the already dry plains. In the meantime, she did not intend to feel guilty about enjoying such lovely weather. Nor did she intend to worry about being forced to leave the village to return to Bellevue.

No one had said a word about it lately, and if someone did, Pitale-sharo would surely intervene and allow her and her father to stay—especially after all they had done to help the tribe through this crisis. Was that what Wetara-sharo and Bon-son-gee wanted to discuss with Pitale-sharo? Maura cocked her head and listened, but could not hear Bon-son-gee coming down the passageway. Certain he was not coming, she slipped back through the tunnel and stood near the antelope skin screening the doorway, from which vantage point she could hear what was being said in the lodge.

Intending to eavesdrop just long enough to be sure they were not talking about *her*, Maura was startled when she heard Pitale-sharo's voice raised in anger. "I don't care anymore what you think, Grandfather. If She-de-a lives, I will marry her. She'll become my wife—my *real* wife. I love her, and I won't give her up."

All thoughts of leaving abruptly fled; Maura edged closer. "The girl does not belong to you," Wetara-sharo disputed. "Will you sacrifice your people for the sake of one of our enemies?"

"She-de-a is no enemy; she saved my life. Were it not for her, I would be dead now. That changes everything."

"It changes nothing, my son. If anything, it only increases her value. She will be the best Morning Star maiden we have ever had. Her beauty and courage will please Tirawa as no other maiden's has ever done."

"Her beauty and courage please *me*, Grandfather. Besides, she may not even live to become the Morning Star maiden. Why do you not send Bon-son-gee to capture another girl, and permit this one to become my wife?"

There was a weighty pause; then Wetara-sharo sighed. "You know why, my son. There is not time to prepare another. In order to become Morning Star maiden, a young woman must first learn Pawnee and willingly adhere to our ways. She must live among us long enough to prove her worth. Most important of all, she must desire the good of our tribe as if it were her own. She-de-a has met every requirement, and thus far, so have you. Do not disappoint us now. What you ask is impossible, a betrayal of us all. More than at any other time in memory, we need a Morning Star who is perfect in every respect."

Another silence ensued. Maura prepared to flee if she heard the approach of footsteps. But instead of footsteps, she heard the shocking sound of male weeping — and Pitale-sharo pleading in a choked voice, "Please, Grandfather . . . I *beg* you. There must be some other way. What will we do if She-de-a dies? Who will be Morning Star maiden then?"

"I do not know, my son. If she dies, it may be a sign that we are doomed, and Tirawa has indeed turned his face from us. The drought shall kill us, or mayhap the spotted sickness."

"If the Sioux dies," said a deep voice, which Maura recognized as Bon-son-gee's, "why not use the White-Eyes woman? She speaks Pawnee, she has learned our ways, and though her looks are not to *my* taste, some might

368

call her beautiful. At least, she would be better than nothing."

Maura clamped her hand over her mouth to smother a gasp. She had not the slightest idea what a Morning Star maiden was or did. But she intended to find out. What if she were to volunteer for the position? Would it free She-de-a to marry Pitale-sharo? Wetara-sharo might not want a white woman to take part in some secret Pawnee ritual, but if she willingly offered herself, might he not consider it?

Ripping back the curtain, Maura stepped into the room. All three men started in surprise. She opened her mouth to speak, but before she could say a word, Bon-son-gee seized her long braid, dragged her into the middle of the lodge, and forced her down on her knees. "Spy! White-Eyes bitch, listening to Pawnee secrets!" He yanked his knife from the sheath at his waist, jerked back her head, and pressed the tip of the blade into her throat. "This is what we do to spies! Prepare to die, White-Eyes bitch. It is long past time that someone slit your throat!"

"Stop!" Pitale-sharo grabbed Bon-son-gee's knife. "Do not kill her."

"Why? Do you lust after this one, too?" Bon-son-gee demanded, refusing to let go of Maura's hair *or* the knife.

Maura hardly dared breathe as the two men towered over her, facing each other across her trembling body. She could feel the blade cold against her skin and knew that any sudden movement would mean instant death.

"The last thing we need is another battle, this time with the White-Eyes. Tell him, Grandfather. Another battle would destroy us."

"Let her go," Wetara-sharo wearily commanded. Though his voice was still powerful, he had to hold on to

369

a lodge pole for support.

Reluctantly, Bon-son-gee withdrew the knife and released Maura's braid. "She has heard what she should not have heard," he said bitterly, defensively. "It is forbidden for outsiders to learn of the Morning Star ceremony. Even among ourselves, we never speak of it unless the subject becomes unavoidable."

Relieved to be free and still alive, Maura rubbed her throat. "I will tell no one what I have heard," she promised, hoping to ease their worries, whatever they were. "I only interrupted because I had an idea that might solve all of your problems."

She looked expectantly from one to the other, but no one said anything, not even to ask what she had in mind. Sensing they were still grappling with the shock of her intrusion—and the fact that she had discovered a tribal secret, Maura plunged ahead. "Bon-son-gee has suggested that I might serve as your Morning Star maiden. I . . . I might be willing if I knew what such a maiden does."

Again, the men exchanged shocked glances. Pitale-sharo's nostrils flared as he emphatically shook his head. "We cannot tell you. As Bon-son-gee says, it is forbidden to speak of it. Besides, you are not of our race, and therefore you cannot—"

Wetara-sharo held up his hand. "Silence! The White-Eyes woman has bravely offered herself in her little friend's place. Such courage in the face of the unknown deserves courage in return. . . . Sit down, child. I myself will tell you as much as I am able without angering the god, Tirawa."

Maura had not actually offered herself—at least, not yet—but she nonetheless knelt down near She-de-a, who slumbered on, muttering now and then, unaware of the tension in the lodge. Maura's own intense excitement more than made up for her friend's lack of awareness; this was just what she had dreamed about back east. She—Maura Magruder—was going to learn about an ancient, secret Indian ritual, unbeknownst to anyone even her father, the renowned Indian expert.

Wetara-sharo and Bon-son-gee both sat down, but Pitale-sharo withdrew a short distance, as if he found the entire matter too distressing for causal conversation. The old chief cleared his throat, and then began. "Tirawa is the god of Morning Star, a bold, vengeful warrior. Atira is his mate, the kind and gentle Evening Star. During the Morning Star ceremony, the two unite, joining their opposing forces to produce balance, harmony, peace, and prosperity in the universe. It is our most sacred ritual, held only once every four summers, at dawn on the longest day of the year."

The summer solstice, Maura crowed to herself, the same time Pitale-sharo is supposed to wed!

"During the ceremony, the duty of the Morning Star maiden is to bear greetings to Tirawa. Thus, she must be able to speak Pawnee so she can intercede for us. She must also be beautiful and possess qualities men would seek in a beloved wife. If she pleases the great god, he will shower blessings upon our tribe and give us good weather so that the corn will grow and the buffalo multiply. He will give us strength to defend ourselves from our enemies and to fight off sickness. But if he is not pleased, he will hold back his blessings, and the Pawnee will suffer."

She-de-a certainly met all the requirements, Maura realized. No wonder Wetara-sharo wanted her to be the Morning Star maiden! "But what happens *after* the ceremony? Couldn't She-de-a first bear the greetings to Tirawa, and then become Pitale-sharo's wife?"

Wetara-sharo mournfully shook his head. "No. Once a

maiden has been dedicated to Tirawa, no Pawnee can marry her. She is *wakon*, sacred medicine, and belongs only to Tirawa."

Maura pondered this a moment and concluded that whoever became Morning Star maiden must be required to live out her life as a virgin, untouched by mere mortals. "Must she stay here in the village? Or could she leave after the ceremony and seek a new life elsewhere, perhaps with another tribe?"

"All of our past maidens have left us," Wetara-sharo gravely responded. "Not one has remained."

"Then I can understand why Pitale-sharo doesn't want She-de-a to participate in the ceremony — and why you have to *capture* girls to fill the role." Maura smiled. "I wouldn't want to stay here either, if I could not marry and live a normal life."

"To become Morning Star maiden is a great honor," Wetara-sharo said. "It is the greatest honor a female can experience. At first, a maiden feels sadness at leaving us, but afterward, she knows great happiness, because she realizes that she has brought health and prosperity to her adopted tribe."

"Yes, I can see how fulfilling it would be," Maura hastened to agree. "Once she gets settled somewhere else, she can look back with gladness, not sorrow. But what of the ceremony itself? You still have not told me exactly what occurs."

Wetara-sharo paused before answering. His bright black eyes probed her face. "I have already said too much, White-Eyes Woman. To tell you more would only anger Tirawa. I dare not risk it. No White-Eyes has ever been told of the ceremony — or ever witnessed it. Even Great Heart does not know of it."

"But if you make an exception for me, I will swear to say nothing to him about it — or to my father. However, if they are here in the village, they might learn of it from someone else."

"It might be possible to arrange for them both to be gone from the village during the summer solstice," We-tara-sharo said, watching her closely.

Maura moistened her lips and willed her voice to remain steady. "Then, if you will accept me, I humbly offer myself to serve as Morning Star maiden in She-de-a's place."

"No!" Pitale-sharo cried. "She cannot do it, Grandfather! I myself will fetch another—an Indian girl, a Sioux or a Mandan, as we have always had. Moe-ra does not realize what—"

"*I do realize what I'm doing!* I'm making it possible for you to marry She-de-a!"

And to learn things no other whites have ever known, Maura added to herself, picturing her moment of triumph in front of the esteemed members of the Anthropological Society. When she told them what she had done and seen, and revealed the role she herself had played in the most cherished ceremony of the Skidi Pawnee, the Society would *have* to admit her—the first woman—into its exalted ranks.

"Let her choose her own destiny," Bon-son-gee argued, surprising Maura with his support.

"She doesn't know what she's choosing!" Pitale-sharo knelt down between Maura and She-de-a. "Moe-ra, this is not right. Do not offer yourself. Great Heart and Silver-Hair would not like it. They will be angry. . . ."

"They will not *know*, Pitale-sharo. Your grandfather said he will find some excuse to send them away."

"But . . . but. . . ." Pitale-sharo glanced wildly at his grandfather.

Wetara-sharo regarded the younger man stonily. His thin lips curled down in disgust. "Are you never pleased, my son? At last, I have found a way to give you the woman you love, yet still you dare argue and challenge me. Your friend, Great Heart, need never know. Excuses can be found for anything—even the unexplainable."

Pitale-sharo jumped to his feet, his face livid, his muscles bunched. Maura could not understand it. He had more to gain from her offer than anyone; why was he so against it?

"It is settled, then," Wetara-sharo said. "White-Eyes Woman, I pledge you to secrecy. As proof of your promise to tell no one what has been said here this day, we must mingle our blood."

"M . . . mingle our blood?"

"Hold out your hand . . . like this." The old chief extended his hand, palm upward. "Bon-son-gee, make the cuts."

Grinning wickedly, Bon-son-gee took out his knife, and before Maura could even prepare herself, reached down and slashed open her palm. The sudden, sharp pain, and the sight of blood gushing from the wound so shocked Maura that she could do nothing but sit and watch silently as Bon-son-gee then slashed the old chief's hand.

"Press your hand to mine." Wetara-sharo held up his bleeding hand.

Fighting a wave of lightheadedness, Maura did so, pressing cut palm to cut palm so that her blood mingled with Wetara-sharo's and dripped upon the floor mats.

"Now, you are Pawnee—one of us, even as Great Heart is one of us. As I have already warned you, he does not know our secret. Only *you* know it, and you must guard it with your very life. Do you swear to do this?"

"I swear," Maura said, and she meant it. For now, she would not tell Luke, her father, or anyone else. But someday, long after it mattered to the Pawnee, she would

374

tell the world. Someday, her treatises would be read around the globe. Every English-speaking newspaper in America and abroad would publish them. They might even be translated into a dozen languages. Fortunately, Wetara-sharo and Pitale-sharo would never know; they couldn't read.

"I swear," she repeated. "I swear with this, the mingling of our blood."

What's wrong with your hand?" Luke demanded the next day. He had unexpectedly sought her out as she was fetching water from the river.

"I . . . I accidentally cut it," Maura lied, hiding the bandaged appendage behind her back.

Luke eyed her skeptically. "How unfortunate! Does your cut look anything like this?"

He held up his own hand and pointed to a scar on his palm that Maura had never before noticed. But then, Luke had so many mysterious scars. Someday, if they ever married and had time to savor each other's bodies, she planned on making him tell her the story of each one. At the moment, she did not want to discuss them.

"It might," she hedged, backing away.

"I'd bet my life that it's identical. Pitale-sharo has one, too. Hell, by now he's probably got two—or he *will* have after this latest cut heals."

"As far as I know, Pitale-sharo hasn't any fresh cuts."

"Then who does—Wetara-sharo? I'm not slow-witted, Maura. I know exactly what you're up to. You've finally figured out a way to stay here, haven't you? You've finally won them all over."

Maura saw there was no sense denying it; Luke might as well know that she did not intend to leave the Pawnee until she was good and ready. After all, her renewed interest in anthropological studies was partly *his* fault; he had not offered any exciting alternatives, such as marriage. Had he insisted upon returning to Bellevue in order to find a preacher to marry them as soon as possible, she would have been sorely tempted to give up her ambitions and follow her heart. Since he had not, all she had left were her ambitions.

"Yes, Luke, I've finally won them over. It's spring now, but no one is insisting that we leave. And no one's going to. We can stay for as long as we like—or until we have a *reason* for leaving," she added pointedly.

"Have you told your father? I haven't noticed him sporting any cut palms. I wonder how he'll feel knowing that his daughter has succeeded where he has not."

"I should imagine he would feel proud of my success. My father and I do *not* compete against each other."

"I wonder if that's really true, Maura. It seems to me you compete with every man you meet. All a man has to do is tell you no, and the first word out of your mouth is *yes*. If he happens to say yes, then you say no. It's a compulsion with you—disagreeing, challenging, proving something to yourself and him, though I don't know what it is you think you're proving."

"Is this the discussion you promised we would have, Luke? The one you've been avoiding? If it is, then you can quit right now. You can't possibly want to marry a woman who rouses you to such anger and contempt."

Snatching her half-filled water skin, Luke flung it aside. Then he grabbed her bandaged hand and yanked her behind a cottonwood, out of sight of the village. "Oh, you arouse me all right, Maura. There's never been any doubt about *that*, has there? You've got me hopelessly confused and muddled, but the one thing I can't escape is my *need* for you."

He pressed her into the tree trunk. His hands locked

around her waist, pinioning her hips against his. Dipping his head, he nipped her earlobe and then rasped in her ear, "Don't you know why I've been avoiding you, Maura? Because whenever I see you, whenever I'm near you, all I can think about is making love to you. I want to release your beautiful hair from those damn, confining braids and run my fingers through it. I want to tear off these old doeskin rags and caress your tender, sweet body. I want to tip you over into the grass, spread your thighs, and enter you. . . . I want to fill your belly with part of myself, so the whole world will know you belong to me and no one else."

His desire for her was sweet as nectar. Maura melted against him, slipping her arms around his shoulders. "I *want* you to do that, Luke—every word of it. Just tell me you love me and want to marry me, and I'll go back to Bellevue with you. We'll find a preacher, and—"

He thrust her away from him, callously slamming her shoulders into the hard tree trunk. "And then what, Maura? *Then what?* Will you have our baby out here on the Plains in some flea-infested dirt lodge or skin tepee? Why, if I got you pregnant right now, you could deliver in the middle of a howling blizzard and bleed to death for lack of a doctor or midwife. Or you could die of snakebite, another Indian attack, a buffalo stampede, starvation during a drought, or a hundred other things I haven't even thought of. And if I tried to avoid all that by taking you back east, *I* could die of boredom and being tied down, and being forced to do work I hate and to live a life I've already rejected. . . . I can't *do* it, Maura! Damn it all, I can't see a way out for us!"

"Luke! Oh, Luke, there *must* be a way to make it work!" Maura clung to him, choking on disappointment and grief, wounded by the hopelessness she heard in his voice.

"Maura, my beautiful, naive Maura." Luke held her and stroked her hair while she ground her face into his shoulder and wept bitter tears. "Don't cry. . . . It tears me to pieces to see you cry." He tilted her face to meet his and wiped away her tears with his thumbs. "Listen to me . . . I need time away from you to think this through. Maybe there is a way, but I need a chance to find it — to figure out how I can provide for you and still be satisfied with who and what I am. My present way of life doesn't allow for a wife, Maura. If I'm to marry you, as I want to, I've got to explore new possibilities. I've got to think and plan. Can you understand that? Can you forgive me for being such a coward? And are you willing to wait until I can find a way to make it work?"

"But where will you go? What will you do?"

"Back to Bellevue — to do what I've always done, help Major Dougherty keep the peace. I have to report back to him about the battle here, anyway. Earlier this morning, I was talking to your father, and I think he wants to come back to Bellevue with me and send for more supplies. He has a notion of arranging to visit the Mandans after the two of you finally leave here, so he can compare their culture with the Skidi Pawnee."

Maura was surprised. "He never said anything about the Mandans to me."

"I doubt he's had time. You *have* been busy and preoccupied, lately. He figures you'll want to stay here anyway and look after She-de-a, at least until he's got everything set up."

Why did men always want to "set everything up", and tell her about it after the fact? Suddenly, Maura remembered the Morning Star ceremony; would Luke and her father be gone for that?

"When will you be returning?" she asked, carefully composing her face so as not to let her secret slip.

378

"I can't say yet. Could be midsummer. Your father mentioned that he'd like to visit the Mandans to see if they'd permit an extended stay like you've had with the Pawnee. It's a long journey to the Mandans, and I'll probably be the one to take him there."

Maura's mind spun; if Luke and her father were going to be gone until midsummer, things would work out perfectly, as far as the Morning Star ceremony was concerned. And after that, she would either be marrying Luke or going off to study the Mandans.

"By the time you bring my father back, will you know if . . . if you want to marry me?"

Waiting for his answer, Maura held her breath. Much as she loved Luke, she did not think she could wait forever for him to make up his mind. Whatever he decided, he would have to understand that she did not intend to abandon her own work in order to marry him. His vehement insistence upon safeguarding his identity had convinced her that she could not change who or what she was, either. Before meeting Luke, she had intended to return to the east, marry Nate Hibbert, and maintain an interest in anthropology. Now, if her study of the secret religious ceremonies of the Pawnee engendered even half the acclaim she thought it would, her future in anthropology would be assured. Wherever she lived, whomever she married, she wanted to study primitive culture.

Luke tugged her closer. "I *already* know I want to marry you. What I'll know by then is if I *can*."

Looking up into Luke's gray eyes, Maura cast aside pride and said what was in her heart. "If you can't, Luke, I don't know how I'll bear it. I want you so much. Take me somewhere and make love to me. For one last time before you go, hold me close. I need memories to sustain me until I see you again."

"Maura, my love, we'll go downriver as we did before. But this time, I won't make love to you in a way that might make you pregnant. So far, we've been lucky, but I won't tempt fate again. We've already tempted it too often."

Taking her hand, he led her away and did, indeed, make love to her in a secluded spot on the riverbank, but without joining their naked bodies in the glorious union she so much desired. At the moment that her body throbbed with intense physical pleasure, she knew deep disappointment and frustration. More than anything she wanted Luke's baby growing in side her, wanted some part of him to keep as her own, in case he decided *not* to marry her.

"Luke!" she cried, wrapping her arms and legs around him, trying to draw him into her.

But he pulled away and wasted his seed on the ground. Afterward, he held her as she wept again, neither of them speaking. Silently, they dressed and returned to the village.

Chapter Twenty-nine

From the moment She-de-a realized she was going to be granted her heart's desire, the girl began to get better. Her fever ebbed, and the wound evidenced healing. Pitale-sharo prepared daily poultices to hurry the slow process, administered herbal brews for her to drink, hunted fresh meat, and entertained her with stories of his childhood and tribal history. Maura found that her own company was not needed or wanted; Pitale-sharo now seemed to resent her presence, and if he was in the lodge, She-de-a had eyes and ears for no one else.

The family from whom Pitale-sharo had first appropriated the lodge finally moved back into it, so there was another woman, Prairie Turnip, to share nursing chores. As Pitale-sharo's and She-de-a's love blossomed like some rare, beautiful rose unfurling its petals one by one, Maura found excuses to stay away. The weather was beautiful and balmy, inviting long, solitary, riverside walks which continually yielded delightful surprises — the first spring flowers, the return of the sand cranes, glimpses of antelope and buffalo babies following their mothers on wobbly legs. The season of rebirth yielded scant rain, but the dewy mornings were as fresh as a shower. Everywhere on the dry plains, new life abounded.

Maura missed Luke and her father terribly — Luke, the most. Without She-de-a to talk to, she discovered that she had few, if any, close friends. Considering what she had shared with the Pawnee, she ought to have had friends aplenty, but it seemed to her that people now looked at her with cool, distant eyes — the same way they had once looked at She-de-a. No formal announcement of her willingness to serve as Morning Star maiden had been made to the tribe in her hearing, yet she sensed that everyone knew, and because of it, were now treating her differently.

She wondered if they were assessing her worthiness and judging her wanting. As soon as She-de-a was past the point of crisis, Maura moved back into Lizard Woman's lodge, but she spent as little time there as possible; even Lizard Woman now treated her in a curiously polite, detached manner, and Small Hand never so much as acknowledged her presence — yet she had saved his life! Without She-de-a in it, Lizard Woman's lodge was a quiet, boring place. Maura cheerfully did her share of the chores, helped repair the damage caused by the Sioux attack, and then spent the rest of the day elsewhere, picking wildflowers or riding Cinnamon. She almost felt like a stranger in the village, and one day, when a group of noisy, playing children fell silent and ran away when they saw her, she knew she must do something to reestablish her fast deteriorating relationship with the Pawnee.

Deciding to have a talk with Pitale-sharo, she caught him alone and unaware as he was returning from a hunting expedition. A freshly killed young antelope hung over his horse's withers. He had just dismounted and was dragging off his kill, preparatory to turning loose his favorite buffalo-runner.

"Pitale-sharo? Could I speak with you a moment?"

At the sound of her voice, he jumped. When he turned to face her, he looked almost guilty. "What do you want, White-Eyes Woman?"

"Not Moe-ra?" she gently chided. "Why don't you call me Moe-ra, anymore? Indeed, why don't you ever speak to me?"

He immediately averted his eyes and went back to dragging the dead antelope away from the horse. She studied him with growing irritation. His blue-black hair had grown longer since the battle with the Sioux. He still wore it in the same way, pulled back and fastened into a taunting scalp lock from which the bushy, startlingly red, false hair protruded, and he still sported the same worn, fringed leggings and breechclout, and the new moccasins She-de-a had made him. Yet, he looked different—and it was not just the scars from his fight with Shon-ka that shone pink against his dark flesh. His manner was that of a man who despised her—but for what reason, she had no idea.

"Pitale-sharo, does everyone know that I am going to be the Morning Star maiden, instead of She-de-a?"

He straightened and gazed at her with hooded eyes across the dead antelope. "They know."

"Who told them?"

He shrugged. "Probably Bon-son-gee."

"Are they displeased? Is that why no one talks to me, anymore? Are they angry because I'm not Indian?"

Pitale-sharo sighed, finally giving her his full attention. "They do not know how to treat you, Moe-ra. Morning Star maidens have always been captured girls who themselves did not know of the great honor awaiting them. In those cases, the people had to test them to prove their worthiness. I myself—or some other warrior—had to tempt them with the possibility of marriage in order to make them want to become Pawnee. That is what we did to She-de-a, only I was not supposed to feel anything for her. But I did."

"I see . . . so I am the first one who has actually volunteered and *knows* she will participate in the ceremony."

"Yes . . . and I still wish you had not done it." Pitale-sharo dropped his gaze to the antelope lying stiff and glassy-eyed on the grass, an arrow sticking out of its heart. "I cannot tell you why, but I wish you had not offered yourself. You opened the way for me to have She-de-a, but it might have been opened, anyway. Had you not interfered, I might have convinced my grandfather to seek another maid from some distant tribe."

"You don't want me because I'm a white woman—is that it?"

Pitale-sharo scowled, but would not meet her eyes or answer.

"I'm surprised at you, Pitale-sharo—and deeply disappointed. Because of your friendship with Luke—Great Heart, I mean—I thought you were a wiser, more visionary man. But you never even told Luke about this important ceremony; you held it back from him, because he, too, is white, and you don't really trust him."

"That is not true! I trust him more than any man I have ever known."

"No, you don't. You don't trust Luke, and you don't trust me—though both of us have fought your enemies alongside you, learned your language, and offered you our friendship. In your heart, you still doubt us, maybe even hold us in contempt. And so long as *you* cannot

384

accept us, your people will never accept us. . . . Don't you see, Pitale-sharo? By not approving of me as Morning Star maiden, you are tossing away a wonderful opportunity to lead your people into the future, to show them that it's possible for two races to respect each other, live in peace, and learn from their differences instead of allowing those differences to drive them apart."

"Cease your prattling, woman! Can you not see that you are blind, foolish, and ignorant? Consider the matter of Great Heart. He takes from my people only those things that suit him. Many times have I invited him to stay among us, marry one of our women, and make his home here, but always he returns to Belle-vue. He is torn between our two worlds, and because of him, so am I, and so, now, are you. The more we learn of each other, the more confused we become. Once, because of my friendship with Great Heart, I thought it would be possible to walk with a foot in each world. Now, I know I cannot. Not only do I question *his* world, I question mine . . . and you do not make my choices any easier. From the day you arrived here, you have sown confusion, the seeds of which will one day spring up like weeds to choke life from the corn that sustains us."

"Why *confusion?*" Maura shouted, exasperated. "What is there to be confused about? You yourself speak in riddles, Pitale-sharo. Why can't you talk plainly, so I can understand?"

"Look at this antelope, Moe-ra. Look at it!"

"What does a dead antelope have to do with anything?"

"Listen and *look*. Maybe your eyes will be opened. It is all I can do for you."

Gritting her teeth in exasperation, Maura looked. It was not a happy sight. The dead antelope had been a youthful creature of grace and beauty. Perhaps it was

385

even one of those she had admired in the distance on her walks along the river. Now, the animal's loveliness was destroyed, for a good purpose, but destroyed just the same. Maura especially hated the expression in the doe's soft, brown eyes; it was one of bewilderment, as if death had come as a great shock, as if it were a rude surprise that anyone should stoop to killing such a harmless, delicate, innocent creature.

"Look well, Moe-ra," Pitale-sharo said. "She died because she was too curious. When the rest of the herd scented me and took flight, she alone paused and looked back. That is when I let fly my arrow to take her life. Had she fled with the others, I would have missed her . . . but she dared to look at me, and so she died."

"What are you *telling* me? Have I something to fear?"

"You and I, Moe-ra . . . we have everything to fear. . . . This very night, I will once again try to convince my grandfather to find another woman to become Morning Star maiden. You have stated the perfect reason: Because you are a White-Eyes, you must not be permitted to do it. You are unworthy; Tirawa will be furious."

The next morning, when Maura went to visit She-de-a, she found the girl sobbing uncontrollably in Prairie Turnip's arms.

"Oh, Moe-ra!" She-de-a cried, lifting her tear-stained face. "Pitale-sharo has left me! He has gone away — and it is all because of you!"

Maura sank down on her knees beside her little friend. "What is it? What's happened?"

She-de-a was weeping too hard to answer, so Prairie Turnip answered for her. "Our young chief came this morning to say good-bye. Last night, he argued and fought with the old chieftain, his grandfather. Wetara-sharo said he must go away to the mountains in the west, a long, hard journey. There, he must fast and pray, begging the spirits to clear his vision and allow him to see the path he must walk, the best way to lead his people, the Skidi Pawnee."

"They didn't fight over *me* — because I'm to be Morning Star maiden?"

Prairie Turnip withdrew from She-de-a and sat back on her heels, eyes lowered, face inscrutable. "It is forbidden to speak of that."

"Well, did they or didn't they? I know Pitale-sharo went to see his grandfather in order to protest. He doesn't want me to participate in the ceremony — or even to witness it."

"I know nothing of any such ceremony," Prairie Turnip denied.

"What do *you* know, She-de-a? What exactly did Pitale-sharo say?"

Groaning and clutching her injured shoulder, jostled in her fit of weeping, the girl sank back on her pallet of furs. "He . . . he said he was no longer a true Pawnee. Even his grandfather has called him a traitor and a coward. I know nothing of this Morning Star ceremony except that Pitale-sharo does not want you to be in it. When he told Wetara-sharo this, Wetara-sharo accused him of allowing a White-Eyes woman to twist his thinking, destroy his manhood, and threaten the whole tribe. . . . Is that true, Moe-ra? Have you lured Pitale-sharo from me to you?"

"No, She-de-a! You misunderstood. Pitale-sharo doesn't desire me; he loves you. That's why I offered to take your place, but Pitale-sharo thinks the maiden should be

387

Indian. He believes Great Heart and I have done nothing but bring confusion to the Pawnee."

"Confusion? Take my place? Oh, Moe-ra, I understand none of this! I only know that he has gone and could not say when he might return, or if we are still to wed as we planned this summer, on the eve of the longest day. Wetara-sharo commanded him to seek a vision from the spirit world. He is not to come home until he has had one and knows what he must do. Until that time, Bon-son-gee will act as chief . . ."

No sooner had She-de-a finished this tearful explanation when Heavy Basket stomped into the lodge, her plain, flat features dark as a storm cloud. Maura had not seen much of her since the attack by the Sioux. When she had seen her, Heavy Basket had been gloomy and subdued, as was only to be expected from a woman who had lost the battle for a husband to someone else. Now, the big squaw came right to the point.

"White-Eyes Woman! This is your fault. Because of you, our great chief, Pitale-sharo, has angered his grandfather, and Bon-son-gee is strutting proudly about the village, ordering this and that, making me and everyone else long to cut off his scalp lock. You are the reason Bon-son-gee has been made chief. You have poisoned Pitale-sharo's thoughts and made him forget his duty. If it were not forbidden, I would take a knife and kill you. . . ."

"Hush, Heavy Basket!" Prairie Turnip warned. "We must not speak of these things, especially in front of strangers."

The latter comment jolted Maura. So that was how the Pawnee still thought of her and She-de-a—as strangers, even after all this time. Maybe what Pitale-sharo had been trying to tell her was that her friendship with these people was all in her head. They never would accept her, never trust her, and probably never permit her to actually take part in a cherished religious ceremony. At least, Pitale-sharo had been honest about his feelings toward her; she was white and therefore alien and unacceptable.

"No, you *mustn't* speak of these things," Maura surprised herself by agreeing. "You are only upsetting She-de-a. I never meant any harm, Heavy Basket. If I have caused harm, I apologize. If there is some way I can make it up to you, I will. In my heart, there is nothing but great affection and respect for your people."

Her apology seemed to mollify Heavy Basket, though Maura doubted that anything could make her smile. Nodding stiffly in acknowledgement, the big squaw said, "Wetara-sharo and Bon-son-gee have commanded me to direct the women in preparing new garments for you, White-Eyes Woman. They are to be the finest ceremonial garments we have ever made, with the finest quill work and the softest leather. Tomorrow, Bon-son-gee will hunt deer fawns for their skins. Each woman in the tribe will assist in the work. We must work quickly; the garments must be ready for you to wear at dawn on the longest day of summer."

Such generosity following a threat to her life amazed Maura. "I thank you, Heavy Basket, but surely fawn skin won't be necessary. . . ." The image of the dead antelope sprang to mind. "Really, I'd rather you not use fawn skin. The skin of an older animal will do just fine."

"It is the Pawnee way," Heavy Basket insisted. "And so it shall be done. We are also commanded to sew wedding garments for this one—the Sioux bitch," she added contemptuously, nudging She-de-a with her moccasin. "Which is proof that Wetara-sharo still has faith in his grandson, even if his future wife has none."

389

At that, She-de-a quickly dried her tears with the palm of her hand. "Wetara-sharo really told you to make wedding garments for me?"

"Yes, but they will not be of fawn skin. Since you have no mother or aunts in the village, you would otherwise have to make them yourself—and as everyone has already seen, you are greatly lacking in skill. If you were to make them yourself, you would only shame your husband with your ineptitude."

"Yes, Heavy Basket," She-de-a humbly agreed. "Then may I at least watch how you do them? I do not wish to shame him in future."

"You may watch," Heavy Basket grudgingly conceded. "But neither you nor the White-Eyes woman may help. The garments for each of you must be perfect—and no one but a Pawnee can make a perfect Pawnee garment."

Alone on the Plains, traveling toward the western mountains, Pitale-sharo fasted and prayed. For sixteen days, he drank only enough water to keep himself alive, and ate practically nothing. The flesh melted from his bones; he had to clutch his horse's mane to stay astride. He carried weapons and a parfleche full of pemmican, but would not touch either. He was now too weak to hunt, and the pemmican would only have made him vomit.

Day and night, he prayed—stopping often to kneel on the plain beside his grazing horse and lift his arms to the heavens. But he received no visions, no answers. He began to think he would die out here on the endless grasslands, in sight of the mountains but without reaching them. He felt that he deserved to die. To obtain She-de-a, whom he loved, he had allowed Moe-ra, the

390

beloved of his friend, Great Heart, to be sacrificed. He knew they loved each other by the look in their eyes whenever their glances met, or they heard the other's name.

Loving She-de-a as he did, what else could he have done? Sacrificing maidens to Tirawa had never been his favorite sport, but the Pawnee had followed the ritual since time before memory. No one knew when it had started, and no one dared end it. As he had pointed out to his grandfather, the Pawnee might already have angered Tirawa by attempting to substitute a White-Eyes for an Indian maiden, though Moe-ra met every other requirement, except, perhaps, that of being a virgin.

Pitale-sharo had stumbled upon a moment of intimacy between her and Great Heart, the day before Great Heart had left to return to Belle-vue. He had seen his friend waste his seed on the ground. Quite possibly, Moe-ra *was* still a virgin. Wasting one's seed during mating was a way of preventing conception, and if Great Heart had done it this time, he had probably done it in the past. However, without examining Moe-ra, Pitale-sharo could never know for certain.

What bothered him most and had driven him to defy his grandfather was not only that Moe-ra must die, but that her death would deprive Great Heart of happiness. It would, in truth, make him utterly miserable, even if he believed the lie Wetara-sharo intended to tell him, that Moe-ra had died during another Sioux raid. Torn with grief, Great Heart would then mount a great army of White-Eyes to wipe out the Sioux, conveniently ridding the Pawnee of the threat of future attack by their old enemies. According to Wetara-sharo, Tirawa had determined everything. The god of Morning Star had planned all along that Pitale-sharo would desire She-de-a, that Moe-ra would love the Pawnee, and that Great Heart would love Moe-ra. His grandfather even believed that the departure of Silver-Hair and Great Heart had been preordained. It would all work out in the end, his grandfather had said.

Pitale-sharo did not believe it. Once, he would have accepted Wetara-sharo's opinions and reassurances without a qualm of doubt. But his association with Great Heart and Moe-ra—Moe-ra even more than Great Heart—had changed his thinking. It had opened his mind to new ideas. From the day of her arrival in the village, she had questioned everything—why a thing was done one way and not another, why the Pawnee lived, thought, mated, and married as they did. . . . He had heard the women—and the men—talking about her endless questions. Her questions had made *him* question, and he had grown to respect her intelligence and curiosity.

But as his respect grew, so also did his doubts. What Great Heart had begun, Moe-ra had finished. Now, he no longer knew what was right or wrong. He even doubted the existence of Tirawa and the spirits who had ruled his life from the moment of his birth. If the gods existed, why didn't they speak to him? Reassure him? Tell him what to do?

Wetara-sharo had told him not to return until he had found peace and certainty within in his own heart that the ancient Pawnee way was the *right* way. "She-de-a will be waiting for you," his grandfather had promised. "As we have always done, we will sacrifice the Morning Star maiden at dawn. At sunset, you can wed the woman who first tempted you to set aside your duty. She-de-a will be my gift to you, for you know that I myself would prefer an older, wiser woman, such as Heavy Basket. If you cannot bear to watch the White-Eyes woman be sacrificed, if you yourself cannot help to send her on her journey to Tirawa, then do not return, my son. If you do, I will shun and disown you. I and all our people will mourn you, as if you were dead."

Suffering from thirst and hunger, swaying from weakness, Pitale-sharo remembered his grandfather's last words to him: *I and all our people will mourn you, as if you were dead.*

Perhaps that was the answer, after all. Because he no longer believed, Tirawa had decreed that he must die. There would be no visions, no shining certitude, no joyous, triumphant return with a brilliant resolution to the entire problem. He would die before he ever reached the mountains, and Moe-ra would die on the longest day of summer.

Chapter Thirty

"There, Major, that's the last one," Luke declared, setting down the heavy wooden crate he had just hauled up from the steamer on the river.

"Three crates of fireworks all the way from Boston." The round-faced major eyed the row of boxes with amazement. Righting his tilted wooden chair, he leaned forward and ran one pudgy hand across the nearest crate. "World's finest illuminations," he read aloud from the faded print stamped on the rough wood. "These have survived a hell of a long journey, Luke. Who would ever have guessed we'd find a use for such genteel entertainment so far from civilization?"

Luke brushed the dust off one of the boxes and gingerly sat down on it. "Out here, fireworks won't be mere entertainment, Major. I think the Indians will view them as messages sent from the gods. Used at the right moment, they'll cause a sensation and turn the tide of battle. I just wish I'd had a few to fire off that day when the Sioux attacked the Pawnee."

"Still say you don't need 'em, Luke. For what these cost, you could stuff enough gourds with gunpowder to blow the whole Plains to kingdom come."

"Gourds are too damned unreliable. As *I* still say, you won't regret this expense. Someday, these fireworks will come in handy, and you'll be glad I talked you into them."

"Better store 'em in that sod hut where I keep fresh meat until I can smoke it. It's the only cool place around. Hot an' dry as it's been lately, these illuminations might just self-illuminate." Dougherty mopped his sweaty brow with a calico handkerchief pulled from the breastpocket of his red, homespun shirt. "Sure wish it would rain. We need rain bad."

Luke got up to leave. "Where's Magruder? What's he been doing for the last two days? I haven't seen him since we got back from scouting the Mandans."

"You haven't heard? George Catlin rode in yesterday, and ever since he got here, Magruder has been thick as thieves with 'im. They're makin' plans to go visit the Mandans t'gether. Magruder's gonna study 'em, and Catlin's gonna paint 'em. Sometimes I think they're both half-crazy; they stayed up all night jawin' about what they'd seen and done among the Injuns since they got here a year ago. I like Injuns, too, but they take likin' 'em a stop beyond normal."

Luke could not resist a chuckle. "So does Eben's daughter. In fact, I think she's worse than her own father."

"She is, eh?" Dougherty shot Luke a shrewd, speculative look. "Well, what have you decided, Luke? You gonna marry that girl, or are you gonna let 'er get away? It's about time t' go back an' tell 'er what you've decided, ain't it?"

"It's past time," Luke acknowledged, instantly sobering. "And I'm no closer to a decision, now, then I was when I left her."

"If I was younger, I know what I'd do. I'd marry her and head for California. Hell, they got Injuns in California, too. I hear tell it won't be long b'fore they also got towns, churches, and ranches. They got 'em now — a string of missions, anyway — an' them Californios won't quit 'til everything's all neat an' tidy, just like back east. You mark my words: for a long time t' come, Bellevue won't be much more than a stoppin' off place for folks headed farther west. California's where they'll be headed. If I was young, and didn't feel so much responsibility to keep the peace here, that's where I'd go. It's the land of the future. . . . B'sides, on the way, you could see some of this grand country b'fore it gets spoilt, see it while it's still wild, and the buffalo and Injuns are roamin' it. . . ."

The major's description fired Luke's imagination. For a moment, he could almost picture himself and Maura riding off into the sunset, heading west to California Territory. But then he thought of all the unknown dangers they would face from hostile Indian tribes, ferocious grizzlies, snowy mountains, and unpredictable rivers. "I can't take a woman on a journey like *that*," he snarled. "I don't know what we'd find."

"You could if she was the *right* woman. 'Course, you know Maura Magruder better'n I do. She may *not* be the right woman for a trip like that."

While Luke was mulling this over, an excited soldier burst through the open door. "Come quick, Major! You gotta come quick! A half-dead Injun just rode in on a half-dead horse."

"*Now* what?" Dougherty grumbled, rising to his feet. "Might as well come along, Luke. Between the two of us, we oughta be able to make sense of his lingo, whatever it is."

396

As soon as Luke saw the horse, he knew the identity of the Indian. The small brown and white pony had been ridden to a state of trembling exhaustion and near total collapse, but there was no mistaking Swift Arrow, Pitale-sharo's favorite buffalo-runner.

Luke dashed out ahead of Major Dougherty and elbowed aside the men bending over the body of the Indian lying prostrate on the ground. "My God, it *is* you, Pitale-sharo!" he cried, dropping to his knees. "What have you done to yourself? You're nothing but skin and bones. Somebody get a water skin. This man is starving to death and probably also dying of thirst."

He lifted his friend's head and cradled it in the crook of his arm. Pitale-sharo opened his eyes and weakly grinned up at him. "I am not dead yet, my friend, just tired. I have been on a vision quest. After I had my vision, I rode for weeks without stopping to get here."

"But why? You've driven yourself and Swift Arrow to the brink of death." Someone shoved a water skin into Luke's hand. Quickly, he removed the stopper and held the neck opening to Pitale-sharo's crusted lips. "Here, drink first. Then you can talk."

Pitale-sharo drank only a mouthful, then pushed the skin aside. "Give some to my horse, then turn him loose to roll and graze. After that, take me somewhere quiet, Great Heart, so others cannot hear. I have much to tell you, and my news is urgent."

"Take him up to the house, Luke, while I look after his horse," Dougherty said. "Put him in my bed. He better eat first and get some sleep, or he'll die before he can tell us anything."

Luke moved quickly to follow the major's directions, but no sooner had he laid Pitale-sharo in the major's big four-poster bed, when Pitale-sharo grabbed his hand. "Do not worry. Once I eat and sleep a short time, i will be ready to ride again. While I sleep, you must make preparations. Sit down, and I will tell you why I've come."

Luke pulled up a puncheon chair, sat down, and waited for his friend to begin. Pitale-sharo did so, speaking haltingly but with more strength than Luke would have thought possible from his frail appearance.

"Forgive me, Great Heart. What I am about to tell you shames me. I should have come sooner. Indeed, I should have told you these things many winters ago, when you first cut palms with me—but I was afraid. I am still afraid. That is why I went on a vision quest. . . . Also, my grandfather insisted that I go. He told me to fast and pray, so I might receive a vision showing the right path on which to lead my people. For many days and nights, I fasted. I rode all the way to the mountains—"

"To the mountains! My God, no wonder you and your horse look half-dead!"

"Yes, we almost died—at least, I did, before the vision came. I fell from my horse and lay on the plain beneath the hot sun for two full days. I thought the gods were angry and had abandoned me. On the morning of the third day, I awoke, looked up at the rising sun, and saw a rim of fire surrounding the yellow ball. Inside the ball, there crouched a wounded, dying wolf. Its howls of pain and terror echoed in my ears. The noise was terrible, the sight more so. I closed my eyes and put my hands over my ears. Still, I heard the wolf's howls and saw its image inside my closed lids. His howls rang with accusation, and I began to think *I* had done this terrible thing to him . . . my own totem and the totem of my tribe."

"Did you?" Luke asked. "Have you done something for which you feel guilty?"

"Yes . . . ," Pitale-sharo's sunken black eyes were piercing, his face haggard. "I am coming to that part. Be patient, Great Heart, and all will be revealed to you."

"Are you sure you don't want more to drink, or something to eat, first? You're very weak. Telling this long, sad tale must be a great strain on you."

Pitale-sharo shook his head. "No . . . let me continue, while I still have the courage. I have done many bad things, but the things I thought were bad, were not, and the things I thought were good, were not. I have fought my grandfather, and then felt guilty, when what I should have done was fight him harder. I have fought my own feelings of love, when I should have loved more, not less. Worst of all, I have concealed things from you, my true friend, and even regretted my friendship with you, when I should have trusted you more and told you the truth."

"What truth, Pitale-sharo? You said your news was urgent. Where is this long explanation leading? Forget the vision; just tell me the important parts."

"Ah, you are right . . . as you always are. The important part is this: I stole She-de-a in order to sacrifice her to Tirawa, the god of Morning Star, in a secret ceremony I never told you about. It is a ritual that takes place every fourth summer, at dawn on the longest day. We dress the Morning Star maiden in fine white garments, as if for a wedding, and then lead her, unsuspecting of what is to come, to the top of the bluff near our village. There, we have a scaffold waiting, in the shape of a five-pointed star. Just before sunrise, when Morning Star gleams its brightest, the women strip the girl of her fine garments and tie her to the scaffold. They purify her with fire. They hold a burning torch beneath her breasts

399

and thrust it between her legs. While the girl screams, struggles, and pleads for her life, we ask Tirawa to accept our humble sacrifice, make the corn grow tall, and the buffalo multiply. . . . Then, as Morning Star fades and the sun rises, the men shoot arrows into the maiden's heart. We compete with each other to see who can fill her body with the most arrows."

"God almighty! You were going to do all *that* to little She-de-a?"

"Yes, Great Heart . . . but let me finish. The worst is yet to come. We always capture our Morning Star maiden and bring her home during the summer before the ceremony, so that she may live among us and learn our ways before she dies. Last summer, when the time came to seek a maiden, I argued with my grandfather. I did not want to go. My grandfather understood my reluctance but insisted it was my duty. So I went and captured She-de-a. I resisted my feelings for her, but from the day I first saw her, it was I who became *her* captive. Still, I could not betray my people. During these troubled times of drought and sickness, I *dared* not risk Tirawa's wrath. So I continued to fight my feelings for her. Then, she saved my life during the attack by the Sioux . . . and no matter what anyone said, I could *not* allow her to be sacrificed. So again, I challenged my grandfather. And Moe-ra overheard us arguing."

"Maura?" Luke's heart almost jumped out of his chest; he had a terrible feeling he was going to hear something he did not want to hear, something awful involving Maura.

"My grandfather had sent her from the lodge, but she did not leave. Instead, she hid in the entranceway. When she heard us arguing, she stepped out and offered to take She-de-a's place as Morning Star maiden."

"She did what? Why in hell didn't you stop her? If she didn't realize what she was doing, *you* certainly did."

Pitale-sharo grimaced. "I tried, Great Heart, but she would not listen. It is true, she does not know what happens to the Morning Star maiden during the ceremony. We never mentioned that part. When she asked questions, my grandfather gave clever answers to deceive her. As for myself, I . . . I wanted to spare She-de-a, so I held my tongue."

"Where's Maura now? Damn it, I'll get her out of that village if I have to blow it up to do it!"

"Wait, Great Heart. . . . Hear the rest before you decide what must be done."

In his agitation, Luke had jumped up and begun to pace. "What more *is* there, *friend?* You just told me that the woman I love is scheduled to be stripped, burned, and shot full of arrows in a sacrifice to one of your heathen gods. Do you now expect me to sit around here twiddling my thumbs? I've got all I can do just to keep myself from wringing your damn neck."

"If you kill me, it will only be what I deserve, Great Heart. I have failed both you and my people. Do you not see? The dying wolf in my vision is *me,* the chief of the Skidi Pawnee. I thought if we did not cling to our old ways, we would die, but the truth is that we will die if we *do* cling to them. In my vision, the spirits told me this: my duty is to lead my people *away* from the old ways— beginning with convincing them to abandon the Morning Star ceremony. However, in this I have a problem. Words alone will not convince them. My grandfather has sworn to shun me if I return and am still opposed to the ceremony. That is why I came here to you, to seek your help. . . . If, at the exact moment when Tirawa comes to claim the maiden, one of your gourd bombs was to explode near the scaffold . . . and if I was to appear in a cloud of smoke, warning my people that the god is angry and will destroy us all in a great explosion if we continue to sacrifice innocent maidens, might they not listen and be convinced?"

Luke could picture it, just as Pitale-sharo was describing: from behind the scaffold, rockets and pinwheels shooting into the sky, the Indians falling back in awe and terror, convinced that Tirawa himself was speaking to them . . .

"You know . . . it just might work! Especially now that I've something a hell of a lot better than gourd bombs."

"What do you have?" Pitale-sharo asked. "What could impress them more than gourd bombs?"

"Illuminations," Luke said. "Bright lights, whirling colors, and huge booms the likes of which no one in the Land of Shallow Rivers has ever before seen or heard."

Pitale-sharo furrowed his brow, trying to understand. "Do you mean something like a shower of stars? Only with noise?"

"Yes, that's it exactly!"

"If we get there in time to try such strong magic, I think it might work."

"We'll get there in time," Luke promised. "We'll leave as soon as you can ride again."

Another day passed before Pitale-sharo was strong enough to climb aboard a fresh horse for the journey back to his village on the Loup River. Even after the Pawnee chieftain proved he could sit a horse without swaying and clutching its mane, Luke delayed leaving for yet another day in order to finish making two special travois—one to carry a crate of the precious fireworks, and another to carry Pitale-sharo, if need be. Major Dougherty, in the meantime, had secured the services of a company of horse soldiers passing through Bellevue en route to an assignment on the upper Missouri. He was adamant that he, too, should accompany Luke back to the village.

"If your damn fool fireworks fail, you're gonna need guns t' back you up. Hell, old Wetara-sharo and Bonson-gee will probably try and take your scalps. You, Eben, and Pitale-sharo can't fight off the whole village. While you're up on top of that bluff puttin' on your pyrotechnical show, we'll ride into the village, like we was just comin' for a visit. An' if you don't signal us that everything's workin' out the way you think it should, we'll start burnin' lodges. That should provide a dandy distraction."

"What it'll do is start that war you've been trying so hard to avoid," Luke muttered. "If the Pawnee see soldiers destroying their homes, they'll come down off that bluff with blood in their eyes."

"Can't help that," Dougherty said. "I can't sit back and let 'em all kill you. If you hadn't come up with this idea of spookin' 'em with fireworks, we'd have to start makin' trouble as soon we rode up. Torturin' and killin' a Sioux maiden is one thing—and a bad practice, I'll admit—but doin' it to a white woman is even worse. Why, there'd be such a hue and cry among white folks that they'd be killin' Indians left and right, no matter what tribe they came from."

"You don't have to warn me of the potential for violence, Major. If our little plan goes awry, and the Pawnee succeed in killing Maura, I myself will shoot every Indian I see. So will her father and George Catlin."

"Sounds to me as if you're even sweeter on that girl

than I thought, Luke."

"It isn't until you're about to lose someone that you finally discover what she means to you." Only after Luke said it, did he realize how similar it was to something Maura herself had once said: *men never seem to realize what they want until they're about to lose it.*

How right she had been! Even knowing that he loved her, he had been unable to commit himself to her; the only time he had felt right about marrying her was when her life was in danger. That was the way he felt now. The threat of losing her had again cleared his vision. What did it matter if he did not have all the details of providing for her worked out? In and of itself, loving was a leap of faith, a risky journey into the unknown, with no guarantees of happiness. Hell, life itself was a risk. Considering that he thrived on risk-taking and had spent the last ten years rejecting the safe and sane, why did he lack courage when it came to marrying the woman he loved?

If they got there in time, *if* his plan worked, and *if* Maura still wanted to marry him, he would marry her *first* and worry about the future, later.

"We're leaving, tonight," Luke said. "Better tell your men to get ready for some hard riding."

"I already told 'em," the major responded. "The way I figure it, if we *don't* leave tonight, we'll never make it. Magruder and Catlin were ready to leave yesterday. Magruder's sure takin' this hard. He and old Wetara-sharo had got to be good friends."

"Pitale-sharo and I are good friends. But friendship doesn't count for much, when it runs opposite to everything you've ever believed."

"When did *you* start gettin' so wise, Luke?"

"When I met a girl with silver-blond hair, blue eyes

you could drown in, and a disposition more stubborn than a Missouri mule," Luke quipped.

"Then let's go save her so you can marry her. After all this, it would sure be a hell of a waste if the two of you didn't get hitched."

Yes, it would be, Luke thought. It sure as hell would be.

Chapter Thirty-one

As the summer solstice drew nearer, Maura's excitement and nervousness rose. She found an odd exhilaration in preparing to participate in an ancient, secret ritual, but was also apprehensive. The ceremony might very well include elements of violence, such as the cutting of palms or the infliction of self-torture that some of the Plains tribes reportedly practised. She wondered if she would be brave enough to endure pain if it was part of the ritual, then laughed at her own lurid imaginings, certain that the gentle Pawnee were incapable of cruelty in the name of religion. She had been living among them for almost a year; if they enjoyed self-torture or watching others suffer, she had never seen evidence of it. Even the cutting of palms had been a swift, business-like gesture, over in a minute and hardly the worst pain she had ever experienced.

On the eve of the summer solstice, when she finally saw the finished garments the women had been sewing for her, Maura realized how absurd her fears really were. Heavy Basket and the other women of the tribe would never have labored so long and hard to produce garments she might ruin by bleeding upon them. The exhaustive tanning process had rendered the fawn skin snow white in color, and thin and soft as satin. Painstaking quill and bead work ornamented the garments. Caressing them with her fingertips, Maura looked up at Heavy Basket and Lizard Woman, and tears filled her eyes.

"I've never worn any garments as lovely as these," she confessed.

"Hold them against your body so I can be sure they will fit properly," Heavy Basket grunted, stepping back in Lizard Woman's fire-lit lodge and squinting her eyes.

Already certain of the fit — she had been measured and fussed over many times — Maura did so without complaint. Heavy Basket nodded her approval and then reclaimed the garments, carefully folding them and handing them to Lizard Woman, who put them with She-de-a's wedding garments, completed two days previously.

"Sit down by the cookfire," Heavy Basket then instructed Maura. "The women of the tribe are waiting outside with presents they have brought for you and She-de-a."

"Presents!" Maura exclaimed, exchanging glances with She-de-a. The girl was lying on a nearby pallet and brooding because Pitale-sharo had not yet returned. "We never expected presents."

Maura sat down near her friend and smiled to cheer her; She-de-a seemed to be the only one in the entire village who doubted Pitale-sharo's return. "Sit up!" she hissed under her breath. "Look happy! There's still plenty of time for him to get here."

Sighing listlessly, She-de-a sat up; the only signs of her terrible wound were a pronounced stiffness in the way she moved and her fleeting grimace of pain, especially when she lifted things. The girl's physical recovery had been remarkable, but her mental attitude left much to be desired. Pitale-sharo's departure had taken the light from her eyes—and only his return, Maura suspected, would put it back again.

One by one, the women of the tribe filed silently into the lodge and gravely made their offerings, first to Maura, and then to She-de-a. Maura noted an interesting difference between the gifts given to her and those bestowed on her friend. She-de-a's were all practical—a handsome parfleche, a finely woven basket, a set of gourd bowls, a small iron pot with a dent in it—while Maura's gifts were ornamental: a necklace of elk's teeth, a quill-embroidered headband trailing white feathers, a bracelet of blue trader's beads, an armband carved of buffalo horn, a pair of beautiful, soft, white moccasins . . .

Maura smiled and thanked each woman but received not a single smile in return. The women hardly looked at her; they seemed furtive and embarrassed. Maura supposed they were trying to show respect, but she began to feel ill at ease and had to force herself to keep smiling. She-de-a accepted her wedding gifts with a hesitant nod, making no effort to conceal her unhappiness over Pitale-sharo's absence. It was almost as if she expected to have to return the gifts in the morning; certainly, they were far too fine to be lavished on a sullen, Sioux maiden with no marital prospects. Maura wondered what would happen to She-de-a if Pitale-sharo did *not* come back. Maybe the young chief intended to boycott the Morning Star ceremony altogether and would appear only for the wedding.

With all of the village women and female children crowded into the lodge, there was hardly enough room to turn around. The air was close and stuffy. Maura breathed a sigh of relief when Heavy Basket announced that everyone could depart and return to their own lodges in order to sleep and prepare for the morning. "You, too, must sleep, now, White-Eyes Woman," the big squaw said. "We will come for you while it is still night, for we must bathe and dress you, and paint your face and body."

"Paint my face and body?" Maura was startled.

Heavy Basket nodded, lifting her hands to her own round face. "One half will be painted black, the other half white, with a red line from here to here." She made a dissecting line from the center part in her hair to the juncture of her thighs. "Black represents Tirawa, Morning Star. White is for Atira, Evening Star. Tomorrow, the two shall be joined, resulting in balance, harmony, and good fortune for all."

"I see." Maura's uneasiness increased.

She had not anticipated being naked in front of all the women in the village. Though she had bathed in the river with them and frolicked with their children, they had all been naked then, their lack of embarrassment providing the impetus for Maura to overcome her own innate shyness. So long as the men of the tribe were excluded from the bathing and painting process, Maura guessed she could manage it.

"Sleep deeply then, White Eyes Woman. . . . Empty your mind of everything save pleasing Tirawa, and bearing our messages to him."

"How will I know what to say tomorrow? No one has yet told me anything."

"Tomorrow will be time enough. After you are bathed, painted, and dressed in the garments we have made for you, we will cover your eyes and lead you to the top of the bluff where the ceremony will take place."

"Why must you cover my eyes? I already know the way; I went there with Lizard Woman to help bring down the household items she had hidden before the attack by the Sioux."

"During the four days and nights before the ceremony, the bluff becomes a sacred waiting place. Even the path there is sacred. No one walks upon it; it is forbidden for the Morning Star maiden to even look upon it."

"Is that why I haven't been permitted to climb the bluff recently?"

"That is why. The men completed preparations five days ago, and none have been there since."

"I see," Maura repeated. Fear slithered along her nerve endings like a snake gathering itself to strike at her heart. She swallowed hard. "I'll be ready when you come for me. I doubt I can sleep at all tonight."

"You must show courage, White-Eyes Woman, or the gods will not be pleased."

Embarrassed, Maura straightened her shoulders. "Don't worry, Heavy Basket. I won't shame you. Don't forget that I volunteered; I *want* to take part in this ceremony."

After Heavy Basket and everyone except Lizard Woman and She-de-a had left the lodge, Maura got out her precious writing materials, carefully hidden during the Sioux attack, and dipping pen in ink, bent over a sheet of foolscap. "It is the eve of the summer solstice," she wrote. "Tomorrow, while the world still lies in darkness, the women will come for me. Though I am afraid, I am also thrilled. And humbled. It is a great honor to be here, the first white woman to live among the Pawnee, to participate in a secret religious ritual, to have actually become one of them. If I achieve nothing else in my life, I will rest content that I have done something no one else before me has ever done. As I think about the

410

importance of this work, my hand shakes, and ink splatters across the paper. . . ."

Maura sighed and set down the pen. She was too excited to write any more, and foolscap was too precious to waste. Besides, by tomorrow night, she would have much more to tell. Putting everything away, she joined She-de-a on the sleeping platform. The girl was curled into a tight ball, facing the far wall. Maura was certain she was not sleeping; she reached out and touched her shoulder.

"Don't despair, my friend. Pitale-sharo will come. It is far more certain you will wed the man you love than that I shall wed the man I love."

"I feel no such certainty, Moe-ra. I feel only fear," She-de-a whispered. "I am afraid to close my eyes in sleep, because when I do, I see the image of a dying wolf. I do not know what it means, but the dream has something to do with you and me, and with Pitale-sharo and the Skidi Pawnee."

"Dreams don't mean anything," Maura scoffed. "If you were a White-Eyes, you would not allow a dream to scare you."

"For once, I must disagree, Moe-ra. If you were Indian, you would know that dreams are messages from the spirit world."

"I am Pawnee. I cut palms with Wetara-sharo, and I know no such thing. Go to sleep, now. If the wolf comes tonight, wake me, and I'll chase him away for you."

As Maura had hoped, She-de-a giggled, her dark mood momentarily lifting. "Oh, Moe-ra! How could you get into my dream? I know what I'll do; I'll bid *him* to come visit *you*. Spirits can do anything, you know."

"Sleep, my friend. Tomorrow night, you'll be lying in Pitale-sharo's arms. So tonight, you need your rest."

411

At that, She-de-a fell silent, but it was a long time before Maura herself could get to sleep. When she did sleep, she dreamed—and amazingly, her dream was also of a dying wolf.

When at last the village below had settled down for the night, Luke stood on top of the bluff and motioned to Eben, George Catlin, and Pitale-sharo, hiding in a crevice halfway down. The four men had arrived only that morning, after a difficult journey, the memory of which still knotted Luke's stomach. One more day of freak encounters, such as the unexpected dust storm that had panicked the horses, almost causing the crate of fireworks to be dumped into a ravine, and Maura would be dead.

Even now, her death still seemed possible, if not inevitable. Preparatory to crossing a river on the journey, they had transferred the fireworks into a bullboat. At one point, the unwieldy vessel had taken on water, drenching the bottom half of the crate. Until now, there had been no time to check the contents, nor was there anything Luke could do to salvage the fireworks if they were ruined. Major Dougherty and his men would have no choice but to attack the village.

Tonight, Dougherty and the soldiers were camping, out of sight, on the open plain. In the morning, while it was still dark, and the Pawnee warriors were riding their buffalo-runners to the top of the bluff, the major would move in closer. The plan made sense, but at the moment, Luke lacked confidence in it. Until he had Maura safely back in his arms, he lacked confidence in everyone and everything.

While Pitale-sharo and Eben carried the crate of fireworks up the path to the top of the bluff, George Catlin dashed ahead to Luke. "Mr. Cutter," he whispered urgently. "What do you want me to do? You just give the orders, and I'll carry them out."

"That *was* my plan," Luke said dryly, wondering anew about the wisdom of bringing along this strange little man.

After nearly a year on the plains, George Catlin still presented a dapper, citified, eastern appearance; he still wore his odd little cap with the turned-up earflaps and pointed brim, sported his distinctive embroidered hunting jacket, and hauled his paint pots and canvases everywhere he went. Luke would have liked to leave him behind in Bellevue, but Maura's father would not hear of it.

"He will be a help to us, Luke. He's marvelous with Indians. They call him the Great White Medicine Man because of the magic in his paint brush."

"Yes, but is he reliable in a tight situation? I don't care how much they fawn over him after this is over; will he shut his mouth and obey orders *during* the operation?"

"I'm certain he will, Luke. Since it's my daughter who's involved, I think I should have some say as to who we take with us to help rescue her."

"All right, if that's what you want, then he goes. But if he *does* do something stupid, I'll hold you responsible."

Now, gazing at the earnest little man in the dim starlight, Luke was still debating how much to trust him. "There's only three of us, Catlin, against a whole passle of Pawnee warriors. Pitale-sharo doesn't count because he can't be holding a weapon when he steps out from behind the scaffold to face his people. A rifle in his hands would detract from his sincerity, so his only weapon will be his tongue. I myself am going to be crouched down, hiding behind the platform, and you and

413

Eben should take positions on either side, where you can't be seen."

George Catlin cast a questioning glance at the bluff's broad, flat surface. Only a few big boulders and rock piles were scattered here and there. Near the edge of the bluff stood the large, star-shaped scaffold, elevated on a high platform, just as Pitale-sharo had described it. The scaffold was a cross-like affair with five points of branches, upon which Maura's arms and legs would be spread and fastened. As the sun rose in the east, its rays would strike her body. By then, if she still hung there, she would be dead, pierced with hundreds of arrows.

"You could hide in those big rocks over there." Luke pointed. "But I don't advise you to stick out your head or your gun until it's time to start shooting. As for Eben, he'll have to climb down onto the ledge that runs alongside the bluff. And he'll have to keep his head down, too."

"Gracious," George Catlin said. "If your plan *doesn't* work, we'll all be killed, won't we? I can't see how we'll get off this bluff alive."

"Want to sneak back down and rejoin Major Dougherty? The rest of us have personal reasons for being up here, but you have only a passing acquaintance with Maura Magruder. No one will think any less of you if you've changed your mind about the extent of your involvement."

"No, Mr. Cutter. I haven't changed my mind. I'm here to stay."

"Then help me pry open that crate. We may be a couple weeks early for a Fourth of July celebration, but I plan to put on a show that will rival anything seen back east on that day."

Barely had Maura fallen asleep when Lizard Woman was shaking her awake. Heavy Basket and the most senior women of the tribe had arrived to bathe and dress her. To her relief, the rest of the women and children waited outside the torchlit lodge, while Heavy Basket helped her out of her old doeskin. When she was naked, the woman washed her with cold river water they had brought with them in clay jars and water skins. Heedless of dampening either themselves or the floor mats, they poured the icy water over Maura, then rubbed her entire body first with sand, which they rinsed away, and then with a strong-smelling mixture of buffalo fat and herbs that made her flesh tingle.

When she had been scrubbed and oiled, they made her stand perfectly still while they painted her and braided her wet hair. The paints had all been mixed beforehand. When Maura questioned what was in them, Heavy Basket motioned for silence. "From now on, you do not speak, White-Eyes Woman, and we do not speak to you. You will be told what to do, but that is all. When there is a need for something to be done, *we* will do it."

Maura nodded. Her stomach muscles cramped, and perspiration popped out on her brow. The torches cast a weird, red light on the faces of the women; even Lizard Woman looked sinister and menacing. The women's eyes seemed to look *through* rather than *at* her. No one was paying any attention whatsoever to She-de-a, but as Heavy Basket took a thin, blunt stick and carefully painted a red dividing line down the center of Maura's naked body, the girl edged forward.

"Moe-ra, you look so different!" she blurted.

"Silence!" Heavy Basket snapped. Jerking her head at one of the attending women, she said, "Take the Sioux girl out of here and make her wait with the other women. When we climb the bluff, she is to come last. Not *yet* is she Pitale-sharo's wife. If he has not yet returned and joined his grandfather in leading the warriors to the top of the bluff, she never will be. The best she can hope for is to serve Bon-son-gee as slave. *That* one will never marry Pitale-sharo's cast-off bride."

She-de-a's cry of anguish was muffled as the nearest woman hurried the girl outside. Maura's heart ached to comfort her friend, but for the moment, there was nothing she could do. If Pitale-sharo *had* returned, he would already be with the men, riding to the top of the bluff. Small Hand must have gone out earlier to join them, because he had not been in the lodge when Maura awakened.

After the painting was finished, the women took turns fanning Maura with feathers to make the paint dry. As it dried, the paint caked on her skin, making her feel itchy, but Maura dared not scratch and disturb the broad swatches of black and white. When the paint was completely dry, the women dressed her in the soft, fawn-skin garments, beginning with the knee-length dress that laced up the middle to conceal her bosom. A short fringed cape went over it, and fringed leggings completed the outfit. Last of all, Maura stepped into the incredibly soft moccasins, and Heavy Basket put on her necklaces and other ornaments.

Maura noticed that the big squaw was still holding the headband with its trailing white feathers. "Turn around," Heavy Basket said, her black eyes gleaming like buttons.

Maura did so, but instead of putting the band across Maura's forehead, Heavy Basket settled it on the bridge of her nose so it blindfolded her eyes. She tied it snugly, so that Maura could see nothing. She experienced a sudden wave of dizziness, and two women immediately stepped forward, one on each side, to support her by the elbows.

"Do not be afraid to walk. The women will safely lead you to the top of the bluff," Heavy Basket instructed.

"I am not afraid," Maura insisted, completely forgetting the ban on speaking. A moment later, she remembered. "Forgive me . . . I should not have said that."

"Do not forget again. The spirits are near; they do not like foolish chatter. It is disrespectful."

When she walked out of the lodge, the silence struck Maura like a stinging slap. She knew the women and children were there; she could smell the smoke from their torches and sense their presences. But no one said a word or made a single sound, not even the babies strapped in their cradleboards. On either side, the women pressed close, steering Maura away from the village toward the rocky path leading to the bluff. Through the soles of her moccasins, Maura could feel pebbles and small rocks digging into her feet. Since she could not see to walk around them, she stumbled once or twice, but the women bore her up, and she did not fall.

The blindfold robbed Maura of courage. Long before she reached her destination, she began to feel more afraid than she ever had in her life. What awaited her on top of the bluff? Why was everyone so secretive? Why had Pitale-sharo so strongly disapproved?

The climb was hard and steep, leaving her exhausted and out of breath, her arms and legs trembling. She heard the snorting and pawing of horses and knew she had arrived; other than that, the only sound was the crackle of the torches.

Then Heavy Basket spoke: "We have brought her,

417

Wetara-sharo. She is here."

"Bring her forward," the old man said. "And I will ask her the Four Sacred Questions."

Chapter Thirty-two

"What do you see?" Hidden in the concealing darkness behind the platform, Luke touched Pitale-sharo's arm.

His friend ducked his head and turned to him. "The women have arrived," he whispered. "I saw Moe-ra. According to custom, her eyes are covered."

"Did you spot She-de-a?"

Pitale-sharo nodded. "She is back with the children and women of low rank."

Luke sighed in relief. He had been half afraid that *her* life might be in danger this morning, too. Pitale-sharo's absence could be a threat to the girl, leaving her as it did without protection from the jealous Heavy Basket. "Better keep your head down. Discovery at this point would ruin everything."

"No one will be looking this way until Moe-ra is tied to the scaffold," Pitale-sharo said confidently.

He resumed spying while Luke checked his tapers of twisted grass and the ember jar. Luke strained to listen to the murmur of voices. Wetara-sharo was asking questions, and Maura was answering in a clear, untroubled voice that left little doubt of her ignorance and naivete.

"Have you chosen to become Pawnee of your own free

419

will?"

"I have."

"Will you be loyal to your adopted people until you draw your last breath, and afterward, when you journey to the Happy Hunting Grounds?"

There was a little pause, and then Maura said calmly: "I will."

"When you journey to the Happy Hunting Grounds, will you speak only truth to the gods, remembering always to plead the cause of your adopted people?"

Again, a slight hesitancy. "Yes . . . I will."

"There is nothing you will not bear—no sorrow or suffering you will not embrace—for the sake of the Skidi Pawnee?"

This time, Maura's answer was long in coming. "I . . . I will try to be brave and endure whatever I must."

Luke clenched a fist. Wasn't she growing suspicious by now? Hadn't she guessed? Or was she just too damn proud to admit to herself that she might have been wrong to get involved with these people in the first place?

"Bon-son-gee, remove the band from her eyes, so at last she may see," Wetara-sharo commanded.

"There . . . her eyes are opened," Bon-son-gee said.

Luke could not keep still anymore; kneeling, he peered over the edge of the platform. Flaming torches illuminated the scene. Maura was standing in the center of the women, facing the scaffold, in front of which stood Wetara-sharo and Bon-son-gee, with their backs to Luke. A half-circle of mounted, painted warriors ringed the bluff. Luke focused his attention upon the slender figure in white. At first, Luke thought Maura was wearing some sort of mask. Then, he saw the wide, frightened eyes staring out of the grotesquely painted face. Except for her eyes, she did not look human, and he could understand better how the Pawnee could callously kill her. The women had painted her to resemble a wooden totem or some other inanimate object.

When they strip her naked, they'll know she's a flesh and blood woman, he thought to himself. He wished he had not agreed to wait until Maura was stripped and tied to the scaffold before setting off the fireworks. Pitale-sharo believed that the crucial moment would come when Heavy Basket was ordered to "purify" the sacrificial maiden. As the big squaw approached the scaffold with a torch, Luke was to ignite the rockets, pinwheels, and smoke bombs set out behind him in a row.

Now, watching Maura, Luke wished with all his heart that he could have spared her this moment of dawning horror. Her eyes fastened upon the scaffold, then darted to Wetara-sharo, Bon-son-gee, the women, and finally, the warriors, sitting with arrows already notched into their bows, and expectant looks upon their painted faces.

"Why have you brought me here, Wetara-sharo? Was it to betray my trust in you and teach me that the Skidi Pawnee are cowards and liars?" Her bold questions startled the onlookers.

"I told you not to speak!" Heavy Basket shouted. "Unless you are commanded, it is forbidden for you to speak."

"Why is it forbidden, Heavy Basket? Because I might demand answers to questions you don't want to hear? You're going to kill me, aren't you? If not, then what is the purpose of that scaffold—and the blindfold—and the warriors with their drawn bows—and the secrecy behind this ritual?"

Ignoring her outburst, Wetara-sharo stepped back and nodded to Heavy Basket. "Let the ceremony begin," he sonorously intoned.

Heavy Basket handed her torch to another woman, stepped toward Maura, and grabbed the front of her white garment. "Seize her!" she cried.

Clawing, shrieking women surged forward and fell upon Maura, tearing at her hair and clothing, holding down her squirming body while some pulled off her necklaces, and others snatched her moccasins. They even claimed the leather thongs binding the ends of her braids. When she was naked, they lifted her above their heads, balancing her painted body on their sturdy shoulders. Maura writhed and struggled, her silver-blond hair sweeping the ground. Luke expected her to be hysterical—he himself was nearly so—but she suddenly went rigid, then collapsed limply into the women's arms.

Carrying her toward the platform, they mounted the three crude steps and bore her to the scaffold. Maura's head lolled back, and her eyes stared sightlessly at the dark sky. As the women lashed her spread-eagled to the stout timbers, she jerked to life again. "Listen to me! I don't care if you kill me in the end, but at least give me a chance to tell you why you shouldn't do this."

Luke could no longer bear to watch. Pulling Pitalesharo down beside him, he indicated that they should get ready; it was almost time to light the waiting fireworks.

"Wetara-sharo!" Maura screamed. "If you kill me without giving me a chance to speak, I'll persuade Tirawa to destroy your people in the worst drought you have ever witnessed. I'll urge him to send the spotted sickness to your village, and to drive the buffalo so far away you will never see them again in your lifetime. Instead of harmony and balance in the universe, there will only be pain and suffering. Do you hear me, Wetara-sharo?"

"I hear you, White-Eyes Woman, but I will not be

swayed. Morning Star maidens have always pleaded for their lives, wept bitter tears, and screamed and struggled. It does no good."

Luke reached for his ember jar and grass tapers, but Pitale-sharo held up a hand to stop him. "Not yet," he cautioned.

Gritting his teeth, Luke waited—and listened.

"Wetara-sharo . . . dear friends . . . I don't plead for *my* life. Instead, I plead for yours and those of your children. If you kill me, Great Heart and my father, Silver-Hair, will bring an army of White-Eyes to destroy your village and kill all of you. . . ."

"They will not know it was Pawnee who did it!" Bon-son-gee shouted. "We will blame it on the Sioux, and Great Heart will then kill *them* and destroy *their* villages."

"No, he will not," Maura argued desperately. "He will blame only you because before he left, I *told* him I was going to be your Morning Star maiden. I promised to marry him, but only *after* the ceremony. He asked me what would happen during the ritual, and I said I did not know, but if any harm should come to me, he must blame it on the Pawnee."

"She lies!" Bon-son-gee shouted. "She is lying to save herself."

"If I lie, may Tirawa strike me dead. I do not lie, Bon-son-gee—but *you* have lied and deceived me, though I came to you in friendship and trust. Is this how the Pawnee treat those who love them, who have stood beside them in battle, lived among them, and shared food and fellowship? No wonder the White-Eyes call you savages. Think on this before you kill me; no other race finds it necessary to kill innocent victims in order to survive and prosper. Why don't you spare me, and see what happens? If Tirawa is angry, let him prove it by striking me dead.

423

But if instead, he approves of his people abandoning this wicked practice, then let him be merciful and allow me to live."

"No!" Bon-son-gee protested. "If Tirawa wants you to live, let him prove it by giving us a sign. Let him cause the heavens to erupt in fire, and thunder to roll down from the clouds. If he sends such signs, then we will believe—but if he does not, then you must die."

"Get ready." Luke nudged Pitale-sharo. "I'll give him fire in the heavens and thunder in the clouds. When I set off these smoke bombs, climb up on the platform and walk out from behind the scaffold."

"I'm ready," Pitale-sharo responded. "Set them off now."

"You see?" Bon-son-gee screamed triumphantly. "There are no such signs. Someone bring a torch, so Heavy Basket can purify this woman!"

"Wait!" Wetara-sharo suddenly cried. "We must give the god a chance. There has not been time enough for him to send a sign."

"Don't kill her! Please, don't kill her!" She-de-a's voice rose pleadingly above the din. "Heavy Basket, Lizard Woman, she is your friend! How can you do this to her?"

Luke heard the arguments and the buzz of angry voices, but he was far too busy to watch what was happening. Lighting the grass taper, he crawled from one explosive to the other, quickly lighting their fuses, and then scurrying to safety near the end of the platform. The fuse on the first rocket sputtered and fizzled, as if it might go out. With a whizzing sound, it shot straight into the sky above the scaffold and exploded. Amber-colored sparks showered down upon Maura's head.

"Look!" someone gasped. "Falling stars!"

The next explosion yielded a whirling pinwheel of

424

silver sparks—the third, a dazzling *pop-pop-pop* of sound and light. Luke stuck a smoke bomb on the platform and lit it. Spinning in place, it emitted long, curling tendrils of smoke.

"Get up there, Pitale-sharo! You'll never have a better chance than this!" Luke grabbed the biggest rocket he had and set it on the platform behind the scaffold. When he lit it, it misfired and instead of going straight up, shot sideways and disappeared over the edge of the bluff. While Luke was lighting another, he heard the explosion down below, so emphatic that it shook the bluff itself. He grabbed another and began lighting rockets, pinwheels, and smoke bombs as fast as he could lay hands upon them.

Some misfired and veered toward the village below, but most shot straight up into the air and exploded with satisfying bangs and a great show of sparkling light. The display dazzled the Indians and terrified their horses. Those who were not mounted on the plunging, rearing animals, pointed and shouted, jumped up and down, or else fell prostrate on the ground and hid their faces. A cacophony of noise assaulted Luke's ears: the panicked neighing of horses, the shrieks of children, the crunch of hooves on gravel, and the shouts of the villagers.

Then he heard Pitale-sharo's voice ringing out with authority. *"Brothers and sisters! Hear me!"*

Luke paused in lighting the fireworks, so his friend could be heard. Silence fell upon the gathering. When even the horses were brought under control, Pitale-sharo continued. "Grandfather, give me leave to speak. I have returned to you from the spirit world, bearing messages from Tirawa himself."

"Speak then, my son. We are all listening. We await your messages with open minds and hearts."

"Grandfather, I did as you commanded. I traveled to the mountains, fasting and praying from the day I left here. The journey nearly killed me, and when finally I lay near death, I saw a vision. It was a wounded, dying wolf, my own totem and the totem of our tribe. While I gazed upon him, my mind was opened, and I realized that I myself had wounded the wolf. If I continued to ignore the will of Tirawa, I myself would slay him."

"What *is* his will, my son? What has he revealed to you? Tell us quickly, for soon the sun will rise, and the maiden still hangs on the scaffold, her journey not yet begun."

"Grandfather . . . ," Pitale-sharo raised his arms in a pleading gesture. "He told me that the old days are finished. They are gone forever, and we cannot bring them back again. In the time that is coming, we must find new ceremonies and customs, new rituals to placate the gods. They no longer desire us to spill human blood, to lie and deceive, to embrace violence and savagery as a way of life. We must learn how to be men of peace, not men of war—"

"Look!" Bon-son-gee suddenly shouted. "The sun is rising! We must kill the maiden, now, before it is too late!"

Snatching his knife from the sheath at his waist, Bon-son-gee drew back his arm to hurl it at Maura. Luke raised his rifle, quickly aimed, and pulled the trigger. Bon-son-gee collapsed in a howling heap, clutching his shattered knee. Shielding Maura's body with outstretched arms, Pitale-sharo stepped in front of the scaffold, a clear target for the mounted warriors. Motivated by the same ancient instincts as Bon-son-gee's, they had drawn back their bows and aimed their arrows at Pitale-sharo's midsection.

426

"Let Tirawa decide!" Pitale-sharo begged. "He has no need of *us* to take this maiden's life. If he wants her, let him take her himself."

"Tirawa! Tirawa!"

Fingers pointed to the east. Women and children began to scream. As one body, the villagers fell to the ground and hid their faces. A great hush descended. In the eerie silence, Luke scanned the brightening sky. Morning Star hung above the earth, twinkling like the brightest of jewels. In the center of the eastern horizon, a stilleto-thin bar of gold signaled the rising sun.

A sudden gust of wind swept across the bluff. A single ray of light pointed a skinny, probing finger across the plains. Unerringly, it found the scaffold, illuminating Maura's silver-blond hair, bathing her face and body in radiance. Moving to one side so he could see better, Luke saw that Maura's eyes were closed, her face serene, as if she awaited death with a perfectly clear conscience— or else, never doubted she would survive this awesome moment.

His heart swelled with love; no other woman could have met this day's challenges with such grace and fire. In the face of torture and death, she had kept her wits about her, using cleverness instead of tears to try and sway the Pawnee from their awful intentions. And she had nearly succeeded—or had at least opened the way for Pitale-sharo. Her courage awed him. Her bravery humbled him. Without any shadow of doubt, he knew that Maura belonged wherever she wanted to be. He had deeply wronged her with his doubts, hesitance, and confusion, and could only hope she still wanted to be with *him*, out here on the plains, or journeying to California, or . . .

"She lives," Pitale-sharo said. "Tirawa has touched her.

Still, she lives. . . . What further proof do you need?"

"She lives!" the women exclaimed among themselves. "She still lives!"

"The maiden still breathes," the warriors muttered disbelievingly. "Tirawa has rejected the sacrifice. It *must* be as Pitale-sharo says; the god no longer desires the blood of maidens. . . ."

"Cut her down," Wetaro-sharo commanded in a shaky voice. "Cut her down, and let her go free."

"Moe-ra! Pitale-sharo!" She-de-a cried joyously, running toward the scaffold.

Luke hopped on the platform and helped Pitale-sharo cut the thongs binding Maura's wrists and ankles to the timbers. "Sweetheart," he choked, gathering her into his arms.

She stared at him with dazed, unseeing eyes and fell forward. He caught and lifted her, cradling her body as he would an infant's. "Maura . . . Maura, sweet, it's over. You're alive and free."

"Luke . . . oh, Luke." She hid her face in his chest. "Take me away from here. Please, take me away."

"Luke! Is she all right? Did they hurt her?" Eben pushed his way through the throng of Indians crowding the platform.

Before Luke could answer, a cry of alarm went up from the villagers. "Look, down below! . . . The village! . . . The village is burning! . . . The White-Eyes are attacking the village!"

"Damn, I forgot about Major Dougherty," Luke muttered. "What in hell does he think he's doing?"

The signal that Dougherty should attack the village was supposed to be two shots, but Luke had only fired one—the shot that had felled Bon-son-gee. Had the major misunderstood? Or had he simply decided that one

428

shot was enough indication that things had gone wrong?

Luke carried Maura to the edge of the bluff, from which vantage point he could look down and see the village, below. There, he saw the truth of the matter: The soldiers were not firing the lodge roofs. They were putting *out* fires. Some were beating at the flaming roofs with blankets and buffalo robes. Others were forming a line stretching from the river to the village, so that containers of water could be passed from man to man.

The misfired rockets had started the blazes, Luke realized. It should be fairly easy to save the lodges, but the rapidly spreading grass fires were a threat to the entire plain. The grass was dry as tinder, and though the soldiers were doing their best, the fires were already threatening to burn out of control.

"Pitale-sharo, do you see what's happening?"

"I see, Great Heart. If we do not quickly stop the warriors, they will be down there *killing* soldiers instead of helping them save the village."

"You had better get moving while I see to Maura."

"Give her to me." Eben jostled past Pitale-sharo and held out his arms. "I'll take care of her. You go help in the village."

"What is it? What's happening?" Maura murmured when Luke tried to switch her to her father's arms.

"Fire," Luke explained. "If we don't get down there and assist Dougherty's soldiers, the whole plain could go up in flames."

"Give me your shirt. I can help, too, as soon as I dress."

"You'll do no such thing! Your nakedness is the least of it; you're in shock. You've suffered severe emotional upset. You need to go somewhere, lie down, and rest."

"I need no such thing!" Maura's vivid blue eyes locked

with his. "Put me down, Luke Cutter! I bet you started the fires with your damn fireworks!"

"Yes, and my damn fireworks helped save your life!"

"Maura . . . Luke . . . ," Eben remonstrated.

"Here, Miss Magruder, take my jacket," George Catlin offered, coming up beside Eben. "Hadn't we all better get down there and help? The warriors went racing down to the village, screaming war cries. I did manage to grab a loose horse, Mr. Cutter. If you want him, he's right over there. That little Indian girl is holding him."

Luke followed Catlin's pointing finger; She-de-a was holding the reins of a prancing buffalo-runner. Without another word to Maura, Luke dumped her in Eben's arms. "Come on, Pitale-sharo, we'll ride double. The rest of you come along when you can."

Chapter Thirty-three

The battle proved easier to stop than the fire. As soon as the Indians got close enough to see what was really happening, they leapt off their ponies and joined the soldiers in trying to battle the flames. By the time Luke and Pitale-sharo caught up with them, the warriors were already forming their own water brigades from the river.

Pitale-sharo blinked in amazement. "I have never seen my people do such a thing. In the past, whenever a plains fire began, we grabbed what we could, fled to safety, and came back when it was all over."

"Maybe you've underestimated your people," Luke scolded, with the wisdom born of experience. "Give them good examples and strong leadership, and they'll be willing to adopt new ways."

Luke quickly found Major Dougherty. He was trying to decide where to start digging a ditch to arrest the fire's spread to the open plains. "It's the only thing I can think of, Luke." Dougherty wiped his soot-streaked face with his shirt-sleeve. "If any of the smaller blazes get away from us, we'll have t' stop 'em this side of the village, or eventually they could eat up the plains. Dry as it's been, we're lookin' at a tinderbox waitin' t' explode."

"You don't have to convince me. I'm a big believer in ditches. For extra protection, we can wet down the grass on both sides of it. Pitale-sharo and I will find a couple digging sticks and get started."

As the women and children came down from the bluff, they were put to work digging the ditch and dampening the grass. Firefighting was hot, dirty, back-breaking work, but soldiers and Indians labored side by side all day under the burning sun. No one quit, complained, fought, or argued. Everyone simply worked, as hard and as fast as they could. No sooner did they get one grass fire under control, when another flared up somewhere else. Capricious, gusty breezes fanned stray sparks in every direction; there was no escaping the thick, gray smoke. The horses had long since fled, panicked by the fire and smoke. Only the people remained behind, laboring in determined silence.

In mid-afternoon, puffy, white clouds with gray underbellies taunted them with the possibility of rain. Luke was sure he scented a brewing storm. When he asked Pitale-sharo what he thought, his friend sadly shook his head. "No rain today, Great Heart. Maybe tomorrow, or three days from now—a small rain. Not enough to put out a big fire. You are hoping for the impossible."

"Nothing's impossible," Luke said, looking around at the exhausted soldiers and villagers. "Consider what's happened, today; we've had one damn miracle after another."

"There will be no rain," Pitale-sharo insisted.

By early evening, the ditch was done, and the winds had died down. Major Dougherty kept everyone wetting down the grass until it grew too dark to see clearly. The only source of light was the line of smoldering grass licking a fiery path toward the ditch and dampened area. Most of the village had been spared; only one small section was a total loss, and if the fire went no farther than the ditch, the danger would be over.

"You think we've contained it?" Luke asked the major.

"Sure as hell hope so. If we haven't, there's nothing more we can do. If there *was* something more, we don't have the bodies; everybody's plumb wore out."

A large, unrecognizable figure padded up to Luke. Upon close inspection of her sooty features in the dim, reddish light, he recognized Heavy Basket.

"Is that you, Great Heart?" she asked.

For the first time, Luke realized that he must be as filthy as everyone else. "Yes, it's me."

"Will you give the chief of the White-Eyes a message for me?"

"He's standing right here. Give it to him yourself."

"I do not speak the White-Eyes tongue."

"He understands a little Pawnee. Go ahead," Luke invited. "See for yourself."

Heavy Basket turned to the major and bowed stiffly. "The women of the tribe wish to leave now and prepare the wedding feast for Pitale-sharo and She-de-a. The work is completed, is it not?"

"Yes, it is," Dougherty responded. "Luke told me about the wedding planned for tonight, but I had forgotten about it."

"She-de-a has not forgotten. That one is determined to wed Pitale-sharo this very night. Though we are all too hungry and tired to celebrate, perhaps we should. . . . It has been a day of new beginnings. New beginnings should always be celebrated."

"You couldn't have said it better, Heavy Basket. I wholeheartedly agree. Of course, the women may leave to prepare the wedding feast."

"All of the White-Eyes are invited. We will celebrate together. If you had not come when you did, our whole village might have been destroyed, and all our food stores and belongings with it."

"We would be honored to attend your feast." Major Dougherty returned her bow.

"Good. Then I will tell Wetara-sharo he may expect you."

"Maybe I'd better find Pitale-sharo and remind him that he's getting married tonight," Luke said, after she had gone.

"No need. He's already excused himself. Said he needed to check on his grandfather. I expect he also wanted to get cleaned up. In fact, if you look around, you'll see that you and me are the only fools left out here. Everybody else has started back to the lodges."

Luke looked around. "I'll be damned if you aren't right, Major."

"You'll be damned if you don't hunt up Maura Magruder and finally settle things between the two of you. I don't see why you're so scared of marrying that girl, Luke. After all she went through this morning, she was out here with the rest of us fighting fires all day long. She's got more gumption than any other two women put together, Indian *or* white. Why, I'd say she's got more gumption than any two *men*."

"Maura was out here working with us? I never saw her."

"Then you must be blind, Luke. She and her father worked all day without stopping. If I was you, I'd marry her tonight, same time as Pitale-sharo marries his little Sioux."

"I *can't* marry her tonight. Who would conduct the ceremony? Who'd witness it?"

"Hell, you're not only blind, you're dull as an old tomahawk. *I* can conduct the ceremony. Why, I was a reg'lar justice of the peace before I ever came out here. I'm the only one with authority to marry folks for miles in any direction. As for witness, we've got a whole tribe of Injuns and a passle of soldiers. We even got the father t' give away the bride. The only other thing we need, is the bride and groom themselves."

"You've got the groom," Luke said slowly, trying to keep a grip on his soaring excitement. "Of course, I can't speak for the bride. Guess I'll have to go ask her."

"Then what're you waitin' for? If you don't ask her, *I* will, and I dare say half the men I brought with me will ask her, too. Ain't none of 'em as dumb as you, Luke."

"I couldn't agree with you more!" Luke tossed over his shoulder as he sprinted toward the village.

"You look beautiful," Maura assured She-de-a as the two of them finished dressing for the girl's wedding in Lizard Woman's lodge. "Pitale-sharo will think so, too."

She-de-a's soft, brown eyes gazed at Maura with beaming pleasure and radiant joy. "I am so happy, Moe-ra. The only thing that could make me happier is if *you* were happy, too."

"I'm happy," Maura lied, lowering her eyes and smoothing down the simple doeskin garment Lizard Woman had found for her to wear.

"No, you are not," She-de-a disputed. "I can see it in your face, but I do not know why you are so sad. Everything has turned out so well. You are still alive, the Pawnee have abandoned the Morning Star ceremony, the village was saved from the fire, and the White-Eyes and Pawnee are now good friends. . . . What is there to be sad about?"

Maura bit back sudden tears. "Oh, She-de-a, I don't know! I . . . I guess I'm just tired. I've made so many mistakes, behaved so foolishly. I've learned so much about myself since I first came here, and I . . . I don't like what I've learned."

"*What* have you learned, Moe-ra?" She-de-a clasped Maura's hands. "Tell me what is in your heart, and maybe I can help you."

"This is your wedding night!" Maura bawled. "You mustn't bother yourself with *my* problems."

"Please, Moe-ra. . . . If it were not for you, I might not be having this wedding night. Tell me what you are feeling."

"*Shame,*" Maura blurted. "And guilt, and chagrin. . . ."

She mixed English with Pawnee, because she did not know if the Indians even had words for what she was feeling. "I thought I alone knew what was best, what was right. In my foolishness, I almost got myself killed, almost started a war between whites and Indians, almost got Luke, my father, Pitale-sharo, and George Catlin killed. Because of me, lives have been endangered. People have fought and argued. I was so terribly stupid and proud. I never heeded anybody's warnings. I forced my father to do things he never wanted to do, refused to listen to Luke when he knew better than I did—"

"But Moe-ra, good came out of your actions—not *bad*. Besides, you did not *cause* everything to happen the way it did. Before you came here, before he even captured me, Pitale-sharo was already questioning the ancient ways of his people. I saw him this afternoon, and he told me how he had argued with his grandfather before he ever left on his journey to find me. He explained about the Morning Star ceremony—what it meant, why the Pawnee have sacrificed maidens. It was time for this change to come, Moe-ra. Pitale-sharo knew it, and I think his grandfather also knew it. But they were afraid. On their own, they could never have achieved it so soon. That is what *you* made possible: The change came *now* instead of later."

"I can't take credit for that, She-de-a. Pitale-sharo loved you, and his love finally gave him courage. *I* did nothing but cause more confusion and upset. I blundered where I didn't belong, and then I even lied about it to Luke and my father—"

"Obviously, you're a very bad person, Maura Magruder," a male voice agreed.

Maura glanced up in surprise. Luke had entered the lodge and was standing there, listening. Coming closer, he said: "She-de-a, would you mind leaving Maura and me alone for a few moments?"

"I would be happy to leave the two of you alone together, Great Heart. Maybe you can make Moe-ra smile again. I hate to see my friend so sad on the most special night of my

436

life." Before she departed, She-de-a gave Maura a small, encouraging hug. "I will come back soon and braid your hair for you, Moe-ra. I am ready, but you are not, and there is still plenty of time before the women come to escort me to the ceremony."

Maura nodded to her friend, and as She-de-a went out, turned her back on Luke. Feeling as she did, she could not look him in the eye. In his dark, sooty face, his eyes were as bright and shining as Morning Star had been that morning. His presence seemed to fill the entire lodge, making her tremble at his nearness. She could not even breathe properly.

"What are you hiding from, Maura?" Luke crossed the lodge, jerked her around, and stared down at her. "Maura Magruder. . . ," he said more gently. "Did I actually hear you admitting that you might actually have been wrong about something?"

"Is that why you're here—to gloat and say I told you so?"

"No." Luke smiled at the question. "It never entered my head to say I told you so. But now that you mention it, I *did* warn you."

"Yes, you did, and you were right, Luke. All along you were right about me. I don't belong out here in the wilderness sticking my nose into other people's business. This morning, while I was hanging on that scaffold, I had ample time to realize what a naive, arrogant fool I've been."

"So now you hate yourself. . . ."

"Hate may not be the right word for what I feel, but if the Pawnee *had* killed me this morning, it would only be what I deserved. I had no business ever coming here, much less volunteering for a ceremony about which I knew *nothing*."

"You should have stayed back east and married that damn botanist."

"Yes, I should have. I don't know what made me think I was capable of handling Indians, snakes, buffalo stampedes, prairie fires, and God knows what else. I was wrong, and

437

you were right, Luke. I'm no match for life in the Land of Shallow Rivers. I should leave immediately for Bellevue and catch the first steamer headed for St. Louis, and when I get home, I should never leave again. Instead, I should marry Nate or some other safe, sane man, and spend the rest of my life wearing lacy white dresses, and attending tea parties where the most exciting thing ever talked about is the newest recipe for teacakes, and when anyone asks me what I *think* about a controversial topic, I should just flutter my lashes demurely and say, 'I don't know, I'll have to ask my husband.' "

"Maura," Luke growled, tipping up her face. "What you're spouting now is one big heap of buffalo chips. You'll never be happy living a life like that. You need a man who's neither safe *nor* sane. Will you marry me and go west to California?"

"Will I *what?*" Maura was not certain she had heard properly.

"Will you marry me?" he repeated. "I need someone to help fight off grizzlies and hostile Indians, hunt antelope and buffalo, help keep a roof over our heads—"

"Are you asking me to be your . . . your *partner,* or your wife?"

"*Partners!* Yes, that's exactly what I had in mind. I'm also asking you to be my lover, my best friend, the mother of my children, the grandmother of my grandchildren. . . ."

"Then you don't think I'm naive, foolish, stubborn, arrogant, troublesome, and . . . and hardheaded?" Maura quavered, still not believing he was actually asking her to marry him.

"Oh, yes, I definitely think you're all that . . . but I love every troublesome inch of you. Together, we can face anything, Miss Magruder. The only thing I *can't* face is losing you because of my *own* foolishness, stubborness, arrogance, hardheadedness, and whatever else you said. Marry me tonight, Maura. I can't go another day without holding you in my arms, knowing you finally belong to me. . . ."

"That you belong to *me*," she corrected.

"That we belong to *each other*," he compromised indulgently.

"But who? How?"

"Major Dougherty. We don't need anything or anyone else — except I'd like to ask your father's blessing."

"Oh, Luke! Let's go ask him, now. I *know* he'll be delighted. He and George Catlin are in Wetara-sharo's lodge getting ready for the feast."

"Can't I wash and get cleaned up, first?"

"I'll *help* you! We'll go down to the river, and—"

"No, you won't. The next time you see me naked, I want it to be *after* we're married — or we'll never make the wedding."

Simplicity characterized both marriage ceremonies. They were over and done with in a manner of moments. However, the dancing and feasting, continued for hours into the night. The weary Indians and soldiers cast off exhaustion and participated eagerly, each side communicating with the other by means of sign language and hilarious attempts at speaking. George Catlin waxed enthusiastic over all the artistic possibilities the feast presented, and Maura's father was equally ecstatic that Luke and Maura had "finally come to their senses."

Maura had known her father would be pleased, but she had never expected he would be quite *this* pleased. As they all sat together, celebrating around a huge village campfire near the river, Maura asked Eben about it. "Father, just when did you decide that Luke and I were perfect for each other?"

"Why, the day we first met him, and he objected so strenuously to your presence. I saw the way he looked at you, and you looked at him, and I just knew. The fact that you both hated each other did not worry me too much; if anything, it only solidified my hopes and expectations. You share the same strength and determination. Whatever the two of you decide to do with your lives, I have no doubt you will succeed."

"But what will *you* do, Father? Are you still planning to visit the Mandans? I hate to think of you going there by yourself."

"Mr. Catlin is going to accompany me. We'll stay awhile and record their tribal customs, and after that, we may move on to yet another tribe. I expect to remain in the Land of Shallow Rivers for quite some time. Indeed, I may never return east. I'll send my treatises home, but I myself have no desire to leave the freedom and beauty of the plains."

"I feel the same way," Maura admitted. She shot Luke a glance of embarrassment. "I didn't mean I don't want to go to California; I just meant I don't want to go back east."

"I know what you meant." Luke entwined his fingers through hers and squeezed them.

"What's this about California?" Eben questioned. "When I think of saying good-bye to my daughter, I get a huge lump in my throat."

"You won't have to say good-bye, just yet," Luke assured him. "For a long journey like that, I want to have the whole summer ahead of us. Weren't you expecting me to guide you to the Mandans? Maura and I could take you there, visit for a spell, then return to Bellevue to pass the winter."

"Oh, Luke, *could* we?" The idea of visiting the Mandans greatly appealed to Maura. She could then compare Mandan customs to Pawnee, write about both of them over the long winter, and send her treatise off to the Anthropological Society before embarking on the next adventure.

"We can do anything we want," Luke answered. "If we winter in Bellevue, it will also give Major Dougherty a chance to find someone to replace me."

"Replace *you?*" the major broke in. "Why, no one can ever replace you, Luke. You're too damned ornery. My *next* right-hand man is gonna be some gentle soul who never cusses, scowls, insults ladies, or talks me into spendin' fortunes on fireworks that can set the whole damn plain afire."

"The fireworks!" Luke exclaimed. "I still have a few left. Wouldn't they be the perfect entertainment for this feast?"

"You ain't thinkin' of settin' off no more of them damn things, are you?" the major incredulously demanded. "Has marriage addled your wits even worse than they was before?"

"If we took them out on the river where the sparks would just fall in the water, we could light them safely."

"I'm plumb sorry I mentioned it, Luke. I got no hankerin' to go out on a raft or bullboat and set off fireworks."

"Come on, Maura!" Luke tugged on her hand. "You and I can do it. After that, we'll just float downstream, where we can be alone together for the night. . . ."

Maura needed no further urging. She had been wondering where they would sleep, and she much preferred the bare ground and the stars overhead to the lack of privacy in one of the lodges.

"Let me get a few things first, Luke. While you get the fireworks. I'll gather what we need to make a small comfortable camp."

"Meet you by the river. Excuse us, everyone. Oh, Major, will you tell the Indians what to expect? I don't want them thinking that the village is under attack or that the grass will start to burn again."

"I'll tell 'em. Maybe they'll think it's Tirawa's way of blessin' this grand occasion."

As Maura hurried toward Lizard Woman's lodge, she heard footsteps behind her and someone calling her name. "Moe-ra? Moe-ra, wait."

441

Maura paused to allow She-de-a to catch up with her. "Where's your new husband, She-de-a? Does he mind that you ran off and left him alone at the feast?"

She-de-a shyly grinned. "No, he does not mind. We are leaving soon, anyway. I just wanted to . . . to say good-bye."

"Good-bye? Where are you going?"

"Pitale-sharo and I are going away together, for a time. Tonight, we will sleep in Wetara-sharo's lodge. In the morning, we will leave here early and ride off by ourselves. For the first few days and nights of our lives together as man and wife, we want to be alone."

"That sounds like a great idea!" Maura rapidly recalculated what she herself ought to take tonight so that she and Luke could do the same thing. "Luke is going to set off the last of the fireworks out on the river, and then we are going off by ourselves, too."

"Moe-ra . . . ," She-de-a said softly. "I wish you and Great Heart a long, happy life, and many fat babies."

"I wish the same for you, She-de-a." Embracing her friend, Maura blinked back tears. "One day, I'll bring *my* babies to visit *your* babies."

"They will be friends—like you and me, like Great Heart and Pitale-sharo."

"We'll make sure of it," Maura agreed, hugging the girl. "No matter what the future holds for the Indians and the White-Eyes, we won't let our friendship die."

"Good-bye, Moe-ra. I must go now. My husband is waiting for me."

Thinking of her own husband waiting by the river, Maura nodded. "Good-bye, my friend. I love you! Be happy!"

She watched She-de-a hurry back toward the wedding feast, then ran to collect her things.

Epilogue

As Maura had anticipated, the canopy of stars overhead was much better than a lodge roof. It out-dazzled the display of fireworks Luke had shot off in the middle of the river, amazing and entertaining soldiers and Indians alike. While Luke hobbled the horses, Maura finished setting up a simple camp, sat down on the spread-out buffalo robe that was to be their bed, and gazed up at the stars. They were the biggest, brightest stars she had ever seen, luminous, radiant jewels studding a black velvet dome.

"Luke—a shooting star!" she cried.

The phenomenon delighted her; the Indians would regard it as a good omen. Deciding that it must be, she lay back on the robe and stretched her arms above her head.

"What's this?" Luke inquired, looming over her. "You still have on your clothes."

"I was waiting for you," she coyly responded.

Luke dropped down on the robe beside her, then rolled over on top of her, pinning her against the soft, thick fur. "Well, I'm here, now. What are you gong to do about it?"

"Let's see . . . I'm going to count the stars, one by

one. Then I'm going to fall asleep and dream happy dreams."

"Like hell you are. I didn't bring you out here to count stars and fall asleep."

"Why *did* you bring me, Luke?" She took his face between her hands and rubbed his rough cheeks with her thumbs. "Tell me what you're going to do to me."

"For starters, I'm going to take you over my knee and show you who's boss in this outfit."

His teasing tone made her grin. It was the first time they had ever gently bantered, without hiding barbs behind every word. Maura loved it — especially as a prelude to lovemaking, which she was sure would follow.

"There are no bosses in this outfit — only partners, remember? I must say we performed well together, setting off those fireworks tonight."

"*Those* fireworks were nothing compared to the ones we're going to set off now."

"Maybe that's what we could do in California — sell fireworks."

"To the grizzlies? No, my love, they don't need 'em. But the folks in those parts could probably use good rifles, powder, and explosives. I've been giving serious thought to starting a munitions business in California. It's the one thing about which I know something."

"Whatever we do, life will be *wonderful*," Maura sighed. "I can study the local aborigines, and you can produce reliable weapons and ammunition."

"In between times, we'll produce our own *special* fireworks."

"You seem to have only one thing on your mind."

Luke nuzzled her neck. "You bet I do, Mrs. Cutter."

His nuzzling became nibbling, and Maura shivered in anticipation. "If I close my eyes, will I see rockets ex-

444

ploding?"

"I don't want you to *see* them, I want you to *feel* them—same as I do."

"You feel them, now—already?"

"I feel the fuses sizzling." He tore at the lacings of her doeskin and freed her breasts, then bent his head and began to kiss them.

Maura raked her fingers through his silky hair. She too was sizzling, now. Each kiss and stroke of his tongue drove her nearer to the brink of explosion. This was what she wanted, what she would always want: to be loved, cherished, and aroused by Luke Cutter, her husband, the man she loved.

Afterword from the Author

Many years ago, while researching another book, I stumbled upon a reference to an incident involving a young Pawnee chieftain named Pitale-sharo, or Knife Chief, and an Oglala Sioux maiden. The girl had been captured in order to be sacrificed to the god of Morning Star in a secret religious rite. Pitale-sharo defied his own tribal customs and spared her life, prompting the young ladies of Miss White's Seminary in a nearby Nebraska town to award him a medal cast in bronze, which they hoped would discourage the barbaric practice.

The story haunted me. Periodically, I researched Pawnee history and customs in an effort to find out more about this incident and the ceremony itself. History books noted the existence of the ritual, but provided only the scantiest details. All that is known for certain is that the Pawnee did in fact sacrifice young women prisoners to Tirawa, the god of Morning Star. The girls were unaware of their fate until the last moment, and the sacrifice followed the lines described in this book. The last recorded sacrifice occurred in 1838.

George Catlin, who traveled the Great Plains between 1830 and 1836, did not mention the ritual in his memoirs, but he was so helpful in providing other interesting data that I could not leave him out of this book. Were it not for him, much of what is known about the Plains Indians would *not* be known. He provided both a written and pictorial account of Indian life prior to the changes brought about by massive, white settlement. Five years after he visited the Mandans, the entire tribe was destroyed in a smallpox epidemic. No other vivid, detailed, eyewitness account of the Mandans exists.

Only through the magic of fiction can we recreate lost civilizations. Thank you for journeying with me into the past; I hope Luke, Maura, and the rest of my characters have made it come alive for you—and that in sharing their story, you have shared a small part of our American heritage.